BY THE SAME AUTHOR

The Female of the Species

Checker and the Derailleurs

Ordinary Decent Criminals

Game Control

A Perfectly Good Family

We Need to Talk About Kevin

DOUBLE FAULT

LIONEL SHRIVER

A complete catalogue record for this book can be obtained from the
British Library on request

The right of Lionel Shriver to be identified as the author of this work has
been asserted by her in accordance with the Copyright, Designs and Patents
Act 1988

First published in the USA by Doubleday, New York in 1997

First published in the UK in 2006 by Serpent's Tail,
4 Blackstock Mews, London N4 2BT
website: www.serpentstail.com

ISBN: 1-85242-911-9
ISBN-13: 978-1-85242-911-9

10 9 8 7 6 5 4 3 2

Typeset by FiSH Books, Enfield, Middx
Printed by Mackays of Chatham, plc

To Jonathan

Whose real name I may use so rarely
to save it for special occasions.
Dedicated in the fervent hope
that we will confine this plot to paper.

AUTHOR'S NOTE

In the interests of storytelling, the tennis ranking system has been simplified in this novel. Readers curious about the complexities of national versus international rankings, or the WTA versus Virginia Slims computers, should consult the copious nonfiction on the subject. A few additional liberties have been taken, for *Double Fault* is not so much about tennis as marriage, a slightly different sport.

"Rarely do you get something if you want it too much. There isn't a tennis player in the world who can't tell when an opponent is frightened."

—TED TINLING

ONE

AT THE TOP OF the toss, the ball paused, weightless. Willy's arm dangled slack behind her back. The serve was into the sun, which at its apex the tennis ball perfectly eclipsed. A corona blazed on the ball's circumference, etching a ring on Willy's retina that would blind-spot the rest of the point.

Thwack. Little matter, about the sun. The serve sang down the middle and sped, unmolested, to *ching* into a diamond of the chain-link fence. Randy wrestled with the Penn-4. It gave him something to do.

Willy blinked. "Never look at the sun" had been a running admonition in her childhood. Typical, from her parents: avert your eyes from glory, shy from the bright and molten, as if you might melt.

A rustle of leaves drew Willy's gaze outside the fence to her left. Because the ball's flaming corona was still burned into her vision, the stranger's face, when she found it, was surrounded by a purple ring, as if circled for her inspection with a violet marker. His fingers hooked the galvanized wire. He had predatory eyes and a bent smile of unnerving patience, like a lazy lion who would wait all day in the shade for supper to walk by. Though his hairline was receding, the lanky man was young, yet still too white to be one of the boys from nearby Harlem scavenging strays for stickball. He must have been searching the underbrush for his own errant ball; he had stopped to watch her play.

Willy gentled her next serve to Randy's forehand. There was no purpose to a pick-up game in Riverside Park if she aced away the entire set. Reining in her strokes, Willy caressed the ball while Randy walloped it. As ever, she marveled at the way her feet made dozens of infinitesimal adjustments of their own accord. Enjoying the spontaneous conversation of comment and reply, Willy was disappointed when her loping backhand tempted Randy to show off. *Ppfft*, into the net.

This late in the first set, she often gave a game away to keep the opposition pumped. But with that stranger still ogling their match from the woods, Willy resisted charity. And she wasn't sure how much more of this Randy Ravioli (or whatever, something Italian) she could take. He never shut up. "*Ran-dee!*" echoed across all ten courts when his shot popped wide. Between points Randy counseled regulars in adjoining games: "Bit too wristy, Bobby old boy!" and "Bend those knees, Alicia!" Willy herself he commended: "You pack quite a punch for a little lady." And the stocky hacker was a treasure trove of helpful advice; he'd demonstrated the western grip on the first changeover.

She'd smiled attentively. Now up 4–0, Willy was still smiling.

The Italian's serve had a huge windup, but with a hitch at the end, so all that flourish contributed little to the effort. More, intent on blistering pace, Randy tended to overlook the nicety of landing it in the box. He double-faulted, twice.

As they switched ends again, Willy's eyes darted to her left. That man was still leering from behind the fence. Damn it, one charm of throwaway games in Riverside was not to be scrutinized for a change. Then, he did have an offbeat, gangly appeal...Ignoring the passerby only betrayed her awareness that he was watching.

Newly self-conscious, Willy bounced the ball on the baseline six, seven times. If her coach knew she was here he would have her head, as if she were a purebred princess who mustn't slum with guttersnipes and so learn to talk trash. But Willy felt that amateurs kept you on your toes. They were full of surprises— inadvertently nasty dinks from misconnected volleys, or wild lobs off the frame. And many of Riverside's motley crew exuded a nutritious exultation, losing with a shy loss for words or a torrent of *gee-whiz*. With Randy she was more likely to earn a huffy *see ya*, but she preferred honest injury to the desiccated *well done* and two-fingered handshake of Forest Hills.

Besides, Riverside Park was just across the street from her apartment, providing the sport a relaxing easy-come. The courts' wretched repair recalled the shattered Montclair asphalt on which Willy first learned to play: crabgrass sprouted on the baseline, fissures crazed from the alley, and stray leaves flattened the odd return. The heaving undulation of courts four and seven approximated tennis on the open sea. Poor surface mimicked the sly spins and kick-serves of cannier pros, and made for good practice of split-second adjustment to gonzo bounces. Craters and flotsam added a touch of humor to the game, discouraging both parties from taking the outcome to heart. An occasional murder in this bosky northern end of the park ensured generously available play time.

In the second set Randy started to flail. Meanwhile their audience followed the ball, his eyes flicking like a lizard's tracking a fly. He was distracting. When the man aped "*Ran-dee!*" as the Italian mishit another drive, Willy's return smacked the tape.

"You threw me off," she said sharply.

"It shouldn't be so easy." The onlooker's voice was deep and creamy.

Abruptly impatient, Willy finished Randy off in ten minutes. When they toweled down at the net post, Willy eyed her opponent with fresh dismay. From behind the baseline Randy could pass for handsome; this close up, he revealed the doughy, blurred features of a boozer.

Emerging from his towel, Randy grumbled, "I've been hustled."

"There was no money on the line," she chided.

"There's always something on the line," he said brusquely, "or you don't play."

Leaning for his racket case, Randy grabbed his spine. "Oooh, geez! Threw my back last week. Afraid I'm a pale shadow..." Zipping up, he explained that his racket had "frame fatigue"; not much better than a baseball bat, *capisce*?

Her coach Max often observed, *When boys win, they boast; when girls win, they apologize.* "I was in good form today," Willy offered. "And you got some pretty vile bounces."

"How about a beer?" Randy proposed. "Make it up to me."

"No, I'll...stick around, practice my serve."

"What's left for you to practice, hitting it *out*?" Randy stalked off with his gear.

Willy lingered to adjust the bandanna binding her flyaway blond hair. The man behind the fence threw a sports bag over the sag in the chain-link at the far end and leapt after it.

"That was the most gutless demonstration I've ever seen," he announced.

"Oh, men always make excuses," said Willy. "Beaten by a girl."

"I didn't mean *he* was gutless. I meant you."

She flushed. "Pardon?"

"Your playing that meatball is like a pit bull taking on a Chihuahua. Is that how you get your rocks off?"

"In case you haven't noticed, I don't have rocks."

The lanky man clucked. "I think you do."

While Randy looked sexy from a court away and disillusioning face to face, this interloper appeared gawky and ungainly at a distance, his nose lumpy and outsized, his brow overhung, his figure stringy. But close up the drastic outlines gave way to a subtler, teasing smile, and elusive, restless eyes. Though his torso narrowed to a spindly waist, his calves and forearms widened with veiny muscle.

"Somebody's got to put loudmouths in their place," she snapped.

"Other loudmouths. You tired?"

Willy glanced at her dry tank top. "If I were, I wouldn't admit it."

"Then how about a real game?" He spun his racket, a solid make. He was cocky, but Willy Novinsky hadn't turned down the offer of a tennis game for eighteen years.

At the first crack of the ball, Willy realized how lazily she'd been playing with Randy. She botched the first three warm-up rallies before reaching into her head and twisting a dial. Once it was adjusted up a notch, threads of the bedraggled net sharpened; scuffled paint at her feet flushed to a more vivid green. White demarcations lifted and seemed to hover. Fissures went blacker and more treacherous, and as it hurtled toward her the ball loomed larger and came from a more particular place.

She played guardedly at first, taking the measure of her opponent. His strokes were unorthodox; some replies came across as dumb luck. His form was in shambles; he scooped up one last-minute ball with what she could swear was a golf swing. But he lunged for everything. When she passed him his racket was always stabbing nearby, and though many a down-the-line drive was too much for him, she never caught him flat-footed on his T just glooming at it.

And there were no *Ran-dee!*'s. He never apologized or swore. He didn't mutter *Get it together, Jack!* or, for that matter, *Good shot.* When her serve was long he raised his finger; at an ace he flattened his palm. In fact, he didn't say one word for the whole match.

The game was over too soon at 6–0, 6–2. Willy strolled regretfully to the net, promising herself not to hand him excuses, but also not to gloat. Despite the lopsided score, they'd had some long, lovely points, and she hoped he would play her again. Before she'd formulated a remark striking just the right gracious yet unrepentant note, he reached across the tape, grasped Willy's waist, and lifted her to the sky.

"You're so light!" he extolled, lowering her gently to the court. "And *unbelievably* fucking powerful." He wiped his palm on his sopping T-shirt, and formally extended his hand. "Eric Oberdorf."

They shook. "Willy Novinsky."

She'd been braced for the usual grumpy terseness, or an affected breeziness as if the contest were mere bagatelle, expressed in an overwillingness to discuss other matters. But grinning ear to ear, he talked only of tennis.

"So your father dangled a Dunlop-5 over your crib, right? Dragged you from the Junior Open to the Orange Bowl while the rest of us were reading 'Spot is on TV.' And don't tell me— Dad's on his way here. Since even now you're nineteen, he still tucks you in at ten sharp. His little gold mine needs her rest."

That she was already twenty-three was such a sore point that she couldn't bear correcting him. "Don't hold your breath. Daddy's in New Jersey, waiting for me to put away childish things. Like my tennis racket."

Which was just what she was doing, when Eric stayed her arm. "Unwind with a few rallies?"

Willy glanced at the sky, the light waning. She'd been playing a good four hours, the limit on an ordinary day. But the air as it eased from rose to gray evoked afterwork games with her father, when he'd announce that Mommy would have supper ready and Willy would plead for a few points more. On occasion, he'd relented. She was not about to become the grown-up who insists it's time to quit. "A few minutes," she supposed.

Eric volleyed. Tentatively she suggested, "Your backswing— take it no farther than your right shoulder."

In five minutes, Eric had trimmed his backswing by three inches. She eyed him appreciatively. Unlike the average amateur, whose quantity of how-to books and costly half-hour sessions with burned-out pros was inversely related to his capacity to apply their advice, Eric had promptly installed her passing observation like new software. She felt cautious about coaching if it manifested itself in minutes, for turning words into motion was a rare knack. With such a trusting, able student she could sabotage him if she liked, feeding him bad habits like poisoned steak to a dog.

Zipping his cover, Eric directed, "Time we had Randy's beer. Flor De Mayo. I'm starving."

"I may have missed it—was that *asking* me out?"

"It was telling you where we're having dinner."

"How do you know I don't have plans with a friend?"

"You don't," he said simply. "I doubt you have a lot of friends."

"I seem that likable?" she asked sardonically.

"No one with your tennis game is *likable*. And no one with your tennis game spends much time holding hands in bars."

"You're going to change all that?" she jeered.

"As for loitering in gin mills, no. But a hand to hold wouldn't do you a speck of harm." Eric grabbed Willy's athletic bag as well as his own, and strode in the twilight with both carryalls toward court three with a self-satisfied jaunt. He had correctly intuited that wherever her rackets went, Willy was sure to follow.

"So where'd 'Willy' come from?"

Her imprecations to consider the West Side Cafe's pleasant outdoor tables having been resolutely ignored, they were seated snugly inside Flor De Mayo. Willy was recovering from a petty sulk that she'd been co-opted into a Cuban-Chinese greasefest. At least the restaurant was clean and not too frenetic; the white wine was drinkable.

"Would you go by 'Wilhemena'?"

"Yikes. What were your parents trying to do to you?"

"Let's just say it's not a name you expect to see in lights. My older sister fared even worse—'Gertrude,' can you believe it? Which they hacked barbarously down to 'Gert.'"

"They have something against your sister?"

Willy screwed up her eyes. He was just making conversation, but she had so few opportunities to talk about anything but open- versus closed-stance ground strokes that she indulged herself. "They have something against the whole world, in which we're generously included. But my parents bear Gert no special ill-will. Their feelings for my sister are moderate. Moderation is what she invites. In high school, she made B's on purpose. Now she's studying to become a CPA. The sum of this calculated sensibleness is supposed to make my father happy. It doesn't. In my book, they both deserve what they've got...I'm sorry, you have no reason to be faintly interested in any of this."

"Oh, but I am."

Afraid he was going to add something flirty and odious, she went on quickly, "I think they scrounged 'Wilhemena' and 'Gertrude' from the nursing home where my mother works. Even as kids, we sounded like spinsters."

Eric knocked back his beer with gusto. "You're awfully young to worry about becoming an old maid."

In the terms of her profession Willy was already shuffling toward her dotage; this man instinctively honed in on soft spots. "I'm not," she fended off lightly. "It's the implausibility of 'Wilhemena Novinsky' on a Wimbledon scoreboard that's unsettling."

"Wee-Willy-Wimbledon. 'Sgot a ring. Besides: shitty name, one more obstacle to overcome. On which you thrive, I'm sure. They did you a favor."

All this assumed familiarity was grating, and only the more intrusive for being accurate. "If I thrive on obstacles, my parents have done me dozens of favors."

The waiter arrived with their baked half-chickens with mountains of fried rice. Eric had ordered two plates for himself, which he arranged bumper to bumper.

"You're going to eat all that?"

"And the remains of yours, when you don't finish it."

"How do—?" She gave up. He was right. She wouldn't.

The rice was marvelous, scattered with pork and egg. The chicken lolled off the bone. "Don't look so greedy," said Willy. "I may finish more than you think."

"Just promise me you won't go puke it up afterwards."

"I'm not that trite."

"No tennis dad, no bulimia, and you're not overweight," Eric ticked off on his fingers. "Too good to be true. You *must* be having an affair with your coach."

Willy was a sucker for any contest, but this was the limit. "None of your business."

His eyes flickered; he could as well have scribbled her response on a scorecard.

"While I'm being crass..." Eric dabbed his mouth with his napkin; she couldn't understand how he could suck up all that rice in such a mannerly fashion. She'd have predicted he'd eat like an animal. "What's your ranking?"

There was no getting away. In tennis circles, this question arose five times a day, though it secreted far more malice than *What's your sign?*

Willy placed her fork precisely beside the vinegar, then edged the tines a quarter inch, as if to indicate the incremental nature of progress in her sport. "I'm ranked 437. But that's in the *world—*"

He raised his hands. "I know! I'm surprised your ranking is so high."

"Surprised! I pasted you today!"

He laughed. "Wilhelm!" He pronounced her new name with a Germanic *V.* "I just meant that I don't expect to run into a top 500 in the course of the average day. Touchy, touchy."

"There's not a tennis player on earth," Willy grumbled, picking her fork back up, "who isn't sensitive about that number. You could as well have asked on our first date how much money I make, or whether I have AIDS."

"Is that what this is?" he asked gamely. "A date?"

"You know what I mean," she muttered, rattled. "A ranking

is . . . like, how valuable a person you are."

"Don't you think you're giving them a little too much power?" Eric rebuked her, for once sounding sincere.

She asked sarcastically, "And who's *they*?"

"*They* are whoever you can't allow to beat you," Eric returned. "And the worst capitulation is thinking just like the people who want your hide."

"So maybe you're my *they*?"

"I'm on your side."

"I've only had one person on my side in my life."

"Yourself?"

"No," she admitted, "I am not always on my own side." This was getting abstruse. "I mean a real person."

"But didn't you like it?"

"Yes." The question made her bashful. "Can we stop talking about me for a second? Like, what do you do?"

"I graduated from Princeton in May. Math. Now I'm taking some time out to play."

"With me?"

"Yes, but play, not toy. Playing is serious business. You of all people should know that."

"Do you . . . have any brothers and sisters?" The low grade of repartee in locker rooms had left Willy rusty and obvious over dinner.

"Three brothers. My father wants to take over the world."

She let slide the implication that a patriarch would only do so with boys. "You," she determined, "are the oldest."

"Good."

What he was applauding, or should have been applauding, was her having made the effort to imagine being in anyone else's shoes but Willy Novinsky's for an instant. Self-absorption was a side effect of her profession. Oh, you thought about other people's *games*, all right—did they serve and volley, where was their oyster of vulnerability on the court. But that was all a roundabout way of thinking about yourself.

"Princeton," she nodded. Extending herself to him was work. "Brainy, then. You wouldn't have two words to say to the people I know."

"I doubt you know them, or they you. Players on the women's tour live in parallel universes. Though they're all pig-thick."

"Thanks."

"The men aren't nuclear physicists," Eric added judiciously.

"Your folks have money, don't they?" The tidy table manners were a giveaway.

"Hold that against me?" Eric lifted his drumstick with his pinkie pointed, as if supping tea.

"I might resent it," she admitted.

"Check: you're not bankrolled by nouveaux riches climbers." He tallied again on the rest of his fingers. "*And* no pushy old man, no eating disorders, and you're not a blimp. Four out of five right answers ain't bad."

That Willy hadn't denied having an affair with her coach had evidently stuck in Eric's craw. "This is a test?"

"Aren't I taking one, too?" he returned. "Princeton: feather in cap. Math: neither here nor there. Money: black eye."

"You're Jewish, aren't you?"

"Technically. Plus or minus? Watch it."

Willy said honestly, "I don't care."

"So why'd you ask?"

He was flustering her. "I guess I'm pig-thick, too." She glared.

"When I asked walking down here if your name was Polish, you seemed to realize that Pole-land was in Eastern Europe and not in the Arctic Circle."

"Stupidity may be an advantage in tennis," Willy proposed, teasing pork bits from the rice.

"The adage runs that it's a game you have to be smart enough to do well, and dumb enough to believe matters." Incredibly, Eric had cleaned his first plate and was making rapid inroads on the second.

"With the money on the line, tennis matters," Willy assured him. "No, I look at fourteen-year-olds romping on TV and think, they don't get it, do they? How amazing they are. They don't question being in the Top Ten of the world because they've no conception of how many people there *are* in the world. And the game is best played in a washed, blank mind-set. *Nothing* is in these kids' heads but tennis. No Gulf War mop-up, no upcoming Clinton-Bush election, just balls bouncing between their ears."

Yet Willy didn't quite buy her own dismissal of tennis players as stupid. Yes, exquisite tennis was executed in an emptied state that most would consider not-thinking. But more accurately the demand was for faultless thinking—since to regard hesitation, rumination, and turgid indecision as a mind functioning at its best gave thinking a bad name. Supreme thought streamed wordlessly from the body as pure action. Ideally, to think was to do.

But the lag between signal and execution was also closing up in Flor De Mayo. Willy no longer heard words in her head before they spilled on the table, and so became as much the audience of her own conversation as Eric, and as curious about what she would say. There was a like fluidity to be found, then, in talk.

Clearly hoping for one more right answer, Eric inquired, "Are you going to college?"

Meaning, *will go*, or *are going*, not *have gone*. After knowing this guy for a few hours, Willy already had a secret. "No," she said flatly.

He took a breath, seemed to think better of the lecture, and exhaled, preferring the remains of her fried rice. She'd left him a few baby shrimp. Something about the sheer quantity of food he consumed was magnificent.

"So which players do you admire?" he asked.

"I'm old school. Still hung up on the last generation. Connors. Navratilova."

"She cries," he despaired.

"So what, if she feels like crying? I bet you like *Sampras.*"

"Who wouldn't?" Eric shrugged. "His strokes are impeccable."

"He's a robot." Willy scowled. "Give me back McEnroe any day, and a decent temper tantrum or two. John taught the world what tennis is about: passion."

"Tennis is about control," Eric disagreed.

"Tennis is about *everything*," Willy declared with feeling.

Eric laughed. "Well, I wouldn't go quite that far. But you're right, it's not the eyes. The tennis game is the window of the soul."

"So what can you see about me in my game?"

"You play," Eric replied readily, "out of love. Sampras loves himself. You love tennis."

"I have an ego, I assure you." She was lapping this up.

"You have something far nobler than an ego, Wilhelm," said Eric, lowering his voice. "Which your ego, if you're not careful, could destroy."

Too mystical by half, Willy retreated. "Sampras—that there's nothing wrong with his game is what's wrong with it. Maybe more than anything, tennis is about flaws."

He laughed. "In that case, I've got a future."

"Your game is...incoherent," Willy groped. "As if you scavenged one bit here and one there like a ragpicker."

"Rags," he said dryly. The bill arrived; he counted out his share and looked at her expectantly.

She stooped for her wallet, abashed by her assumption that he would pay. "I didn't mean tattered. You made me work today."

"My," he said drolly. "Such high praise."

"Praise is praise." She slapped a ten-spot on the check. "Take what you can get." Willy was offended in return. She doled out flattery in such parsimonious dribs, to anyone, that she had expected him to run home with the tribute and stick it under his pillow. He wouldn't bully her into a standing ovation. He was better than she expected. Period.

Eric offered to walk Willy to her apartment, but up Broadway the air between them was stiff with grudge. "That was good food," she said laboriously at 110th.

"You thought it would be ghastly."

"I did not!"

"*Cuban-Chinese? Beans and stuff?* You whined, like, *Sher, I mean, if you wanna.* Vintage Capriati."

She laughed. "OK, I thought the food would be revolting." The air went supple. Willy strolled a few inches closer to her companion, though he'd still have to reach for her hand.

His arms swung free. "What are you doing tomorrow?"

"Heading up to Westbrook, Connecticut, for the weekend. I train up there."

"Let me come see you."

She felt protective of Sweetspot, but a visitor would serve a purpose. "Maybe."

Eric crimped her phone numbers into the margins of his New York City tennis permit.

She lingered at her stoop for a kiss. It was not forthcoming. In the glare of the entrance light, Eric's woodsy eyebrows shimmered with mutated stray hairs, some up to an inch and a half long. Intrigued, not really thinking, Willy reached for the longest eyebrow hair to pluck it.

He slapped her hand.

"Sorry," he said as Willy rubbed her knuckles. He'd hit her hard. "I like those."

Cheeks stinging, Willy studied her tennis shoes. "I guess I liked those weird hairs, too," she mumbled. "Maybe that's why I wanted one."

When she glanced up again, he was pinching the same overgrown straggler; he plucked it and laid it in her palm. "Then it's yours."

Her fingers closed over the specimen. She didn't know what to say. Willy didn't go on dates.

"Eric?" It was the first time she'd ever said his name. The

syllables felt ungainly on her tongue, their use a monumental concession to the young man's existence. "I did go to college. My father made me. I quit, after my junior year, to go pro. I'm not nineteen, I'm twenty-three. I'm way behind. I have very, very little time left."

In reward for the successful exchange, one eyebrow hair for one confession, he kissed her. Willy could only hold one broad shoulder. The other hand fisted Eric's peculiar gift. Unaccountably, once in her apartment she would store it in a safe place.

TWO

MAX UPCHURCH CALLED SWEETSPOT a "School of Tennis," dismissing Nick Bollettieri's more famous Florida academy as a *camp*. The education Sweetspot students received was better than perfunctory; Max couldn't bear colossal forehands at the expense of confusing Tiananmen Square with Chinese checkers. Max eschewed Bollettieri's reform-school trappings, dispensing with Bradenton's sniffer-dog drug checks, five-dollar fines for chewing gum, and restrictions to one TV program per week. As far as Max was concerned, if parents wanted to pay two thousand dollars a month for their kids to pop bubbles in front of *The Munsters* it was no skin off his nose. Should his students turn pro they might as well get practice at the tube. Isolated in an indistinguishable string of hotels waiting for the rain to clear or their draw to come up, most journeymen on the tour spent more time watching American reruns than they did on court.

Despite Sweetspot's unfashionable liberality, Willy was not alone in regarding Max's operation as more elite than his competition's in Florida. Bollettieri accepted 225 would-be champions a go; Max admitted seventy-five. Max Upchurch himself had had a distinguished career, ranked number six in the world in 1971, and making a solid contribution toward pulling the U.S. ahead of Australia playing Davis Cup. As a young aspirant in the late sixties, he'd made a name for himself behind the scenes, finagling with a handful of other infidels to drive this snooty, exclusive, stick-up-the-ass amateur sport into the crass, low-rent, anything-goes, money-mad and cut-throat Open era that was now so happily upon us.

But the biggest difference was tennis. Bollettieri's protégés blindly cannoned from the baseline like ball machines. To Max, *crash-crash* was not what tennis was about. Sweetspot emphasized cunning, style, finesse. While Nick assembly-lined bruisers, Max handcrafted schemers and ballerinas. Willy's coach believed that in every player lurked a singular tennis game struggling to get out—a game whose aberrations would prove its keenest weapons. He regarded his mission as to coax those idiosyncratic strokes from unformed players before their eccentric impulses were buried forever beneath the generic "rules" that constituted common coaching.

When Max first took Willy on at seventeen he demolished a game twelve years in the making and reconstructed it from the ground up. Willy had grown up fighting—fighting her parents; fighting her extraneous algebra homework when she was on the cusp of a breakthrough with the slice backhand; fighting the USTA for transport to junior tournaments that her father hadn't the remotest intention of financing; and later, fighting her height, when it became crushingly apparent that she would never exceed five-three. The appetite for battle Max encouraged. He drew the line at Willy's fighting herself. He insisted that she stop overcoming weaknesses and start playing to strengths.

All through high school, Willy had rushed forward at every opportunity, to prove a dwarf could cover the net, and she'd clobbered every ball with pleasingly improbable pace. It was Max who'd convinced her to stop defying physical fact. She was short; she should approach selectively. She was light; she'd never overpower heftier, Bollettieri blunderbusses. What Willy had going for her was that she was fast, that from scrapping with Daddy and the USTA and Montclair High School she had tremendous reserves of spite, and, scarcest of all, that she was intelligent.

Sure enough, Willy could pummel juniors into submission, but on the pro circuit she would never win a slugfest. She had a higher percentage trading on her wits. Though it took absurd restraint to keep from hauling off and slaughtering every ball—if only for the sheer sensation of hitting any object that hard without being arrested—Willy discovered delights in delicacy as well, until certain backspinning dinks slithering over the tape made her laugh out loud. Max played her a video of the Ashe–Connors Wimbledon final of '75, where instead of belting Jimmy's shots back laced with his own medicine Arthur deliberately slowed the points to a crawl. The long, easy returns drove Connors wild, and he'd slash them to the net or overhit. In the end, of course, the tortoise beat the hare.

In fact, Max was not coaching her in anything new at all. Players who specialized in craftiness—drops, lobs, disguises, and change-ups—were playing old-style women's tennis, for the sport had been routinely won on guile before the advent of oversize rackets and hunky grunters like Monica Seles. Yet the standard, abandoned long enough, becomes fresh. Willy sometimes suspected that his shaping her into an icon of bygone tactics was an exercise in nostalgia—for the days when women players were lithe, limber, and ingenious; and for the days when women players were women.

Thus it was thanks to Max Upchurch that Willy didn't spend every passing day in a state of hysteria. While she moped through another unwelcome birthday, Max had serenaded her with tales of Kathy Rinaldi, Andrea Jaeger, and Thierry Tulasne—young hopes-of-tomorrow who fizzled out as fast as they once burned brightly. "Early to rise, early to bed," he'd assured her when she turned nineteen, and was glowering at yet another year wasted at UConn on Spanish verbs. "Tennis is for grown-ups. You won't peak until you're twenty-five, Will. There's time."

***

As of six weeks ago, a tarnish had mottled her memories of those first trips to Sweetspot that Willy couldn't quite rub off. Though she and Max had agreed to go back to "normal," when Willy stepped off Amtrak in Old Saybrook it was an older student who waved her to the car. Once again, Max hadn't met her train, and that wasn't normal, but one more petty reprimand.

"What do you think of Agassi taking Wimbledon?" the boy bubbled. "Nobody thought he had the goods for grass. I was sure he'd show up in, like, fuck-you orange check or something, but no..."

Desmond was so eager that he forgot to pause for the answers to his questions. Willy observed enviously how in the last two years his dark mop had bobbed nearer the roof of the car. He'd be well over six feet, and had the compact, long-limbed figure for his sport. Had she a taste for little boys, she might have helped herself to Sweetspot's choice morsels. But Willy spent her own teenage years so virulently disdaining the likes of Desmond that cradle-robbing would amount to a post-deadline rewrite. Wistful, she admired but didn't quite covet his naive enthusiasm, not yet seized by savvy terror.

At any rate, the envy worked more in the opposite direction. Desmond was still undistinguished from the common ruck; Willy belonged to the select stable of older pros whom Max was grooming for the tour. Many of these were handpicked from the graduating class, though a few, like Willy, were bagged on Max's cross-country shopping trips. Willy herself had never been a Sweetspot student, and often wondered how much more advanced her game might be now if she hadn't been marooned at Montclair High School, which didn't even have a tennis court. Making use of the nearby public park, the school had offered one tennis gym course, for which in her sophomore year she'd maliciously signed up. That memory tweaked her now, reminding her why that Eric person had been right, that she'd never had many friends. Little wonder—she'd assaulted the lot of them with such contemptuous serves that they rarely had the luxury of losing a proper point. Toward the end of the course, with an odd-numbered enrollment, no one would play her at all, and she spent gym class pounding a ball mercilessly against the backboard, as if to break another barrier less tangible but just as impassable, it seemed, if she remained a public school student in suburban New Jersey.

They were drawing into Westbrook now, a small, tucked-away community on Long Island Sound whose property values were astronomical, but whose houses had been kept in families; the town retained its middle-class, unassuming character. Downtown, such as it was, included an ill-stocked drugstore with superlative homemade fudge, one Italian restaurant that overcooked its spaghetti, the obligatory military monument though few residents would remember to which war, and the beloved Muffin Korner, whose loose eggs, hot biscuits, and forgivably weak coffee cost $1.49. On the outskirts, where unprepossessing clapboards weathered by the shore, sturdy dowagers paddled the lapping surf in underwire swimsuits.

That Westbrook, Connecticut, was a steady, settled place may have inspired Max to select this location for Sweetspot. Pro tennis was such a roller-coaster, packing the events of what ought to have been a lifetime into perhaps ten frenzied years. It was sedative to bring students of age in an atmosphere of the reliable, the ongoing, and to coach them in the calming context of a place where tennis didn't mean much—the public courts by the firehouse looked like landfill.

Desmond was asking her to take a look at his serve. Doubtless he was hoping that Willy would put in a good word for him with Max. Desmond was entering his last year, when his mentor would be either asking him to stay on or merely wishing him the best, and so would take incidental privileges like being trusted with a school car this evening as auspicious. Willy had the urge to warn him, bitterly, that her good word would have meant a great deal more six weeks before, but a stray grumble would ruin months of discretion. When she glanced again at Desmond's yearning, mysteriously unwritten face, she ached. The first cut at Sweetspot was just the beginning of a cruel, sometimes savagely short process of elimination through which eagerness and even, by laymen's standards, awesome ground strokes counted for nothing.

This counsel, too, she swallowed. Willy had heard the poor odds enough times from her father, and the remonstrance was hateful. Desmond would have to find out for himself the staggering unlikelihood that he should ever be ranked at all, much less be deciding, after his idol, whether to concede whites to the fusty All England Club.

Threading outside of town, they curled the drive of the school, whose buildings blended with Westbrook architecture: green-trimmed white clapboard Colonial Revivals, each skirted with a wide wooden porch. Below the overhangs, rockers listed with curled afghans, and wicker armchairs beckoned with quilted pillows, calling out for long, fractious games of gin rummy. Nothing about this lulling, serene laze suggested the sweat shed on these grounds except that it was two hours after the dinner bell and the porches were deserted. Any student worth his salt at eight o'clock was back on the courts.

Willy drifted into the dining hall, to spot her coach at a side table, next to the horrid Marcella Foussard. He was scraping up the last of his meal—so once again they would not be snuggling into their regular booth at Boot of the Med to pick languidly at flaccid linguine. Willy grabbed a tray, brightening her laughter. Max would see through her insipid vivacity without looking up. What a disaster. What an awful mistake, though she wasn't certain which of them had made it.

The cafeteria betrayed that this was a sports academy and not a prep school. No vats of brick-solid cheese macaroni and liquefied kale; no lime Jell-O. Since Max had bought into high-protein theories, replacing the old saws about carbohydrates, they confronted skinless chicken breasts and lean flank steaks, undressed snow peas, and an inexhaustible mound of bananas.

Facing down the bananas one more night, Desmond moaned, "You know, Agassi lives on junk food."

Willy slid her tray next to Desmond on the side of the hall opposite from Max. She might have braved Max's table if it weren't for that Foussard creature, who surely spent more time on her nails—the back of her hand—than on her backhand. The hall recalled a mess in more ways than one, and Willy was frantic to get out. Shredding her chicken, she asked Desmond to hit a few after dinner. Ecstatic, Desmond chucked his flank steak merrily in the trash.

On the way out Willy forced herself to turn to Max's table. He was watching her steadily. She wiggled two fingers. He didn't wave back, his expression unreadable. She made a swinging motion and pointed at Desmond. Max dipped his chin a half inch, and as Willy swept through the screen door she at least had the satisfaction that with Marcella jabbering away Max had not heard a single word the silly girl said.

Sweetspot's twenty hard and four clay courts were built right on the sound, which made them breezy. But Max believed in the strengthening of adversity. He'd situated his school in the Northeast because, he claimed, European civilization had surpassed southern cultures due to rigorous, hard winters. Cold had invigorated northerners to activity and enterprise, while tropical layabouts lounged beaches munching pomegranates. According to Max, Tahitians would never have invented tennis. But Willy was confident the whole pro-winter hoo-ha really just meant that Max hated Florida.

Stars were emerging, the glow from the powerful floods fissiparating into the salted air. The lights projected a blue halo that could be seen from miles away. Closer up, the bulbs produced a low-level collective hum, like a chorus finding its note before the song. As the floods on their four corners flickered, starting gray and warming to hot white, the court blazed with the tingling theatricality distinctive to playing at night.

"No, Desmond," she declined when he challenged her to a match. "Let's just hit." The boy deflated. Later he might treasure his few offers of carefree rallies; now he craved a showdown. But Willy, for all her reputed keenness for head-to-head, tonight hankered for reprieve from a world with no choice but to vanquish or be vanquished. There had to be a haven in between.

"Why the cold shoulder?" Willy demanded. "I thought we were going to go back to the way it was."

"I wasn't the one who sat on the far side of the cafeteria," Max returned coolly.

"I wasn't the one who chose to eat in the cafeteria."

They were in the library, which Max adopted as his lounge after lights-out. Though the kids instinctively hid their bottles in racket covers, there were no booze bans on the books; Max was treating himself to solitary bourbon.

Looking up, he closed Winston Churchill's *The Gathering Storm*. "You expected that I would meet your train and scoop you off to Boot of the Med, where we'd order the fried calamari and Chianti and then—"

"We'd practice a few drunken overheads at midnight. Why not?" Willy's T-shirt was limp with clammy sweat; she rubbed her arms.

"What would we talk about?"

"What we always talk about. Primpy Marcella, and your ex-wife, and...and we'd draw point diagrams on napkins before the zabaglione." Her tone had taken a defeated turn. To Willy's own ears, the reprise sounded ridiculous.

"Our agreement was not to 'go back to the way we were' but for me to 'treat you like everyone else,' which I had never done, from the time you were seventeen. So I could hardly go *back* to anything."

"You're always so aggressive and nasty lately."

"I've always been aggressive and nasty. You used to like it. Don't go soft on me, Will. It's not good for your tennis."

"Do you even care about that these days?" she entreated. "My tennis?"

"I thought it was for the sake of your goddamned tennis that we've had such unimpeachable relations for six weeks."

"See? 'Goddamned tennis'—"

Max slammed his hardback to the table. "Enough! You practice your forehand, but the bust-up is blessedly a one-time-only. It doesn't improve with repetition, it just gets old."

"Gets old! We haven't discussed this since May!"

"Will." This time he implored her. Meeting his eyes, she pondered once more how this man contrasted with the photographs of Max's heyday twenty years ago. Many an evening she had marveled through his tour album, where his *Sports Illustrated* and *New York Post* profiles were preserved under plastic sheets. Max had maintained the same compact physique, with a dense torso whose dark hair sprang from his Lacoste shirt then as now. His face remained right-angled, and had acquired none of the fleshiness that invaded most middle-aged jowls. The beginnings of those eye crinkles were to be found in yellowed clippings. Though he'd axed the seventies sideburns, Max hadn't even restyled his no-nonsense haircut. The before-and-after pictures were, in their strictly physical detail, almost identical. So what made him look so unmistakably forty-five?

"It's late, I should get to bed," she said, and at the mention of the word *bed* Max poured himself another finger. "I may have a visitor tomorrow. Is that all right?"

He might have wanted to ask who or why, but Max Upchurch had made millions of dollars on self-control. He shrugged. She left.

In their on-court session the following afternoon, Max didn't refer to the evening's tiff, and no one observing the two would have picked up on anything amiss in this fruitful, vigorous coach-client relationship. His very capacity to put sentiment aside when business required a cool head may have contributed to his looking his age, though if Willy didn't miss her guess the faculty faintly depressed him.

But Willy knew the difference. Since May a formality had invaded their sessions. Briskness prevailed, though the tightening of the interval between drills may have only been a matter of fifteen seconds. Max no longer tucked strands into her bandanna but ordered gruffly, "Get that hair out of your face." He was hard on her—always had been—but now his criticism was knifed with genuine derision. He seemed glad for her mistakes, and Willy submitted to his abuse with uncharacteristic meekness.

They were working on corner-to-corner backhand drives, and as Willy spotted a peaked hairline sifting across the field to their court she bent her knees lower, drew her backswing more quickly, and forced the whole of her weight onto her right foot. The ball skimmed an inch over the net, and scooted from underspin.

"That's more like it," Max commended, though he sounded annoyed.

She put something special on the next one. It kissed the corner and skipped at a cockeyed angle beyond Max's racket. By the gate, the gangly Jew whistled, and Willy realized that she was showing off.

"I'm afraid we'll be another hour!" she cried.

Willy had orchestrated this exhibition, suggesting Eric take a train that would get him into Sweetspot before her afternoon's drills were done. Now she felt obvious, demonstrating what a *real pro* hits like with a *real pro coach*. The ensuing hour was painful, as her visitor bounced his back against the adjacent court's fence. Rather than gawk in slack-jawed awe, he looked put out. She could as well have been a little girl oppressing a house guest with her piano études. Moreover, while she'd intended Eric's visit to accustom Max to her new admirer, the ploy abruptly appeared tactless. From the age of five Willy had learned to control a tennis ball, and had virtually abandoned the more challenging project of managing people with the same aplomb.

Between drills, Willy bent and grasped her calves, bringing her forehead to her knees. The tension of the antagonism she'd contrived was tightening her tendons. Max rolled his eyes and flicked his finger, commanding her to the net post. Pulled hamstrings could put you out of the game for weeks; Max took no chances.

As she braced against the net post, Max kneeled at her feet and cradled an ankle on his shoulder. Gradually he stood nearly upright, which brought his groin level with her open crotch. Willy grunted at the ache in her thigh. As Max lowered her leg and prepared to lift the next, she glanced over at Eric, who was intently rewrapping his grip.

When the recital was mercifully over, she abbreviated introductions. "Max Upchurch, Eric Underwood."

Eric's mouth twitched.

Max skipped the so-you're-a-friend-of-Willy's-are-you and how-do-you-two-know-each-other and went straight to all he cared about in regard to anyone. Nodding at Eric's racket, he squinted. "You play?"

"No, I use this to catch butterflies." Deadpan.

Max sprang his palm against his strings. "How about a game?" The casual inflection was a lie. He had never challenged anyone to a match casually in his life.

In reply, Eric began whisking practice balls to the next backcourt, implying that Willy was to pick them up.

Willy hated watching other people play tennis. It consumed her with jealousy. Though she'd flagged minutes earlier, now she summoned a second wind, and how dare anyone abscond with her partner while she still had a stroke left in her?

Thus as the two men warmed up—Eric insolently relaxed, Max inscrutably impassive—Willy could not tell for which player she was rooting. She detested them both. This sucked: sulking cross-legged on the sidelines, the court hard and hot. As the match commenced, Willy gazed at banking seagulls overhead. However, it was impossible to screen out the familiar grunts that were Max's version of flattery, or the *pooch*-puh-*poom*-puh-*poom*-puh-*poom-poom-poom* of a protracted point.

In that Willy's calculation of a tennis score was automatic, neglecting to keep track of who won what took a concentration of its own. (Gentlemen did not announce the score.) She'd have expected Max to dispatch the parvenu in thirty-five minutes, though once Willy had realigned her racket strings and bounced a ball off the face five hundred times without missing, the half hour was long past and those two were still batting away. Max was moist. Eric was playing plenty of trash, but it sometimes worked. At last, after another point during which she had found a rally two courts away more compelling, she turned to find them shaking over the net, stiffly.

Willy picked herself up, dusting off her shorts, and the two gladiators ambled to their bags.

"You're a pro," said Max.

"Yes," said Eric.

"Ranked?"

"972."

Max cocked his mouth. "Ways to go."

"I'd never picked up a racket with any seriousness until I was eighteen. My first year at Princeton I was on the basketball team."

" Eighteen. Late."

"As in better than never."

They were both ignoring Willy, who was looking daggers at her new friend, *the pro*. She should have sensed it. At her stoop, his right palm had scratched her neck with lumpy calluses. He had not arrived at Sweetspot toting one racket but three, and as he zipped the Prince into its expensively padded case, she recognized the classic asymmetry of his arms: the right so comparatively overdeveloped that it suggested a skewed proportion of mind, as if a tennis player placed too much weight, literally, on one side of his life.

"I'll show you the showers," she offered. Eric didn't respond. His motions were jagged, his manner curt. The last time he was hammered he'd been jubilant; perhaps she was to infer from this truculence that he'd won the match.

As she traipsed with her guest toward the locker rooms, Max motioned her back. "I know his strokes are rough," he warned her quietly. "Sleazy. But underneath the junk, that kid can play."

Trudging across the field, Eric walked ahead, indulging the naturally extreme stride of a man at least six-two. They were trapped in the estranged silence of two people who had played tennis, but not with each other. And Willy could hardly make conversation about a match she had declined to follow so belligerently that she didn't know who had won.

"So what, we're supposed to shovel institutional slop with a bunch of pampered, brain-dead sportsmen of tomorrow?"

"There's an Italian place in town. Max would lend us a car."

"Upchurch would lend *you* a car." Eric kicked the ragweed.

"For a sport in which you apparently have aspirations yourself, you don't seem to have much respect for the folks who play it."

"You respect *these people?*" he asked incredulously.

"*Respect* may be the wrong word. But the game itself—"

"Is a pretty doable business. Sometimes you beat people at their own game not because you think it's so all-fired marvelous but because you don't."

Scurrying to keep up, Willy was mesmerized by the long, loose legs eating the ground with such blithe assurance. Surely it behooved her to defend the crowd in which she ran, but for a moment Eric's contempt was liberating. He was right, in a way. The lofty regard in which most pro players held their calling was insupportably pompous. The majority of her "colleagues" were narrow, fatuous, and catty. All they wished for Willy was defeat, and in truth she owed them nothing. Though she'd always tried to keep the sport and its practitioners separate in her head, Eric lured her with the giddy freedom of seeing even tennis itself as "a pretty doable business," a skill she had mastered but did not master her. For Willy's reverence for tennis was a tyranny—the more gravity she gave it, the more it crushed her when she fell short of the sport's uncompromising standards. Any man who found the diversion ordinary would have a peculiar power.

Eric waved his hand over the manicured lawns. From this distance the school's tidy Colonial Revivals looked contrived, self-consciously New England, precious. "This crowd makes me puke."

"Then why would you yourself want—?"

"To whip them where it hurts most."

"You don't think there's something special about someone who can play spectacular tennis?" asked Willy, nervous that to join him in denouncing this crew was not necessarily to escape being lumped in with them as well.

"I think there's something special about the way you play tennis." He stopped. "Or maybe I just think there's something special about you, and fuck the tennis."

Willy had long regarded herself and her strokes as synonymous. "Love me, love my game," she said warily.

He conked her lightly on the back of the head with the heel of his hand. "You're warped."

"That waitress knows your name," Eric charged.

"There's not much to choose from in Westbrook."

"Who'd you come here with?"

"*Various* people," said Willy stolidly.

"Uh-huh." He stabbed four calamari rings on the same fork and drowned them in hot sauce.

"You regard yourself as a jealous man?"

"Not especially. But when a situation calls for jealousy, I can rise to the occasion."

The Boot of the Med subdued her. She'd had second thoughts about coming here on the drive over. The hideaway had once seemed so enchanted, despite garish red lighting and clichéd Chianti bottles fat with candle wax. Maybe she'd have better left the past undisturbed, and not disillusion herself by discovering this was a tacky dive with bad food.

"I'm sorry I kept you waiting at the courts today," Willy submitted, prepared for reassurance that he hadn't minded.

"Just don't let it happen again," Eric said instead, and did not wait for the next subject to be gracefully introduced. "Overgrown boys like Max Upchurch piss me off. They go out and make scads of money doing for a living what in a sane world is leisure amusement, well, okay. They didn't make the rules, I guess."

Willy smiled. "Max did make the rules. He helped bully Wimbledon into Open tennis."

"So he's a scam artist. It's not against the law. But what gets me is these muscleheads turn forty and still expect little girls to whisper, *He used to be number six!* They convince every brat who's ever hoisted a ball over the net with the help of a forklift that he'll be swelling in a limousine before he's twenty. Meanwhile, his parents cough up twenty thousand a year for a third-rate education. All right, I'll give Upchuck this: for a geezer he can still play. He beat me cold today and I don't even think I taxed him. I tried, too. But I don't like the way he acts as if he owns you and I don't like the way he touches you and before I get into this any deeper I think you'd better tell me what's going on."

Willy discovered that she was pleased Max had won. *Here*, she had offered up to Eric. *This is my coach; his excellence is my excellence. Take defeat at his hands as evidence of my worthiness for yours.*

THREE

"So, WHAT, UPCHUCK'S BEEN schtuping you since you were twelve?" Eric snapped a breadstick.

"We didn't meet until I was seventeen." Willy folded her arms in front of the gummy pasta that Eric was bound to finish for her.

"Beyond statutory. A stand-up guy."

"Exasperatingly so, if you have to know."

"How'd you hook up with him, anyway?"

"Max was the one serendipitous result of my father's determination that I not turn pro. Max and I were both on vacations that made good on the emptiness of the word."

Having become the number three amateur in the New Jersey juniors by sixteen, Willy had exhausted most of the local competition but was not allowed the financing or time off from high school to participate in tournaments far afield. With the U.S. Open nearby in Flushing Meadow, in 1986 Willy had anticipated skipping her usual ballgirl stint to take a last crack at the junior title, even if that meant plowing through the qualifying rounds. Naturally this was also the summer that her father resolved to take his family on a cross-country car trip, into which Willy was summarily drafted.

Outraged at being denied the National Tennis Center, she spent the long, hot drives hunched in the backseat saying nothing. Willy particularly froze out Gert, who'd made a great show of being willing to come along as a college sophomore and had urged Willy to be, as Gert would say, *mat-yure*.

Willy hadn't been *ma-cher*. She left the family stranded in the Mount Rushmore souvenir shop to go for a six-mile run. Her sole interest was in finding a motel with a court, and in completing the day's loathsome sight-seeing before the light waned and it was too late to scavenge a partner. Like the rest of her high school gym class, neither Gert nor her father would play her anymore.

Chuck Novinsky was tightfisted, but limited vacancies in Nevada drove him to a luxury motel. At least The Oasis would mollify his second daughter, since it harbored three tennis courts.

The resort also hired a resident pro, a former 600-something who preyed on wealthy travelers working off their afternoon ice creams. Though Ed Sanders was going to seed from rum sours, he strutted those three baking hardcourts as if taking a second bow at the Foro Italico. As Willy later remarked to Max Upchurch, "Big prick, small pond."

Willy skipped a canvass of the old bags and brats in the lobby and went straight to Sanders. He was practicing his serve; the sizzling topspins all landed two feet deep.

"Hey, mister." Willy sidled to his baseline. "Game?"

"I charge sixty bucks an hour, sweetheart. Better check with your daddy first." She was treated to the beefcake smile for free.

The Oasis was already bankrupting her father. At the additional expense of some charlatan's worthless counsel her father would blow a gasket.

"Tell you what," Willy proposed, tossing a Wilson hand to hand. "You win, I pay you double. I win, you pay me."

"Okay, darling. You're on."

Those were the days when not a cloud of hesitation had shadowed Willy's sunny certainty that she could take all comers.

She sometimes supposed that had she sustained her adolescent sense of peerlessness by now she could be in the Top Ten. It was astonishing how far blind self-regard could take you, even if the braggadocio was arguably unfounded. For Willy had made the common error as a teenager of mistaking for excellence what was merely potential.

"I wasn't as good as I thought," she told Eric. "Still, playing Ed Sanders was like taking candy from a grown man."

When the bill arrived at Boot of the Med, Willy dived for her wallet, Eric held up his hand. Apparently he would pick up checks as a kindness but not as an obligation.

"Halfway through this wham-bam-thank-you-mister match," she resumed in the car, "a face appeared behind the fence. Just like you. Beady eyes, fingers crimped around the wires. I gave the guy a show. I was so pissed off. The junior qualies were starting in Queens, and here I was glowering out car windows at the Painted Desert.

"I'd no idea who the guy was. When he saw Sanders fork out the sixty bucks, he asked if I was tuckered out. So I put the sixty back on the line, figured I'd double it. Like fun. This time I'd been hustled. I was playing Maximilian Upchurch. He put me right in my place, which at the time was the only way to get my attention.

"Max took the sixty bucks to teach me a lesson. Then he bought me a soda and grilled me about my training. It was such a relief to find anybody who gave a damn. My parents and teachers were goading me to learn the Pythagorean theorem; I'd never had a serious conversation about my forehand. I felt like the ugly duckling who'd finally met a swan."

Willy parked the school car at Sweetspot. Ambling, she instinctively drifted toward the courts.

"We met up in the piano bar that night," she rambled. "Max and I were in the same boat. His wife had refused to spend one more summer schlepping to tournaments and buying his clients corn kits. She wanted a real holiday, with nothing to do with tennis. To salvage the marriage, he'd agreed."

"My wife has no interest in tennis," Max had explained. "Or, I take that back. She hates tennis. Which is a kind of interest, I suppose."

Willy had stirred her Virgin Mary. "How could anyone marry a tennis coach and dislike the sport?"

He smiled, dismally. "You're too young to understand, but it makes perfect sense. Why, it's almost inevitable." He reveled in her naïveté. Max told her anything, the way you confide in a dog.

"But I'd think turning against tennis would be the same as turning against you."

"Duh," he said.

It seemed the Upchurch's marriage wasn't flourishing on their edifying scenic drives, since every evening Max wolfed his dinner and rushed back to the motel to scan cable channels for Ivan Lendl. As a reprieve from Taco Heaven and Navaho beadwork, he'd loiter soulfully on public courts to side-eye local talent. But his subversion of their "vacation from tennis" into the stalking of a new junior discovery was the last straw. At the end of the couple's stay in The Oasis, Max was free to tail the Novinsky's Chrysler to Yellowstone, since his wife had flown back to Hartford to file for divorce.

"So when you returned to New Jersey," Eric prodded as Willy led him to the Sweetspot courts, "Max proposed."

"To be my *coach*, dickhead."

Having plowed up their Montclair drive, Max had offered Willy a contract: he'd coach her pro bono in exchange for 20 percent of her winnings the first five years of her pro career. "You're pretty," he'd observed cynically, lounging against his Saab Turbo. "The money's in sponsors. Your face would sell." Max had appraised her clinically up and down, as if she were a head of cattle. For months after she'd act more temperamentally than came naturally, if only to be recognized as a girl.

"Max offered me a full scholarship to Sweetspot for my senior year." Willy kicked open the chain-link gate. "But my father wouldn't hear of it."

"Upchuck made him nervous."

"His worries proved unwarranted. Contrary to your sleazy assumptions, Max never laid a hand on me. And I was dying for him to. I used to lie in bed at night fantasizing about winning some big tournament, and Max would sweep down from the stands and lift me over his head—"

"Like I did."

"Like you did," she said shyly. "But I never earned better than a clap on the shoulder and a slug of Gatorade." Even now, her voice was melancholy. "At any rate, I was allowed to take the bus to Connecticut on weekends if I promised to go to college. Later I tried to renege on the deal, but Max was on my father's side. Max said he wasn't grooming an imbecile. Later I wondered which slot he *was* grooming me for. He didn't push his other students to go to college."

"So far I don't understand why I'm not speaking to the second Mrs. Upchurch. That's the usual program."

"He was waiting. He wanted me to make an informed decision as an adult. That was his mistake." The deserted facility was lit by the single floodlight of the moon, and Willy sank onto what for no rational reason was her favorite court. She laid her palms flat, soaking up heat from the tar.

"By this spring, the tension had become unbearable," she continued, leaning against the fence. "Pausing outside the women's locker room, he'd repeat some coachy tip I'd heard a million times, just to keep talking. Or we'd dawdle by my dorm before I hit the sack and stand a little too far apart because any closer and we'd have had to do something." She shrugged. "So finally we did something."

"But it didn't last long," she went on quietly. "Weeks. Oh, I won't pretend that the first few nights weren't a dream come true. But during practice nothing was the same. We started quarreling. I balked at his advice; I didn't like his pushing me around. I'm sure he'd told me to 'move my fat ass' before, but suddenly I got offended, and I'd stomp away in a snit. Then one

morning in May ... Still chilly, I guess. It was eight-thirty, late
for me. I started to get up. He reached for me and mumbled,
'It's cold. Come back to bed.' That was the end."

"You lost me."

"It wasn't cold. Not especially. And what did I care if it was
five below? It was time to practice, and he didn't give a damn
anymore. I'd started questioning everything: why he chose me
in Nevada, whether he really thought I was gifted or just liked
my legs. His every stingy compliment sounded in retrospect like
a pick-up line. I was convinced that other players were laughing
at me behind my back. For years I thought that all I wanted was
Max. I wanted one thing more."

Willy reclined flat onto the court, its warmth steeping
through her jeans and cotton shirt. Eric lowered himself on top
of her and exhaled. "You're warning me that I better not get on
the wrong side of your racket?"

But sandwiched between Eric and number seven, Willy had
her first intuition that it might be possible to have a man on one
side and a court on the other. "I'm tipping you off," she
murmured, "that I'd rather play tennis than have sex."

"I'd rather play tennis," he said, tugging her shirttail from her
jeans and sliding his hand up her rib cage, "*then* have sex." He
was a math major, a calculating man; he prized a small foil
packet from his watch pocket.

"Right here?"

Eric flipped her on top of him. "I've wanted to for years. After
all, tennis is like sex, isn't it? I think that's why you like it.
Thrusting across the net—the ball is just a medium, a messenger
of love and loathing all rolled up in one. That antagonism—
you're enemies but you need each other. Listen to the language!
Long-body, sweet spot, throat of the racket. *Dish* and *shank*, *stab*
and *slice*, *punch* and *penetrate*—it's pornographic!" Eric sidled her
Levi's down her thighs. "*Approach* and *hold*, *break*, *break back*,
stroke, *regain position*, and *connect*—it's romantic. And we both
know that libidinal high from finally finding the right partner,

and how you raise each other up. You never thought you could
be so good, and they never thought they could be so good, and
more than caring who wins, most of all you don't want to
stop... Good God, Wilhelm." He had grasped her buttocks, one
in each hand. "Your buns are about as pliant as Goodyear
radials."

Willy faced the fact that she'd always wanted to do it here as
well. It was significant that she and Max had never thought to,
as if they'd sensed that number seven and Max's bed were
incompatible. When she wriggled from Eric to step from her
jeans, being naked here felt normal. She always felt naked
playing tennis, each blemish on her character laid bare: every
unjustified conceit or nascent timidity, the least laziness,
flagging, or despair. The body, in comparison, was a trench coat.

In one motion Eric shed his grungy black T-shirt, and so
revealed an unsuspected artistry of torso, as the sly elegance of a
surprise drop-shot is covered until the last moment of opening
the face. While Willy had indulged a few flings with other
athletes at UConn, the dullness of their conversation had cast a
pall over their anatomies, the idealized bodies prosaic and
lifeless as line drawings in *Gray's*. With more than one Adonis
she'd remained so unaroused that she'd dragged her shirt back
on and trudged off to her own dorm. Willy had supposed it
took some aching flaw—a belly sag, an appendectomy scar—to
capture her imagination. But while Eric had no flaws to speak
of, an intriguing stir across his shoulders flickered the
moonlight from plane to plane, like the facets of a mirror ball,
or a series of complex, interlocking ideas.

Eric pulled his own jeans off, balancing on one leg, then the
other. He seemed to enjoy her watching. Willy had often found
the prick, both its shriveled button of retreat and its strangely
dissociated waving and poking when in heat, ridiculous. But
Eric's, at halfmast, drooped down his thigh at that unhurried
and luxurious stage of excitement that was a man's most
alluring.

As he kicked his clothes to the side and glided toward her where she rested against the net, Eric didn't strut with the gut-sucking, chest-thrusting swag she had learned to associate with the vain male athlete who has taken his clothes off. At the same time the confidence of his stride, the wryness of his smile signaled plenty of vanity. But those vacuous hard bodies had flexed their deltoids as if to make up for other lacks. Triangular pectorals were all they had to offer and so seemed paltry, like lone finger sandwiches on a picked-over platter. Eric Underwood instead uncloaked his body as if it were a pleasant incidental, like free leather upholstery when you buy the car.

If Eric considered his physique a trifle, Willy was in awe of it. Awe in general had not been a prevalent emotion in her life, and she wore the sensation awkwardly. She scanned his body for some restful ugliness. His feet were long, but this attenuated body should have big feet. Willy was ordinarily content with her own figure; it was taut and neat. But as Eric approached in the moonlight, she was aware that her breasts, while small, sagged just enough to fail the pencil test. She recited to herself that she was in good shape, that all women have a layer of subcutaneous fat; when Eric put his hands on her waist Willy heard in her head the very phrase, *subcutaneous fat*. Her own trunk was smooth and bland, with none of those conniving, thinking ripples musing over his chest. Eric sighed as he traced her hip, but Willy found the slight flare too wide and envied him the clean, parallel shoot to the thigh.

The foil packet in his right palm scratched when he stroked her ribs. From the shading of dark hair, his forearms loomed in relief, while hers, blanched in the wash of the moon, looked flat, paper-doll. He smoothed his left hand from her hip to her thigh, teasing his fingers up and inward, and she panicked at what he could possibly find in the absence between her legs that could compete with the whole fifth limb that arced against her stomach. Maybe, in sufficient thrall, it was impossible to imagine that so riveting a sex could conceivably be attracted by one's own.

"Oberdorf," he said cryptically. She didn't recognize the syllables, which sounded like an incantation, an open sesame from *The Arabian Nights* that would move boulders from caves.

"What?" Her voice was thin and vague.

"My last name is Oberdorf," he announced. "'Underwood' is for deviled ham."

Something about this new name oppressed her. Underwood had been a flimsy, easily manipulated infatuate who had pursued her all the way to Westbrook on the basis of one Cuban-Chinese meal; an adventitious young man who might eventually prove a pest but whom she could employ usefully as insulation from Max Upchurch's forbidding disappointment. Underwood's phone number would be scrawled on scrap paper, later accidentally thrown away. An Underwood sent her flowers that she forgot to water. And an Underwood had a gutsy but goofy and entirely forgettable tennis game. An Underwood wouldn't have had a prayer in pro tennis—but with a name like that an Oberdorf could improve.

"Eric Oberdorf," she said faintly. Her acknowledgment of his real name seemed to satisfy something he'd been waiting for, and he tore open the foil.

If condoms once indicated consideration for the girl, they did no longer; and here Willy was yielding to a man she knew so slightly that she couldn't be sure if he'd have bothered to protect her from pregnancy if he weren't primarily protecting himself from disease. Nor could she tell if he was packing contraceptives with the specific arrogance of expecting to fuck her or if he simply went everywhere with the generic arrogance of expecting to fuck somebody. But it was too late to worry what she was getting into because something was already getting into her.

Willy's back pressed the net cord; it groaned. Eric Oberdorf lifted her to cradle the small of her back on the tape, crouched, stood, and closed his eyes. Consequently Wilhemena Novinsky discovered what a match was like without the go-between meddling of a tennis ball.

The following morning Willy insisted that Eric leave. To have imported a man she was pretending to be interested in was tacky; to foist under Max's nose a man she was genuinely interested in was sadistic. Eric dispatched, she warmed up with Max that afternoon on number seven with an irrepressible smile. In her mind's eye the net cord retained a telltale dent from the pressure of her back, and she could still hear it creak from her pleasure. Though Willy had contrived the intersection of their paths, she now resolved to keep these two men as far apart as possible.

"You're hitting well," Max accused her. "Unusually well."

Willy begged off a day early, claiming she had paperwork to post for a satellite tournament in August, but in truth she wanted to try tennis again without the ball.

FOUR

THERE ENSUED A COURTSHIP in every sense. After Willy just missed making the semis of the Fresca Cup in Dayton, Eric met her plane at LaGuardia toting his Prince, and dragged her from the taxi directly to Riverside Park. Since by wristing and framing and stabbing he got the ball back more often than not, she had to agree with Max that though Eric's technique was raw, somewhere in this Neanderthal was a tennis game.

As for the game off court, he had no pride, or so it seemed when he announced that, barring his own tournaments, his schedule was at her disposal. Eric was unabashedly eager to see her every day she was in town and, rather than emphasize that he had his friends and many professional matters to attend to, cheerfully volunteered to sweep any other considerations aside if she had time for him. Initially this carte blanche had struck her as shameless, groveling, foolishly self-abnegating, and bound to backfire.

Eric bludgeoned her with invitations to have spaghetti with his roommate, or to pick up a slice of pizza for lunch, and was eternally available to practice in the park, even if that meant canceling other partners. He fanned nightly tickets to the U.S. Open before her like a deck of cards, of which she was free to avail herself. And he was thoughtful in a way that somehow meant more because the gestures were so minor and instinctive;

he didn't expect pats on the back. If he fixed himself a drink in her apartment, he refilled the ice cube trays. He replaced the lining in the garbage pail without being asked, washed his own coffee cup, and never left toothpaste globs in the sink. One afternoon in August, when she was pressed for time packing for the next satellite in Norfolk and was out of clean sports socks, he bundled to the basement with her reeking shorts and tank tops, returning with her laundered clothes folded and the sock pairs matched.

Willy's new boyfriend showed up at her door with tokens on evenings they went out—a silk bandanna the same crimson as her favorite sweatshirt, or a pirated Janis Joplin cassette, on which he'd written out all the names of the songs. The presents were always small, inexpensive, and beautifully wrapped.

Willy had grown up among the enemy, and initially regarded his generosity with suspicion. If Eric was trying to wrest something from her, she felt bound to keep him from getting it. And Willy had developed many a woman's instinctive disdain for niceness. Men who treated her too lavishly well were patsies. Yet one lunchtime when Eric tossed her a new jar of mayonnaise, she did a double take. Remembering the condiments for their sandwiches was considerate. Noting that her own jar was scraped to the dregs had been attentive. What was the problem? She would prefer a cad, a moocher, some heedless creep? At last Willy entertained the notion that there wasn't something wrong with niceness, but something wrong with her.

So on their next date, shyly, Willy handed Eric a package in return. Coming up with a gift had been hard, and while the modesty of Eric's presents was always charming, the paltriness of her own gift seemed niggardly. She kept apologizing. It was only a Sweetspot T-shirt, and maybe she'd been insensitive; Eric didn't, after all, have much time for the school. But Eric was overjoyed, and insisted on wearing it to Flor De Mayo. In fact, he wore the shirt for days after, until it was filthy and smelled. Willy didn't mind. She was proud of herself. She even wondered if all Eric's little gestures weren't meant to ingratiate himself so much as to teach her to make one back.

Besides, through the summer Willy came to understand that her suitor's strategy was sourced not in self-abasement but conceit. Eric Oberdorf was a single-minded man who once bent on a project did not relent until its object was achieved. He did not court Willy with an eye to his own self-protection, because it never entered his head that he would fail. This proclivity for unreserved full-tilt at what he would not be denied was both winning and unsettling. Willy's experience of getting anything she wanted was always over somebody else's dead body. But Eric evidenced no signs that anyone had ever stood in his way. Simply, he was spoiled.

If Eric boasted few former girlfriends, he was given to infatuations of other varieties. In his early teens he had thrown himself into politics, devoting himself to Ronald Reagan's reelection campaign of 1984. (To Willy's Democratic horror. Unusually for New York Jews, the Oberdorfs were Republicans. While the Clinton-Bush campaigns heated, he and Willy's electoral joustings were regularly sidetracked when Eric snidely marveled that here she was a pro tennis player and she knew who was running for president.) At fourteen, every weekday Eric had leafleted his Upper East Side neighborhood after school let out at Trinity. His homework essays had detailed how to increase defense spending, decrease taxes, and still reduce the national debt—papers that presaged Eric's aptitude at Princeton for imaginary numbers.

Subsequently Eric had become consumed with basketball. "Rick the Slick" was apparently a legend at Trinity still. When in a stroll through Riverside he and Willy happened upon a rough-house four-on-four that lacked an eighth man, she had the opportunity to verify that Eric was no slouch at hoop. Though jostled by colossal, trash-talking homeboys tingling with fast-twitch muscle fiber, Eric racked up more points than anyone on his team. Notably, Willy had no trouble watching him swish baskets, in contrast to following his tennis match with Max. God, Eric was graceful, so precise and fleet; his head fakes were comic, though wickedly effective. Willy shouted, "Go, Slick!" and burst into spontaneous applause so many times that she embarrassed him, but she was relishing not only the game itself but her own clean feeling: pure, free-flowing adoration.

Eric clearly excelled at whatever he put his mind to. A resultant summa cum laude assured Willy that once he concentrated on mathematics at Princeton he was adept at his equations. In fact, he emitted an arithmetic coolness even on the tennis court, where he maintained the implacable remove of a programmer entering information in his banks, and defeats were mere data, blips no less relevant than victories for the graph that he was plotting in his head.

Fundamentally, Eric Oberdorf liked to play games. That concluded, Willy considered a more cynical view of this no-holds-barred woo. Was romance just another contest to him? If Eric was given to infatuations, was Willy one such passing amusement in a string? For her boyfriend's capacity to shift energies willy-nilly from one engrossment to another was perplexing. It was inconceivable to Willy that anyone should aim to become a bankable tennis player without having nurtured the ambition from the age of five.

Willy appreciated that Eric seemed to be going about the project with some seriousness. He played for hours every day. He trained every other morning in Gold's Gym, with light weights and eight thousand skips of rope. He had scheduled out the whole next year, as she had, with a series of successively more challenging satellite tournaments. Though his ranking sounded abysmal to a layman, Eric had managed to accumulate a handful of computer points after graduating only in May, and through his disappearances in July and August scraped up several more. The bookshelf over his bed was crammed with how-to and tennis history; his knowledge of tennis stars and statistics was encyclopedic. But despite his laudable whole-hog, she was dubious whether such a capricious embrace of what for Willy had been a lifelong passion ought to be too readily rewarded.

Accordingly, in Flor De Mayo—or Flower of Mayonnaise, as they had now dubbed their regular dive—Willy inquired how he might feel if his aspirations failed to flourish into a career. She observed what Eric, with his thorough research, would have ascertained already: that although Top Tens raked in $10 million a year, the earning curve in tennis fell off sharply. With rankings from 11 to 25, a man might pull in $1 million a year; a woman, Willy noted wrathfully, half that. From 26 to 75, a player's total income came to no more than $200,000 to $300,000, though that depended on staying in the top 75, and in tennis, standing still could wear you out. However, by 125 you could expect no more than $100,000, half of which would be consumed by economy-class airfare and overpriced hotel breakfasts. If they both didn't scramble into the top 200 neither would do much better than break even.

Unperturbed, Eric reached for the remains of her rice. "You pay your rent, don't you?"

"Barely. I made thirty thousand dollars last year, which included winning two satellites. Five thousand went to Max. Another five to expenses. If you factor in what I don't pay for—his coaching time, my dorm at Sweetspot—I'm in the red. How do you plan to make ends meet?"

Eric hunted out chunks of pork. "My father."

"What?"

"Why look so shocked? My dad's backing me my first two years on the circuit. If I succeed, I won't need him. If I don't, I do something else. But I doubt that will prove necessary." Eric licked his fingers.

"Don't you want to make it on your own?"

"I never said word-one about wanting to 'make it on my own.' I said I wanted to make it. How that is achieved is of little consequence. If you're short and need to fly to Indianapolis,

who hands you a ticket? Upchuck. Me, it's my father. What's the
diff?"

Willy went quiet.

Eric lifted her chin. "The profession's rigged anyway. How do
you earn computer points? By winning tournaments that award
computer points. How do you get into tournaments that award
computer points? By having computer points. That's not the
only catch-22. How do you make a living playing tennis? By
getting into the top 200. How do you get into the top 200? By
devoting one hundred percent of your time to tennis, and
thereby *not* making a living. You can't get there from here with
a day job, Wilhelm. This is still an upper-class sport. I'm sorry
your own father hasn't been supportive, and I'm glad, financially
anyway, that you've got Max. But you won't make me feel lousy
about my dad. Patronage is how it's done."

She dropped it, eaten by a new curiosity. "Underwood? Why
do you want to play tennis professionally? After an Ivy League
degree in math?"

"You wouldn't go out with a computer hacker, would you?
Reason enough."

"I'm serious."

Eric drummed his fingers. "It's challenging. Keeps me in
shape. I could stand to make a packet of money. And I'll have
to retire by forty at the latest, so it allows for a second career."

"You *like* that? Being forced to quit?"

"Sure. I need variety. I get bored easily. Who'd want to play
tennis all day until they're ninety-two?"

"*I* would!"

"Well, you're a nut," he said affectionately.

"God, I dread retirement. When I think about how few years
I have left, I feel like I'm on death row."

"Why do *you* want to play pro, Wilhelm?"

"What kind of a stupid question is that?" she snapped.

Eric laughed. "The same stupid question you asked me."

"In my case that's like asking why do I insist on breathing."

Eric examined her with real incredulity. "You've really never asked yourself that, have you?"

"Not once," Willy acceded. "I don't have reasons, though I was pretty sure that you would. I'm a tennis player. I can't envision being anything else and still being me. If I thought up explanations, they'd come afterwards. They'd just be something to say."

"OK, but *unreasoning* isn't generally a compliment."

Willy had the queer impression that he was jealous. "You grew up with a whole series of ambitions," she said softly, taking his hand. "Politics, basketball, mathematics. Me, maybe you'd call me limited, or obsessive. I've always had one true love."

His eyes narrowed another millimeter, and he slipped his fingers out from beneath her palm. "Are you accusing me of being a dilettante?"

"I'm not accusing you of anything!" Willy cried in exasperation. "I'm sure you're more adaptable than I am. You're brilliant at all kinds of stuff, and that's hardly a criticism. But I'm not the only one who's irrational or less than candid with themselves. Because you've never answered *my* question. What if it turns out you don't have the goods in tennis? What if your two years go by and you're stranded in the 800's? Or unranked altogether? That happens, and to decent players. How would you take it?"

"Told you," he said. "Do something else." Eric didn't usually speak with his mouth full; the garbling of his answer seemed deliberate, as if he didn't want to hear it himself.

"Like what?"

"Dunno," he said tersely. "What about you?"

"What about me what?"

"If you don't make it."

Willy was tempted to defend that $30,000 didn't sound like much but it was plenty for her rank and she was starting to make a living and so she had already, to some degree, "made it," unlike some people who still got a monthly check from their *daddies*.

"I can't imagine, I—try not to think about it."

"Exactly." Eric dabbed his mouth with a teachery expression, as if he'd been putting her to a test again and she'd barely passed. "I don't believe in contingency plans. A little imagination is a dangerous thing. Picture the future where you're foundering and before you know it this bleak landscape is framed on your living room wall. Put up travel posters. You'll do great. I'll do great. We'll do great."

He spanked rice grains off his hands. Though only a year his senior, for once Willy felt appreciably older than her boyfriend.

The National Tennis Center had a wretched reputation among players—the crowds were rambunctious and disrespectful; the stadium was plunked smack-dab under LaGuardia Airport's flight path. Willy had long turned a deaf ear to such carping. She herself had been forced to focus through a foofooraw of wailing car alarms, plinking ice cream trucks, or thumping outdoor rock concerts in nearly every scrappy tournament she'd entered. As far as Willy was concerned, the National Tennis Center was as reverent and hushed as St. Peter's. If Steffi Graf groused that she couldn't concentrate there, Willy Novinsky would happily take her place.

Willy loved Flushing Meadow. She'd been a ballgirl there in the McEnroe era, and had a crush on the volatile bad boy of tennis when she was fifteen. Since then, she always ducked behind security tape to say hello to the man who still managed the ball-retrieval team, and brought him up to date on her career. Though she'd never been a contender here, familiarity with the tunnels and locker rooms, of which the public were ignorant, infused her with a proprietary sense of access. At the NTC she dared to believe, as Eric did daily with such unnatural ease, that center court was her destiny.

With amazement, Willy was led by the hand on September 7, not up switchbacking ramps to the upper tiers of rowdy proles, but to the hallowed courtside seats reserved for corporations and blue-blood families. Screwed on the backs of their chairs gleamed two plastic plaques: OBERDORF. In that it had become customary to hand on permanent U.S. Open seats in one's will, some day these thrones could belong to Eric. Willy conceded that privilege did not seem altogether obnoxious from the standpoint of its beneficiary.

Yet Willy and Eric seemed destined to remain on opposite sides of the net. As he supported the incumbent Reagan in '84, Eric promptly backed Stefan Edberg, the obvious favorite, who had won the U.S. Open the previous year. Eric *knew* she was rooting for the challenger, Larry Punt—a modestly ranked hopeful who had battled his way through the qualies into the round-of-sixteen.

"Are you being deliberately contrary?" she asked. "Every time we watch a match, you back the other guy."

"That's because you have such a soft spot for long shots, Wilhelm. Whenever some poor slob is ranked 4,002, or is coming back from an injury that will eventually put him out of the game forever, you take his side. Who's being contrary?"

"Since your ranking isn't far from 4,002 you might sympathize with the player who isn't famous."

"For most of these people, this is entertainment," he murmured, leaning forward. "For you and me, this is a vicarious exercise. So it's a question of with whom you identify. That piece of kelp out there, even if he freakishly took this match, would only get cut to ribbons in the quarters. Why go down with the no-name in your head? Make it easy on yourself, and identify with the front-runner. If you throw your mental lot in with the lowly, there's no logical limit. You may as well imagine yourself as an aspirant ballgirl."

"I was a ballgirl," she said icily, tugging the empty arms of her sweater around her shoulders and jerking them in a knot. "Edberg is drab. Typical Swede. He has no personality, and his face is about as expressive as set cement."

"Who needs personality with a volley like that?"

"Tennis should be a test of character."

"Character, maybe. Not personality."

"What's the difference?"

Eric assumed a patient tone. "Personality involves frilly quirks like I-have-to-wear-my-lucky-headband. Character entails flushing all that emotional froufrou down the toilet and getting on with the job."

She turned to Eric's face with amazement, which had assumed the same rigid intensity that he wore on court. Eric was a great admirer of technique, the exterior game, and if the interior existed for him at all, it was to be obliterated. Presumably in Eric's view the most exemplary tennis players didn't, themselves, exist. But Willy was riveted by the storms of frustration, beleaguerment, and redoubled determination washing over a player's face like island weather. To Willy, the interior game *was* the game—your feelings could be played like a violin, or they could play you. Eric's solution was not to master the emotions but to make them go away. If he himself could pull off such a vanishing act, he was either a shaman, or a machine.

When she turned back to the game, Punt had been given a warning for racket abuse. The underdog was screaming at the umpire, who gazed unconcernedly at an airplane overhead.

"No class," Eric hissed.

"It was a bad call!"

"Which wouldn't be overturned if Edberg's shot had landed so far wide that it bounced on our picnic basket . . . Christ, what a trashy outburst."

"Punt is 5–1 down! He's frazzled."

"So if he can't play tennis, he could at least behave himself. Losing all the more behooves him to be gracious."

"Gracious defeat is always insincere, and if I were being humiliated at what I cared about most in the world in front of thousands of people, I'd blow off a little steam at the umpire myself."

Meanwhile, Larry Punt was giving his all. He was drenched in sweat, and lunged for every return, if reliably to no avail. For

Edberg was in a zone, and deep lobs drove him to his backcourt for only the one winning overhead. Willy tried to get Eric to appreciate that at least Punt didn't roll over.

Eric shrugged. "Makes for better spectating, but doesn't affect the result."

"God, you sound so contemptuous...when he's playing his guts out—"

"Quiet!" shushed a woman behind them.

"Keep it down," Eric muttered.

"Oh, who cares what the buttinsky thinks?"

"*I* care," he scolded.

"Of course you do; anything to do with what other people think and how somebody appears. All this stiff-upper-lipping tut-tut when you're not even British—" Willy burst into tears.

"Willy! What's with you?" Apologizing to their neighbors, Eric ushered her from the stands.

"Honey." He wrapped his arms around her under what might have been the Open's single spindly tree. "What's wrong? I thought we were having a nice time."

Now that Willy had the most to say she couldn't talk. "All you care about is—" Her throat caught. "All you care about is—" she would have to choose single words carefully "—*winning.*"

She expected the usual *There-there-I-care-about*-you-*sweetheart!* but instead he laughed and smoothed her hair and said, "Oh, Willy. Not nearly as much as you do."

Her sniffles subsided and they resumed their seats, where Willy discovered that she didn't revile Edberg quite so virulently any longer. Yet on the subway back to Manhattan, Willy was reserved, choosing to stand and read the MTA's Poem of the Week even when two adjacent seats became available.

"Little Miss Macho," Eric muttered in her ear, swinging from the next strap to dig a forefinger discreetly into her ribs. "Can't be caught sitting down."

He meant lighten up; she couldn't. Some bitter pill from

their outing was still undissolved. "Happy?" Over the clatter
of wheels, she had to shout. "The impertinent nothing was
crushed. More laurels for the automaton."

"I'm delirious with joy," he said, flouncing into one of the
seats. Eric wouldn't be lured into another public confrontation,
and grabbed a discarded *New York Times*.

Willy grew alarmed that in reviving the antagonism she'd
gone too far, and now Eric wouldn't come home with her. At
that prospect, her face drained and broke out in a sticky sweat.
The train jostled her clenched jaw, and her teeth clacked. When
Eric didn't tromp out of the car at Grand Central for his connection with the number six, she went so weak-kneed with relief
that she dropped into the seat next to him, with only one stop
to go. Something awful was happening. It shouldn't have
mattered so much, whether he stayed over. Willy had slept
complacently alone most of her life.

"OK, I give up!" he declared, slamming the door of her
apartment. "Truth is, you don't give a rat's ass about Larry Punt.
So what's this really about?"

Eric switched on the overhead, and in its blaze Willy felt
pasty and exposed.

"I'm a little distressed that we admire such different players,"
she said haltingly.

"You like Boris Becker?" he fired at her, bombing into the
couch.

"Yes, I—"

"Bingo. We have something in *common*. Feel better?"

"There's one other player who we may not see eye to eye on."
Willy stood staring down at her hands.

"I can't see what better to unite any couple than mutual revulsion for Andre Agassi, so who do you have in mind?"

"Me," said Willy quietly.

"Hey, come here." Eric reached and pulled her to his side,
and then thought better of the overhead light. He lit a candle
and killed the third-degree glare.

"You like these stony, stoic types," she went on in the crook of his shoulder. "But I stamp my feet, leap up and down—"

"And talk to yourself all the time," he finished for her with a smile. *"Take your racket back! Kill the son of a bitch! Follow through on that volley!"*

"You're making fun of me."

"Of course." He kissed her forehead. "You charm the pants off me on the tennis court, you know that."

"But you're so contained. I've never seen you display a single emotion in a match."

"That's illegal?"

"It's inhuman! If your face never tingles with humiliation when someone slams an ace down your throat, if you don't experience a trace of exasperation when you muff a simple drive that you'd hit right since you first picked up a racket—well, then, I can't see how you could have feelings about anything!"

"Like what?"

She squirmed. "I don't know, whatever..."

"Like what?" he needled into her neck, teasing up under her chin, where he knew she was ticklish.

"Me!" Willy tried not to laugh. "Me, me me!" He moved to her ribs, which precluded addressing this very serious issue in their relationship with proper gravity. "All your fascist blather about *control*...and that snotty, antiquated bullshit about *dignity*..." She wriggled out of his clutches long enough to deliver, "And on top of that, you need 'variety' and get 'bored easily'!"

Eric backed off, shaking his head. "So if I could possibly get bored with tennis, of course I'll get bored with you."

"Well, how do I know? You play like a martinet. You have no commitment to tennis, since you *look forward* to quitting. Where's the devotion, the fire? Taken to its extreme, self-possession is mentally ill!"

In a single motion, Eric slipped one arm under her knees, the other behind her back, and lifted her off the couch. He marched with Willy bundled against his chest to the bedroom and dropped her, bouncing, on the mattress. He dropped on top, stretching her arms overhead with both her wrists manacled in his hands.

"*Mentally ill,*" Eric lectured, "is not knowing the difference between some stupid little sport and real life. One of the main reasons I like Edberg and Becker is they keep their careers in perspective. They recognize that the rest of the world would roll merrily along without them or tennis, if it came to that.

"Now, do I feel anything on the court?" he asked rhetorically, his forehead pressed against her own. "Sometimes. I don't show it, and that's a gambit. I play better when I don't give my reactions away. But tennis is not about 'everything,' you moron, not by a mile. Sure I like control, and dignity, in its place. This," his hands slid down her arms, "ain't the place."

Grappling under her shirt, Eric popped a button. Willy decided this was not a very good time to go look for it. When he unzipped his fly his cock sprang forward, and for once Eric didn't seem self-possessed but simply possessed. He wouldn't wait for them both to get all their clothes off, and plunged into her with his jeans still binding his thighs. Willy had always considered fucking partially clad tacky, but now she changed her mind. Urgency took precedence over aesthetics. Apparently Eric did not always bother about appearances, about what people might think; he groaned loudly enough to titillate adjoining tenants. Yet his consideration was not so readily shed as his sense of decorum; even in the heat of the moment, he'd managed to slip a condom on.

Eric flipped her gracefully on top, and grasped Willy by the waist. He raised her whole body until the tendons in his arms stood out. Bringing her pelvis back tight to his, he bellowed. In the echo of his exclamation, a rich, round cry she had never heard issue from that throat, Willy gaped wondrously at Eric's face. The muscles spasmed. The sharp planes of his brow and cheekbones sloughed and blurred. His countenance was almost unrecognizable; he didn't look clever, caustic, or *contained*. Some people would have found the contortion of his features ugly. To Willy, it was the most beautiful thing she'd ever seen, and she came.

Turnabout was fair play. If the seemly Eric Oberdorf could wake up half of 112th Street with an orgasmic roar, the volcanic Willy Novinsky could keep the lid on for one tennis game. The next day she tempted Eric into another match at Riverside. Willy insisted on the northern courts, whose surface eccentricities her boyfriend detested. To Eric, a court was an idealized graph from which the ball should take predictable trajectories if you'd got your equations right. This Oberdorf was Germanic by nature and liked order. A Novinsky had a genetic Eastern European predisposition to chaos. Willy was only delighted that overhanging branches had recently baptized number eight with a shower of purple berries, whose pits were rolling across the composition like violet ball bearings.

Rather than click her heels at a winner or bop her forehead when she botched a gift put-away, this afternoon Willy set her face into the very impassive mask she had learned from Eric himself. No whistles of admiration, racket twirling, or knocking the frame on her shoe. Instead, Willy marched woodenly from serve to serve without one stomped foot. Stifling her running monologue, today she straightened her mouth in a line so flat that were it an EKG the patient would be dead. When Eric asked if his serve was a let she would only nod.

"Are you upset about something?" he worried on the second changeover.

She shook her head rigidly, though whether or not she was upset had nothing to do with *getting on with the job*.

Whatever Eric seemed to want she denied him. He loved to dive for low, whistling passes, so each time he rushed the net she lobbed—exquisite topspin arcs cresting a few tantalizing inches from the tip of his racket. He'd streak to his baseline, plow back again, *bloop*... When he paced up his game, she dragged the points to a crawl.

And Willy had never been more coldly conniving. Her sidespins were given a happy assist when they landed on berries. She'd sweep her racket back as if for a doozy and at the very last second bring it to a shrieking halt; *dink*, the ball would cough over the tape and wheeze to Eric's feet. Finally, when he'd been lulled into anticipating only junk, she'd let tear, jangling the ball into the fence. Composed and serenely mechanical, Willy dispatched the first set 6–2.

Receiving in the second at 5–1, Willy reflected that she'd aimed only to enrage him, to teach Eric that he could be fervid once he got out of bed. Yet her methods had begun to backfire. The score was sweet enough; she needed only to break him this game, or hold the next. But instead of at last revealing his wit's end—by kicking another of her winning balls at the net, or at least shooting her a glare—Eric had started to laugh.

His serve went wiggly and folded into her service court, as if itself doubled over in hysterics. She flattened it. He didn't even attempt to retrieve, and wiped away a tear. Willy narrowed her eyes to make them all the more steely, and disciplined her mouth to a bar. Meanwhile he had started to hoot, losing his balance and gasping for breath. At love–40, match point, he shoveled a fat, juicy floater to her midcourt. She squashed it. Barely able to get the words out through his guffaws, he said something.

The match over, it was now permissible to speak. "What was that?" asked Willy courteously.

This time he shouted unmistakably, "Marry me!"

Willy cartwheeled her racket fifteen feet in the air, and caught it neatly by the grip. Oberdorf had finally displayed a little passion on the tennis court.

FIVE

I F TWENTY-THREE WAS YOUNG to marry for 1992, Willy did not situate herself in modern history any more than she regarded herself as American. She owed allegiance to the tennis court, whose lines described a separate country, and to whose rigid and peculiar laws she adhered with the fervor of patriotism. Likewise Willy conceived of her lifespan in terms of the eighteenth century. As a tennis player, she would at best survive to forty; twenty-three was middle-aged.

That the institution of marriage had been thoroughly discredited by the time Willy was born didn't delay her acceptance of Eric's proposal by ten seconds. Granted, her own parents set a poor example; Willy envied neither her glumly patriarchal father nor his cheerfully submissive sidekick. But she might have envied her parents at their first meeting, in 1961: when her mother, Colleen, was a flighty modern dance student, leaping through recitals to the beat of bongos inside a helix of scarves, and her father, Charles, was an undiscouraged beatnik scribbler, whose pockets bulged from squiggled napkins and leaky ballpoint pens. Willy clung to the notion that nothing about marriage itself condemned her mother to dismiss an ambition to dance as vain folly, nor her father to turn on his own credulous literary aspirations with such a snarl. And surely had she wed in this more liberal era, the acquiescent Colleen might have told Charles to get a grip and stop moaning and sometimes gone her own way. Despite overwhelming evidence that both true love and domestic balance of power were myths, Willy still believed in the possibility of an ardent, lasting union between equals, much as many religious skeptics still kept faith in an afterlife because the alternative was too unbearable.

So all through a militantly independent young adulthood Willy had been waiting. At last along came Eric Oberdorf, who radiated the same clear-eyed courage that shone from pictures of her father in the early sixties—before Charles joined the opposition in celebrating his own defeat. Willy had inherited her mother's grace, and given it structure and purpose. Together she and Eric could rewrite history, which may have been what children were for.

As for Eric, Willy's primary concern was that he might regard marriage, like his so far useless degree in mathematics, as an end in itself. Eric had a modular mind. He might not conceive of pro tennis as death row, but he thought of his life in blocks, and therefore as a series of little deaths. But Willy knew enough about the altar to be sure that marriage demarcated not only the successful completion of a project, but the beginning of another, far more demanding endeavor.

"Daddy, it's Willy."

"*Hola!*"

Willy let the receiver list. Her father had never forgiven her for majoring in Spanish. "You're going to interpret for the UN?" he'd inquired dryly when informed of her decision. "No, I'll sell veggie burritos in Flushing Meadow," she'd snipped back. "Which by the time I finish this BA is the closest I'm going to get to the U.S. Open." Her father held nothing more against Spanish people than against anyone—meaning he held a great deal against them, indeed. But he knew that she'd chosen an easy major to have maximum free time for the tennis team.

"*Qué tal?*" asked Willy.

"Nothing ever changes here, Willow, you know that."

"You could always get old and die," she recommended. "At least that would get it over with."

"It's important to keep something to look forward to."

"Listen, I have someone I want you to meet."

"Another brain surgeon?"

"Yes, he's a tennis player, Daddy," she said impatiently. "But with a degree from Princeton."

"A tennis player with a degree!" he exclaimed. "You told me that was impossible."

Willy almost hung up. If she could barely make it through this phone call, how was she going to survive the whole evening she proposed? "How about Friday night? We'll take the seven-twenty from Port Authority."

"I'm sure I can squeeze you and your young man into my busy social calendar."

"Listen, Daddy," she added effortfully. "I really like this guy. Could you... be friendly?"

"Willow, I'm always—"

"I mean, don't be quite such a gloomy Gus? Like, don't rain on any parades for one night."

"Gloomy! After an electrifying week of teaching budding car mechanics commonly confused words, I'm sure to be happy as a clam."

"Oh, never mind," said Willy, and hung up with a sigh.

"When you first talked about your father, I thought he was some working-class stiff," Eric swung the Chateauneuf du Pape in its plastic bag, "not an English professor."

"I'm sorry if I seem dismissive of his job," Willy mumbled. "But that's the product of careful coaching."

They were standing in line at Gate 413. Willy was relieved that the bus was late. Her stomach knotting, she now wished they'd brought two bottles of wine.

"When I was a kid my father sensed I admired him," Willy

went on, "since any little girl would. I must have been—oh, eleven, alone with my father in the car. He explained that most of his classes could barely read, so if teachers were judged by the quality of their students my father was, I quote, 'the bottom of the barrel.' He announced that with a weird, vicious pleasure."

"What's his problem?" asked Eric as the line began to move. "Bloomfield College isn't a great school, but it's not disgraceful."

"To Chuck Novinsky it is. I didn't understand until I was fifteen. Nobody had told me. I was pottering in the attic when I found a box of duplicate hardbacks. Unappealing cover—plain; I think it was cheap. *In the Beginning Was the Word*, by Charles Novinsky."

Eric chuckled. "A little inflated, if you don't mind my saying so. What was it, criticism?"

Willy glanced at her fiancé in the light streaming through the door of Gate 413. A fresh feeling came off of him that had nothing to do with having ironed his shirt for the occasion. His mental basement wasn't knee-deep in naysaying bilge; the storage in his parents' ritzy East Side apartment wouldn't breathe musty disillusionment.

"A novel," she said sorrowfully, climbing into the bus and snuggling by a window. "Begpool Press, 1962—never heard of them."

"Did you read it?"

"I had a feeling that I shouldn't mention the books to my father. So I sneaked up to the attic with a flashlight."

"Was it any good?"

"I don't know," she puzzled.

Had her father's book been any good? Naturally the novel had commented on the nature of literature, and there wasn't a soul who wanted to read about *that*; likewise it celebrated the power of language, a power he now derided. The plot was playful, about a novelist whose every printed word came to life. (She loved it when a mixed metaphor gave rise to a grotesque behemoth slouching toward the narrator's house until he frantically rewrote it.) But the prose clanked with thesaurus plunder, a whole paragraph conceived to accommodate *stereotropism*. Still, the slim volume seemed an eager, trusting effort and couldn't have deserved the scathing reviews shoved down the side of the box.

"The reviews were hideous." Willy shuddered. "All in local papers, fly-by-night magazines. Probably by young journalists trying to make a name for themselves, and so acrobatically snide. One reviewer called *In the Beginning Was the Word* so awful that it was 'a bit of a giggle.'"

Newly curious, Willy had located a second box, where four different rubber-banded typescripts were crammed into water-logged cardboard, their pages folded and specked with roach eggs. She'd been reluctant to paw those reams, once treasure, now trash—thousands of offbeat adjectives mined from *Roget's*, only to slump in this carton and rustle with insects. She'd scanned only the most recent manuscript, on top, heart-breakingly protected with "Copyright© 1967 by Charles Novinsky" on the title page.

The End of the Story had been more of a slog. The prose was dry and spare, recalling the cutting, droll sarcasm of the father she knew. The satire described a mythical population grown so vicarious that content was extinct. An automated world whose only work was entertainment divided between the watcher and the watched. Consequently, all art was reflexive: films concerned screenwriters, TV programs followed the "real lives" of sitcom actresses, and novels, the author noted with special disgust, exclusively detailed the puerile pencil-sharpening of literary hacks. The manuscript had left off on page 166 in the middle of a sentence. Little wonder; with its theme that storytelling was dead, the narrative dripped with such self-loathing that to finish such a book would be antithetical.

"That last manuscript was depressing," said Willy. "He'd even worked the phrase 'a bit of a giggle' into the text. He was smart-ing. I'm not sure he's smarting anymore, which is probably what's wrong with him."

"You think all those failed novels explain why he's discouraged you from playing tennis?"

"I wouldn't be that simplistic. I'd give my parents some credit for genuinely wanting to protect me. Original sin in my family is *getting your hopes up.*"

"Honey?" They'd been sitting on Willy's bed; her mother had patted her hand. Willy was seventeen, and still feuding with her father over college. "Every young person wants to be a celebrated artist, a fashion model, or a big-name sports star. All but a very, very few end up working for IBM, or teaching youngsters who themselves want to be famous that they still have to learn to spell, like your father. And there's nothing wrong with having an ordinary life. We'd just like you to be prepared. If you set your heart on being Chris Everest—"

"*Evert,*" Willy corrected, twanging her racket strings with her fingernails.

"We're just afraid you'll get hurt."

"You're afraid, all right." Willy had stood and zipped her case. "Afraid I might *make it.*"

She'd stomped out; but later her father had been adamant.

"I have nothing against tennis," he said, which was a bald-faced lie. "But as for going pro, you could as well announce that instead of earning a degree you're taking your Christmas check to Las Vegas."

"Max thinks I'm playing with more than a Christmas check," she returned hotly.

"A gamble is a gamble, and this is a poor bet that will only pain you when you're older. In my day we wanted to join the circus—"

"Or write a book," Willy spat.

His double take was steady. "Or write a book," he repeated coolly. "And then we grew up."

"Spare me your adulthood."

"I would if I could, Willow." For a moment he sounded

dolorous. "But you are not throwing away a college education for a childhood hobby, and that's final."

"Do you think he had a point?" asked Eric.

"Now you, too?" Willy groaned. "My father didn't have a problem with tennis when a sports scholarship covered my tuition, did he?"

"It's just, I still don't understand why after three years at UConn you dropped out."

"My father didn't want me to have credentials to rely on after I'd made a name for myself in tennis. He wanted me to have a degree for when I fell on my face. I had to drop out and turn pro. To finish college was to believe him."

Eric smoothed her hand, uncomfortably like her mother.

"What I still can't get over," Willy gazed out the window at the darkening buildup of industrial New Jersey, "is he taught me to play. When I was little, we hit three times a week. We had a great time."

"So why the hostility?"

"I could say he was mad that I've beaten him since I was ten. But I don't think so. I found trouncing my father upsetting. He seemed to find it marvelous."

The memory remained a queer color. They were playing at that lumpy macadam court nearest Willy's house. She didn't remember the game itself, only standing on the baseline after match point feeling dazed. Her father had come toward her in wonderment, climbing over the net instead of going around the post as if approaching an apparition that might vanish. He knelt at her feet, his voice hushed. "You have something special, Willow. I don't know where you got it; not from me. But you be careful, and don't let *anybody* take it away."

Her mother bustling from the car broke the spell. "Chuck, whatever are you doing on the ground? Dinner's been ready for an hour."

Her father spread his hands. "She beat me."

"That's nice, dear. She's a regular little whirlybird with that racket, isn't she? Now, no dawdling, you two. The potatoes—"

"Colleen, you don't understand," he said irritably. "I didn't *let* her. Ten years old, can you believe it? And I tried. I gave it my best shot."

"Chuck," her mother scolded. "You'll give her a swelled head."

Yet at the very point her father recognized that his second daughter was gifted he began to stand in her way. He found fewer afternoons after work to hit. He refused to cover her dues for the Montclair Country Club, and Willy was forced to collect balls for tips to pay her way. Half the players she fetched for didn't really want a ballgirl, and she became something halfway between mascot and pest. Arguments over entering local junior tournaments that "interfered with her schoolwork" were incessant.

The antagonism came to a head on Willy's sixteenth birthday. She sat before the usual sagging cake; her mother never quite went all the way in cooking, and had whipped the egg whites for the coconut icing to insufficient peak. As the whites subsided to raw slime, the icing slurped down the sides with a dispiritedness that encapsulated the Novinsky gestalt. Likewise each fallen layer was lined with a streak of dense, rubbery sad cake, as if nothing in this household was destined to rise from perpetual depression. Before her lay a single envelope, labeled *Wilhemena*.

She should have known better, but it was May; Willy leapt to the conclusion that inside was at last permission to attend the Vitas Gerulaitis tennis camp in Queens. When she ripped open the envelope, her face fell as noticeably as the cake.

"This way Gert gets her birthday present early," her father blustered. "But you're not quite old enough to go alone."

The offer of three weeks in Europe with her dreary older sister could as well have been an all-expenses-paid to Newark. Willy mashed a bite of cake with her fork. "There are only three places I want to go in Europe," she delivered levelly. "Roland Garros, the Foro Italico, and the All England Club—*on tour.*

Other than that, I have no intention of spending three weeks of the best weather of the year shuffling through moldy museums with *Gert.*"

Conventionally her father used composure as a weapon. This time he turned crimson, knocking back his chair and barking that Willy was thankless, that at her age he'd have given his eyeteeth—

Willy had learned icy calm at his own knee. "If you can afford to send me to Europe," she'd pushed away her uneaten cake, "you can afford to send me to tennis camp."

Once at camp, Willy instinctively gravitated to the scholarship kids, and lied that she came from poor white trash. The fib came easily; Walnut Street constituted poverty of a kind. Yet there was something inevitable about her family's low emotional income, and Willy didn't know what besides bitterness she might expect from her father. His own hopes had been crushed. How could she insist that he be generous in defeat when she herself decried gracious losers as insincere?

Since having discovered her father's secret body of work slowly rotting in the attic like a murdered corpse, Willy envisioned the young, determined Charles Novinsky as a different person altogether. She stood sentinel over the innocent predecessor, fending off ridicule from the mordant man he became. She cherished her picture of the stranger: a tirelessly ebullient aesthete, bursting with ideas, destined to become a great writer. This was her real father. The ornery Chuck Novinsky she grew up with was an impostor. In paging through those mildewed manuscripts, Willy could as well have unearthed documentation that she was adopted.

Maybe Chuck in adulthood was attempting to remedy his own parents' optimism on his account, which he described as a kind of abuse. Willy's grandparents had been hardworking Eastern European stock whose modest dry-cleaning business had grown prosperous by the fifties. Their unanticipated comfort, and the classically American structure of their lives whereby this year was always better than last, encouraged them to buy wholesale into the country's claim that any boy could be president. They must have lauded little Charlie's lucid first few words, taped his poems to the refrigerator door, and cooed to relatives about his editorship of the high school paper. Alfred A. Knopf anxiously awaited. Willy's father blamed his parents for having sold him a bill of goods, a mistake he would not repeat with his own children, who were raised to glower squarely at the low, unremarkable horizon that humped outside the windows of their frumpy New Jersey house.

Her mother, however, had preserved a girlish purity, which Willy happened upon when she was twelve. Her tennis game rained out, Willy came home earlier than expected. Hot-blooded salsa music pounded from the living room. Willy peeked through the doorway to find her mother in bare feet and leggings; the ancient black leotard was a little tired, and falling off her shoulders. She was switching her hips in figure eights, and snaking her arms in *S*'s. Eyes shut, she slithered into a full split. Wow. She could still bring both thighs to the floor. Though the choreography was eclectic—Desi Arnaz meets Twyla Tharp— she was actually a pretty hot dancer.

When Willy whistled, her mother shrieked, then blushed and fumbled to turn off the stereo at once. Willy was immediately sorry that she'd given her presence away; she should have treated herself to a longer show, slunk off, then theatrically slammed the front door a second time. Willy wanted Mama to keep her secret. Colleen O'Hara's dreams of being a dancer had been conceived in private, and in private they remained intact. No wonder she urged Willy to play tennis just for fun. Colleen herself preserved a few minutes a day as a *première danseuse*, and she wanted at least the same secluded limelight for her daughter. The afternoon's improvisation had mimed urgently to her second child: keep within you the tiny court where you are queen; be a star in the night sky of your own eyes closed. If it weren't for me, that box of *In the Beginning Was the Word* would have been carted long ago to the dump, or burned gleefully as fire starter. Your father bared his heart for an instant, to have it dashed against his sleeve. Shut anything dear to you safe from the catcalls of strangers; *only dance when the house is empty.*

Willy and Eric disembarked at the corner of Walnut, a leafy, stable street of Second Empires and Dutch Colonials. Nothing about the humble but attractive neighborhood was intrinsically dour. Clutching Eric's hand, Willy dragged her feet. "I should warn you about the house," she said. "It's brown."

The house was brown. It was brown outside, it was brown inside. When her parents first bought the two-story Queen Anne, they spoke of replacing the chocolate wall-to-wall carpet and ripping off the cheap umber paneling that made the rooms look cheerless and small. But the very oppression of the interior steeped its residents in lassitude, and their grand renovation schemes dwindled. Faced with objectionable decor that was bothersome to revamp, it was more expedient to revamp their tastes instead. Her parents now claimed they liked brown-everything, and had invested in matching mahogany furniture and beige drapes. That redecoration was all talk was hardly surprising: they were both given to vague propositions, but never suggested cleaning out the garage *this Saturday.* Her parents had mumbled for years about traveling to Japan, but the only trips her father could be troubled to take were those that actively conflicted with his daughter's tennis matches.

Willy tromped up the brown steps, shuffled over the brown porch, and poked her head in the brown door. "*Hola!*"

Her father dwelt on the paper in his lap a beat before looking up; she supposed it took him a moment to ready himself. Willy always seemed to drain him, and before he rearranged his features into arch remove, he looked stressed.

Crinkled snapshots of Charles Novinsky at Willy's age looked like portraits of some brave eldest later shot down in a war. The young man's eyes were searing and his bearing was vertical; there was no presentiment in that face of the mortars to come. It took effort to see any relation to the jaded veteran she faced now. Her father's rich curls had thinned to a dry frizzle, as if he'd been singed. Though his complexion was naturally ruddy, he had a psoriasis condition, and shedding skin flaked his cheeks gray.

Her father adjusted his spectacles down his nose. "Say, I've been reading a Chomsky book that pertains to your calling. According to Noam, in the secular era sports are the opiate of the people. Seems the masses are enervated by vicarious gladiatorial contests, much the way they were once mesmerized by mumbo-jumbo in church."

"Eric," said Willy, "this is my contentious, curmudgeonly father, who is trying his best to offend you before he even knows your name."

"Princeton, I hear." They shook hands. "What possessed you to join the yahoos after earning a degree from a place like that?"

"Willy and I plan to make millions in endorsements for deodorant," Eric tossed easily back.

They each took a seat in brown chairs, and Eric nodded at the term papers in her father's lap. "That doesn't look like Chomsky. What are you reading?"

Don't get him started, Willy almost intruded, but Eric liked to get people started.

"Reading may be too dignified a word. I play little games to keep myself amused, though. My charges divide into those who think commas are states of catatonia after a car accident, and others who regard them as decorative curlicues—in which case, the more the prettier. So I sponsor home contests. This is a prizewinner." He held up an essay. Whisked with red deletes, from three feet away the paper was pink. "Thirty-five super-fluous commas on one page. A record."

"What are you trying to do, Daddy, impress us with your powers of punctuation, or get us to feel sorry for you?"

Frankly, his keen of condescension was so familiar that she turned it off. Willy had grown up with the vague impression that their family was superior, although not in a worldly way. Theirs was a loftiness that left them outside of things. Her father had the aura of an Old Testament prophet who had tried preaching a time or two, was paid no mind, and now, spitefully, would deliver no more tidings. If that meant leaving the hordes to floods and locusts, very well.

The cornerstone of her father's supremacy was his valiant realism. He recognized that the planet was teeming with acned adolescents all planning to be film directors, industrial magnates, and Pulitzer prize-winning foreign correspondents, and he set his students straight on the odds. Only the frail and simpleminded clung to their delusions. Chuck had insisted that his offspring grow up in the world the way it *was*.

Willy's mother scuttled from the kitchen, wiping her hand on her apron before extending it to Eric. Colleen Novinsky carried herself at a forward angle, stooping with her whole body so that you always worried she was about to fall over. She clasped her hands at her waist in an attitude of perpetual supplicant. After accepting Eric's bottle of wine with a gasp about how he shouldn't have, she saw to their drinks with an attentiveness bordering on hysteria.

As Eric lengthened across the central recliner her parents shrank from him, edging their chairs and glancing askance. It was that *freshness*. Eric wasn't brown. He floated above his seat with a faint white outline, as if snipped from a glossy magazine and pasted on Novinsky newsprint. Eric straightened his long legs and crossed his ankles, locking hands behind his head; his articulated Adam's apple caught the lamplight. This household managed, congenitally, to be both phlegmatic and agitated, and they regarded her boyfriend's graceful, interweaving banter with mistrustful awe.

"You must be pretty pleased with your daughter, Mr. Novinsky," Eric purred. "Last week she got to the semis in Des Moines. Her performance was stupendous. It isn't easy to yank your ranking from 612 to 394 in one year."

Her father waved his hand. "I can't make heads or tails of all those sports numbers."

"It's simple arithmetic, Mr. Novinsky," Eric reproached him. "Rankings are comprehensible if you can count."

"We're just worried how she's going to keep body and soul together."

"Body, maybe," Willy grumbled. "You've never seemed too bothered about my soul."

"I am concerned about how you will make a self-respecting living," he shot back.

"Is that what your work is? Self-respecting?"

"It is a living," he countered. "I don't see why you can't get a proper job to have something to fall back on."

"You can't play pro tennis part-time," Eric intervened. "You're always on the road, and it takes unequivocal devotion." Exactly what Willy had said for years, but when Eric said it her parents listened. "And Willy's doing well for herself, Mr. Novinsky. I shouldn't have to remind you, but she's got something— something special."

"But she's in debt to this Upchurch fellow up to her eyeballs," her father objected. "And what if she breaks a leg?" On Walnut Street, "break a leg" really entailed breaking a leg.

"Everyone lives with uncertainty," Eric returned smoothly. "In the meantime, imagine being able to support yourself playing tennis! It's almost as outrageous as being paid to write stories."

Her father assessed Eric gamely, then tapped some paperback novels on the table beside him. "What's outrageous is being paid to write these stories."

"And you, Mrs. Novinsky? What do you do?" Put to women of her mother's generation, the question was a risk. Forced to admit they were housewives, they were embarrassed, for the very question implied that vacuuming wasn't enough. If instead you neglected the inquiry and they had jobs, they were insulted as well. But Eric didn't take gambles he didn't think he could win.

He knew Mrs. Novinsky worked in a nursing home.

"The way the age structure is shifting," Willy's father chimed in cheerfully, "pretty soon we'll all be working in nursing homes, if we're not committed to one already. Colleen's ahead of her time."

"Mother originally studied modern dance," Willy volunteered.

"That was years ago," her mother scoffed. "I didn't have the talent to join a company. And I'd never have refrained from all those cookies."

Willy rolled her eyes. This tried routine had hoodwinked both daughters for years into insisting that no, no, she had a lovely figure she might have kept, and come on, she moved like an artist. "Sure, Mama. That's just what your instructor said when he gave you the lead in 'Pavane for a Dead Princess' your senior year: this klutz belongs munching Oreos with old people in diapers." That her mother always made other people stick up for her was a kind of laziness. "Now, can we eat?"

"We're waiting for Gert."

Oh, great.

If Willy didn't detest her sister she might have felt sorry for the woman. Born around the time that those typescripts would have been shoved in the attic for Roach Motels, Willy's older sister had suffered the initial brunt of her father's barbaric practicality. He could just as well have kept a foot on her head. From the start, Gert had been overly grown-up, with that restrained, well-spoken modesty that in a child is a little disturbing. In the early days when the girls still played together, Gert would never agree to rambunctious reenactments of *Kojak* chase scenes, but insisted on playing Mary Tyler Moore. In junior high, she never wanted to be a rock star, but a schoolteacher. Her tennis game was safe and soft, and as soon as Willy got good Gert quit the sport without a fight. In high school, she dressed with a matronly mutedness all through the era of wacky New Wave clothes. Her garb in her twenties was still sensible, like her marriage—her husband and shoes alike would wear well, so much better than heels that were flashy and precarious. Willy's father had succeeded: Gert was a bore. Her single pretension was to claim that she hadn't one.

When Gert efficiently whisked in the door (her suit was *brown*) she asked Willy while fussing keys into her pocketbook, "How's tennis?"

"Fine," said Willy.

That was that.

At dinner, so assured and fluid was her fiancé's patter that Willy wasn't needed. Inspecting him, she had the irrational impression that she'd brought not a prospective son-in-law but a surrogate—rather than their surly, guarded, too-private second child who always made life so prickly, here was a self-possessed, engaging young adult in whose presence her parents, incredibly, *laughed*. At previous family mealtimes, whenever Willy launched into insider tennis scuttlebutt Gert would ask for more potatoes and her father went back to harping on how deconstructionism was blessedly kaput. But when Eric gossiped about Agassi, they all three leaned forward and asked questions ("Who's Agassi?"). Presently her father was exploring with convincing curiosity how Eric tamed his nerves before a game, a question he had never bothered to ask his own daughter.

Having sucked up to her mother by eating three helpings of inedibly undercooked chicken cacciatore, Eric expanded back from the table. In the pool of light at his open collar, shadows swam in his clavicle like the darting of small fish. Willy grew alarmed. Eric's extreme features could be regarded as either striking or overdrawn. In the past she had bestowed him with a provisional handsomeness, which she was thereby free to rescind. Yet tonight, like it or not, the branched veins over his broad forearms made Willy's mouth water as surely as an open candy dish of licorice strings. If his beauty was a present, it was one he would keep.

"At the January '89 Buenos Aires Davis Cup match with Argentina?" Eric opined. "Agassi was playing Martin Jaite, a heartthrob local talent. Andre was whitewashing the poor bastard, 6–2, 6–2. At 4–0 in the third set Jaite had a chance to win a game. Down 40–love, Agassi shouted to his coach, 'Hey, Nick, watch this!' Jaite served, and Agassi *caught* the ball with his left hand."

"Why would he do that?" Gert frowned, fascinated.

"Twisted charity. To humiliate Jaite and offend the crowd. It worked. Then he'd the nerve to claim to journalists that the trick was 'just something he always wanted to do.'"

Willy's brow creased as well. She'd tried to tell this exact same story at Thanksgiving last year. Her mother had continued clearing the table, Gert had rifled through sample questions for her next accountancy exam, and her father, far from readjusting his chair at a rapt angle, had turned absently to *The New York Times*. Willy had abandoned the anecdote well before she got to the punchline.

If only to get a little attention, Willy *pinged* and raised her glass. "Hey. A toast. We're getting married."

They were thrilled.

When everyone went to bed, her mother pointedly directed the engaged couple to separate rooms. Willy might have staged a scene, but the chummier her fiancé became with her father ("Eric, please call me Chuck") the more she was inclined to tolerate the arrangement.

"Well, you charmed the bejesus out of my family," Willy growled in the hallway.

"They're not so bad," he whispered.

"Maybe to you they're not," she muttered. "Good God, I'm engaged to Eddie Haskell."

"Willy—?"

She didn't kiss him good night. Willy had been nervous whether her family would like Eric. She hadn't thought to worry that they'd like him too much.

SIX

WHEN WILLY NEARED MONTCLAIR, New Jersey, she dwarfed, as if mere proximity to her mother's womb shrank her to fetal dimensions. In contrast, as Eric swept into the polished lobby on East Seventy-fourth Street and hailed the doorman by his first name, her betrothed seemed to grow taller with every step. By the time he strode in the door of his parents' apartment she was afraid he would hit his head.

After much shoulder-clapping and bear-hugging of his firstborn, Axel Oberdorf turned to greet the girlfriend. "Pleasure. He does bring home the lookers." Axel winked.

She had expected a lanky, balding version of Eric. Instead Axel ("Axe") Oberdorf was a head shorter than his son, compact and stocky. With the stance of a linebacker, he was hard to get past. His full head of black hair matched his arms, which were matted in thick animal fur. A senior surgeon at Mt. Sinai, Axel exuded the sharp scent of a rigorous detergent, a two-layered smell of harshness masked by a cloying but insufficient perfume. He pumped Willy's hand; his nails were short and clean. Through initial small talk, his face explored a restricted range of expressions: the self-congratulatory beam of aren't-we-all-grand; a stolid wait-and-see, indicating a withholding of judgment that wouldn't last; and the occasional flicker of suspicion.

"What'll it be, Eric? Laid in two sixes of that Pickwick Ale you said you liked. Or you on some health kick? Wheat-grass juice? Boys be glad to run out and fill special orders." It was a small matter, but had Willy ever let on to her parents that she was partial to Pickwick Ale, they'd have gone out of their way to stock Old Milwaukee.

Axel led the couple into his capacious living room, whose plush ivory carpet looked as if it were vacuumed three times a day. The fluffy furniture was modular, like Eric's mind. Bright, primary-colored rectangles, cones, pyramids, and cylinders, all stripped with Velcro, could be whimsied into a variety of configurations. It was easy to picture Eric working out geometric theorems here as a child, or designing his own Rubik's Cube with furniture. Eric's mother ran an art gallery, and the walls were spaced with original canvases that themselves might have passed for math diagrams or magazine puzzlers—abstract impressionists mazed with triangles, Russian prints whose Cyrillic phrases challenged anyone in the room to pronounce them, and white-on-white grids more witty than beautiful. Though the room was splashed with an array of hues, not a single cushion or painting was brown.

Eric set about building himself a chair. Willy perched on a plain cube, a poor choice. She couldn't lean back; already jittery, she was now literally on edge.

"So bring me up to date, my boy," said Axe, on a big-armed throne. "What happened in Toronto?"

"Oh, I won," said Eric. Drizzling his beer, he was determined to drain the whole bottle into his glass. When the last drop trembled at the rim, he looked victorious.

Axe nodded vigorously. "Good, good. Not surprised, mind you." Eric's father often left out the subject of such sentences, as if his centrality were a grammatical given.

"It wasn't an important tournament," Eric deflected. "Chump change, meager computer points."

"He was terrific," added Willy. "And there was more depth of field than Eric's letting on." While on Walnut Street she'd been grateful when Eric stuck up for her, on Seventy-fourth her support felt thin, surplus.

"Winning's winning," said Axe. "It's a habit, one I'm glad to say you got into at an early age. You gotta hand it to this guy." Axe gestured with his vodka and tonic. "Picks up a racket at eighteen, two years later he's on Princeton's tennis team."

"Pretty amazing," said Willy.

"Could just kick myself I didn't get him started as a brat. Maybe now he'd be giving Agassi a run for his money. When you learn to play, Willy?"

"At four. Though I didn't start to play seriously until—"

"And you're ranked what?"

"386."

Eric intruded, "That's likely to go up after this month, since Willy's entered in—"

"Three hundred and eighty-six." It sounded like a long number.

Mrs. Oberdorf glided in with a tray of tea sandwiches, whose triangles of salmon, accents of black olive, and strips of daikon reiterated the Russian prints. Here was where Eric got his looks: she was tall, spare, and stately, with strong cheekbones and the same grand, angular nose. Alma Oberdorf dressed with a simplicity that costs. Her manner was collected, her voice murmurous. When she leaned over her eldest and kissed his forehead she teased that he'd lost more hair—the first intimation of the evening that Willy's fiancé had a single failing.

"Willy, I'm so glad that Eric has somebody to play with," said Alma good-humoredly, and Willy accepted a sandwich.

"Your mother's making that polenta mush for dinner again," Axel groaned. "I've tried to tell her that cornmeal porridge is peasant food, but you can't fight chichi New York."

"The recipe is from the Union Square Cafe." With the obdurate calm of her delivery, Mrs. Oberdorf must have been accustomed to standing her ground, although perhaps not gaining any either. "And it's only a side dish, dear." Obliviously, she slipped away.

When Axe began to extol his son's renown as "Rick the Slick" on Trinity's basketball team, Eric interrupted impatiently, "Dad! Look alive—Willy *already likes me*. Though she may not continue to, if you don't give it a rest."

Eric muscled the conversation back to Willy. He rattled off that she'd been the number-three junior in New Jersey without being allowed to compete outside the tristate area, that she'd been number one on the tennis team from her sophomore year at UConn, and that she'd recently made the semifinals in the Norfolk Masters, which was worth gobs more computer points than his own lowly satellite in Toronto. Though flattered, Willy was perplexed as to why Eric felt compelled to blurt this rush of statistics. They were supposed to be getting acquainted, and here Eric could as well have printed out her résumé, as if she were applying for a job.

"Your dad your coach, Willy?" Axel topped up his V&T with tonic at the bar.

"Willy's coached by Max Upchurch, one of the best in the business," Eric interceded, adding effortfully, "They're very... close. Willy's his bright and shining hope for the nineties."

"What's your father do, then?"

"He's an English professor," Willy jumped in to answer for herself. "Head of department."

"Rutgers?"

Willy's cheeks warmed. "Bloomfield College. He writes novels, and doesn't much care about the academic—"

"What's his name?"

"Chuck—Charles Novinsky."

Axe rubbed his chin. "Can't say I ever ... What's he published?"

Willy slumped as much as the backless cube would allow. "One book. You wouldn't have heard of it. But it's very good. It went underappreciated at the time."

"Never met a teacher who didn't have three novels stashed in his bottom drawer. At least your dad managed to get one published."

Willy straightened her shoulders. "Well, I think my father is a pretty gifted writer. But you know, we can't all be famous."

"Yes." Axel smiled; his teeth were small and perfect. "Many a worthy man's toil is thankless, isn't it?" he added grandiloquently. Floweriness neither suited his style nor served the sentiment. He raised his V&T. "To the unsung."

Willy didn't take a sip of her wine.

Before they were called to dinner, Eric gave Willy a tour of the two-floor condominium. When he showed her his old room, she was struck by its bare walls and bald surfaces. Had his mother cleared all trace of him away?

"No, I always kept it neat and simple," he explained.

But the real explanation did not emerge until they ducked into the master bedroom. Prominently displayed across one wall was every award Eric had ever earned: his straight-*A* report cards, his grade school Advanced Reading Group assignment, the covers of his gold-starred essays from Trinity on Ronald Reagan, a letter of thanks from the Republican National Committee, several blue ribbons in track, eight consecutive dean's list notifications from Princeton, his Phi Beta Kappa certificate dangling with a gold key, and a freshly framed summa BA in mathematics. A table underneath was crammed with sports trophies. Willy stared at the display agog. She was reminded of devout Catholics who kept novena cards, candles, crucifixes, and statues of the Virgin Mary cluttered in a hallowed corner of their homes. No doubt about it: this was a shrine.

"What is all this doing in *your parents'* bedroom?" she asked incredulously.

"Personally, I count my blessings that this worthless crap isn't plastered all over the goddamned living room." Eric seemed both irritated and embarrassed, but he had shown her this array on purpose. If they were going to be married, there was something he wanted her to understand.

"But why didn't you want to keep your awards in your own room?"

"I did, or I tried. I shoved them in my desk, but my father always filched them. When he helped me clear out of my dorm in May, he bullied me into forking over the Princeton stuff, claiming he'd paid for it. And in high school, he got so intrusive that I started throwing little bullshit tributes away. No use. Those blue ribbons in track? He rooted them out of the trash, banana peels and all. See?" Eric pointed. "That one's still grease-stained."

"Have you always been so humble?"

"It's not humility; it may be the opposite, to tell the truth. I'm not interested in anything I've already done. I keep my eyes on the next hurdle. Ask any horse what happens when you run looking backwards, congratulating yourself on how well you cleared the last hedge. This is dross, Wilhelm. And rinky-dink dross at that." He sounded disgusted.

"God, I can't imagine my father even—"

"*Don't,*" Eric cut her off sotto voce, "get envious too fast. Sure, these trinkets are in my father's room. Because they're his. You can't imagine that he was bragging about me down there." Eric gestured to the floor. "He was bragging about *himself.*"

When they returned downstairs, Eric's three brothers were already seated at the sleek teak dining table, where the two younger boys were fighting over which building was the tallest in the world.

"Wrong! The Sears Tower! One thousand four hundred fifty-four stories—"

"*Feet,* you moron. Think it goes all the way to the moon?"

"*Nobody cares,*" Eric interrupted. "You guys? This is Willy. Willy? Robert, Mark, and Steven," he introduced from youngest up.

They were all roughly attractive boys, though the two older ones had more of Axel's build, short and square. Maybe they'd not grown into themselves yet, but not one of his siblings possessed

Eric's arresting angularity and confident ease. They all three turned to Willy with expressions that mingled admiration with resentment. So Eric had brought home another good-looking girl. Big surprise.

The second eldest, Steven, was perhaps the most homely and about seventeen. Steven began drilling his brother Mark on which five American presidents had been shot, but when Axel arrived, drying his hands, their father took over as referee. "Begins with a *G*," Axel prodded.

"No clues!" Steven complained. "You never help me!"

"Garfunkel!" Mark guessed.

Steven hooted. "So everyone in the sixties was listening to Simon and Garfield?"

As Alma delivered the first course, a venison tureen, Willy's attention began to stray. Mark had begun to list every Robert De Niro film ever made. Steven had apparently memorized George Bush's cabinet. Something about the banter disturbed her. At the Oberdorf's, all fact was on a par. It didn't seem to matter whether in which film De Niro played the devil was important, only that Mark knew it was *Angel Heart* and Steven didn't. When knowledge had value only as a weapon, all inform-ation was cheap and fungible. These kids threw facts the way unrulier kids threw food.

Only Robert, the scrawny, sullen twelve-year-old at the end of the table, had ceased to joust as soon as his father appeared. Having mashed his venison into turds, he neglected his dinner for the notebook computer in his lap.

"Boys!" Axel called the family to order. "I'll have you know that your brother Eric here just won a big Canadian tourna-ment."

"Enough!" Eric despaired. "It was a piece of shit tournament, and I *told* you that, Dad!"

Robert's notebook wheedled. "I bet all the girls threw flowers and wet themselves," the youngest muttered. "We can't wait to hear *all* about it."

"Gosh," said Mark, "did you win, like, a million dollars?"

"I won squat," Eric insisted. "You didn't even have to be ranked to get in, the draw was overrun with amateurs, and what I won wouldn't buy Robert a copy of 'Microsoft Golf.'"

But Eric's protestations washed off his brothers like rainwater. Willy supposed that modesty made him only a little more irritating.

"My debate team won the first round against Dalton, Dad," Steven piped up.

"I got my paper back on *GoodFellas*," Mark intruded. "My film teacher gave me an *A* plus!" The "plus" had the tinny ring of an embellishment.

Though in the early hubbub Willy couldn't quite keep the brothers straight, she now discerned that their interests were cautiously discrete: tennis, politics, movies, and computer games. Each son dwelt in his own preserve, like animals in a zoo that had to be fenced from one another lest they eat each other up.

Alma presented the main course, which to Willy's surprise was a stuffed tenderloin. Eric had said his family was ultra-secular, but pork seemed ostentatiously so. Robert excepted, the children's table manners, like Eric's, were impeccable. Alma refilled her sons' Pellegrino, quietly pointing to a little chunk of venison on Mark's chin. He brushed it off with a collusive glance of gratitude at his mother. She is the real family, Willy thought. The one who picks up the pieces when one of these paragons shuffles home having been, perish the thought, denied the lead in the school play.

Willy was seated next to Steven, who might have picked up his ambition to become a politician from his older brother's discarded fascinations, like a hand-me-down jacket. When she asked whether that meant a law degree he went vague, as if already oppressed by the mandatory admission into Harvard. He doubled back to that afternoon's debate coup, the details carefully loud enough for his father to hear. Yet though Steven extolled his own lucidity, never once did he mention what the debate had been about. More, through his bluster she detected too high a ratio of relief to relish. Willy had seen it in tennis players before: with sufficient dread of a drubbing, victory inverts to not-getting-egg-on-your-face-this-time; triumph becomes a squeaking-by, more reprieve than reward. The conversion was deadly. Any defeat you put off rather than preclude takes on all the inevitability you accord it. There may even come a point when, just to get it over with, you invite your ruin with open arms like an old friend.

Inspecting her future husband across the table, Willy searched for signs that Axel's summary dismissal of losers, his apparent lack of interest in complexity or excuses, had rubbed off on her fiancé. Despite the sharpness of its planes, there was gentleness in Eric's face, in contrast to his father's, whose round, jolly contours were punctuated by a merciless, impatient twitch around the mouth. Axe promoted a Darwinism that only a life of untrammeled success could afford. Willy speculated that doing well could be bad for you, should it result in this callous disregard for also-rans. If Eric seemed unbattered by such an upbringing, he had rarely disappointed his father. Mark, by comparison, had the wince of a boy who had failed to make first-chair clarinet, and the furtive fidget of a liar. Though infirmity had hitherto appeared universally unjust, Willy looked forward to their robust, barrel-chested father getting long in the tooth. For the harsh intolerance of weakness to which he had subjected his own family, Axel deserved old age.

"If you're walking off with trophies," Willy overheard Axel say to Eric, "you must have toughened up that tender heart. Had me worried with that track business."

"That was back in high school, and I wish you'd let it go," said Eric.

"Get this," Robert muttered in Willy's direction. "Not only is big brother Magic Johnson, Albert Einstein, and Andre Fagassi all in one, he's Manhattan Gandhi, too."

Axel brought Willy in. "The night before a big track meet, this guy starts limping from a sprain. Wraps the ankle with an Ace bandage; even gets himself a crutch. Day after the race, I find the little bastard running laps in the Trinity gym. Ace on a bleacher, crutch on the floor. Took him by the collar and said, leave the props, kid, you've got some explaining to do. Thought he'd chickened out. Figured he was just afraid to lose.

"Alma here squeezed it out of him. His best friend, What's-its—"

"Yossi Brenner," said Eric, bored.

"*Yossi* was running the same race. Eric's sure he can beat the guy, but doesn't want him to feel outclassed. Fakes an injury. Gives him the event. I had to tell Eric, you're not doing that guy any favors. If you don't beat him, somebody else is going to."

Eric sighed. "He did win, Dad. And the ribbon meant much more to him than it would have to me. I only ran track to help my basketball."

"I always thought Eric's bowing out for a friend was lovely," said Alma quietly.

"It was sweet," Axel granted. "But I'm sorry to say, there's little place for charity where Eric's headed. Where *any* of you boys are headed," he added, as if just reminded that he had three other sons.

Willy caught Eric's eye. "I wouldn't worry about Eric's competitive drive. To really give his friend satisfaction, he'd have *run* the race and dropped behind. Obviously, he couldn't stand that. Compromise: a sprained ankle. He still wins the race in his head."

Eric remarked to his father, "I told you she was smart."

Alma offered Willy more polenta, and Axel stayed the platter. "Willy doesn't want seconds, Alma. She's got to watch her figure."

"Actually, Mr. Oberdorf, I rallied for three hours today and I'm famished. I'd love some more polenta, which, by the way, is delicious." Willy lifted her plate and exchanged a smile with her hostess.

"Can you tell me why so many girl tennis players are *fat*?" Axel nodded at her dinner. "Capriati is a load. Seles is a cow. Even Sanchez-Vicario is dumpy."

"Well." Willy smoothed the polenta in her mouth. "Sponsors pressure women players to look sexy. Sometimes that pressure backfires into eating problems. But we're not paid to be fashion models."

"Of course not," Axel concurred heartily. "But a pretty face like yours sure brightens up a game. Nothing wrong with looking good, is there? And it must help your speed, to stay light on your feet."

Willy resolved to be agreeable. "It did improve Martina's agility when she dropped a few pounds."

"Bit of a shame about the lesbianism, though," Axel reflected innocently. "Mean, I'm as liberal-minded as the next person, but never thought Martina and Billy Jean were much good for the game's rep. Every fan's not as *tolerant* as we are."

"Lesbianism in the WTA has been greatly exaggerated by the press." Willy paused, placing her tongue between her molars to keep from grinding her teeth.

"I bet Willy's not a dyke, Dad," said Mark, raising his eyebrows. "Ask Eric."

"Say, Willy, when you play Eric here," Axel pried, leaning forward, "who wins?"

The boys had fallen silent, and with no other course immediately forthcoming it seemed that Willy was for dessert.

"Willy beats me easily, Dad," Eric provided.

That this information registered Axel signaled by ignoring it. "Must be difficult," Axel commiserated, "struggling in a profession with a number like 386."

Willy's voice rose despite herself. "It's murderous to be ranked at all!"

"No need to get exercised," Axel soothed his guest. "Just being sympathetic with the frustration of being relatively unknown."

"I don't mean to be rude, but how many people have ever heard of Axel Oberdorf?"

"Every other vascular surgeon in the country," said Axel gruffly.

"Exactly. I've been noted by my peers myself."

"Sure you have," Axel purred. "With plenty of tournament experience, since my son tells me you're twenty-three. But I was wondering, isn't that pretty mature in women's tennis these days?"

"Dad," Eric interjected, "I'm glad Willy's twenty-three. I wouldn't want to marry a thirteen-year-old nitwit."

"What's that, son?"

"I said, the woman you are insulting is going to be my *wife*."

The subsequent bottle of champagne failed to bring Willy's blood pressure back to normal.

Relieved to be on their own again, Eric and Willy debriefed on the crosstown bus. It was almost worth submitting to such an evening for the pleasure of dissecting it afterward.

"Your brothers sure have a lot to measure up to," Willy ventured.

"They don't, really," Eric objected. "So I've got a college degree, big deal; I'm the oldest. I've been on some school teams; I have a decent academic record. Now I'm on the very outer margins of a long-shot career. What's so intimidating?"

"They just seem, I don't know, wary. Are you very close to them?"

"How could I be?" Eric exploded, and the bag lady in a RESERVED FOR THE HANDICAPPED seat looked up. "Steven's too nice a guy to flat out despise me, so Steven I simply depress. Mark's a little gaga, but that won't last; he's shifty, always looking for a shortcut. He's convinced I've mastered some kind of trick, and he wants me to share my secret. He'll be plenty pissed off when he finds out the 'secret' is hard work. As for Robert, he thinks I'm a smarmy, ass-licking goody-goody. Christ, he's probably right."

"You're not exactly James Dean," Willy conceded.

"I'm not going to screw up my life just to rebel against my obnoxious father. I sometimes even wonder if that's what he really wants. If he's baiting me to go out and be a zero to spite him and so show I'm a real man."

"It's a shame." Willy sighed. "Those kids could probably use a big brother."

"My father's taken care of that. Shit, I don't blame them for resenting me. If I were them, with that fucking exhibit in my father's bedroom? I'd take out a contract on my anointed brother. And Dad knows exactly what he's doing. He wants them to hate me. He never wanted the four of us to make allegiances, potentially against him. Divide and conquer, that's his motto, keep them at each other's throats. And damned if it hasn't succeeded. You noticed how he asked you, when we play, who wins? He's trying to stir up trouble, pit us against each other."

"You know, that story about your friend Yossi surprised me. To be honest, I'd have never expected you to forfeit a contest of any sort."

"Well," Eric admitted, "the real story's a little more complicated." He pulled the cord for their stop, and suggested they walk uptown from Eighty-sixth Street.

"Yossi was my best friend for a couple of years," Eric continued up Broadway. "We were always rivals. Towards the end I thought it was all his problem, but by then I'd gotten the edge, so it was easy to feel lofty. Maybe if it were the other way around, I'd have been just as big a pain in the ass—you're never aware of being 'competitive' when you're winning. Still, it got pretty tiresome: who was getting taller, who got the hot-number girls into bed. You know, it was everything but whip it out with a measuring tape. Trite, in retrospect, but it didn't feel like *Happy Days* at the time. I'd make the honor roll when Yossi's GPA missed by .15, and he'd be surly for days, making bitter little digs and pointedly hanging out with the dope-smoking lowlifes in the stairwell."

Hands in his pockets, loose legs swinging, Eric looked up at the sharp fall sky. Willy would have assumed he was terribly popular, but she realized now that Eric had, until recently, no one to talk to.

"So when Yossi *had* to go out for track, too, I almost quit the team," Eric carried on, lengthening his stride. "But I needed to work on my conditioning for basketball. The whole feel of the track team that year was contentious, kind of nasty. Everybody was always dropping their times in conversation, and lying, of course, making the other guys nervous they were slow. Yossi and I were both working on the 800 meters. It's a difficult distance—long enough to require pacing, but short enough that you still have to sprint. I knew Yossi's personal best, since he was *always* bringing it up; and I knew mine, which I kept to myself. I had him by several seconds.

"That race my dad went on about, it wasn't important—a two-school meet, though that only made it more intense. We cared more about races against teammates than the big state meets. At any rate, my sprained ankle ruse was the product of eleventh-hour disgust. When I pictured leaving Yossi in the dust, I could just see that closed, black, murderous look he'd get when we cooled down. I thought, Let him have it. Maybe I'd had enough of Yossi, period."

"You don't think you were being nice?"

"Condescending, maybe. Or sick and tired. Hey, you got my number back there. If I were *nice*, I'd have let him beat me on the track. And you were right: I'd opt out, but I wouldn't lose. I don't think I'm capable of losing for anybody." Eric sounded morose, as if his own constitution depressed him.

"Besides," he went on, his cordovans scuffing the sidewalk, "I'd feel prouder of myself without the epilogue. Afterwards, Yossi went on about that 800 meters so relentlessly, like he was so glad to have something over on me for once, that I finally told him that I'd faked the injury and given him the race."

"How'd he react?"

Eric shrugged. "He called me an asshole—which I *was*—and claimed that he'd have won anyway. But I'd burst his bubble. He didn't brag about the race again. I know I was a prick, but I was a kid."

His mother's delicate portions inadequate, Eric stopped at a vegetable stand and bought some fruit.

"What happened to the friendship?" Willy asked.

"It died fast after that nail in our coffin," Eric confided as he inhaled a banana back up Broadway. "I didn't miss him. Constantly comparing notes, who got this, who won that, it was gross. You never got to be real buddies. And that kind of game, it's only fun so long as it's a toss-up who's ahead. Like, when we met, we'd have races doing the *Times* crossword, and it was neck and neck. But by senior year, I'd handicap myself by referring exclusively to the across clues, while he got to use the downs, too. I'd still beat him by a quadrant. I made him feel like crud. He made me feel sheepish. What was in it for anybody?"

Willy found this tale unaccountably disquieting, and changed the subject. "Do you think your family was happy as they pretended, that we're getting married?"

"My mother, sure. She liked you—if only for standing up to my dad. Of course, you must have noticed that my brothers went ashen with dread. Dad will just use the event to make a fuss over me and they'll feel like earthworms in comparison. My father? Can't marry me himself, so I guess he'll get used to it."

"Has he gone for the jugular of every girl you've brought home?"

"No, you're the first woman I've shown up with that he's goaded like that. I'm awfully sorry. And I was impressed—you handled yourself great, really kept a cool head. It's just, he tests people. His version of taking you seriously is to take you on. I'm sure it didn't feel like a compliment, but you ought to be flattered. He sized you up as a contender and thought you could take it."

"But how can he make fun of *my* ranking of 386," Willy puzzled, "when *you're* ranked 927?"

"Why do you think you got under his skin? You make me look bad."

"Eric, you just started—"

"That's what he's telling himself. Too loudly. He's nervous about this tennis thing."

"Aren't you?"

"Not especially."

"Why *not?*"

Eric tossed her an apple. "You know the first thing you learn on the high wire? *Don't look down.*"

SEVEN

Clamorous sweetspot students having sifted off to dinner, the weight room was silent but for the squeal of the shoulder pull and the compressed hiss of exhalation through Willy's teeth. Max's shadow fell from behind her onto the facing wall.

"You're tilting to the right," Max observed wearily.

Willy released the bar to dangle overhead. She rested thirty seconds between sets—plenty of time for a single sentence. "My right shoulder is three times stronger than my left; a tilt is inevitable." The wrong sentence.

"Since my advice is *impossible* to follow, I'll leave you to it." The shadow shifted, bloated, and faded.

"Wait! See if this is better." Willy clutched the slippery grips and bowed her head. With her eyes shut, the position was prayerful.

"Yes. That's straight." His voice dragged. When Willy resisted his coaching he got angry; when she did what she was told he got sad. Go figure. The shadow expanded again. The doorknob clicked.

"Max, we need to talk." Willy wiped her hands on her shorts, working her shoulders in circles. The left one ached. She swiveled to the upright bench press, adjusted to five more pounds of bullion than she usually raised. But the clink of pins would reverberate unbearably, so she left them as they were. Nestling her back on the padded rest, she grasped the squishy, foam-covered handles.

Max remained by the door. He wasn't slumped; he never slumped. Still there was a preternatural relaxation about the man that was almost deathly. She had seen it in coaches before. They all struck a been-there-done-that posture, like a soul reincarnated one too many times. Maybe the post-everything otherworldliness was not to be envied. Max looked conclusively like a man who had nothing left to prove, and she didn't understand what you did with your life if not prove something.

Facing him now, arms open, her pose was frank. She got the impression that he still liked looking at her breasts.

"Max, I'm getting married."

The sentence didn't take anywhere near thirty seconds. Since Max's face registered no change, Willy wondered if her dread of this exchange for the last month was pure hubris, and he didn't give a damn.

"Underwood?" Max asked dispassionately.

"Oberdorf. I got it wrong. Though one and the same."

"Good idea, if you're going to take it, to learn his name."

"I'll stay Novinsky."

"You've thought this through, then."

"I've thought of little else."

Max transferred his weight from his left to right foot, as if torn between Willy and the door. "That sounds distracting." He shifted to the left again. "The New Freedom satellite is next week."

Willy hefted her arms forward. On this contraption the asymmetry of her strength was the most glaring. Her right arm plunged to its full extension; the left quaked catching up. The disparity was another reminder that, in focusing on one goal only, she had refined a single proficiency at the price of ineptitude at a great deal else.

Willy squeezed out between breaths, "I've done nothing— but think of tennis—since I was five."

"And look where it's got you."

The metal slabs clanked still. "Not far enough."

"It's got you ready. The next two years are your big push. I find your timing on this marriage business peculiar."

"Marriage isn't a business."

"It is," he objected. "And it will affect your business; it may affect mine." Max, who seemed to have made up his mind about staying, straddled the leg pull three machines away, twisting her towel.

"Might you consider that I get lonely?" asked Willy. "None of the girls in locker rooms will speak to me—"

"A good sign. If they're friendly, you're not intimidating enough."

"Well, maybe—I could use—a hand to hold, maybe—a happy tennis player—is a better—tennis player." The iron clapped to rest.

Max squinted. "You know, I couldn't name a *happy* tennis player."

Willy traced a handle with her forefinger, elbows limp at her waist. Her whole upper body was burning. "When I was a kid, tennis was ecstasy."

"Meaning it's different now."

"When I haven't been on a court for two or three days I still tear my hair."

"When did you last go *three days* without tennis?"

She smiled. "I don't know, five years ago?"

"Grown-up tennis isn't concerned with ecstasy," Max hazarded, tightening the towel into a rope. "Facing down what you're made of on a daily basis doesn't lend itself to peace of mind."

"None of which—explains why—I shouldn't get—married." Her chest had begun to shudder; her left arm was trembling so violently that the vibration rattled her jaw. This was too much weight, but she was not about to stop shy of twelve repetitions under Max's scrutiny.

"Don't talk pressing that much weight, Will. I mean, it's hard enough to wrestle the gremlins in your own head without living alongside somebody else's heebie-jeebies, too."

Willy forced herself to ease the weights down with a controlled sigh. She caught her breath. In truth, she felt a bit nauseated.

"Eric doesn't have heebie-jeebies," she recited. "Eric is sure that he'll do very well. And that I'll do very well, too."

Max eyed her. "A few months ago, a hand to hold was the last thing you wanted."

"*Your* hand!" Max had her towel, so she wiped her face on her shirt. "My *coach's* hand."

"I guarantee," Max went on in that horribly moderate voice that reminded Willy of her father, "that if you came to me and said you'd found a nice boy who didn't hit you and had some grasp of the dedication demanded by your career—a decent fellow who would tend to his own dog food factory or whatever and would wait loyally for you to come home from Tokyo—I would wish you the best of luck."

"Eric is nice and he doesn't hit me and understands better than anyone the demands of my career, since it's his career, too. So when do I get the good wishes?"

Max slapped the vinyl of the leg pull with her towel. "You are being *deliberately* stupid!" The restraint in his voice had given. Willy appreciated that they were at least conducting their first legitimate conversation since that wretched morning of *It's cold, come back to bed*, and instead she'd left his bed forever.

Willy adjusted the sit-up board at a severe angle, banging the hooks on the rungs. Tucking her ankles under the padded brace, she rested her little fingers on her temples and her thumbs under her jaw. As she rose her elbows drew forward; they sheltered her breasts. Though Willy did sit-ups like this every other day, there was a suggestion in the fenced arms, hands over her ears, that she didn't want to hear what Max had to say.

Max was badgering her by the board. "You're the only girl I coach who has an inkling that a successful tennis career is a miracle of God. Half these poor whelps honestly believe they will waltz out my gate and straight into an Evian contract worth three million bucks a year. You're not that retarded. So I am shocked by your shabby imagination."

"I have no idea what you're talking about." With her stomach muscles contracted, Willy's voice was squeaky.

"You've always had this precociously cynical bite to you, Will. It's not like you to be so trusting."

"Of Eric?" she wheezed.

"Of *yourself.*"

"Trusting yourself is tennis in a nutshell." She flopped on her back head-down.

"Only at its best."

The blood rushing to her head made Willy dizzy. She raised to clutch the ankle brace and bowed her head.

"He's a tennis player, Will."

She clapped her palms back over her ears, bent her knees, and resumed wrenching up and down. "Isn't that fabulous," she grunted. "He's good, too."

"All the worse."

Willy toiled through her sit-ups, eyes shut, but still Max preyed at her elbow as the embodiment of all she didn't want to consider. She was happy, and the novelty of the emotion slapped the rest of her life with reproof. Willy had never regarded herself as miserable in the past. But now it turned out she'd led a barren young adulthood; she'd never had boyfriends even in high school. All the guys thought she was stuck up, or involved in something that didn't pertain to them, which it didn't. At last she had a lithe, lean, lovely man, and sleep had never been so gorgeous, a luxury in itself rather than one more drudgery to dispense with. She was only twenty-three but already fatigued; perseverance required respite. And here Max would convert her sole salvation into one more obstacle.

Willy rolled off the board and turned into the staple-shaped dip bar. Laying her arms across its corners and gripping the iron, she stood facing Max with her chin thrust, willing to make him the enemy if the alternative was to return to a life that, had it been palatable before, could only seem destitute now.

"If nothing else," she said steadily, "I have found an excellent hitting partner whom we don't have to pay."

"A husband's just a cheap addition to your entourage, then," said Max sardonically, hands on the hips of his sweatpants. "An economy."

Willy withdrew an inch. "We can work out together, run together—"

"Really." Max grasped the dip bar, leaning to her ear. His cheek brushed her hair. He'd not dared come so close since May. "What other paradisiac visions do you have of a life together in the same sport?"

"We can enter the same tournaments—"

"On the satellite circuit, there are a handful of coed events. But your ranking is better than twice his, and Oberdwarf's not going to get into the same gigs. Moreover, you don't intend to *stay* in satellites, do you?" Max spoke with a measured enunciation, as if addressing a child or an idiot. "Isn't the plan to amass enough points in the coming year or two and hit the WTA international tour?"

"Of course."

"And Oberdork, he wants to get on the ATP tour?"

"Naturally..."

"Do you realize, aside from Grand Slams, how few international events invite men and women to compete at the same place and time? *Two.* I guess you'd really look forward to them."

"I was hoping you'd congratulate me, but I should have known better."

"I'm just being practical." One of her father's favorite words. "Let's take the possibilities one at a time, shall we?" Max pressed back forefinger with forefinger. "One: you both succeed splendidly. Top 200, maybe better. So you're on the road, *different* roads, all but December. Merry Christmas. Meanwhile you'll both have umpteen affairs from Munich to Tel Aviv, since that's the only way either of you will feel anything from the waist down. After fifteen years, you'll retire to a bald stranger with bad knees and back problems, who you're right back to calling 'Underwood' because you no longer remember his name."

"I already call him 'Underwood,'" Willy objected. "It's a joke."

"Very cute," said Max, and bent back his middle finger. "But let's peek behind Curtain Number Two. Let's say, tennis being tennis, that you both fall on your butts. Oberklutz never does get his backhand cross-court on the more profitable side of the alley. You go back to charging a net you can't cover—"

"I can, too—"

"Shut up. So you're both washouts, wandering about in the 700's, where you can't make a living like just about everybody else can't make a living at this sport. Maybe for a time you get along because misery loves, etc. But I bet that after a year or two, unable to get your constricted, furious hands around the throat of the whole world, you'll start going for each other instead."

"These fully furnished dioramas are a hell of a wedding present, Max. Remind me to send you a thank-you note—"

"But let's look behind the *third* curtain," he barged on, bending the next finger. Max was double-jointed, and its angle was shiveringly obtuse. "Will hits the tour. Underwood, tragically, falls short. But that's lucky in a way, isn't it? Because now your cut-rate hitting partner is free to accompany you around the world—booking your practice courts, massaging your shoulders, and balancing your burgeoning bank account. Shall I go on?"

"No thank you," she said coldly.

"Excuse me, have I left an alternative out?" He wiggled his remaining pinkie.

"That will do." Willy about-faced to the running machine, whose hum would mercifully mute her coach's malicious monologue. The treadmill began at an easy lope, but as she sped from 5.2 to 7.4 mph she did not manage to run so much as a yard from Max, or from what he was saying.

The jolt of her step gave Willy's voice a huffiness. "There are plenty of tennis couples on the tour."

Max crossed his arms. "Name one."

"Chris Evert and John Lloyd."

"They're divorced," said Max flatly. "And what is John Lloyd best known for?"

Her flush was covered by a natural reddening when she accelerated the treadmill still faster. "Being married to Chris Evert," she admitted. "But they made a good team for a while!"

"Since when do you join any team, Will? You can't even play doubles. You compete with the girl on your side of the net."

"I'm not in love with the woman on my side of the net," she puffed.

Max sneered. "And I thought you liked classical music and proper literature. The way you talk you've been listening to Top Forties and reading Harlequins—*baby, baby, baby*. Now you think that love conquers all? I refuse to believe that being over the moon about some horny hunk has turned your mind to mush."

"Liz and Peter Smylie!" More speed.

"Liz made it to 36. Peter quit."

The machine rose from a rumble to a whine. At 10 mph the tromp of her shoes and the rasp of her breath made it necessary for Max to shout: "You forget how well I know you! You'd compete with a fly if you thought it was trying to climb walls faster than you. All the world's a contest. A fine quality in a sportswoman. Not in a *wife*."

She thumped the stop button. "Nobody's asking *you* to marry me!"

The mat had come to an abrupt halt; Max steadied her when Willy lurched forward. He kept his hand on her arm. The treadmill silent, he spoke quietly. "Do me one favor. Fill out the

picture in your head of this glorious future of yours. See if it
doesn't include Underboy shouldering your luggage to Kennedy
and requesting your wake-up calls in ten different languages.
When your career takes off and he's still hacking away in the
900's, you think he's going to be all meek and supportive, from
the sidelines? Because Will, my friend, if you're this gaga over a
kid after years of being Miss Frosty, I'll bet my bottom dollar
that he's *just like you.*"

"That's so terrible?"

"It is," said Max, dropping his hand to his side, "disastrous."

The New Freedom Championship was held in the disheveled
town of Worcester, Massachusetts, where Willy's beige and
umber hotel recalled her parents' living room. If an event
backed by panty shields was embarrassing, the WTA was not
nearly so flush as the men's ATP, and couldn't be choosy about
sponsors. The WTA had still not kicked its habit, Virginia
Slims, despite frequent placards picketed outside Slims tour
venues: WOMEN'S LIVES ARE GOING UP IN SMOKE, or YOU'VE
COME A LONG WAY, WTA: DIVORCE VIRGINIA SLIMES. In comparison with a cigarette company, a promoter of menstrual
hygiene was a godsend.

But Willy would have entered if the tournament were
bankrolled by a company that produced assault weapons or
child pornography. The New Freedom paid its winner only
eight thousand dollars, but made up for the poor purse with
computer points. Besides, points were money; they were better
than money.

This fortnight was as Max foretold: the Worcester satellite
had no men's counterpart; if it had, Eric's ranking would have
precluded him. Instead Eric was in Oklahoma, competing in
the Jox All-Comers. Jox paid a pittance in every respect, but Eric
couldn't afford to skip any tournament that earned points at all.
Willy couldn't manage a ticket to Oklahoma City to applaud
him through his first two rounds, and until she started hauling

in substantial prize money this was bound to be a standard fiscal constraint. Her original visions of urging each other on all over the globe began to cloud.

Until the Jox–New Freedom overlap, they had managed to spend a misleading amount of time together. For the previous three months their tournaments had been fortuitously staggered, and in the rash prodigality of headlong romance they had each flown to watch the other play. Sweet but irresponsible, their mutual admiration society couldn't last.

Sudden isolation in Worcester demoted Willy to a single life grown hollow and torpid. On the train up, she had half-turned to share a snippet from the paper with an empty seat. Time yawned between check-in and dinner. The food, too, was brown. More time yawned between dinner and bedtime. Finally Willy lay down, bored and wide-eyed, perplexed how she'd ever gone to sleep without first getting laid.

The idea of allowing her own fingers to wander down there was repellent. Not only did the notion present itself as a betrayal, but any sex without Eric no longer qualified as sex, in Willy's new grasp of the term. To Willy, even the word *fuck* could no longer function syntactically as an intransitive verb. That was the difference: Eric was always having sex with *her*. In earlier encounters, Willy could as well have thrown her partner a piece of Portnoy's liver and got up to read. In fact, had she on some occasions Willy would have had a better time. But Eric often called out urgently, "Willy? Willy!" to remind her that he knew she was there. He never cried *Oh, baby!* the way one athlete at UConn had done, and she'd recognized at once that this guy shouted *Oh baby!* with every girl he took to bed. Besides, with previous men the whole operation had become so physically complicated—first he would go down on her and next she would go down on him and then they'd have to try exotic positions. But Eric displayed no interest in exchanging favors like nervous neighbors, who borrowed cups of sugar and then returned them the next day. Rather than get tangled in an elaborate macramé of limbs, both their bodies seemed to melt away. When Willy closed her eyes and opened her legs, the part of her that Eric entered was her head.

So in her Worcester hotel room, Willy shut her eyes and let the perimeters of her body bleed into the room, until its walls dissolved and her fingers ventured not to her own nether regions but across state lines. Over the darkened country, Willy reached from these cold sheets to Oklahoma, groping until she found Eric's hand. Clutching it warmly in her grasp, she slept.

Tennis, as ever, brought Willy to herself. Max had sent Desmond up on the early train to warm her up. Later that afternoon as she tied her shoes in the locker room of Worcester State, the jerk of her tightened laces yanked Willy back to who she was and what she was, which to Willy were the same thing.

Willy's opponent, Robin Lascombe, had finally stopped yammering about her devoted father, only to outline her all-protein diet, including a long list of much-missed contraband like sausage pizza and frozen Mars bars. Willy hid a creeping smile by stretching out her calves. At maybe seventeen, Robin was young, but fatally so—skittish young, too-friendly young. Maybe Max had a point, that adulthood remained an advantage. Had it not been so absent, the girl's face might have been pretty. Instead, any fetching curve was fogged by fear, which clouded off her cheeks as steam wafts from hot tarmac after a downpour. A profusion of moles splashed her skin like mud spatter. One unpronounced feature slurring into another, hers was a roadkill face, pulpy and boneless. Willy's own features were sharp; her nose sheared in a straight ridge, her chin pointed, her cheeks jutted, her brow cut a clean shelf; even her eyes had edges, flashing vertical highlights like bevels. Glancing in the basin mirror, Willy concluded that on the basis of looks alone she would slice through this girl's game like a knife through pâté.

Willy tucked the last wisps of hair under the crimson

bandanna from Eric, pulled the elastic of her underpanty to wedge snugly under her buttocks, and tugged the plain white sleeveless tennis dress to smooth over her jog bra. Bandaged with elastic, her breasts were solid and immobile; it was like being ten again, or a boy. She double-checked that her kit bag was equipped with four rackets, a towel, water, and a sweater—in the nip of October, the danger was getting heated and sweaty, then chilling on breaks. As Willy shouldered her bag and headed into the small sports stadium, Robin trailed behind her and shouted, "Good luck!" Willy rolled her eyes.

Willy arranged her gear on a single fold-up chair, set starkly on the sidelines as if to emphasize how from here on she was on her own. At the first round of an only modestly known tournament, the audience was small and scattered, but Willy had never relied on fans to get psyched. She was sorry that Max couldn't get here until the quarters; she was sorrier that Eric was in Oklahoma. But Willy made her offering not to ticket buyers or well-wishers but to Tennis itself—an abstraction, but with all the intangible presence and mute observation of God.

Even in the warm-up Robin kept hitting the ball out, then grinning at a bruiser in the front row. "*Shift your porking ass, Rob!*" he'd bark back, or "*Anticipate!*" Robin's grin only got wider and more sickening.

Willy won the toss and just about everything after. Lascombe started wobbly and proceeded to disintegrate altogether. A few shots she botched would have taken effort to miss; stick out the racket and the ball would bounce back, but Lascombe seemed more intent on getting out of the way. There was something almost erotic about the way Robin presented the vulnerable flank of her backhand side naked and unprotected, always with that unnervingly thankful smile. It took concentration not to feel sorry for her, but Willy knew pity was death. Sympathize with your opponent and before you know it they're feeling sorry for you.

Only back in the locker room did Willy permit herself a gentler glance at Robin Lascombe. She was seated with her legs splayed, her skirt hiked carelessly to expose an aging, ocherous bruise, wide as a hand. At first Willy thought the girl had been playing connect-the-dots with the moles on her face, until Willy realized that Lascombe's mouth and fingers were covered in melted chocolate.

On the phone with Eric late that evening, Willy nattered about the match, the high from the afternoon's shutout not yet subsided. "The audience was dead bored, getting up for Cokes. I almost felt guilty."

Eric was strangely unresponsive. When she'd finished spilling her victory, the conversation was clumsy; silence would be succeeded by both talking at once.

"I'm sorry," she remembered. "Your quarters were today. How'd it go?"

"Eh. 6–4, 6–7, 6–3."

"So it went three sets, but that's not bad."

"Not bad for John Reilly. I was the 4 and 3."

Shock was too strong, but she was surprised. Eric had entered three minor tournaments since she'd known him, and taken two trophies; Jox was the sorriest of the lot. Out of the way, too easy to get into, and with little to offer, the draw could only have been weak. "What went wrong?"

"It's that cross-court backhand—just wide."

"Take something off it."

"I don't *want* to take something off it," he said edgily. "Without pace it's not effective. I'll work on it."

"*We'll* work on it," she offered.

"Right." His voice was clipped. "There's no point in my hanging around Okie City now, so why don't I schlep up to Worcester? Catch the end of your gig."

"I could use a hitting partner."

"And a ballboy, too, I'm sure."

He sounded so sour that she gave him the option to take it back. "What did you say?"

A long, slow breath rushed in Willy's ear with a low roar. "That I miss you, Wilhelm."

"I miss you, too—" She was about to call him Underwood, and thought better of it. "And I need more than a hitting partner. I need a partner."

She was signing off when the receiver yipped, "Hey! I'm glad you won, Willy. Keep it up." A funny firmness marked his tone, an underscoring that was excessive.

That evening she had no trouble dozing off by herself. Naturally Eric's loss at Jox had saddened her, so it was odd how his misfortune sent a warm lull creeping through her chest. Maybe sadness was like that.

Meeting up with Eric in the hotel, she sensed a strain, evidenced in a forced bubbliness on her part, a terseness on his. They'd been out of each other's company a mere two weeks, yet Eric kissed in an alien tongue, and their teeth clacked. When they made love, it didn't feel safe to make jokes. At first he hadn't fit inside, as if their bodies in the interim had grown slightly shy of interlocking shapes. It took the whole next day to locate the lucid, easy banter that had seemed like breathing before they'd parted.

Eric had shrugged off the All-Comers as of no importance. He could box and bury disappointment six feet under, well aware that in the open air of his head it would begin to smell. Whenever results did not square with his ascendant vision of himself, the event, not the vision, had to go. But aspects of Eric were opaque. Willy was uncertain whether he had truly cast the defeat aside, or merely appeared to have done so. Barring the odd backhand, Eric did all things well; if his insouciance was fake, it was seamless.

As promised, Max drove up for the quarters, but choreo-graphy was cumbersome. Eric insisted on stretching Willy's hamstrings; he'd not allow her coach to leer into his fiancée's crotch. When Max gave her the low-down on her opponent's shortcomings and Eric chipped in what he'd picked up spying on enemy practice, Max contradicted that what Eric had seen was an aberration and in fact the girl's backhand volley was extraordinary. Willy was left with no idea whether to pass on the forehand or backhand sides and decided to lob.

Lobbing turned out to be the ticket, and to celebrate Willy's victory in the quarters they dined as a threesome in the hotel. A nightmare; never again. Max expressed aggressive sympathy with Eric's loss in Oklahoma, and name-dropped former Top Ten confederates with the nimble regularity of Hansel sowing crumbs. Eric was stonily polite, and declined to mention that his parents had been good friends of Ted Tinling's. Some games were best won by refusing to play.

The morning after she won the semis, Willy was rallying with Eric on a practice court, when Max marched onto Eric's backcourt with an unsheathed racket and stood on the T as Eric collected a ball by the fence. Eric looked briefly confused. Max held his racket out for the ball. Eric didn't hand it over. Instead he advised across the net, "Willy, you might take those approaches even earlier—"

"If you take an approach too early, you lose control," Max interrupted. "Placement in an approach is everything—"

"I wasn't talking half-volley, Upchurch—"

"Willy, come here!" It was the stern command of calling a dog to heel. Willy padded over. Max didn't often shout, and he didn't now. "You can fuck him. You can even marry him. But if he's going to be your coach as well, you'd better tell me now."

"Of course not, he's just—"

"All right. Today's the final. It may only be worth eight thousand dollars, but sixteen hundred of that is mine. You need those points, badly. If you need those points, I need those points. So get that man off this court."

"Eric, maybe you'd better..."

Eric zipped up his racket, his motions quick and tight. Max called after him, "Ever hear the adage about too many cooks?"

Eric was right: tennis was like sex. You mostly remembered the times it was awful. After matchmaking reached its heady climax a successful encounter blurred; all that was left was the score. Awkwardness, missed connections, the wrong partner at the wrong time lasted longer, pricking into memory point by point with all the precision of a child's pin drawing held up to a lamp. Calling up her year's tennis highlights, Willy saw only drop shots that hit net cord, break points she failed to convert, lunges that sent her sprawling. No matter how many trophies she had accumulated, the year-in-pictures cataloged disaster. It was as if nothing about competence was worth retaining; as if memory existed exclusively for the purpose of self-torture.

Consequently, as soon as Willy's racket followed through her match-winning overhead in the New Freedom final, the game behind her shrank to a statistic. Shaking hands with her opponent and turning to her chair, Willy searched the twilight for the afterimage of match point before it faded forever. It must have been gratifying, but she could no longer be sure. As with sex, maybe that's what kept you coming back for more: when it was good, you couldn't keep it.

Toweling down and shaking hands thrust from the stands, she spotted Max ambling toward her with an understated sketch of a smile. But when Willy searched the front row, no Eric. Though his seat was empty, he hadn't bounded to her side.

Meanwhile, Max was working the elastic of her sweatpants over her shoes.

"Max, these look ridiculous with a tennis dress."

"You'll get cold."

Once she was swaddled, her skirt lapping over the gray sweats, Eric threaded from an exit and apologized as he unseated neighbors to reach his chair. The cheesy *Chariots of Fire* sound track was already *PUM-pum-pum*-ping through the speakers, and there was no time to exchange a word before she had to waddle to the mike and accept the cut-glass trophy.

Arm around the bowl, she flicked the skirt with her free hand and curtsied. "I know you must get tired of players thanking their coaches and fiancés," she began, "but I face the music if I leave either of them out."

The crowd chuckled. American audiences were putty in the hands of any victor; she could obviously say anything.

"At least I'll spare you the ritual gratitude for my father's support," Willy continued, her voice booming into the stands, "since for years he had his heart set on my becoming a certified public accountant. *[Huh-huh-huh.]* But most of all, I want to thank everyone for coming out to a satellite. We all like watching the stars, but Top Tens have to come from somewhere, right?"

She raised her fist in the air, and they cheered.

"Where *were* you?" Willy exclaimed when they were finally back in their hotel room. "At the end of the match, I looked everywhere. You'd vanished."

"I had to take a leak," said Eric, tossing his bomber jacket on the bed.

"On the *last game?*" They didn't have time for a fight. The end-of-tournament party was in half an hour, and the winner was obliged to be on time. Hurrying, Willy pulled off her sweatpants, and they got stuck around her sneakers.

"It wouldn't have been the last game if you'd lost it," Eric explained with suppressed impatience, pitching clothes. "It was 5–3 in the second set, you were down love–30, and with a break Patterson would be back on serve. I'd put off dashing out for an hour, and I was about to bust a gut."

"If you could wait an hour, you might have waited five more minutes," Willy grumbled, wrestling from her sweatshirt. " You wouldn't have left your seat coming up to *Edberg*'s match point."

Down to his boxers, Eric turned with his hands on his hips.

"I wasn't watching Edberg, was I?"

"What's that supposed to mean?"

"All that 'I'm gonna be a Top Ten'—"

"I didn't say that—"

"It was a bit much."

Her cheeks tingling, Willy bound her arms over her bare breasts. "The crowd expects rah-rah. So does the WTA."

"I came all the way up here to see you play." Eric stepped into his dark suit pants, zipping them up officiously and slapping the leather belt. "For a week I've had nothing else to do but grab a few pick-up games with local losers. And now you're riding my ass for barely making it to the men's room—"

"I'm sorry." Willy reached out to touch his arm through the starched white shirt, letting her breasts swing free. The few inches between them seemed uncrossably vast. Her portable electric clock shuddered as if every second were more effort than the last, and the air in their shabby brown hotel room had gone to pudding. She wasn't used to touching Eric being difficult; that she had to force her hand came as a shock. "I'm grateful you're here," she added, holding firmly to his sleeve and employing the same peculiar emphasis with which Eric had stressed "I'm glad you won" from Oklahoma. "Very grateful. You helped inspire me. Maybe that's why I did better than...I mean, I had a cheering section. I like to perform well for you. Then you missed the last game. So I was disappointed, that's all."

Eric didn't throw his arms around her, but at least he had not drawn back. His own motions had the same creakiness of hers, as if their joints lacked oil. Why had simple conversation grown so laborious? "I am doing my best," he said heavily, "to support you in every way I can. Sometimes I have to *tend to my own needs*, as they say. Okay?" The exhausting exchange completed, he pulled away.

"Aren't you glad it matters to me that you're watching?" Willy asked softly.

Eric whipped his tie around his raised collar. "Delighted."

Willy slithered silk over her head in silence. A lascivious red, this was one of her favorite outfits, but just now the dress glared; it looked garish, too low-cut and showy, as if she thought she was hot stuff. She tugged the skirt down brusquely, and would only toss an offhand glance in the mirror, not to be seen preening. Willy smoothed the white tights up her legs. Eric's back turned, she traced an admiring finger under the hard disc of her calf muscle, and then felt guilty. She shook out her hair, as if to get a spare part rattling in her head to clunk into place. This wasn't the way she usually felt after winning a tournament. There was no elation, no relief, and her only relation to this upcoming party was dread. It was almost as if, since the victory was only hers and not also Eric's, she had only half won.

In fact, for a fleeting instant Willy wished that she'd missed that last overhead—that she'd lost the final. In a flush of regret both alien and unnerving, Willy imagined this evening otherwise, telling the WTA to stuff their stupid party and sweeping off with Eric to splurge on a compensatory dinner neither could afford. In mutual commiseration, they might not feel exactly jubilant, but at least they'd feel close.

Though that very morning they'd winked like gold bullion, with the New Freedom's computer points now in hand they clinked cheaply in Willy's palm like spare change. Her momentary impulse was to give them away. Standing in her stocking feet and staring helplessly at Eric's back as he worked his broad shoulders into his jacket, Willy lifted a hand as if to offer him a gift—one that would make more difference than some flimsy Sweetspot T-shirt. But the computers weren't programmed that way; just because the points were yours didn't mean you could donate them where you liked. Willy was stuck with them, and maybe the fact that they were nontransferable was what made the points feel trifling.

"Honey," Willy whispered at her future husband's side, "you don't have to go to this party if you don't want to."

"I never said I didn't want to go," he said stiffly, readjusting the Windsor knot more tightly around his neck than seemed necessary.

"It's only a cheapie WTA cocktail affair for a second-rate tournament. It's bound to be dull..."

"Isn't the event to celebrate your achievement?" he asked stolidly.

"In a way, but mostly to keep the sponsor—"

"Then my presence is more or less required, is it not? A given? Why would I not want to go?"

She shrugged and peeped, "No reason."

"All right, then. Get your coat."

The victory party was in the student union, and infiltrated by sophomores with an eye for free drink. The glasses were plastic, the wine poured ominously from carafes. Indifferent to the low-rent catering, Willy concentrated on shepherding Eric.

There was clearly no need to. He was perfectly well behaved—too perfectly. He was gracious and demurring. As pruney, overtanned WTA administrators chattered about Willy's technique, he maintained a courteous if vacant expression. But Willy kept him hooked on her arm, inserting into every exchange, "*Eric* plays pro as well."

"That so?" asked the rep from New Freedom—a man; men were bound to take an interest in women's periods when there was money in them. "What's your ranking, bud?"

Since Eric's adjacent competition had also dropped points, at least his poor performance in Oklahoma hadn't cost him lost ground. "926." Eric's enunciation was even and neutral.

"Good for you. Best of luck, keeping up with this little powerhouse. Don't let her get away from you."

"I don't plan to," said Eric with a distant smile. She could not put her finger on it, but through the evening Eric kept his arms close to his sides, drank a single glass of wine, and spoke only when spoken to, all with the composed distraction of a man who was making resolutions.

EIGHT

"**O**F COURSE YOU'LL BE invited," Willy promised. "But I was concerned you might find it difficult to watch."

"I make my living as a voyeur."

"How can you stand it, Max?" she ventured. "Looking on while other people play?"

"It's the best of all possible worlds." In the confines of Sweetspot's library, his cigar smoke was noxious. "I get credit when you win; if you lose, you're easily replaced. I make lots of money; I risk nothing."

"That's how you see your job?"

"Increasingly."

Willy had glimpsed another side of Max those few weeks in spring—a side that would risk the whole game on a single play at her dormitory door; the side that hit the ball in his prime, gladly putting himself on the line instead of placing these cowardly hedged bets on proxies. Little of that bravery glimmered now. Settled in his usual corner, cupped in lamplight that hugged his chair, he looked complacent and safe, and she saw again why she had to marry Eric. Remembered anxiety and immediate anxiety were chalk and cheese. Max, in his retirement, could never understand her.

"Why don't you have it here?" he volunteered. "Save your pennies." She'd have been touched, except he met her eyes flippantly, tapping his ash. The offer didn't cost him. Maybe her romance had already foreshortened to another match he'd follow from afar.

"You're too kind," she said formally.

"Use this library for the reception. It's small, but you don't have many friends."

"When would I have had time for them?"

"You regret that?"

"Not enough." She hefted her kit bag. "Max? You're my friend, aren't you?"

"I'm your coach. Turning a relationship like ours personal is *ruinous*. Remember? It was your word."

Eric was uneasy about getting married at Sweetspot; Max's donation of the school radiated an obscure vengefulness. But Willy was more uneasy about asking her father to spring for a commercial venue. All her childhood he'd denied her bus fare and Motel 6 bills, forcing her to save babysitting money for the spare racket he considered an extravagance. She needed to preserve the impression of her father as cheap to keep from finding him spiteful.

At any rate, for their ceremony neither a synagogue nor a Methodist altar was appropriate. Eric had never owned a yarmulke; the temple on Seventy-fourth Street promoted ascension on earth. Willy was raised in the church of abstention, where the kingdom belonged to immaculates who declined to participate. While the Novinskys subscribed to the faith of the spurned, and the Oberdorfs to the faith of the spurning, their families sat on opposite sides of the same house of worship, and Willy was uncomfortable in either pew. There was something ghastly about Axel's clawing up New York's ladder and kicking aspirants on lower rungs; there was something unpersuasive about her father's sulking at the bottom with his arms crossed.

For their own parts, Eric and Willy had gravitated to sanct-

uaries of austere design: great green open-air chapels exposed to
passing airplanes. The commandments of their bible were not
always easy to keep, but its catechism was crisp, its theology
straightforward: thou shalt not double-fault; thou shalt not
question line calls. Theirs was a religion both of ruthlessness and
equal opportunity, and if they revered a material grace bestowed
on an elect, they were both members of the chosen people.
Should their marriage be blessed on hallowed ground, it made
perfect sense to say their vows on a tennis court.

So the two settled on Sweetspot, and scheduled the event for
December, the only downtime in the tennis calendar. As they
compiled the guest list, it evolved that Eric had scads of
acquaintances, but few intimates. Eric's loyalties were few,
absolute, and sequential. The majority of his confidants he had
either finished with, or finished off—one contentious best-
friendship had ended in a fistfight. Eric pursued his every
project with blinkered intensity and then one way or another
brought it to conclusion. (It was like him, for example, to flat-
out propose to Willy, and not suggest they live together first.
Anything short of ultimate struck Eric as namby-pamby and
disturbingly indefinite.) This proclivity for closure suited him to
a career in tennis, and to marrying, less well to marriage itself,
with its undemarcated forevermore and its slight haziness about
what, beyond *I do*, the project is exactly.

They settled on a smattering of peripherals, since shy of a
quorum a wedding felt dinky. Accordingly, the preponderance
of their guests—hitting partners, Princeton and UConn ex-
teammates, Sweetspot grads, steeds of the Upchurch stable
whom Willy could abide (*not* Marcella Foussard), all
descending on Westbrook in Vuarnet sunglasses—were tennis
players. While the bride and groom had invited no one whom
they despised, even individuals you like can be revolting as a
group. One wedding guest and his Mazda Miata was neither
here nor there; a roomful of people all of whom owned flashy
cars was gross.

After the guests had warmed themselves with coffee in the library, they trooped up the hill in muffs and fur-lined hoods to court number seven, where Willy and Eric awaited with a Westbrook justice of the peace. At a distance, Willy recognized the shrill, showy laughter of athletes accustomed to being interviewed. The phalanx of taut bodies approached like a mobile paste-up from *Vogue*. Trailing, the single dowdy clump in this army of mannequins was Willy's family. Her father's suit was rumpled from the trip up (why was no one else's?), and his hair scraggly to match the crabgrass at his feet. Her mother's excess of costume jewelry was heartrending. For once Willy was even grateful that Gert was plain. The Novinskys were their only wedding guests who looked like people.

Maybe it was gimmicky, but Willy had enjoyed decking out for the ceremony. The sleeveless shift with its short flared skirt replicated her tournament dress in white satin. For an outdoor event in December, she'd special-ordered a sweatshirt in pearl angora. The shoes had taken days to locate—slight heels, but the toes, tied with ribbon, laced like sneakers.

Eric was leaning on the net post with the inaccessible composure that any tennis court fostered in him. He really should have played in the sport's aristocratic golden age. Those long legs were made for white flannels. In the bone cable-knit sweater with maroon and navy trim, a starched white collar sheering from its V-neck, Eric might have been lifted straight from a frame at Forest Hills—Ellsworth Vines, 1930. Like dapper gentlemen of yore he'd slicked back his hair. All he needed to complete the portrait was a laminated wooden racket.

It was cold, though fitting to marry in weather that drove you to bed. Isolated snowflakes drifting to the court recalled previous winter afternoons when Willy would push the envelope of the season. At the end of many a December session with Max she'd had to prize her rigid fingers from her grip, much as they would unclench a racket from her rigored hand when she was dead. Sweetspot had four indoor courts, but they were airless, protected, and sterile; not-tennis. Until number seven was blanketed, Willy hit outside. Tennis as well as marriage was "for better or for worse."

The JP rushed their ceremony, stamping to warm his feet. In kissing Eric to seal their vows, Willy defied the elements as she had through December tennis. Despite adverse conditions, she would prove to Max that icy outside forces could not freeze out a passion. Despite the many superb rallies that had eluded her retention in the past, this time she was determined to keep what was fleeting.

Willy's memory of the subsequent reception would soon blur. The Novinskys and Oberdorfs assumed opposite corners, as if social climbing or stunted ambition might be physically contagious. Max may have been attempting an air of remote amusement, but his urbanity was strained. By the end of the festivities he was bulwarked in his armchair reading sports psychology in spectacles, with all the unpersuasive aloofness of a brainy adolescent at a school sock hop who was afraid to dance.

Surrounding Max was an entire library full of wrist sprains, regrooved forehands, and winter suntans. Willy was disconcerted that she clung so tenaciously to her place in this vacant lot. Likewise in the flotsam of finger sandwiches and slow tide of champagne, she had often to float her eye toward Eric to remind herself what this sea of chat, yet another cocktail mumble that resembled too well dreary victory celebrations like New Freedom's, was meant to mark. Ordinarily, the game was the prize; the trophy was chaff. This time the game had been incidental. The trophy was a lifetime.

But one memory would remain sharp. Whites gleaming, a chapped hand grazing tape for the ring, the JP intoning, "I now pronounce you husband and wife": in their very union Eric and Willy stood on opposite sides of the net.

***

The halcyon period of the next few months evoked a ball at the top of its toss: steady, serene, balanced. Though at its apex the ball's repose appears eternal, its very arrest implies a rise and fall. At no point did Willy take herself aside and whisper, *These are the good times*, but it may be definitional of good times that they never get labeled as such until they are over.

Eric shifted officially into Willy's apartment on 112th, where he had been moving in sock by sock for five months. Marriage or no, she took a breath when the sanctum of her mailbox was invaded by a man with a duplicate key. The flimsy locks that had hitherto gated her from any other person had been picked. His flipping of her mail or striding in the door unannounced were physical tokens of the fact that Eric now knew her well enough to intuit anything from which she might attempt to bar him. Eric had the keys to Willy herself.

Suitably for them both, Willy's efficient one-bedroom was designed for hasty departures, red-eye arrivals, and weeks of desertion in between. Her freezer routinely stocked a dozen microwave lasagnas and one half-eaten carton of Häagen-Dazs laced with frost. After coming home to enough liquefied onions and shrunken, testicular potatoes, Willy had learned to line the pantry with only a few cans of tuna fish. And having swept numerous black mangles from her windowsills, she'd dispensed with thirsty plants, retaining a single cactus, which could survive on neglect. Bulbous with spurts of erratic growth from irregular waterings, the prickly, misshapen lumps alerted Willy to the dangers of the itinerant marriage, by describing the thorny deformities you fashion when tenderness is too sporadic.

Emblems of intermittent absence grew poignant on nights Willy was left on her own. Desultorily, she'd pick a packet from their overflowing basket of uneaten USAir peanuts, select one of the many Sheraton shampoos and Hilton soaps in the shower, and treat herself to a nightcap from their copious store of airline miniatures. Though they both liked order, when Eric was on the road Willy missed his sweat-soaked T's, ragged tube socks, and crenulated jock straps drying on the curtain rod. She yearned for his dank sweats to drape the hissing radiator, their yeasty must infusing the apartment like rising bread. She'd delay disturbing the bed; though the wide white spread had once invited only the deep, self-righteous sleep of physical exhaustion, the sheets underneath now rippled with a more delicious stir. Restive, Willy would wistfully rewind her husband's jump ropes into neat coils in the foyer, pausing to sniff the foam handles, funky with his perspiration. When she was lucky, they'd still be wet.

If anything, Eric's presence was not intrusive enough. His one mutant eyebrow hair Scotch-taped to the wall remained his sole contribution to her bedroom collage: Polaroids of Willy and her Davis Imperial hefted on her father's shoulders, clippings from sports pages, sittings for Sweetspot annuals. He demurred from miscegenating the trophies over her bureau with his own. He was content for the two frames that predated him to brighten their living room: an attractive poster rescued from the New Jersey Classic, her first satellite victory in 1990; and a lively, buoyant print from the Museum of Modern Art. The painting portrayed a Gay Nineties sportsman leaping out of the frame with a ball at his fingertips. His red-and-yellow-striped bathing costume resembled long underwear, and his handlebar mustache was off-center. Though the orb was actually a volleyball, the comic abandon of the figure, his carefree exuberance, captured the unfettered explosion of pure joy that Willy identified exclusively with a tennis court.

Aside from distributing its every surface with drying sports clothes, Eric assisted in decorating their apartment only by helping to fill Willy's offbeat coffee table, of which he became inordinately fond. She'd glued it together herself: a large clear Plexiglas box whose top was perforated in the center with a three-inch-round hole. Popped through that hole over the last two years, spent tennis balls crowded against the walls of the box, tinted rust from clay, violet from Riverside's berries, or gray from afternoons it had begun to rain and Willy couldn't bear to stop playing. Gradually the level of discards rose, and balls pixelated behind the plastic like the dots of a photograph enlarged to the point of absurdity.

In sum, Willy's space had hardly been invaded. Eric was away more than half of every month, and Willy herself was out of town a proportion of the time he was home. So the estrangement and reacquaintance of Worcester became routine, and Willy no longer expected to quite recognize Eric's face when it poked through the door. In continually reappraising its planes, she never achieved the classic wife's blasé familiarity with her husband's countenance, tantamount to no longer seeing it at all. Searching for a prompt to jog her memory, she often discovered a fresh feature that might otherwise have escaped notice—a new wild hair wending from an eyebrow, the first faint track of crow's feet, the purple undertones in his sockets that told he'd taken the late flight from Houston in order to spend the next day, for once, at her side. They both cleared the decks for these reunions. At Flower of Mayonnaise, Eric would eat two plates of fried rice and half of hers, and the two would trade results of forays far afield.

Nineteen ninety-three began to shape up as a successful year, though also Willy's most strenuous. For there comes a point with any native gift where you get nothing more for free. Willy had plundered her bequest in her teens. By twenty, she could no longer trade entirely on talent. Suddenly having to work for improvement had been frightening at first, but maybe sailing on ability alone was cheating.

Moreover, as she narrowed the distance between her ranking and the Top Ten, each increment cost more than the last. Eric had explained the calculus: as she approached a limit, half the gain might take twice the effort. Surging from a ranking in the latter 400's in April '92 to 355 after the New Freedom had been arduous enough, hut clawing from 355 to 321 in the same number of months proved debilitating.

The competition was bound to get more vicious still. Willy was not the only woman on the domestic circuit who was determined to join the international tour. It was technically possible to hit Kennedy Airport ranked anywhere in the top 500, but fiscally prohibitive when you were well down the list. Max refused to fly her to Argentina only to hack through qualifiers. She had to be able to enter on points and have a chance at payback prize money. For Max to bankroll her abroad, she had to break into the top 200. Though aging, anxious, and impatient, Willy regarded his stipulation as fair. Max was right: he wasn't her friend but her coach, and a businessman.

While Willy could no longer cash in on the "something special" that had brought her father to his knees when she was ten, Eric was barreling along on his genetic gravy train. His game seemed to mature by itself. Naturals who are still flourishing on knack alone do not understand, as Willy did not in high school, anyone who fails to grow new skills like fingernails. Too, the athlete who has finished mining the seam of his gift has a dronish aspect, marked by sedulous, painstaking progress, as if scaling a cliff with no chinks for sudden ascent; the precocious find handholds to make breathtaking leaps in a day. It was prettier to be effortless, and she worried that Eric found her monotonous two-hour net drills pathetic.

Walking in on just such a drill at Forest Hills (where, to Willy's silent consternation, his father had finagled him a membership as well) Eric had taken the notion, whimsically, to "work on" his diagonal lob. He strolled to the baseline, and beckoned Willy to shoot him backhands. After three or four experimental sweeps that from the first showed brilliant instincts, adding a touch of top like a cook throwing in a pinch of salt, he had promptly potted his lob in the exact opposite corner. The stroke had taken him ten minutes, not the morning, much less the next two years. Eric was flying on the wings of inspiration, and in comparison Willy must have seemed landlocked, as if he could hop in his private Lear Jet while his wife took the bus.

Consequently, while Willy sweated from 355 to 321, in the same six months Eric slashed his way from 926 to 708. The aberration of the Jox All-Comers was not repeated, and soon Eric would be able to enter a better quality of tournament with more appreciable points on offer without submitting to qualifiers. While there was something magnificent about her husband's growing into his game, Willy couldn't shake the sense that his burgeoning was a little horrible as well. She suffered the increasing ambivalence of watching a cute puppy with huge, awkward paws loom by the week into a sinewy monster of a dog.

Though their "casual" matches with each other were more and more rare, as of the summer of 1993 Eric had yet to beat his wily, agile wife. Yet they always went three sets; tiebreaks were frequent; games went to deuce. The tactics she was forced to employ were fiendish. Worse, she had come to rely too heavily on Eric's unforced errors, which were decidedly on the wane. He was at last tightening that cross-court backhand, and when it was in it was unreturnable. Frankly, he was breathing down her neck. The closer Eric came to an upset, the more crucial that Willy stave off defeat. Surely something more considerable than her pride was at stake. For there is no parity in tennis. From early in the marriage their matches with each other had ceased to be quite fun. When Willy prepared to play her husband, a lump beneath her rib cage formed as if she'd been punched.

Willy had always been in her element coming up from behind. Thanks to the ball and chain of her dismal family, Willy excelled most when the least was expected; she thrived on being thwarted. That lately no one was trying to stop her was destabilizing, as if she'd been hurtling against a locked door suddenly unbolted from the other side. Adversity was focusing; opportunity was too wide and undefined. She missed her father as archenemy, and was sometimes subject to the lost, evaporating sensation of an agoraphobic in a football stadium who yearns for a closet.

Hence the crick in her neck from looking over her shoulder at Eric. Aiming to overtake, change is your friend; protecting a lead, change is intrinsically disagreeable. All that can happen to number one in the world is that he should become number two. Heelchasers are optimistic and fearless, with nothing to lose; frontrunners are naturally conservative and paranoid.

A marriage should not be a race. That didn't keep it from being one. "He's only 708," Willy would mumble on her way to LaGuardia. But in the same taxi Willy would calculate that Eric had rocketed 218 rankings in the same half-year she'd hobbled up 34. At this rate, in two years Eric would be on TV, and Willie would be adjusting the vertical hold.

Meanwhile her husband proved offhandedly superior at everything that shouldn't have mattered. When they retreated to the Walnut Street backyard, Eric threw ringer after ringer that knocked Willy's horseshoe off the stake. When they dropped into a pool hall on Houston Street, Willy spent the evening chalking her cue. When they bowled in New Jersey, Willy hooked gutterballs, while Eric's scorecard was stitched with little X's.

So for one precious evening together in June, Willy proposed staying home to play Scrabble, at which she had always slaughtered her sister. From the first round Eric drew all the high-value letters, while Willy was stymied by rackfuls of vowels.

"I've been hoarding this for half an hour," Eric admitted when only three tiles rattled in the bag. "I was afraid I'd get stuck with it." He placed down the only Z. "*Zwieback.*"

"What's *that?*"

"Some kind of nasty cracker... So that's twenty-eight points, spanning two triple-word scores: 174."

"Get out, what—?"

"Times six, of course. Then I used all seven letters, which is a bonus of fifty..." For a math major to take any time to add it up was pure sadism. "224."

"You mean you now have a *total* of 224."

"No, that's for the one play."

She flipped the board off the coffee table.

Eric hadn't finished aligning his *zwieback* tiles in anally precise parallels; he drew his hands to his lap. His expression of infantile glee took a few seconds to evanesce. "Willy. It's only a game."

She was breathing harder than the exertion of hurling bits of plastic quite merited. "Is there *anything* you're not good at?"

Eric's very pause told all. "Languages," he said at length.

"Ever tried to learn one?"

"I satisfied degree requirements." On his chest, he scouted consonants from under the couch. "Two years of German."

"But you made *A*'s."

"So? I watched a lot of war movies."

His deflection convinced her only that had he concerned himself with Chinese or ancient Greek he'd have been a whiz at philology as well. All that seemed to determine Eric's expertise was whether he turned to a given field. Willy had long been dimly aware there were such people, but never expected to share a bed with one. From close up, the grotesque facility was so inhuman that she was tempted to regard her husband as born not with something extra, but with something missing.

"Would you really prefer," he inquired from the floor, "that I were a shitty Scrabble player?"

That was easy. "Yes!"

Looking up, he scrutinized her critically. "That would make for a poor game."

"Which I would win."

"Beating someone who's crummy? I can't see the satisfaction."

"It would satisfy me to beat you at *something*."

"You beat me at tennis. Which is what we both do, or one of us does rather, for a living." That their tiebreaker tennis games were her sole purchase on equality was cold comfort. "And even if I did beat you at tennis," he added, maybe remembering the last 7–6, 4–6, 7–6 score, "what would it matter?"

Eric may have graduated summa cum laude, but his question indicated an idiocy of a kind.

"Can't you imagine how it might feel if *I* excelled at everything you didn't?" Willy implored. "If I could read faster and run faster and add faster? If I went to one of the best universities in the country, and you barely squeaked into a state school on a sports scholarship?"

One tile had fallen through the hole in the coffee table; Eric removed the top to retrieve it from the balls. "In that case I'd simply be proud of you."

"And in this case?" she asked softly. "With a wife who's rotten at everything? Eric, what do you see in me?"

"What's all this you're rotten at, Wilhelm?" Eric replaced the Plexiglas and joined her on the couch, wrapping his arm around her shoulders. Willy hunched, hands sandwiched tightly between her knees.

"That computer of yours," she said. "All I get is error messages...I can't preprogram the VCR...My checkbook doesn't balance...*I* never remember which year Bill Tilden was caught messing with little boys—"

"Years," Eric corrected; he couldn't help himself. "He was arrested twice."

"See! And I won't make 224 points on one Scrabble play until hell freezes over!"

Eric pecked her forehead. "And if you ever did, I'd fling the board out the window to the Hudson River."

That was the concession she was waiting for, and she rewarded it with a lingering kiss.

"I'm hungry," he mumbled. "Any zwieback in the house?"

Willy biffed him playfully on a pectoral, but the punch landed harder than she intended. Eyes flashing, Eric wrested Willy's left arm behind her back. He yanked her wrist just high enough that she yelped more from surprise than pain. For a moment she was helpless. With a twist she wrenched free, but he must have let her. Willy socked him in the gut, though this jab was cautiously calibrated merely to wind him a bit.

Eric lunged for his wife and tackled her to the open floor. They'd done this before. They liked to tussle. It was always both serious, and not; aside from the odd bump or scratch, no one ever got hurt. Eric pinned Willy's wrists, hooking his feet around her calves. She slipped her legs free and thrust her knees under his chest, rocking to use his weight against him. As they flipped over sideways, Eric's hand shot out to make sure that she didn't nick her head on the table.

With Willy's knees on his elbows, Eric's arms were long enough for him to work her shirttail out. Willy used her free hands to grab the sides of his T-shirt, and when he toppled her once more she held on. As planned, Eric could escape only by letting her pull the T-shirt over his head. Another familiar game: who could get whose clothes off first, and with Eric now bare-chested Willy already had the edge. A tirelessly entertaining cross between pro wrestling and strip poker, the sport never quite descended to play-rape.

In no time, Eric was standing with a grip on the hems of Willy's denims, her back and head on the floor. The jeans were so snug that to get them off Eric began dragging her across the carpet like a dray pulling a plow. Traction suffered from a couple of waxy Scrabble tiles skating under Willy's bare back. Though her shoulders would probably show rug burns later, she'd started to laugh. Cracking up was deadly, and in the end only the fact that Eric wasn't wearing boxers kept her one article of clothing ahead.

Panting and sweaty and down to socks, they concluded in a prone, tensely immobile clutch, exerting force for force. Willy could feel he'd got hard under her stomach. For an instant, however, the rest of Eric's body relaxed, of which she took full advantage to whip off his last sock. She dangled it victoriously in his face.

"Bitch," said Eric fondly. In this contest, they both won. "Get your diaphragm," he advised.

When she emerged from the bathroom a minute later, Eric was still laid out on the living room floor, which he evidently preferred to the bed. Willy spread herself on his chest, and they locked hands. Eric tried to bend her wrists back; she resisted. He applied more pressure; she held.

"God, you're strong," he said admiringly, though he looked beyond her rippled arms, as if the actual muscles were unimportant.

But Willy didn't like this duel because he was humoring her. At any time he could have easily cocked her wrists back and made her cry uncle. Meanwhile she was pushing as hard as she could, and his own wrists didn't bend a millimeter. Hands trembling, she cast her eyes down his lean, beautifully proportioned torso. Of course he wouldn't be much of a man if he weren't the stronger. It still wasn't fair. Willy would keep the upper hand in any cat fight, but this draw was artificial, and she relaxed her grasp.

Eric insinuated his prick inside her, but the battle was not quite over. For the next twenty minutes they played Who's on Top, another struggle from which even the loser benefited. When their rolling around grew more earnest, Eric drew on his superior strength. Once they were done—with Willy on the bottom—she climbed unsteadily upright to collect her clothes in sublime exhaustion, brushing off the Scrabble tiles stuck to her back. Willy would never admit it, but after all their horseplay those 224 points still irked her a bit.

NINE

WILLY HAD LEARNED THE relativity of success from her parents, who for all their seeming resignation to obscurity had both organized themselves into notables among dross. At Bloomfield College, Chuck Novinsky rose head and shoulders above student bodies for his splendid sentence subordination alone. He'd never sought higher status employment. A colossus among dwarves had no motivation to go seeking other giants.

Likewise, her mother's choice to become nutritional advisor at The Golden Autumn may also have been sly. Daily, Willy's mother confirmed the futility of ambition, destined for so much gnarling and drool. Whatever her charges might have accomplished was encoded by senility, reduced to garbled scraps of ill-remembered better days to which their overseers would attend with distracted tolerance. When Willy had visited The Golden Autumn she could barely breathe from the oppression, but her mother took in the stale, medicinal air as if it braced her, and clipped briskly down the gleaming halls of the home, beaming at her slack-jawed wards with a wave. In the leveling of old age her mother seemed to find vindication.

So her mother mightn't pull off a grand jeté, but she could control her bowels; her father didn't wax eloquent in the *Paris Review*, but his subject-verb agreement was unimpeachable.

Willy's own profession determined that you were as good as you were better than the girl behind, as wanting as worse than the one in front. Greatness was context.

Previous to her marriage, in the context of other avids at Sweetspot, Willy had reasonably considered herself a disciplined, focused athlete. As of December 14, 1992, that context changed. For when Eric Oberdorf ran he covered not four miles, but six, and in better time; Eric preferred to rise not at 7 A.M., but 6 A.M.; and on the road he traveled with a jump rope, lassoing more than one hotel room overhead off its screws.

If Willy was focused, Eric was fanatic. His reading matter consisted of tennis bios, tennis history, *Tennis* magazine, *Racquet*, and *Serve and Volley*. When he returned from LaGuardia, his carry-on was padded with the *Austin Star* and the Cleveland *Plain-Dealer* folded to the sports page. Their VCR was pre-programmed in their absence to record ESPN and USA, and his idea of a relaxing evening at home was to rewind and take notes on Indian Wells. If he rented a video, Eric would cart home, not *Last Exit to Brooklyn*, but the McEnroe-Borg Wimbledon final of 1980, of which he'd continually replay single points. In context, therefore, overnight Willy Novinsky—who had rather hoped to see *Last Exit to Brooklyn*—could reasonably consider herself a dabbling, flabby slacker.

Adjacent zealotry drove her in two directions at once. On the one hand, when Eric threw back the blankets and leapt upright while the light outside was still the color of old, overcreamed coffee, Willy was inclined to loll sullenly abed till noon. On the other, she was tempted to set her own alarm for total darkness and complete an hour's calisthenics while Eric snoozed. After vacillating between defiance and triumphalism, she marched to a slightly quicker beat and made a soldierly effort at keeping abreast. She, too, rose at New York's version of cock's crow (when the garbage trucks yawned), ran six miles instead of four, and took up jumping rope.

***

Axel's wedding present had been a family membership in the Hamilton Jordan Indoor Racquet Club, to which Willy began to accompany her husband midday when they were both in town. Eric booked a regular sixty-minute training session in a squash court, an enclosure, he assured her, large enough for them both. Skipping rope together presented opportunity to spend precious extra time in the same room, and Willy had assumed that Eric's bouncing up and down entailed such drudgery that he'd welcome companionship. Yet the first time Willy came along in June, she discovered the *ta-dum-ta-dum* tedium of her imagination required some touching up.

For the initial few hundred, he skipped in the left-hand service square until the slim black plastic tubing churned like an eggbeater. As he accelerated, a low whir rose to a high-pitched whistle, and his heels seemed to hover, immobile, three inches above the floor.

Eric had lent her a leather Everlast, knotted to accommodate her height; that through the next few months she continued to cadge his rope instead of investing in her own was a reminder that the regime itself was borrowed. She assumed the opposite service square, their ropes clicking the boards as one. But Willy was left well behind after the first 250. As she disentangled the thong from her socks, the whine of Eric's whip continued to rise in pitch.

Warmed up, Eric zigzagged up and down the court on the tips of his toes, like the nimble electric stitch of a sewing machine with special attachments. Next, he sliced a set of scissors kicks, his long legs held stiff as shears, his Lycra cross-training shorts switching like beveled blades. Through her own plodding *tu-dum, tu-dum*, Willy cut her eyes askance as Eric repeatedly clicked his heels together in midair, as if he had just won the lottery. Then he plunged deep on each thigh, extending the opposite leg like a Russian Cossack. When he crossed his arms over and back, *s-swip, s-swip*, the loops closing and opening out again in an unbroken snake, Willy's Everlast once more hit her shins.

Her eyes narrowed. Willy centered again in her own square, gathered momentum, and crossed her arms.

Pthwack.

This clearly took more than one go. Willy built a rhythm, trying to shut out Eric's *whoo-ooo-PUM, whoo-ooo-PUM* of double-jumps by counting in her head:... *6, 7, 8, 9—CROSS!*

Pthwack. The rope circled her left leg, wrenching the wooden handle from her grip; it clattered to the floor.

Despite the clamor, Eric didn't falter, but went into a mixed routine of doubles, arm crosses, Cossack dips, and heel clicks. Behind the squash court's transparent back wall, a small crowd of club members had gathered to watch.

Retrieving her rope from the floor, Willy studied her husband. His lips were delicately parted. Half-closed, his eyes fixed on a midpoint in space. The pupils weren't quite cold; perhaps that pure a concentration qualified as an emotion. The lone indicator of his exertion was a dimple dented between his eyes, as if an invisible divine finger were touching his forehead. As the black whip blurred an oval halo around his body, he looked blessed. She might have never seen his face more tranquil, more affectionate, or more attentive—but all that engrossment converged inward. He was oblivious to her grunts of exasperation when her own rope hooked her toes. Willy beheld the part of Eric that was concerned with Eric, and it was unnerving to encounter this contented, self-congratulatory grace outside her embrace. Willy had previously indulged the fiction that in her absence Eric was not quite there.

Ssee-ow-sseee-ow, ta-hooo-ta-hooo, SMACK. Eric wound the rope around its handles, dried his dripping face on his shirt, and turned to Willy as if she had just walked in the door.

"Eight thousand?" she inquired.

He shrugged. "The usual."

Willy had managed only six thousand in the same period.

"You didn't mess up *one time*, did you?"

"I do, some sessions," he defended.

"What, like once? In eight thousand?"

"Is there something *wrong* with that, Willy? Do I not have permission?"

"Don't be absurd. Here, this is yours." She held out the Everlast with distaste.

"You just need some practice!" he shouted after her. "I've done this for years!"

But Willy did not easily resign herself to shortcomings, or readily concede superiority. Through the summer, in breaks between tournaments she accompanied her husband to the sweltering squash court and bore down on his variations one by one. She mastered the zigzag and the scissors step; her speed and consistency improved. But as soon as she got the knack of the double-jump, Twinkletoes moved on to triples.

Though her skipping had become more lucid, Willy never quite attained the Zenlike perfection of her husband. Eric's claim that he did miscue "some sessions" proved accurate only in the strictest sense. Once or twice a month the whirling dervish would sputter to a halt. Though his fumbles flooded her with a brief, malignant joy, his very errors came to serve as reminders of how rarely they occurred. More, through a flub he was so unflappable, his pupils riveted on their fixed point in space, his lips angelically parted, that when he resumed as if nothing had happened, it really was as if nothing had happened.

By November, Willy demanded the same seamless dexterity from herself, refusing to forgive the few stumbles that regularly blighted her routine. As a result, their skipping sessions were increasingly poisoned by Willy's outbursts of bilious rage. As Eric cavorted into his Polish polka, Willy would punctuate her regime by chiding herself, "Klutz! Bonehead! You stupid, clumsy slob!" The interjections were mumbled at first, but grew louder as her temper flared, her timing crumbled, and Eric vaulted into a wizardry correspondingly more balletic and baroque: "You dishrag! You worthless, stinking, steaming pile of dogshit!" Spit spattered the floor; a sharp pain pitched between her eyes; red splotches bloomed in her field of vision and spattered the walls. The day Eric mastered skipping with the rope moving backward, Willy considered that a squash court, with its stark white paint and vivid crimson markings, would make an excellent setting for a chain-saw massacre.

Once the session drew mercifully to a close, sweat drizzled down her temples and Willy was drenched in shame. In private she contemplated her tantrums, disquieted by the dark, sticky place in her head that they uncovered.

So the first week of December Willy experimented with booking a squash court by herself. The air felt cooler. The cube looked cleaner, simpler, whereas with Eric the sperm-shaped ball smudges above the service line had seemed to squiggle and worm. Willy was reminded that she had never harbored any aspirations to become a rope-skipping wunderkind—that her skill at this exercise was of no importance to her whatsoever.

Spared Eric's flights of fanciness, a halting regularity returned. The requisite eight thousand completed, Willy stared at the limp rope in confusion. Her performance wouldn't have taken any prizes, but she was hardly inclined to call herself a butthole. Aimlessly, Willy tried the crossed-hands. After a few failed efforts, she shrugged and wound the Everlast around its handles. So she couldn't do the crossed-hands. Big deal.

Fortified by the revelation that rope-skipping was Mickey Mouse, Willy next accompanied Eric to the Jordan on Eighty-sixth Street with a lift in her stride. In a spirit of fresh repose, Willy began jumping in unison with her husband. She fashioned a blasé regret on discovering that in company she couldn't quite smooth through the first five hundred without goofing up. Resolved, at each error Willy placed the rope behind her heels, took a deep breath, and silently recited, *It doesn't matter.*

Breezy aplomb persisted through the first one thousand, until Eric dipped into his Cossack step. The tips of his toes kicking at the corner of her eye tickled something in her head; her Everlast *thwacked* and lay still. "Dipshit!"

The rebuke had escaped; she had not meant to say it; she would say no more. She resumed, but as Eric bounced into a fox-trot Willy's breathing constricted, a discrete bull's-eye below her rib cage beginning to heat. Though training her gaze to the front wall, Willy was unable to elude the message drumming through the floorboards: *he never makes a mistake.*

In contrast to a certain someone. Swiveling, Willy forced herself to face him as an extra punishment for having screwed up three times in the last one hundred. She would make herself confront real agility in order to feel that much more of a toad.

Eric's muscles rippled as if a spectral pianist were playing arpeggios across his thighs. Beneath the blazing squash lights, shadows striated between the tendons in his forearms. His hair was wet and splayed, but flopped into the inspired disarray of genius. If he had always looked striking skipping rope, now Eric exuded a more menacing beauty: the tortuously exquisite good looks of a man who is denied you.

Granted that she possessed him in a way; Eric was her husband. Still, this was the part of Eric that was his and only his, that indeed she could not have. Now, by reputation at least, a woman in generations past had derived her status from her spouse, assuming his achievements as transitive achievements of her own. But as Eric segued into a series of three hundred consecutive hand-crossings—now the totem of her own limitations—Willy could not see how her husband's adroit, superhuman grace conferred on her one little bit.

Meanwhile, a larger than usual audience had collected in the back bleachers and overhead gallery. Under observation, Willy herself abandoned any tricks. She would only appear an apprentice struggling with elaborations over her head, attempting poor forgeries of the maestro, who had himself begun his most magnificent confabulation: the mixed routine, weaving boxes of waltz, lunges of polka, sashays of Irish jig, and reversals of forward to backward, climaxing in ten consecutive triples.

At which point the onlookers exploded into spontaneous applause, and all the blood vessels in Willy's head swelled to bursting with revulsion.

While one might speculate, in the droll composure of a glass of wine after dinner, that aversion for your lover is merely devotion flipped upside down, Willy couldn't find the barest resemblance between this splenetic antipathy and the warm, vertiginous rush of adoration. There was no use having a word for love if its synonym was hatred. And hatred such as she had never felt before, a hatred that challenged whether she had ever hated anyone else really, not a single opponent however forbidding or unworthy, not even Marcella Foussard. She hated his self-righteously sweaty clothes, she hated his smarmily perfect body, she hated his fancy-schmancy exhibitionist theatrics raised to a power just because a lot of nobody pseudo-sportsmen were gooning at him. In a spreading tide of anathemas, she hated his priggish recitation of who won the Italian in 1963, his look-at-me-I'm-so-dedicated posing in front of tournament videos with a pen and pad, his chuckling superiority slipping out those *zwieback* tiles when he'd merely lucked into the Z, and most of all she hated his conceited, swaggering upper-class assumption that just because he deigned to pick up a tennis racket at eighteen he could sashay into the pantheon of her profession when she'd been busting her ass since she was five.

Eric was cooling down with plain skipping, the floor on his side of the court flecked with dark drops of perspiration. Though a few spectators drifted off, the show was not, quite, over.

That gorge of odium had not done wonders for Willy's flow. "Goddamn motherfucking hell!" she cried, bungling once more.

"Willy," said Eric quietly, at last breaking his code of silence.

"People can hear. Watch your language."

"Watch your own." The remark wasn't clever, it didn't even make sense; but the first thing to go in rage is your wit.

Eric turned his back, as if to disavow her.

Willy had begun to fling the rope as fast as she could. When the rope convulsed from nicking her heel, it lashed her forearm, raising long red welts above her watch. In the impromptu flogging was a vindictive, almost erotic pleasure.

"You shit!" Even Willy wasn't sure if she was speaking to Eric or herself. She could no longer hurl the rope around more than a handful of times without tripping, and with each blunder the rope scourged her left arm, which was glowing a crisscrossed pink and starting to swell. "You piece of garbage! You nothing!"

At Eric's hand on her shoulder, Willy leapt back.

"Hey." He assumed the fake-reasonable tone of a doctor cornering a mental patient, or a cop coaxing a suicide risk from a ledge. "Call it a day, huh?"

"I haven't done my eight thousand. I can't go home until I've done my eight thousand, can I?" Willy was panting.

Eric glanced furtively to the glass back wall. The onlookers had retreated to behind the bleachers, and were side-eyeing the squash court as if they weren't really watching. Members met one another's eyes with complicitous amusement, exchanging whispered incredulities. *Well, screw them.*

"You're worried I'm making a spectacle of myself. Isn't that what you just did? Made a spectacle?"

"Willy, this self-abuse—it doesn't help."

"What, I should be like you? Patting myself on the back every minute for what a glorious athlete I am?"

"Yes."

"So that's the answer. Be a preening asshole."

"Yes."

She was taken up short.

"Because it's a better life," he added. "And it works." Eric tugged his Everlast from her hands.

They walked home without speaking. Eric draped his sopping sports clothes over the radiators and left to hit a few balls. When he returned that evening, Willy wanted to say she was sorry, but could not quite get on the other side of something to get the words out.

Eric, by contrast, was resolute. "Willy, you mentioned that you jumped better by yourself, right?"

Willy wrestled with a jar of spaghetti sauce. She wasn't in the mood to ask Eric to open it. "Some."

"Why don't we book separate sessions, then? My companionship doesn't seem to have a great effect on you."

"You don't have to put it in terms of my interest. You want your serenity back, don't you? Your happy, complacent self-communion?"

"As a matter of fact, I do."

The lid wouldn't budge. "OK." She had failed to rise to enough challenges for the day, and put the jar down.

Willy bunched up on the sofa to flip through *Tennis* magazine. Her left arm was hot; a few lashings had broken skin. As she swung her foot, it kicked the Scrabble box, which had been shoved under the couch post-*zwieback* and remained there since. Neither of them had suggested the game again.

He was right, of course: they ought to jump rope in different slots. Her behavior today was appalling, he shouldn't have to put up with it, and indeed she had done a better job at skipping on her own. An era was over. Then, it had never exactly been a barrel of laughs, skipping together. Good riddance, she supposed. So why did Eric's proposal depress her?

The answer to Willy's Scrabble tantrums was to no longer play. The answer to jump-rope rivalry was to separate. Both activities in themselves were niggling, expendable. But Willy wondered if it was not so much the nature of their problems that measured her marriage as the remedies they chose, and these solutions were ominous.

TEN

"I DON'T THINK SO . . . No, Tuesday's my wedding anniversary, but that's not the problem. I just think we've reached the end of the road, John. If it's no longer competitive, there's no point. I've got some other names if you—Yes, they are my 'discards,' if you insist on—Hello?" Eric put down the phone. "Bastard hung up on me."

It was a small apartment; Willy couldn't help but listen in. "Can you blame him? I thought John Lance was a friend of yours."

"He wasn't a friend, he was a hitting partner. You should know the difference."

Well, she did. The decorative pregame natter about romances or weather camouflaged the utilitarian character of the sports "friendship." Beyond a post-match beer, itself only tolerable if the score was close, hitting partners were rarely invited into your social circle. Because hitting partners got used up. But Willy had never seen anyone consume as many partners in such short order as her own husband. He chewed them up and spit them out, ingesting morsels of strategy or technique along the way as he sucked oysters from a chicken back and left the bones.

"Why not beg off that you're out of town?" Willy suggested. "Anything but, 'Your game stinks, don't call again.'"

"He'd know I was making excuses. I double-bageled him our last match. John's ranking will never rise from the late 700's."

"You were in the 700's six months ago. Why now the pee-yew?"

"Because I'm pushing to the 400's by early next year," Eric explained impatiently. "*You* can't bear partners you shellac."

"There's just something hideous about telling someone point-blank that they're not good enough for you anymore."

"This is a ruthless sport."

"Which brings out a side of you that makes me nervous."

"What should make you nervous is if out of some misplaced altruism I keep playing inferiors and bring my progress to a standstill."

"What if John improved?" she pressed. "Games wax and wane. He might overtake you again."

Eric snorted. "Never happen."

It never happened. Eric had yet to be surpassed by any opponent over whom he'd established dominion. In no endeavor had her husband ever experienced a stall, much less a setback; the prospect of regression was as preposterous to him as the notion of waking up two inches shorter. Willy had been in this game longer, and herself knew the brief, shuddering horror of watching your ranking slip the wrong direction for a month or two. She had shared a locker room bench with plenty of has-beens, once in the top 200 and wandering, bewildered, in the wasteland of the 800's. They all had a distinctively stunned, battered look, like accident victims in shock. Particularly to Americans, for whom life was definitionally a series of betterments, a shift into reverse defied some hitherto immutable rule of physics—as if time itself had run backward. Regression was betrayal, bequeathing the shaken trust of earthquake survivors, for whom the solidity of the very earth is newly unreliable. But the ground under Eric's feet had never rumbled; his second hands plowed unremittingly clockwise. While his innocence gave him power, it accorded him a callousness as well.

"So I boot some no-talent from my list," Eric pursued. "Why does that rattle *you*?"

"Maybe you plan on going through wives the same way," she said dryly. He laughed, but she hadn't meant to be funny.

Eric raised his wife by the armpits, extending his arms until her pale, flyaway hair grazed the ceiling. "I *use* hitting partners. I *love* you."

She supposed that made her lucky; Willy was officially the object of Eric's whole ardor. He wasn't very interested in friendship; since their marriage, he had failed to keep up with his old roommate, and never evinced any enthusiasm about dinner parties or having someone over for a drink. If she did arrange a social occasion, he got annoyed; Eric was possessive of intersections with his wife and stingy with their evenings. He was an absolutist, and valued efficiency. He had solved his emotional requirements like one of his equations. There was of course his family, to whom he was dutifully attentive, but the Oberdorfs were stored in their own unit and allocated the broader, fuzzier affections of blood. Eric had invested all his passion in his wife, like sinking his life savings in a single stock.

The lack of diversity in Eric's emotional portfolio, while not a burden precisely, was a responsibility. Eric had no other great love. Tennis for her husband retained its clinical aspect, and never sent him careening on the tempestuous roller-coaster of rapture and desolation that for Willy served as a parallel romance. Though he'd been vexed with her at times, she was sure he'd never inflamed with the raging antipathy that had engulfed her skipping rope. The memory of that loathing still smoldered, an ugly secret she had vowed to keep. Had Eric stepped into the blaze of her mind at that instant, he'd have seared his heart.

Like so many men, Eric respected only those who thrashed him. Once he'd wrested the advantage, his interest dwindled, he grew derisive and restive when vanquished adversaries called, irritable when their appointments came due, until finally with a crumple he tossed their numbers in the can. Eric was fond of stalking tennis courts for choice, unravaged talent, just as he'd prowled Riverside before pouncing on his wife-to-be. Every month or two he would return from these safaris clutching a new phone number, wearing the grin of a tom chomping a live mouse, with which he planned to toy before the kill.

While Eric acclaimed the genius of his newest acquisition, Willy ground her teeth. He may as well have drooled over some other woman's sexy gams and pert breasts. That her promiscuous husband's practice opponents were male merely brought Willy's jealousy to a boil. Only men could feed Eric the pace he craved; only men could dish out serves at 120 mph. Willy couldn't compete.

With his voracious appetite for fresh meat, Eric and Willy played each other no more than every six weeks. Since for months she'd beaten him by a hair's breadth, Willy had suffered the growing unease through the autumn that in this infrequency was reprieve.

On their first anniversary, however, Eric cleared his calendar for a ceremonial rematch. December dictated an indoor date at Jordan. As she strode to the net post at the same time of day that they had wed, Willy's hands buzzed with the tremble that ordinarily signaled the onset of a vital finals match. When she peeled the flip top, a rubbery breath exhaled from the Wilson can. Commonly the perfume of opportunity, just this afternoon the smell was spiked with an acrid tinge.

The same sharp, acid scent exuded from Eric's new togs, fresh from the package—his Lycra cross-training shorts, cotton overshorts, and roomy designer sports shirt were all solid black. As Willy had worn her plain white tournament dress, the aesthetic of the classic Western prevailed. A triangulated black bandanna obscured his receding hairline, Eric's sole physical flaw. When he smiled, his teeth, under artificial lighting, flashed like little knives.

In the warm-up, rather than rally to groove their strokes, Eric continually put the ball away. If Willy initiated a point with an easy midcourt forehand, Eric cracked his return to skid the alley line, and Willy would trudge to fetch the ball. He hurried the racket flip for serve, though Willy had not remotely hit her stride.

Leaning forward to receive, twirling his racket, rocking side to side, Eric had the shiny eyes, tensed muscles, and spittle-flecked mouth of a hound with the hare in sight. Willy bounced the ball, unable to put her finger on why something felt wrong. The toss was a little low, and as she wound up at its crest Willy recognized her sensation, one that ritually afflicted her as the number 66 bus drew into Montclair.

She felt short.

Her double fault was inauspicious. Eric trotted to the ad-court, leered forward again, juggling his grip. He *broke her* the first game, and today the expression was resonant.

"Do you have to chew gum?" Willy implored on the change-over.

"I always chew gum," Eric smacked.

"It's obnoxious."

"It's supposed to be." He blew a bubble, and popped it with a relish that usually comes with bursting someone else's.

Her trouble was sourced in the preliminaries, which Eric had truncated to five minutes. Eric could switch his game on like a radio. But Willy's strokes didn't sing instantaneously. Until a melody gathered in her body, the racket felt clunky, apart.

Eric was so eager to punish the ball into oblivion that their rallies were rare. The fits and starts of the first few games had no music. Willy had gone down in the first set 4–6 before the object in her right hand felt like a racket and not like a shovel.

Between sets they toweled down. "Of course, you *know* I need fifteen minutes to find my game," she said. "I've even told you."

"No need," said Eric. "I've seen it. In a quarter of an hour, you improve by a factor of five."

"On the stock exchange, you'd be arrested," she sniped, walking off to serve. "It's called 'insider trading.'"

"It's called marriage!"

In the second set, Eric's famous relaxation took a twist toward the snide. As he sauntered back and forth to receive, he took his time. His commonly erect posture was compromised by a cocky slouch. Picking up balls, he flipped the Wilson with the tip of his frame, then ponged it off the strings with a twirl between bounces, as if he needed some extra amusement to keep himself entertained. Smacking gum on the baseline, he looked more like a street-corner tough than a tennis pro.

While Eric pursued his usual policy of saying nothing, there was a new development: every time he missed a shot, no matter how taxing, he laughed—as if muffing such a piece of cake were hilarious.

Willy's forehead began to pinch with a telltale headache. Anger in sports ran all the risks of nuclear power; before her building fury blew up in her face, she had to harness and channel it. But no matter how much weight she threw behind her shots, that was at most 108 pounds. Eric was used to playing other men; no amount of zing fazed him. Willy could hit a heavy ball, but heavy for a girl. In male terms, her pace was no better than respectable.

It was crucial not to be lured into playing his game; she would never overpower him. So Willy switched to cold fusion. Though it was gratifying in the moment to fry the ball, the only enduring satisfaction was to win. At 4–4, she dialed back the voltage, playing percentages, opting more to press than to destroy.

Though this cagey hunkering down elicited multiple chortles from her husband, she could still do no better than hold serve, and likewise in the tiebreak. Impatient with a tit for tat that at $35 an hour could last from now till doomsday, Willy saw her chance and threw her switches. Instead of sending his deep lob to her backhand safely down the line, Willy ran around to her forehand for an inside-out overhead. That left the rest of the

court for the taking; if he hauled ass to return, she was dead.
Max would have turned purple.

As it happened, the overhead did clear the tape by the
requisite half inch and nicked the line. Eric was nowhere nearby,
but back on his baseline chewing gum, adjusting his black
kerchief at a jaunty angle. Propped against his knee, his racket
was not even in his hand. "Touché," he said, with an indulgent
smile, as if she had just done something cute.

It may be no coincidence that there are both three sets in most
dynamic tennis matches and three acts in the classical play. Each
set completes a discrete subdrama, whose intricate ins and outs
can distract from the larger story. Hence Willy's triumph in
taking the second was quickly washed away in the briefest of
intermissions, after which the players took their places.
Dramatically, at 1–1 there is no telling whether the second set
represents a turned tide, or a red herring.

In the first two sets what had got Willy's goat was Eric's
apparent leisure—his insolent, ball-bobbling nonchalance, the
sort of hip, slovenly posturing that most people could only
manage with a cigarette. What dismayed her in the third was his
exertion. Eric sloughed off his disguise of so-fucking-what to
reveal how fantastically hard he was trying. He leapt two feet in
the air to intersect a damned good lob; he never once conceded
that her volley was too sharp to chase down, and surely he risked
injury in some of the heaving changes of direction that his
incredible retrievals demanded. Lunging for passing shots, he
threw his whole body as if rescuing a wayward toddler from an
oncoming bus. Of course she wanted him to make an effort;
lack of application was an insult. But somehow he was going too
far; he let her have nothing; he was even willing to hurt himself
if that's what grappling a single point from her clutches cost
him. Frankly, in none of the tournaments she'd watched him
play had Eric put himself out quite so extremely as in trying to
sandbag his own wife on their wedding anniversary.

And he had memorized her game like a poem. No matter what she hit, he seemed to know before the ball left her racket precisely where it was headed. Even when she aimed deliberately to surprise, he looked like a sneaky child who had peeked inside his Christmas package and failed to feign delight on opening it a second time.

Worse still, Willy kept recognizing her own esoteric shots, retooled and refurbished. Of course she didn't *own* the slice-drop, barely clearing the tape like a pole-vaulter grazing his back on the bar. Still Willy felt robbed when Eric duplicated her trademark, and not only reproduced but improved upon it, the way the Japanese manufacture an American car: one of Eric's slices had so much underspin that it somersaulted back to his own court. All her helpful hints of the preceding year Eric had faithfully installed, and Willy resented how kleptomaniacally Eric had *taken* her advice. When they met his game was scrappy; now that she'd shared her professional secrets, only to have them used against her, she wanted them back. Surely usurping so many monogrammed shots wholesale was as unseemly as dressing up in her clothes.

A year before Eric's strokes were potent, but his strategy was predictable. Now between his blasting masculine drives he slyly interwove the female cunning of impetuous dinks, neurotic spins, and last-minute improvisations, when it was conventionally the prerogative of women to change their minds. Yet these feminine wiles were grafted to muscle. The result was a game that glimmered with sexual ambiguity, like a construction worker with a few incongruously effeminate mannerisms, whose buddies can never quite decide if he's gay.

Willy could not even console herself that her own game was crumbling in return. Eric was hitting so fabulously well that he lifted her with him. Though her tactics were increasingly defensive, these were still very effective tactics. Rather than be disgusted with herself, in the main of the set at 2–3 Willy considered that she may have been playing, wastefully, the best tennis of her life.

Best wasn't good enough.

Unlike the fits and starts of the first set, now their points were drawn out; every game went to deuce. But Willy's anger was spent. Try as she might, she couldn't despise him. It was easy to detest a braggart jumping rope, because rope-jumping was stupid. But as an aficionado of fine tennis, Willy couldn't revile an artist on the court. Her dark, dashing husband himself looked only more exquisite, and his beauty was murderous.

At 4–2, Willy's arms went limp. Eric served to her ad-court. She didn't feint in the ball's direction, but allowed his ace to burst splendidly undefaced to the netting. She smiled, weakly conceding with a quaver, "Terrific serve."

This and the final game were tribute. If Eric wanted her soul he could have it, though it grieved her that more than anything that's what he craved: her dignity like a lamb on an altar. On match point she deliberately popped him a sitter, that he could fall upon it to his greater glory, and watched, sacrificial, as the ball hurtled from his overhead. Transfixed, she didn't realize it was rocketing straight for her until it clocked her on the breast.

He ran over. "Are you all right?"

"Since when did you worry how I was?"

"Honey—" He touched her cheek.

She brushed him away. "Happy?"

Eric shrugged.

"No, tell me. Are you *happy*? You got what you wanted. You won. It's our anniversary. Have I made your day?"

"Sweetheart, you've been pasting me for over a year. And somebody has to win, don't they?"

In her own mind, Willy had not been "pasting" him; she'd won nothing but delay. Willy shoved her racket in its case; the zipper stuck. She wasn't furious; she was doleful. Something more than a tennis match had been lost. "Congratulations," she mumbled. "No one could say you didn't put your whole heart into it."

He touched her sleeve. "Aren't you glad that I regard being able to best you once in a while as an achievement?"

"Once in a while" was false modesty. None of his other partners had ever broken back. Eric would see to it that she never outplayed him again.

Through the funereal unwinding of her bandanna, Eric pressed, "You wouldn't want me to *let* you win, would you?"

"Of course not," she answered brusquely, but something bruised and girlish in her whispered, hissing, *Yesss*.

ELEVEN

"FOR YOU, TENNIS," MAX barked, his voice echoing over the empty indoor court, "is not a spectator sport."

"I wouldn't have gotten it," Willy objected.

"Not planted on the baseline like an azalea bush you won't. You're wasting my time. What did you come up here for, Christmas shopping?"

These few days were a window of opportunity—the season over, students home for the holidays, Max available. During the last year Willy had spent fewer days at Sweetspot than since she and Max had met. Her coach had grown icy. In marrying, she had written herself off.

"Can we have dinner?" she pleaded at the net post.

He eyed her, and appeared to detect something strange. "The mess is shut. So it's Boot of the Med, or a sandwich in my digs. But that might make Mrs. Undershorts nervous."

"I told you, I kept my own name."

"Today that's about all you've kept."

"Max, I've had a good year."

"That's what I don't get. In six months you should be ready for the international tour. With my blessing, not to mention my money. So why are you quivering in the backcourt like a cube of Jell-O?"

She saved an explanation for a glass of wine, which she

needed more than usual.

"Don't you get lonely through the holidays?" she asked polite-ly as they crunched the grounds patched with snow. "You must miss your family."

"I told you about my family. You've forgotten."

Willy colored. "It's coming back to me." The pillow talk of the jilted had a tendency to float off and disperse like so many feathers.

"They detest me. All the world loves a winner except his own kin. You should know that."

"Would they like us any better if we failed?"

"No, you only get to choose between teeth-gnashing at your success and malicious pity for your downfall. Take your pick."

"You don't have very high hopes for people, do you?"

"I've always had the highest hopes for you."

Max spoke so rarely from the heart that Willy glanced to make sure that he wasn't being caustic.

At Boot of the Med, Willy delivered the blow by blow of her anniversary match the day before.

"That's all? He's a man, Will. It's staggering that you held him off so long."

"You always say it's no coincidence that people who make excuses are the same people who need them."

"He's a foot taller than you! And Oberdork would never have a chance on the tour if he couldn't clobber a girl. You should be relieved on his account."

Willy twirled spaghetti on her fork. When one strand was wound, the others flopped down.

"You've had men get the better of you before," Max badgered, mashing his own spaghetti into inchworms. "You haven't shown up the next day holding your racket like a dead fish and watching my groundies with a pair of field glasses."

"This is different."

"You understood that other hitting partners could muscle you, but not your own husband. Whose masculinity I assume you have sampled from close range."

"I know he was bound to beat me eventually, but the dynamic—" Willy dipped a mussel in marinara. "Walloping me gave him so much pleasure."

"Didn't you enjoy beating him?"

"Not really. Winning only filled me with foreboding. It put an onus on me to keep it up, and I knew I couldn't. Yesterday, he tried so *hard*, Max—he hurt my feelings."

Max studied her with the concerned, diagnostic expression of a doctor who had received unsettling lab results. "Maybe you shouldn't play together anymore."

"You'd like that, wouldn't you?" she snapped.

"I would like that," he measured, "if it meant that your tennis game did not get all fouled up, your head all morose and hangdog just because you couldn't win some private domestic trophy that wouldn't put ten cents in either of our pockets even if you came out ahead. Which you won't. I don't often recommend that you resign yourself to anything, but this time you'd better. Fixating on being able to rout Doberman is like setting yourself the long-term goal of growing a dick."

The wearing family festivities were dispatched. Willy wryly bought Eric a copy of *Learn Tennis in a Weekend*, and Eric gave his wife her own jump rope. Between Christmas and New Year's both their pools of hitting partners had drained out of town, and Willy would not return to Sweetspot until after the first. They were stuck with each other. Not long before, Willy could have conjured no more delectable a curse; now she prepared for the Jordan as if for the gallows.

On court, Eric looked worried; his high forehead rippled as he kissed her temple. This was the last she would see of his solicitous persona for the duration, since as soon as his feet touched baseline Eric transmogrified. Willy told herself that she shouldn't hold it against him, that this alternative Eric was the one who won tournaments and without a Hyde to his Jekyll his natural kindness would destroy him on the circuit.

Still it was disturbing when she faced him and his mouth set with a ravenous twist. The way he leaned and swayed as if tethered suggested that the net was strung between them for her own protection. This time he allowed her to warm up as long as she liked.

Through the first set, a whole new sensation began to snarl in her lower intestine: a mistrust akin to nausea. Even when easy balls came her way midrally, she clutched with misgiving before impact: *How did I hit this shot all those other times? I can't remember!* Infinitesimal hesitation often sent the ball deep. By 0–5 she was calling her every instinct into question, and so began to play more cautiously, popping her lobs, pushing her volleys, and going for safe, flabby shots that landed prostrate at midcourt with such a please-let-me-make-your-day degradation that she might as well have taken off her clothes. By the time he blanked her in the first set she had become such a full participant in her own disgrace that the second took on the feasting self-hatred of a bulimic binge.

Eric treated her soft, shallow returns to the abuse they deserved. Freshly cut, his hair flickered black fire. Willy kept telling herself that a killer instinct was in his nature; that to demand that Eric desist from slaughtering her helpless, bleeding sitters was as absurd as putting a wounded antelope before a lion and expecting the beast to turn its head. Still she glanced across the net with bafflement that this man she had married was now the agent of her abasement. By the time his last dazzling cross-court whistled past her backhand, Willy was too devastated to lift her racket.

As his adrenal rush subsided, Eric's hair fell limp to his scalp. Yet while his claws retreated and his pupils contracted to normal size, the two zeroes in succeeding sets continued to stare back at her with wide, accusing eyes.

"Yo." Eric touched her arm, and Willy sprang away as if from a hot poker. "This doesn't feel so good. You make me feel like a bruiser."

"You got what you wanted," she charged. "Willy's magic on the court revealed as smoke and mirrors. I'm debunked, like all your other entrancements. One more disposable practice partner, all used up. Like a box of Kleenex."

"You win a few, you lose a few," said Eric sharply. "Comes with the territory. Take it like a—" he seemed to think better of his phrasing, and amended "—like a good sport."

Willy hung her head. "I'm sorry. I was being childish. You played fantastically well. I wish I could have given you a better game."

"So you had an off day." Eric raised her chin. "But next time let's just rally. Do some drills. We'll help each other. No more matches for a while."

They both knew he meant: forever. They both knew as well that even rallying was volatile, not disengaged from victory and failure, good shots and weak, and as a consequence they'd each find themselves strangely busy in the next few weeks, unable to make much time for playing each other. By February they'd have tournaments to play in different states... When he was no longer challenged, Eric got bored, and Willy couldn't bear to be regarded as tedious on a tennis court. Grieving, she would certainly decline to attend the Oberdorfs' New Year's Eve party that evening, crawling miserably to bed before the knell of twelve.

"So, then," Willy encapsulated softly. "Resolutions for 1994: we can't play Scrabble, or horseshoes, or billiards, or go bowling. We can't even jump rope in the same squash court. And now we can't play tennis. What is it that we'll ever do together besides fuck?"

"We could do worse." Eric pressed her head to his chest, and she cried.

To Eric's dismay, Willy packed up on January second to head back to Sweetspot.

"You're taking *ten* running bras," he observed, fingering into her suitcase. "How long will you be gone?"

"Maybe two weeks," she said offhandedly, stacking T's. "The school laundry won't be staffed yet, so..."

Eric's face folded like a Coney Island hot-dog stand, battening down against the elements for a cold, windy winter. "That's quite a while," he said at length. "This is the only time of year—"

"This is the only time of year that I can have Sweetspot to myself, and Max as well."

"So nobody else will be there? Just you and Upchuck, stretching your hams, chumming in low-lit restaurants?"

"I suppose Marcella will be up," she noted, crossing briskly to the closet. "She never misses an opportunity to slime herself into Max's good graces."

"What are you taking that red dress for?"

"Eric, I can't wear sweats all day."

"You do for me."

Willy sighed, and tossed the red silk on the bed. "Would it make you feel any better if I left it behind?"

"Take it, I'm not going to wear it." Though his tone was gruff, Eric rearranged the rumpled silk fondly on the spread, tugging out wrinkles, removing specks of lint. "I thought you weren't going to compete with Marcella any longer over who can be Upchuck's darling.'

"I don't need to compete. Marcella's game is repulsive. She only wins because she drives her opponents mad, and tempts them into doing something rash if only to stop her blobbing at them. Max prefers sting and drive to witless attrition."

"But, Willy, *two weeks*!"

"You saw my game yesterday. It's diseased. I need a doctor."

"Then maybe," he proposed shyly, "I can come with you."

Willy bustled, wrapping a pair of tennis shoes in plastic. The bags crackled white noise.

"Wilhelm?"

Socks. "That's not a great idea."

"But why—?"

"I need to concentrate. The next six months—"

"You want to get away from me, don't you?"

The remark was not remotely like him. Eric was a great one for letting sleeping dogs lie, and conventionally accepted Willy's explanations at face value. He didn't like problems. He expected a marriage to simmer murmurously on the back burner, and when situations like Scrabble and rope-skipping and now even tennis stirred the pot, his solution was to avoid those situations. For Eric the observation was brave, and she had to reward him with honesty in return.

"Yes, I do. For now. Since our anniversary—I've been disturbed. You're having a nasty effect on my game."

"I know you, Wilhelm. That's the same thing as saying that I'm having a nasty effect on *you.*"

"Sweetheart, I just need to get my head on straight." She reached for an inch-long eyebrow hair and tamed it against his face.

Eric insisted on seeing her off at Penn Station, and as he waved from the platform for once he didn't look trim and taut but scrawny. Tufts of cropped hair cringed over his bald spots in lonely, desolate curls. It took all her willpower to keep from dragging Eric in the door, throwing her arms around him, and whispering feverishly that she'd been terribly foolish, that their time with each other was far too dear to waste, and of course he must come along. One by one she would ease the worry lines from his forehead with the tips of her fingers and apologize that now he hadn't any luggage, but they could pick up a toothbrush and a shirt or two in Old Saybrook. Flopping into a booth and propping their feet on facing seats to ward off strangers, they'd do the *Times* crossword together. She'd admire his memory for Civil War generals, one hand scribing and the other resting reassuringly on his inside thigh for the whole trip up.

Instead, the rubber edges of the train door kissed, and Willy was banished to the overheated car. She rushed to a window and waved at Eric, though the reflections of the station lights probably masked her hand. As the train drew into the tunnel, she pressed against the cold glass, and the condensation of her breath fogged a last glimpse of her husband as he shuffled toward the escalator. His posture was unusually poor. The car went black, and for an instant Willy was afraid of the dark—a grown-up sort of dark. Once the lights flickered on, she opened her *New York Times* halfheartedly to the crossword. Unable to get one-across right away, she closed her eyes, slumped into her leaden independence, and folded the paper over her face.

Willy's original idea was to return to the old days, she and Max against the world. Yet though they put in long sessions on her strokes, evenings rang hollow. When she dined out with Max, the twittering Marcella Foussard often came along. Even after Marcella left for a fat farm their nights felt roomy, like an oversized coat; hours hung off either side of dinner like sleeves off her hands. Getting ready for bed, Willy's ablutions went too swiftly and she was pestered by a sensation of having forgotten something.

Her game did, after shuddering and sweating as if shaking off a flu, return to its muscular surety. But when she brought off a barreling down-the-line pass, Willy would turn to the side as if to say, "Did you see that?" and no one was there.

With Max, she was often at a loss for conversation. Sometimes they'd resort to current events; while Willy was sincere enough in her disappointment that Hillary Clinton's leadership of health care reform was turning out a disaster, newspaper chatter between old friends felt desperate. Ten days into her stay, after a gaping silence over calamari, Max finally ventured, "How are you two getting on?"

"We've refrained from clawing each other's eyes out."

"I didn't realize it was quite that bad."

"Between me and *Marcella*?"

"Between you and Underwood."

"Oh, God no. Eric's doing terribly well." Willy's voice lilted. "In the quarters of the Mennon in Detroit? He was down a set, 1–5 in the second. But you know Eric, the Comeback Kid—"

"As a matter of fact, I don't know *Eric*."

"Whose fault is that?"

"Nobody's. I'm not remotely interested in the man."

"I'm very proud of him," she recited, in the monotone of the multiplication table.

"I repeat: how are you getting on? Are you still having trouble?"

"I didn't say we were having trouble."

"Not in so many words."

Near the end of her stay Max threw his racket in disgust. "Not one more word!"

"What are you talking about?"

"*Everything* I tell you, it's '*Eric* doesn't do it that way,' or 'That's one of *Eric*'s favorite shots,' or '*Eric* hates it when I . . .' Stop thinking about Underfuck!"

"I'm not!"

"Listen to yourself, woman! Because I only want to hear about how *you* hit the ball, what are *your* favorite shots, which bad habits drive *you* up a wall."

Newly mindful, Willy was shocked to discover how frequently she stopped herself from describing *Eric*'s underspin. At dinner, she refrained from mentioning how *Eric* would have vacuumed up her pasta. And at the end of the evening she excused herself, naming no names, with "I have to make a call." Deleting Eric from her discourse required great vigilance and self-control. Before she was married, Willy had lived in a world with a population of 1.5; Max was the .5, and in keeping him pruned to a partial, cipherous extension of her own ambition, she had nipped their romance in the bud. So maybe the novelty of a whole other human being in her universe had not worn off. In any case, having waved from the platform or not, her husband had accompanied Willy to Sweetspot after all.

She'd so looked forward to seeing him. Her head overrun with visions of grateful, torrid reunion on the train, Willy reread the same page of her novel about twenty times before casting it aside and gazing longingly out the window even through the extensive black tunnel into Penn. But when she walked in the door, Eric barely looked up. The *ATP Rulebook* splayed at his elbow, he was feeding forms into his Bubble Jet. He didn't so much as say hello.

"Some tournament promoter," he mumbled instead, aligning the page, "Bob Evanston? Saw the two of us play on our anniversary. Seems he was impressed."

"He wouldn't have been impressed with *me*."

"He wasn't." When Eric glanced up, he looked tired, and irritated with mandatory diplomacy. "I mean, he may well have been, but didn't mention it. The point is, there's a small ATP tournament in February at Madison Square Garden. They've got Hans Sörle seeded first. But there have been last-minute cancellations, injuries. Evanston offered me a wild-card slot."

"Sörle—he's ranked, like, twelve, isn't he?"

"Ten. He's in the Top fucking Ten."

Willy dropped her luggage. "What's the draw?"

"Thirty-two. In New York; expenses negligible."

"Since when do you worry about expenses?"

"I do work within a budget, Willy."

"But how did *you* get into a draw of thirty-two?"

Eric took a deep breath. "It's sort of a decorative tournament—like Mahwah, only with a few points on the line. So the audience get their money's worth, it's best of five sets. Sörle's agent is trying to attract endorsements; Sörle's slipping. And Evanston liked the drama of a low-ranked challenger. Said I'd only have to win one match to pay off as entertainment. This is the break I've been waiting for, Willy. The satellite crawl is for suckers."

"Suckers like me."

"That you've gotten as far as you have playing grade-B tournaments is obviously to your credit." Having to compliment her seemed to try him. "But satellites are tooth-and-nail. It's far more efficient to beat a highly ranked player. Jesus, it pays points like a one-armed bandit coughs quarters, Willy. The trouble is getting at the bastards. Now I've got a Top Ten within arm's reach."

"What, you expect to *beat* Hans Sörle?"

"Why not?"

Willy shrugged, and dragged her valise to the bedroom. "I guess you'll find out."

Eric had hitherto an attractive breeziness about his upcoming tournaments, which may have helped him overtake opponents who tossed the night before. For six weeks, his cool vanished. He had trouble sleeping, and Willy would wake to find him with his feet hooked under the bed frame, tucking into tight, panicked sit-ups. Previously a human garbage disposal, he became picky and superstitious about his diet. He never suggested practice with his lowly wife; for the period before Madison Square Garden, Eric selected hitting partners with the same finicky care with which he inspected T-bones in D'Agostino's for the slightest marbling.

When Willy departed for LaGuardia to enter her 1994 inaugural tournament, an indoor Har-Tru affair in Chicago, she was relieved to flee the self-importance that thickened the air in their apartment and stuck in her throat. Eric was *getting his hopes up*, for which Willy felt a genetic disapproval. But Willy had taken her share of knocks, and maybe it was time Eric took the odd blow on the chin himself. It would keep him human.

By the time she returned from Chicago, Eric had played his own indoor warm-up in Paterson, New Jersey. That she was now ranked 265 seemed a little less of an achievement when Eric announced that as of Paterson he had broken into the 400's. That was the *plan*, of course, but Willy was a little tired of everything slotting so cooperatively into her husband's designs. Where were those famous slings and arrows that typified everyone else's life? Besides, he provoked the same optical illusion as heading up to Westbrook, when her train was traveling alongside another Amtrak going the same direction. If the adjacent train started to go faster, it induced the impression that her train was going backward.

The field at the Garden was motley, though Eric was the darkest horse in the running. There were several other players, however, in the top 75, all of whom would net Eric generous bonus computer points if he serendipitously outdid them. When he drew one of these for his first round—ranked 54— Willy commiserated that it was an awfully bad break to face such stiff competition at the start, which could stop him from playing Sörle. Her husband shook off her consoling hands. "Don't be ridiculous," he said. "This is *great* luck. Pounding 54 will net points at the start."

"But you've never played anyone in the top 100. You don't know how good they are."

"Willy, they're just tennis players. You can seem so savvy sometimes, but you still buy into this bullshit mystique. Some greaseball climber gets into the upper rankings and you go timorous with Messianic wonder. You think playing 54 is supposed be an honor. Well, screw that. They're just like us. Where do you think we're headed? He should be honored to play *me*."

Willy stepped back; whenever Eric blustered like this she was torn between wonderment and recoil. "A little humility could go a long way, Eric. Pride goeth—"

"A little humility is poison. What do you think this game is all about? You're the one who claims I concentrate too much on technique, always pointing out how what makes tennis fascinating is character. You say the distinction between players isn't in their forehands but their heads. Okay—you're right. So the last thing I'm going to do is to quiver into the Garden simpering 'Thank you, Mr. Fifty-four, for stooping to hit me a ball.'"

Whether Eric's arrogance was magnificent or odious was nugatory. All that mattered was it worked. He got his bonus points, with games to spare. That 498 had upset 54 sent a ripple of curiosity through the crowd. Clearly Willy's husband had made another of his breathtaking leaps. For the Eric Oberdorf who played in the Garden was not the same promising but still ragged-edged athlete with whom she was so recently neck-and-neck. No, this Eric she couldn't have touched with a barge pole.

In the round-of-sixteen, he made mincemeat of 87 in straight sets. The quarters went to four sets, the semis to five. Meanwhile, Willy barely saw her husband. Between rounds he was practicing, after victories swept off on the arm of this Bob Evanston creep for celebratory dinners. She might have come along, but her headaches were genuine. Only when Eric slipped in at 1 A.M. did Willy get her hands on her husband, and then exclusively on his more public parts.

The night after the semis, Eric disrobed and slid under the coverlet, where Willy lay still awake. She turned and smoothed his rib cage, tickling the scrub on his chest. As she grazed her fingertips over his left nipple, Eric grasped her hand, pinning it firmly to his clavicle. She wriggled free, and ran her palm to his stomach, whose muscles hardened at her touch.

"Willy," he whispered. "I've got to get to sleep."

"Eventually," she said slyly, easing down to cup his scrotum, rolling the glands like marbles in a bag. "But what better way to doze off? You always say you sleep more soundly after, right?"

"Honey," Eric censured. "I have to play Sörle tomorrow."

"The finals are tomorrow *night*. You can sleep in, late as you like." As her fingers padded up the shaft, it expanded as if inflated with a bicycle pump.

Eric grabbed her wrist and wrenched it from his groin. "Stop it! That's enough!"

Willy immediately retracted, recoiling into a ball like a sea anemone when poked at. "You haven't so much as kissed me since this tournament started," she mumbled, knees clutched to her breasts. "And we haven't made love for weeks, not since before I left for Sweetspot. What's wrong? Did I do something? Are you still angry at me for leaving in January? Did you meet someone while I was gone?"

Eric lay on his back, and his controlled sigh suggested that among other things he was not in the mood to tick down her list of insecurities one by one. "I realize I've been distracted. But I don't think we should have sex before the finals."

Willy lifted her head. "You buy into that bullshit?" she asked in amazement. "That you can't allow your precious elixir of manhood to drain your strength?"

Eric raised on his elbows. "I know it's probably an old wives' tale—"

"Better believe it! Doctors say sex is good for you, that it *gives* you energy!"

"But on the off chance there's something to it..." Eric appealed. "Sometimes those old wives knew a thing or two, and if it makes any difference at all—"

"The *old wife* was always trying to get out of fucking any way she knew how." Willy heaved out of bed, stripping the top blanket, and caped her shoulders. "But in case it makes *any difference at all*, you can sleep by yourself. I wouldn't want to accidentally turn in bed and disturb His Majesty's rest."

She flounced from the bedroom, dragging the blanket. Eric stepped on it from behind and said, "Stop being a baby and come back to bed."

"*Me* a baby! You hear some asinine superstition when you're seven years old and you still believe it."

"I know it's probably nuts, but if you could only indulge me my little—"

"I've been indulging plenty. If it's any comfort, I wouldn't let you lay a hand on me now with a knife to my throat. Good *night.*" She yanked the blanket out from under his feet and sent him sprawling in the hall.

"Willy, goddamn it, you could have hurt me!"

"Oh, tragedy, falling on your million-dollar butt." Willy trundled to the sofa.

Eric picked himself up and stood uncertainly in the moonlight hazing from the bedroom window. His prick had shriveled in the cold to an unalluring knot of blue gristle. Willy bunched on the couch. Teetering in the hall, Eric was clearly torn between cajoling her to bed and talking it out and no doubt fucking after all to reconcile, versus leaving her to her huff and at least getting a decent night's sleep for his first Top Ten match. His indecision lasted only a few seconds. It wasn't much of a contest.

As if success in a lucrative sport were not already cushy enough, pros in the upper echelons could often rely in a crunch on "winning by reputation." It wasn't unheard of for a no-name like Eric to blast through the first few rounds, only to come up short against one of the hallowed Top Ten, who might well be in poor form and ripe for picking. Yet the halo surrounding the anointed could blind a challenger to opportunity. To participate in a sports hierarchy was commonly to endorse it; no one wished to climb a ladder whose rungs were diaphanous. In sweating blood to obtain them, players needed to regard computer points as laden, and thereby to perceive the Chosen as blessed. Underlings often threw matches in acquiescence not just to the elite but to the status quo, in preference to spinning the sport's painstaking arithmetic into disarray. Most tennis players, in submitting to the ladder, believed in the ladder, and would sacrifice their own glory for the greater glory of an orderly universe.

Eric had no such qualms. He did not believe in tennis exactly; it was a vehicle for his own beatification. He readily admitted to his wife that, unlike Willy, he did not worship the game. Tennis happened to be something he was good at; what Eric worshiped was that he was good at it. Eric's sole religion was Eric. That's what Willy found glorious and that's what Willy found repugnant. Her ambivalent crackling between those poles may have generated the very electricity of her passion; maybe Willy loved her husband because she could never quite decide if she could stand the man.

And if Eric did not even honor the absolute god of tennis the sport, much less did he bow before its worldly manifestation in the ATP. The last thing he suffered was an overabundance of respect. Eric didn't care for tennis players in general, and would gladly blow the myth of the Top Ten to kingdom come. For though the Association produced plenty of megalomaniacs, folding before "reputation" was ultimately a failure of vanity.

If Hans Sörle was counting on his opponent seizing up in insecurity after Eric took the first set 6–4, Sörle hadn't done his homework. Eric's face betrayed no spasm of incredulity. As he held serve through most of the second, the eyes of this Oberdorf kid didn't glaze with stage fright; the upstart never reached to pinch himself to check he wasn't dreaming. And even when the 400-something neophyte was put in his place at 7–5, his shoulders didn't slump with I-knew-this-couldn't-last. The jaw squared slightly, that was all.

Willy perched in a front row seat, where Alma Oberdorf kept patting her hand. Between the anxious parents of this astonishing long shot, Eric's three brothers were arranged in order of birth and at rigid attention, all with scrubbed-pink skin, wetted cowlicks, and fresh haircuts. A price tag trailing Robert's sleeve betrayed bright sweaters bought for the event. Alma folded his collar down. Robert squirmed and tugged it tough-guy to his chin.

Axel stretched to swat the twelve-year-old's crown. "Sit still!" All three boys snapped upright.

The score even, Willy's mind wandered back to the days before her marriage, watching her boyfriend play tennis. Certainly she had admired him; and Willy being Willy, she had not solely been enchanted by his devious smile or his nervy claim on her every available evening. Something in his *game* had struck her fancy. Yet in the old days her admiration hadn't seemed to cost so much. Choosing to love him, she had reveled in her own creation. It was almost as if she'd made him up.

But in the Garden Willy couldn't have retracted her adulation if she tried. This love was helpless, sucked from her at a glance. Eric no longer flourished under her benevolent eye like her own art but gleamed under the radiant floods with such a hard, separate clarity that it was Willy who felt invented. Amid hundreds of other onlookers, Eric didn't need her one more pair of pupils to call him to life. In fact, through double break points Willy would read Kodak billboards on upper tiers, anything but allow her gaze to seek his face, as her mother had warned her not to look directly at the sun. To follow his fluid grace around the court for the entire match was more draining than she could afford. The more Eric Oberdorf awed her, the less she was impressed with herself.

In the clench of this compulsive desire Willy resisted where before the wedding she had happily capitulated. She was no longer giving, but given. So many ordinary people fell in love and married; how did they manage without resentment, without struggling against their own defenseless ardor, no longer a freely written check but a monthly debit drawn from their accounts? Eric had worn his new black gear, and Willy wilted at his good looks. Once proud to be associated with such a striking man, now she cowered before his bony shoulders, binding her jacket about her stomach, its little round folds in contrast to the lean sirloin on court.

"Look at that retrieval!" cried Axel hoarsely to Steven, prodding the boy's thigh. "I couldn't have touched that shot with a broom handle tied to my racket!"

Nor could I, thought Willy. That was the problem: her every homage left a negative afterimage. Each rally echoed through the hall, *I could never reach that high, I could never run that fast, I could never hit a ball that hard.* When Eric made an aside to a linesman, Willy could think only that playing her first Top Ten she'd never have possessed the easy élan to toss off suave retorts. Any adjective she might apply to her husband slid to the comparative—he was *more* talented, *more* intelligent, *more* athletic, for there was no such thing as specially gifted without someone to be more gifted than. Was that why Eric had scooped her up in Riverside? Had he been shopping not for a partner but for a fan?

Axel jumped to his feet, pounding fist in palm. "That's my *boy!*"

Startled by the roar of the crowd, Willy looked hastily at the scoreboard to find that Eric had taken the third set. Now that her husband needed only one more set of two, she couldn't enjoy the luxury of a peripatetic attention. When first Eric broke, then Sörle broke back, Willy leaned off the chair until her knees hit the forward rail. She crushed the empty Coke cup to shed wax in her lap. Alma squeezed her daughter-in-law's arm, and risked a glimpse away from the game to share a look of sympathetic solidarity. Alma obviously understood that for Willy watching her husband on the very cusp of acclaim was agony. Imagine what a sad night it would be if after all this buildup, coming so, so close, he moped home having missed by a hair. Willy would be left nursing a disconsolate hulk, powerless to moderate his disappointment.

The crowd, which loved an underdog and the eventfulness of an upset, exhaled and whistled when Eric won a point; they inhaled, then groaned faintly when his net-corder wavered, then dribbled to his court.

Willy jumped at a hand on her shoulder.

"Are you really his wife?" When Willy nodded, the young woman behind her added, "You must be thrilled!"

Willy was Eric's wife, so she must be thrilled. Yet her respiration was out of synch with the crowd's. When the Oberdorfs sighed, Willy took a sharp breath. When the surrounding throng drew a strangulated sough, the air eased from Willy's lungs, *ah-ah*.

Eric was jaunty enough in the 400's and 500's. Should he lose this evening, Eric would recover his self-esteem in ten minutes. But if he swaggered back to 112th Street triumphant, the man would be insufferable. The girl in the row behind could go home with her own lover, their felicity independent of an entertainment's results. It was Willy who had to live with the consequences of this match for months to come.

Willy was rooting for Sörle.

TWELVE

WHIPPING NUMBER TEN DIDN'T make Eric number nine. But he did skip from 498 to 293 in one week, which in tennis terms was leaping tall buildings in a single bound. At 265, for the first time Willy shared that crucial initial digit with her husband.

After the mandatory fête with the tournament promoters and another lavish spread at the Oberdorfs, who invited the entire Upper East Side, Eric and Willy scheduled their own celebratory dinner for two days later. Though overfed, Eric was flush with his $50,000 first place, and proposed Lutèce. An evening at New York's chicest French restaurant was a generous gesture, so Willy repressed a grumble when Eric instructed her to lug along his tux and meet him at Jordan after his practice match. Herself catching a plane to Florida the next morning, Willy had her own errands to run, but time was short.

When Willy arrived with his black-tie rig over an arm the game wasn't over. Though Lutèce was picky about punctuality, he had to complete the set. She harrumphed into a chair, scowling. Terrific. One more compulsory audience conscripting Mrs. Eric Oberdorf. Lately what she wouldn't give to watch him lose, just once.

He lost.

Willy sat immobile in dull shock. She hadn't seen her

husband defeated in months. It was as if a fairy had read her mind and granted Willy's wish. Or maybe Eric had looked into his wife's eyes and been so disheartened at what he saw there that he tanked the match.

The tuxedo still draped her arm, and under its clinging dry-cleaner plastic her skin had gone juicy and reeked of guilty anxiety. She kissed her husband and handed him the tux. "Are you feeling all right? We could do this another time."

"I'm fine," he said lightly.

"But the way you—"

"I don't know, something fell away. The whole business seemed—silly, all of a sudden. Eh. Let's get some chow."

"The few times you've lost," Willy observed, "you imply that you didn't apply yourself. Not once have you admitted to coming up against your limitations."

Eric prized a fishbone from between his teeth. "I may never have confronted any limitations. Not absolute ones, anyway."

"You would have if you were a girl."

"I'm not."

Crammed with fragile floral china, Lutèce was a poor setting for a fight. Willy folded her hands over her linen napkin. "Have you ever envisaged yourself born as a woman?"

"Certainly not."

"You think women are that different? Don't we share the same emotions, the same ambitions?"

"You might have more emotions."

Willy poked at her squab—a rash order, but dining at Lutèce on one of the filthy, ratlike pigeons that splatted the public library had appealed to her as pleasantly perverse. "So, say, I love you more than you love me?"

"Willy, we're supposed to be celebrating. Why are you trying to start something?"

"Why, does the idea of yourself as female repel you?"

"The idea strikes me as ridiculous!"

Willy leaned back from her plate. The squab had been a mistake—tiny, brown, and withered. The only way to get any meat off the scrawny thing would have been to pick it up in her bare hands. Already in chasing the pigeon about the plate she'd slopped port sauce onto her favorite red silk dress. She didn't dare admit it to Eric—her menu had no prices, so God knows what this cost—but she'd have had a better time, with heartier food, in Flower of Mayonnaise. If this was their new champion's lifestyle, there was something to be said for struggling instead.

Willy looked enviously at Eric's salmon trout with vanilla sauce, a more intelligent order, then up at her husband, dashing in his black tie, and pondered the thin line between icon and nemesis. Why of all people had she married this Princeton-alumming, triple-jumping, hoop-swishing, math-whizzing tennis prodigy? Had she been searching for the one person on earth of whom she was bound to feel unworthy?

Or might she feel inadequate with any man? Since girlhood Willy had chafed at being female, and for a tennis player the resentment was rational. For the better portion of this century the women's game was considered a frivolous sideline; even now, women's prize money came to little more than half of the men's. Besides, who wouldn't choose to serve at 120 mph instead of 85?

"You like movies," Willy admonished her husband. "Films invite you to imagine being someone else for an hour or two. You don't march out of the cinema because being expected to identify with someone different from you is 'ridiculous.' So why is my asking you to picture yourself as a woman so absurd?"

"Maybe it's not absurd, but it's a dead end. Even if I did wear a dress in my head, I couldn't know if the image was accurate. Since I have no idea what it's like to be a woman."

"Do you think I'm so alien?"

"I don't think *you're* alien."

Willy tapped her tines on the tablecloth. This was true. Eric had demonstrated little use for women on the whole. He had never had a single close female friend, nor, previous to his wife, one regular female sports partner. Willy was the exception, and thereby an honorary boy.

For her own part, Willy had always suspected that she was either born in the wrong body, or born in the right body as a penalty for not being quite up to masculine snuff. Which was why Eric's smug security in his sex riled her, though any woman might be offended when at the prospect of swapping genders her husband became derisive. On the other hand, had Eric confided that he was "trying to get in touch with his feminine side" she'd have gagged. Willy didn't so much revile his patrician self-assurance than covet it for herself.

"You know," Willy changed the subject, "your match at the Garden irked me one more time about this guarantee business. You can bet that Sörle was paid far more than you, just for showing up, and you won the tournament."

"I'm not complaining."

"*I'm* complaining. If he's paid oodles for walking to the baseline, there's no motivation for a Top Ten to put out any effort. He can just tank and collect his check."

Eric leaned back from his trout, its skeleton picked surgically clean; he and his father had skills in common. "Pride," he noted, "is its own guarantee."

"The trouble is, the Rule of Fourteen encourages slacking."

Now that players who could afford the expense of more than fourteen tournaments a year were free to eliminate poor performances from tabulation of their rankings, Willy's assertion wasn't controversial. Many a big name had been accused of accepting a guarantee and then just going through the motions when a loss wouldn't affect his standing. Yet Eric didn't chime in.

"Sörle didn't try?" he asked soberly.

"Well, of course he did!"

"Are you saying he handed me the match? I thought I played pretty well." Eric's eyes were small.

"No, no! Sweetheart, I didn't mean that!"

"It sounded to me as if that's exactly what you meant."

"Honey! I was just making conversation! I thought it was time I stopped hacking on you for—"

"You're an efficient woman," he interrupted. "Or *person*. Whatever you are. I have never known you to simply make conversation."

"*Please* forget it."

He didn't.

Willy was on good behavior for the next few months but disliked watching her p's and q's with her own husband. As she treasured the unedited flow of tennis in a zone, so Willy valued immediacy in banter at home. Amid forced compliments, hastily masked flashes of who-do-you-think-you-are, and double-checkings of impulse remarks to make sure they weren't malicious, Willy's domestic discourse was marked by the same infinitesimal delay between thought and action that characterized both second-rate tennis and tactful cocktail chatter. Talking to Eric was becoming depressingly like talking to anyone else.

Willy herself had a fruitful spring. She'd heavily booked the season, hell-bent on breaking to the pivotal number 200 that Max insisted she achieve before he backed her for the international tour. Thus the couple shared a few luminous spring evenings aglow with mutual victory, launching to Flower of Mayonnaise in the hand-in-hand rah-team spirit that had powered the early days of their relationship.

But this sensation of joint accord was fleeting. If their careers were parallel trains, the nose of Eric's engine was steadily edging up Willy's cars. He had drawn attention to himself as the dark horse who outran Hans Sörle. Tournament promoters were *asking* Eric to play, whereas Willy had to enter solely on the basis of her ranking; likewise, he was invited into a better class of contest than his statistics should have permitted. Further, for 1994 Eric was already making substantially more money than

his wife, and no longer leaned on Axel. That Willy had supported herself with her winnings while Eric hit his father up for rent
had provided her title to a moral high ground that she was
reluctant to share.

In all, the spring of 1994 duplicated a sensation common to
runs in Riverside Park. Tripping nimbly around gasping
anorexics and jiggling hefties, Willy would occasionally discern
a *pad-pad* at her back. Often a touch of application was enough,
and the jogger who'd been gaining ate dust. Still, though she
outpaced most of the park, at five-three Willy was no sprinter.
In running as in tennis, she applied constant, steady pressure
with an eye to the long haul. Admirers would call her relentless;
detractors, dogged.

So if Willy hated being overtaken, it happened. As the *pad-
pad* grew louder, she pushed a bit harder, training her eyes to the
front. But the man drawing alongside—it was always a man—
was generally much taller and racing his own clock. Sometimes
the runner waved appreciatively as he surged in front, or slapped
her palm with a fraternal high-five, but Willy's returning smile
would be wan. Fight the impulse as she might, chasing his heels
it was almost impossible not to flag a little in disappointment.

The Chevrolet Challenge was held in early June, nestled
between the French and the Stella Artois. Scheduled when
public consciousness of the sport was high, the Chevy was the
highlight of the hopeful's calendar, having helped hoist dozens
of names to international scoreboards. Not only was the tournament specifically designed for the up-and-coming to break out,
but it was one of the only events all year in which the ATP and
WTA operated in concert. Conventionally the organizations
were distant, if not antagonistic. But it was difficult to attract
attention to any tournament without highly ranked seeds
sprinkled in the draw; only shoulder-to-shoulder cajoling convinced ESPN to broadcast the Chevy to showcase promising
unknowns.

The year before Eric had had nowhere near the ranking to enter without hacking through the prequalifiers, but his progress up the ladder had been so rapid that this year he was admitted to the draw. Willy was of two minds about Eric's eligibility. It would be nice to enter a tournament together for once, catch the same train to D.C. At the same time the Challenge was the jewel in the satellite crown, and victory in the Chevy was a virtual guarantee of rescue from the exhausting treadmill of the lower circuit—three-week marathons for a handful of points like coins thrown to beggars. Having been in the game longer, Willy felt she should get a shot at the Challenge first. Tennis, of course, only modestly rewarded diligence and positively punished seniority. Still, Willy had always regarded the Chevy as awaiting her, and with Eric entering the men's singles as well she felt crowded.

This sensation was alleviated somewhat by a solicitation from *Slick Chick*, an upmarket glossy building a story around the Chevrolet Challenge and featuring a particular player who, according to the editor on the phone, "was emblematic of the next generation of sportswomen, and who represented the values of their magazine." As for what the magazine "valued," Max Upchurch had tipped off the staff that Willy Novinsky was not only set to do well in the tournament, but was, *ahem*, "presentable." Several more highly ranked women had been dismissed, the editor despaired, for being too "chunky, mannish, or plain."

So Willy would be a fool to expect a serious profile, but attention was attention, and wannabes had to take what they could get. A puff piece, however sickening, would be an enticing addition to her portfolio should Willy become prestigious enough to court panty-shield sponsorships. Yet it did rankle a bit when the journalist arrived at 112th to twitter into her microcassette about Willy's cute ball-discard coffee table. The lady wasn't interested in Willy's game; she grilled her subject instead on dieting tips and hairstyles. It was hard to imagine that were Eric ever interviewed he'd be pressed for his opinions of this year's tennis outfits.

A photographer arrived an hour later. He was toting a sequined wardrobe of evening wear, as well as a makeup case swelling with pots of pink and maroon glop. Willy had assumed he'd want action shots on the court, and had cleaned a plain white tournament dress for the occasion. Bad call. Helplessly, she submitted to being poked at, powdered, and primped. Willy wore little makeup ordinarily, and at the end of this ordeal the mirror revealed a vapid, vampish stranger. The dresses were too long, and had to be pinned; the photographer was displeased with her muscular shoulders, and insisted she drape them with a shawl. When they dragged her to the Boat Basin for outdoor shots, Willy begged the man to at least photograph her with the clay courts in the background. Instead he posed her in a slatternly slouch on the rail, the George Washington Bridge forming a tiara behind her moussey, teased-up do.

Being prepped, painted, and arranged was humiliating, but still a taste of fame, inspiration to someday do well enough to tell these pretentious fuss-budgets just where they could shove their mascara brush. After all, the only thing worse than being approached for a four-page glossy layout was *not* being approached for a four-page glossy layout.

Willy was still removing smears of blue shadow from around her eyes that night when Eric arrived home from another of the ATP's Challenger Series, this one played in Philadelphia. The upward swing of his head after he set down his bags was a giveaway.

"You won."

"I won. Hey, I did a little calculating on the train."

"When are you *not* doing a little calculating?"

"These numbers are soft, of course, dependent on the competition's performance; you and your buddy Marcella are neck-and-neck. But it looks as if when you take the Chevy, you've made it, Willy—to 200!"

"The Chevy isn't cake, Underwood. It's the most coveted trophy on the lower circuit."

"So what? Who's out there you can't handle? But this is even neater, Wilhelm. If I take the men's singles in D.C.? *I'm* 200. Isn't that great? You and me, dead even. It would make great publicity, too: husband and wife win the Chevy together and head for the big time at identical rankings. Barcelona, Tokyo, here we come!"

"Aren't you counting chickens? We're not through the first round."

As Eric extolled a positive attitude, Willy didn't admit that she'd come up with these numbers herself. But she hadn't quite the same festive reaction to the arithmetic. Something about the perfectly parallel digits seemed unlikely. Now that she was so close to what she'd wanted all her life, Willy's stomach didn't yowl with appetite, but clenched in clammy, dyspeptic fear.

Though Eric won the final of the Chevy with his usual detachment, he gambled like mad: dozens of his shots barely grazed the absolute outer edge of the line, and with a less scrupulous umpire the score would have turned out otherwise. Scrutinizing her husband from the front row, that night Willy finally glimpsed his secret: *he didn't care very much.* Eric's game was beside him; tennis was something he did but not what he was. He had the advantage of any poker player who could easily bluff through his hand, because while bettors like Willy had put their very souls on the table, for Eric the chips were plastic.

Trembling into the trusty white tournament dress for her own final the next afternoon, Willy was constitutionally unable to avail herself of Eric's indifference. Eric was now number 200; he had as of fourteen hours before exceeded her ranking, and the next two hours would determine if she kept pace. It was impossible to convince herself that it didn't matter.

Poetically, Willy's final opponent was Marcella Foussard. Marcella was too hoity-toity to dress in the locker rooms provided, and had primped in her hotel. She had just ducked in to touch up her vermilion lipstick. Strapping and buxom, Marcella must have spent an hour arranging the coils of her bottled-red hair over her peach silk headband. In the last six months Marcella had starved off some of her baby fat, and was now sucking in her cheeks under the misguided impression that a gaunt bone structure would finally emerge from her lollipop face. Slimmer, yes, but Marcella was stuck with those hammy thighs for life.

"So your hubby took the men's singles, Wilhemena!" Marcella cooed. "He's doing awful well, isn't he? I thought he was kinda funny-looking at first, you know, a little knobby. But lately he seems sorta debonair, you know?" Marcella smiled. "I guess he'll be watching." The lipstick had smeared on her teeth.

Playing Marcella was lucky in a way; Willy would face no surprises, though the two rarely practiced together at Sweetspot. Willy couldn't stand it. She found Marcella's style aesthetically deplorable. If the ersatz redhead had dropped a few pounds, her game was still fat: her looping moonballs plopped on the baseline, monotonous and unabating as weather. The texture of Marcella's shots was wet, formless, and soft; like oversized snowflakes, they melted on the bounce. Any energy in a point had to be generated by her adversary, who often found the job debilitating. And no matter how much pace you fed Marcella, she ate it, blocking back these plump, languid blobs. Yet Marcella's placement was nefarious, and though she appeared to move about the court with the lazy boredom of an overfed cat, she was tall, and faster than she looked.

Through the first set, Willy held to Max's advice: resist the impulse to massacre the ball right away. Marcella's approach was taunting, and Willy's Pavlovian urge to strangle her was dangerous. Ease it right back, Max had said of moonballers, naming no names. Moonballers love zip, they use it against you. Don't give it to them. Lie in wait. Only mow down the ball full-throttle when you're sure you've got your opening. Until then, bide your time.

Adherence to this counsel took fantastic self-control, but the strategy worked. Fighting her instincts aided concentration. Willy took the first set with a comfortable margin of 6–3, though it must have been a tedious exhibition to sit through. From the front row, Eric discreetly raised his thumb. He could see what she was doing; he meant, keep doing it.

The second set began almost too well. Breaking Marcella in the first and third games, in no time Willy was leading 4–0. She had got her tactics down to a formula: press, press, and press, until you get one ball just a tad shallower than the others and slam a severe, short cross-court, which Marcella couldn't handle even if she could see it coming; at best her desperate stab would dink back, and Willy could close at the net. But with the luxury of such an ample lead, Willy's mind began to stray. Too far ahead and it is actually hard to pay attention. This blancmange tennis still didn't suit Willy's palate, and if the sport were always so toothless she'd have opted for a career in squash.

More than once between points she turned to Eric and smiled and that was a mistake. Though she should have savored spooning Marcella's thick, heavy game point by point into her own pudding dish, Willy was not enjoying herself. She wanted this match over, badly. Something twisted in her middle, as if a Phillips-head had tightened a screw.

Receiving at 4–0, Willy broke again, but the game went to deuce. The game should not have gone to deuce. Marcella's serve had spin and placement, but no verve. Nobody but Willy seemed alarmed that the fifth game was close. A few onlookers were gathering their picnic baskets, assuming that at 6–3, 5–0 the match was pretty much over.

The screwdriver twisted another turn. Willy shook out her arms, jumping up and down on the baseline. A mysterious shadow crossed Max's face. Eric looked horribly encouraging.

Fifteen–love, yes. Thirty–love, *yes*! But Willy knew that she was rushing. Her play was impatient, and in yearning to conclude this ordeal, to fall into Eric's arms in relief, at triple match point Willy lunged at Marcella's obese corner forehand, now wandering into the backcourt and heading for the stands. Any midmatch coaching, even with hand signals, violated WTA rules; Max sat duly mum and immobile in the front row. His low, ragged voice whispered in Willy's ear all the same: *This isn't the opening; you don't have time to set up. Press deep to her backhand, recover ready position, and wait for a ball on a silver platter to come clanking over the net.* But Willy wanted out of this match, wanted her number 200, wanted to go to Europe, wanted to hold her head high with her husband, to keep him tight up against her ranking as he wrapped tight to her back in bed. Crouching, she whipped the ball cross-court for the same short, sharp angle that had netted her so many points this set.

What was netted was Willy's shot. She'd arrived too late to throw her weight forward. Still, there was no need to be flustered. Two more match points. No problem. Cake.

But there was a problem. Each time Willy pounced on the wrong ball, overhitting in her anxiousness to be done. Willy didn't want to win so much as to have won. Deuce.

Ad-out.

Game.

Stupid, bonkers. Three match points in a row donated to charity. Well, let Marcella have her one game. See if it keeps her warm at night, that she got that one off me. Now let's close that prissy doughball out.

At 5–2, a few of the spectators who had gathered their things sat back down. Marcella's hanging in there was the kind of gritty spitting in the face of the inevitable that audiences always admire. And look at that! Imagine breaking back a second time that far behind!

But 3–5 wasn't far behind. For tennis arithmetic is insidious. Huge leads seem to collapse in one game. At 5–2, the odds of your beleaguered opponent catching up appear laughable. At 5–3 you stop laughing.

A familiar rope-skipping headache pinched Willy's eyes. "Idiot," she mumbled under her breath, rather than the usual uppsyching "Stay on your toes." One more game was all Willy needed, but having let three match points slip through her fingers grated and kept grating. If Eric's maxim was "Don't look down," Max's was "Don't look back." "Never cry over spilled milk," he always said. "Let it go. I can't say about the rest of life, but in tennis regret will destroy you." Yet Willy was awash in spilled milk, rapidly souring in the muggy June afternoon. Her own perspiration had the rank, turned smell of yogurt.

Her coach's visage, commonly impassive, had sagged from grave to deathly. A dimple of concern dented Eric's forehead, on which the TV cameras hungrily zoomed in. Willy could have delivered the commentary herself: *Here we see the Chevy men's singles champion, displaying perplexity that his wife is allowing a bimbo with a game like porkpie to nuke a lead the size of North Dakota...*

At 5–4 Willy had to ask herself what was wrong, but she asked too late. She had forsaken her strategy. She was no longer lying in wait. She was trying to clobber every one of Marcella's flabby baseline shots, to haul off and clout them with the spanking they deserved, but Willy was hitting out of frustration. *I am out of control,* she admitted. But by the time you admit you are out of control, you are—obviously—out of control. What you have lost is not substantive but mechanical, the very means by which any end like "control" might be achieved. In such a state, it was as absurd for Willy to demand she "get herself together" as to insist that she try once more to reel in a fish when her entire rod and tackle had fallen into the sea.

On the changeover, more ESPN broadcast in Willy's head: *Oberdorf is already drafting his European itinerary, and promises to call home from time to time, where his wife will be knitting sweatbands for her man on the tour...*

After losing the second set 5–7 Willy went into shock. She could not have been more ahead in the match without winning outright. Victory had lain in her lap, a gift for unwrapping, and now as the sky grumbled with displeasure, out of some dark miracle she and Marcella were dead-fucking-even. No one in the stadium was packing to go home.

Between sets a thundercloud exploded, and though the rain was brief the army of young boys who squeegeed and blasted the court with hot-air dryers took half an hour. The delay gave Willy a lethal amount of time to think, and Marcella the opportunity to change her outfit. As Foussard bounded to her baseline in a tutti-frutti skirt and fresh lemon headband, the air was cooler, almost chilly. Marcella's cheesecake for the cameras revealed that she'd wiped the lipstick off her teeth, and it seemed as if they were beginning a whole new game.

"Willy, I guess it goes without saying that you thought you had the match?"

The microphone was shoved aggressively in Willy's face, and she reared back as from a loaded gun. "If I ever did, that was my error. It's only over when it's . . ." she swallowed, "and all."

"Willy, you're married to Eric Oberdorf, who beat then number ten Hans Sörle earlier this year, and just snagged the Chevy men's singles title last night—pretty effortlessly, by all appearances. How do you feel after this setback?"

How did she feel? She stared incredulously at the ESPN reporter, but television mesmerized you into pro forma inanities. "I'm very happy for my husband, and I'm just sorry that I couldn't make his trophy half of a matched set. That would have been—romantic."

"You likely to hit the road with your husband, or will you keep working on your own game?"

"I think," another swallow, "Eric is plenty experienced with packing his own suitcase by now. There's lots of tennis left in this old girl." Which was Willy's way of claiming that she was still alive.

"So would you say that you choked?"

"Choked?" Willy repeated, her voice strangled. "Marcella has a deceptively crafty game; she wears you down. I think midmatch she started playing really, really well and I'd just like to commend her for an impressive performance, especially recovering from behind like that. I gave it my all, but she got the better of me this time."

"You don't believe you choked?"

"Sometimes," she stammered, eyes darting to his badge, "Mr. Dawson, the gods switch sides."

In answer to her imploring gaze, Dawson thanked her and proceeded to glad-hand the winner. The last five minutes had been the most supremely adult of Willy's life. In front of millions of viewers, she didn't cry.

THIRTEEN

WILLY INSISTED ON ACCOMPANYING Eric to the victors' reception, though even Max, to Marcella's dismay, skipped the party altogether. Max claimed he felt unwell; he certainly looked it. Eric was mobbed. Unchaperoned, Willy drank too much, and her jovial self-deprecation masked a more vicious self-deprecation that's a little frightening. The guests were so grateful. Discussion of her real devastation would have been *awkward*. Edgy, truncated chat quickly moved on from shame-about-your-final to neutral subjects like whether Monica Seles would ever return to the game after being stabbed. No doubt Willy's *yes isn't my husband amazing yes I have terribly high hopes for him* was as enervating as it was obligatory.

Back in their room at the Marriott, Willy collapsed on the bed as if all night she'd been holding her breath. "Christ, I could have spread that bitch across that court like tartar sauce on a bun."

"Then why didn't you?" Eric demanded. "What's a better definition of what you *could* do than what you *did* do?"

Willy had looked forward all evening to when they could finally be alone, and now Eric was being as insensitive as that ESPN reporter. "Don't you ever see a discrepancy between your ability and how well you played a match?" she pleaded.

"If I do, I shouldn't. If you discriminate between the two, what you 'could' do is infinite. You're capable of what you actually do. If ability is a finite, measurable quantity, it's the same thing as performance."

"So if Marcella beats me, she's better than I am. Period." Willy had meant her formulation to sound ridiculous. It didn't.

"Marcella is better than you are until you prove otherwise on the court. Not in your head. And not in mine."

"You're being a jerk," Willy accused him sulkily. "You know Marcella plays like a marshmallow. She didn't win, I lost. I had a bad day—"

"Your bad days are also your days," Eric interrupted sternly. "They count. I don't see why you want me to humor you. You're as good as your execution. This is sport. It's external. That's its strength and that's its limitation. I agree there's a lie in it. But there's a lie in the interior as well. You know yourself that people who are all talk, who sit around feeling *valuable* and busting with *potential*, are full of shit."

"What happened today was a travesty, an outrage! Why can't you agree? Why can't you have confidence in me?"

Eric dragged Willy by the wrist to sit up. "I do have confidence in you, which is why I'm not going to pander to post-match rewriting. Yes, it was a travesty, but it happened. Something went wrong. Turn your mind to what that was. My patting your hand about how awfully more gifted you are than Marcella won't help. Because, damn it, if she clouts you again, and again, no matter how tawdry her devices, then you are *not* better. There's only one way to prove otherwise. Beat her."

Willy slumped back to the pillow. "I was beating her," she observed glumly.

"Willy, it was 5–zip, 40–love!" Eric exploded. "What happened?"

Folding her hands funereally across her chest, Willy announced to the ceiling, "I was afraid."

If a simple explanation, it was plausible. In sport, fear alone could raise a dread to life. That Willy would squander so vast a lead had seemed farfetched. Yet by merely entertaining the possibility, she had called the unimaginable into being. Since she only needed one point of three, and from long thereafter a single game, which she should have picked up along the way if only from habit, the scale of the terror must have been monstrous.

"What could you *possibly* be afraid of, at that score?" asked Eric incredulously.

"I don't want you to leave me." Willy's voice, ordinarily a sturdy alto, was frail.

"I wouldn't leave you over a tennis game!"

"That's not what I mean. You're going on the ATP tour—"

"Which is part of the deal; we discussed this before we got married. You fly off to plenty of tournaments yourself. I don't like separation any more than you do, and some day soon this will all be over and we'll—"

"No. You'll leave me behind. You'll be famous. If you pull far enough in front, you'll be thousands of miles away when we're in the same room."

"Nonsense," Eric dismissed. "Besides, you lost one match. You can make up the points this summer, in the Tanqueray, for example—"

"Then you agree. In order for us to stay together, truly together, I have to keep up with your ranking."

"I didn't say that."

"Your answer to what if such-and-such happens is just to say it won't happen," Willy spoke to the overhead light. "You're nervous that I'm right."

"Willy, you've been more highly ranked than me by a yard the entire time we've been together. It's been the other way around for twenty-four hours, and you're going off the deep end. We can obviously manage not being exactly on a par, because that's the way we've *been* managing."

"You knew you were gaining on me." Willy's voice had gone flat and factual. "It's psychologically apples and oranges, coming up from behind and overtaking versus starting out in front and being surpassed. You know that from tennis. You're being intentionally thick."

"You can wear the shoe on the other foot for a month or so after two years of my playing second fiddle."

"You're mixing your metaphors," said Willy wearily. "You must be rattled." As if to demonstrate, the phone rang, and they both jumped.

Willy picked up. "No, it's not too late... Yes, I can see your point... Well, I'm sure she'll be perfect... No, the whole thing wasn't my cup of tea anyway, I don't mind. Yes. Goodbye."

Willy dangled the receiver on two fingers and dropped it *c'est la vie* in the cradle. "That was *Slick Chick*. The editor said that if we'd both won the Chevy it would have been a great story. But the way it shook out would make their readers 'uncomfortable'—a fractured fairy tale, you know. So she was schmoozing with Marcella at the party. They'll do a spread on Foussard instead."

"Willy, I'm sorry."

She shrugged off his arm. "It was stupid anyway. I looked like a whore."

"Honey..." Eric loitered helplessly at her side; for once Willy wished that she smoked. "What I said before—I only meant that your tennis game is as good as you play. I didn't mean that you are."

"The distinction is lost on me."

"I love you, sweetheart. I don't care if you win tournaments."

"That's love? My career doesn't matter?"

"It only matters to me because it matters to you. If it would help—I'll come to the Tanqueray. To give you support."

"You'll be in Europe."

"I'll come back."

She hadn't the heart to tell him that his courtside presence was kryptonite.

***

When Eric left for Switzerland, Willy fled to Sweetspot to train intensively for the Tanqueray in July. Fewer than half the points were on offer as she might have collected at the Chevrolet, but Willy needed a win like a fix.

In practice she had the shakes. Willy no longer quite believed that her shot would arrive where she aimed and, lo, it did not. Max called this self-fulfilling failure of faith the "Tinkerbell Syndrome"—in *Peter Pan*, unless children believed in fairies Tinkerbell would die. Putting a successful stroke on a par with the supernatural, his coinage recalled Willy's recurrent flying dreams, to which she was both prone and partial. Yet lately, soaring over mountain ranges with her arms outstretched, suddenly it would occur to her that people couldn't fly. At the instant of misgiving, her body would plummet, and Willy woke with a start, her heart thumping and the bedclothes dank. If the fatality of hitting bottom in falling dreams was apparently a myth, certainly in its metaphorical sense hitting bottom would be a death of sorts.

The cancerous mistrust was periodic, and bred itself. Hesitation begat poor shots, which begat more hesitation, which begat more poor shots. Often the only way to break the cycle was to quit, an impractical solution in a match.

Admittedly, Willy's game always had its ups and downs. When Willy was on form, a point flowed like water; when she was out of kilter not the point but the atmosphere went liquid, and slogging toward the alley she might have been hoofing it in a swimming pool. The gods of tennis were capricious, their gifts no sooner bestowed than withdrawn. Yet this latest invasion of doubt seemed the more human failing of Thomas than divine neglect. Sensing her diffidence after an especially atrocious practice session, Max sat Willy down in the library that evening and regaled her with, of all things, tales of dentistry.

"I have good teeth," he began. "As a kid I never had a cavity. Until I was twenty-nine, when I was mortified to be told that I needed a filling."

"I asked my dentist, why after all this time? He explained that molars are formed in pieces, and grow together to make a solid tooth. In my case, the pieces had never quite united. For my whole life a little pocket had waited, hidden. Finally some bit of flotsam invaded the gap, and the tooth decayed."

"I assume this is another of your parables, and not a lesson in the importance of floss?" asked Willy tolerantly.

"I've never coached a woman who wasn't riddled with holes," Max declared. "Sometimes the missing chunks are gaping, and the poor girl can't comb her hair without bursting into tears. You, though—I thought at first I'd found a female whose ego wasn't Swiss cheese. Now I wonder if you aren't like my molar—no pits on the outside, but in the very center, there's a hollow."

"If they're 'riddled with holes,' why coach women?"

"I'd have made a good dentist. And hey, the holes aren't their fault. Most girls have been blasted with buckshot by the time they're five."

"You sound as though you're coaching the Special Olympics," Willy grumbled. "So what's the answer? To my 'hollow'?"

"Well, it's ultimately a Daddy thing, but Chuck's not going to change much at this point. You've sealed him off. You've sealed everyone off, even me," Max volunteered cheerfully. "That's been your secret. Keep fending us away, then. And fortify your enamel with the fluoride of victory." Max clasped his hands over his stomach, in a gesture of literary repletion.

The time had long passed when Willy's leaving for her own dorm room was noticeably painful to either of them, and she dragged herself unceremoniously upright. "If a man had been stabbed by his competitor's fan," she posited, "not horrendously, but unnervingly, would he quit the game?"

"No," said Max. "I doubt a man would be 'traumatized.' I think he'd be *angry*."

"So Monica Seles has a hollow, too. Backhanded comfort."

"Will," he called behind her. "I don't like to say I told you so. But you know what 'bit of flotsam' is the catalyst for your decay, don't you? Who's worked into your hollow like a husk of popcorn?"

"That's a lie," said Willy before slamming the door. "You love to say I told you so."

As promised, Eric did fly back to attend the Tanqueray after his tournament in Zurich, where he'd made the round-of-sixteen— a reputable showing for a greenhorn on the tour. For his July return, Eric sacrificed his next European foray. Superior ranking had made him kinder. Magnanimity is to some degree a function of what you can afford; with a few moving exceptions, rich people buy more extravagant presents than the poor. Much as the gesture touched her, Willy envied him the luxury of generosity. How nice to be nice.

The Tanqueray was played in New Haven, though any town on the circuit came down to a price tag—how much it cost to get there, how much it cost to stay. To Willy, New Haven didn't mean grand Ivy League university, notorious drug problem, and quaint, resuscitated downtown. It meant cheap—within an hour's train ride of New York. Otherwise it simply meant comedown. Though with poor depth of field its trophy was ripe for picking, winning the Tanqueray would confer less prestige than losing the Chevrolet finals.

As Willy's first round began, no one in the stands would have noticed anything amiss. Oh, it looked dismal, playing in that enormous Yale stadium before such a tiny crowd; and perhaps 223 versus 522 going on to three sets was unexpected, though not unheard of. Eric beamed from the sidelines, punching the air after Willy's winners. But Willy herself kept hearing that deep interior hollow echo in her ears as if someone were pounding on an empty oil drum.

Granted that in tennis you were always making decisions, since most oncoming shots could be returned in a variety of canny directions. Several variables had to be calculated at once: where were this opponent's weak spots; how had you contended with similar configurations earlier in the match, and so what was your adversary expecting; could you handle the probable replies. Yet a good player hit with the illusion of making no decisions at all. Compacted into a split second, all that geometry, game memory, and espionage condensed into gut, spontaneous instinct.

But in the opening round of the Tanqueray, Willy was thinking too much. The summer's incipient uncertainty, the self-conscious decision-making, was back. Just before impact with the ball, she could have listed her alternatives on paper.

It was 3–4 in the third set, on-serve, Willy receiving. The game went Willy's way, until at 15–40 she confronted a vital break point.

Willy drove deep, and came to net. Her first volley was gettable, though the returning lob was weak. Willy could either streak back and take it on the bounce and so be driven to the baseline, or smash it midcourt and resume the net. Willy went for the more aggressive overhead. Keeping the ball in view, she backed into position.

But then Willy remembered that midcourt volleys were inherently risky, and a spin was beginning to curve the ball unpredictably to her right. Maybe take the bounce instead. Not having firmly opted for one course of action or the other, Willy was torn literally in two directions at once: her torso swiveled toward the baseline, while her feet danced forward to smash.

Her scream was still reverberating around Yale Stadium when Willy discovered herself splayed on the court. Her right knee was twisted in an implausible posture, like the figure drawing of an inept art student. Of the last few seconds she had no memory; she did not understand how she'd landed on the court, until a second wave of pain broke over her leg, oceanic and obliterating.

"Willy, sweetheart, don't move" came a familiar voice. Her vision spotted and the lines of seats wavered; she couldn't make out his face. "Don't try to get up. Wait for a doctor. Here, hold my hand. That's right. Squeeze hard. Stay still. Everything's going to be all right."

Funny how people always said that. They had no idea if everything was going to be all right.

The gold band was warm under her fingers. She squeezed his wedding ring harder, as if it were in danger of falling off. "Eric?" she whispered. "Did I make the shot?"

"Sure you did. A real killer."

Before blacking out, she knew he was lying.

Willy didn't realize she was going into surgery until she was out of it. Groggy from sedation, she worked her way up on her elbows as 3–4 in the first set swam into memory. A break, didn't she break? For a moment she was ready to serve for the match before a tear in the narrative appeared, as if someone had ripped out a page. What had happened was still unclear. That something had happened was certain, and as certainly it was bad. As she grasped the reality of her hospital bed—the stiff, scratchy sheets, the squashed pillow, the blare of neon that made even nurses look sickly—Willy was smitten by the primitive ignorance of a Civil War casualty. Her right leg...she couldn't feel it! When she lifted the sheet, what a relief that the leg, though bandaged at the knee, was still there.

Had Willy been able to maintain this variety of crude gratitude—she had all her body parts, she was in her right mind, she was alive—the next few months would have gone more gently. But crude gratitude was the stuff of crude expectations. The terminally ill could feast on surviving another day in however stuporous a fashion. For a young, ambitious tennis player abruptly unable to hobble to the bathroom without a crutch, thankfulness was fleeting.

Finding herself in Yale Medical Center instead of proceeding to the second round, Willy was dizzied by an emotional kaleidoscope; it was impossible to fix her feelings for more than an instant. Livid anger vied with duller grays of lethargy and gloom. Brief silver flashes of determination lit up the room, only to give way to inky hatred for every pedestrian within eyesight blithely striding about the ward on two legs. For moments her panorama washed clean with wide, white, annihilating denial. Others Willy was blanketed by a soft, beige, biding sensation—the patient numbness of waiting for a bus in cold weather. Yet gradually the miasma behind her eyes turned an ugly, sulfurous yellow, and for minutes Willy couldn't move a finger from pure, perfect terror.

When the orthopedic surgeon came to chat at her bedside, Willy didn't interrupt. She caught at the term *cruciate ligament*, with its semantic aura of importance. She was trying to pay attention, but there was only one question she wanted to put to the man.

"Doctor," Willy rasped. "Will I—" She considered putting off the inquiry for later, but in that case she wouldn't sleep. "Will I be able to play tennis?"

"Oh, a little recreational sport, taking it easy—"

"No, Doctor, I play for a living. Can I go back to it?"

The young man sniffed the air, as if he might smell her fate on the wind. "Oh," the surgeon supposed, "probably."

"*Probably!* What does that mean?"

"It means probably," he repeated with vexation. "Medicine isn't exact; all bodies are different. One of the things that's compelling about being a doctor—"

This was hardly the time to explore her surgeon's fascination with his job. "Can't you pin it down better than that? Like, what are the odds?"

"Generically, with this sort of injury? Fifty to sixty percent," he stabbed, shrugging. "But odds on an individual basis are meaningless. I have hopes for your recovery, but that depends on how you respond to physical therapy. You may feel twinges for the rest of your life, and your right knee will always be a weak point. You'll have to be careful."

"I got here being *careful*," she muttered.

"If you build up the muscles around the knee you may well return to normal, or nearly normal."

Willy's stomach lurched. The distinction between "normal" and "nearly normal" could easily be the difference between rankings of 215 and 902.

"I'll tell you this much," he assured her, moving off her bed. "If you'd snapped the cruciate completely, you'd be out of the game for good."

Having administered another dose of *crude gratitude*, he left her to the roll of a die.

Willy had made a poor Methodist, and so her prayers were offered to a presence she was not sure was out there, with the instinctive dumb crooning of a dog baying at the moon. *Please, please, if I can play again I'll*—She was not sure what she was promising to do for whom. If she was vowing to never take tennis for granted again, she knew better. Permitted back on the court, Willy would take the sport for granted in five minutes, chafing when a volley landed wide. But maybe it was that very chafing, the fight toward an ideal game that no player achieved, that she would most miss.

The sensible vow was to trust. Doubt itself had shuttled her to bed. But now that very mistrust had materialized, another monster roused from her imagination to lumber the world. Being "careful" meant that she could no longer trust her right knee. In this way the punishment was apt. By the time Eric arrived for visiting hours, Willy had convinced herself that she deserved it.

Her husband bore treats, for which Willy had no appetite, and she was loath to put on weight via the sedentary, bored nibbling of the bedridden. Although she'd lain here less than a day, she could already feel her muscles decomposing into jelly.

"The doctor says you're going to be fine," Eric purred, stroking her cheek.

"That's not what he told *me*," said Willy.

"He said the percentages were on your side. Come on, you're in great shape and perfect health. I bet you'll heal like time-lapse photography." Eric fluffed her bedclothes, but looked away when the sheet rose, avoiding a glimpse of the bandaged knee. Despite her husband's go-get-'em-champ, the errant strands of his eyebrows were sticking straight up in alarm. His hair greasy and coloring wan, Eric probably hadn't showered or slept.

Sweeter and as carefully selected as his gift of Godiva chocolates were Eric's tales of miraculous injury comebacks, which he must have stayed up researching overnight. But for every Pat Cash or Thomas Muster, Willy could name a Peter McNamara, who also turned to chase a lob, also tore up his knee ligaments, and was thereafter qualified for little more than hawking frozen yogurt at Flushing Meadow.

"Recuperation has a lot to do with attitude," Eric asserted, pouring her a glass of grape juice she didn't want.

"Maybe so," Willy agreed. "All the worse. My attitude already sucks."

"Wilhelm, this mess just happened yesterday, of course you're depressed. But later, recovery is fifty percent character."

"That's what worries me."

"It doesn't worry me." For a man who wasn't worried, Eric's forehead was awfully crimped, folded between his eyes like an accordion. "You're the most persevering woman I've ever met."

"It was character got me into this," Willy grumbled. "'He who hesitates is lost.'"

"You're talking crazy. It's the sedative."

"I was graceless."

"Hey," Eric separated the fine pale hairs at her temple, "think I've never had a minute when I was ungainly on the court?"

"I've never seen one. You know when you want to volley and you go volley. You don't hand-wring and change your mind and sprawl on your butt in the shape of a pretzel."

Eric swiveled from his chair and raked his fingers over his scalp. "Willy, you think this is humility, I'm sure. So you hurt your knee because you did something *wrong*. Anything that happens to you, you made happen. But that's not humility, it's hubris. There's such a thing as an accident, an event outside your control. This country is so litigious and so secular lately that any disaster has to be some poor bastard's fault. But it isn't always. There's such a thing as a bad break."

"And a good break?" Willy prodded softly. "You're doing well yourself because you're lucky?"

Eric's pace around her bed came up short. "I haven't been unlucky. Maybe that's the same thing."

"You most certainly don't attribute your own successes to the fates," Willy insisted, "or to a well-worn rabbit's foot. You earn what you achieve. Likewise, I got what I had coming."

"For some *bizarre* reason this way of thinking makes you feel better," Eric ranted. As his volume rose, the visitor at the next bed pulled the curtain. "I thought I was the ultra-rationalist, but you're the real culprit. Everything has to be ordered: rightful rewards and just desserts. No randomness, nothing from left field. That sort of rigid one-two-three makes no sense of the world, because it doesn't add up. But I'll leave you to it for now. As if this ordeal weren't hard enough, on top of everything you have to be to blame! As if it didn't hurt enough already, make you nervous about your career already! But stew if you have to, whip yourself if that provides you some masochistic, flagellistic satisfaction. Christ!" He was back to pacing. She could tell this was not the spirit in which he would have wanted to depart.

Willy held out her hand. "Kiss me."

He did so and muffled into her neck, "I'm so sorry." Willy drew back in amazement. It was the first time she had ever seen him cry.

FOURTEEN

"M AX?" WILLY RASPED, her Face contorted and her breath shallow. "You don't think I was looking for a way out, do you? That secretly I wanted a rest, or to quit?"

"Why?" Spotting her down the parallel bars, Max hovered with his hand an inch from Willy's shoulder. He was forcing himself not to help. "Are you telling me that you want to quit?" Whenever she distressed him, Max sounded irritated.

"No." Sweat drizzled down her neck; through the pain, it tickled. "But maybe subconsciously—"

Max rolled his eyes. "So I guess the interstates are overrun with drivers *subconsciously* hankering to plow into jackknifed tractor trailers."

Having shuttled the length of the bars placing a few pounds on the knee, Willy hopped to the leg pull and sank onto its bench. "Oh, Max. This equipment," she gestured at the fitness suite, since July grown crowded, "rented for me; that physiotherapist three times a week; your time, when your new summer school is still on—all because I was a klutz."

"Kid, this compulsion to regard that spill as your fault—"

"I was indecisive!"

"What do you want from me?" Max despaired. "Absolution? Or for me to agree that yes, you were a clumsy oaf, serves you right? I'll do either. Whatever will get you to *drop it.*"

Willy tugged at the elastic brace to peek at the scars, still bright pink, then snapped it against the tender skin. "I want to know what you really think."

"I've coached you for eight years. I've never had a student who was faster or more surefooted. Even that choke of yours with Marcella—which will dumbfound me to the day I die—you weren't *awkward*. No, you were agile enough, always getting to the shot, and I may never have seen you hit the ball harder—straight into the net, as if you were aiming for it. So over eight years, you're ass-backwards for three seconds. Does that mean you deserve to be taken out of the game for six months, go through this hideous rehab and then retraining this winter, and meanwhile your ranking plummets to a number requiring scientific notation to fit on one page? I bet you think shoplifters should get the chair."

"Thank you," she said shyly.

"Grow up." This irritation was not feigned.

Eric had offered to stick around—or not exactly. Rather, he asked diffidently, "Should I stay with you?" with the pleading expression of a child who has done his chores and is begging to go play. He had already sacrificed a tournament by flying back for the disastrous Tanqueray, and she could not conscionably demand that he hold her hand at such severe cost to his ranking. As ever, Eric had to keep in the running just to stay in place, like jogging on the Sweetspot treadmill, which punished a single pause with ejection from the track.

As for Willy, maybe a compassionate computer would put the rankings of injured athletes in suspended animation through recovery. But desperate players might too easily falsify incapacity to preserve their standing, so the associations had to keep the clock ticking come what may. As the season marched on, points dropped from Willy's name, for the computer tabulated accrual on a rollover basis. Her subsequent sinking heart resembled the despondency of a stalwart wage-earner abruptly laid off, watching his once robust savings account dwindle to nothing.

But if Eric would not submit to the monotonous business of tugging on her foot to lengthen her reattached ligaments, if he declined to spot her at the parallel bars as she pulled the heel toward her buttock until tears streamed down her cheeks, then he had no right to squawk when she accepted Max's offer to recuperate at Sweetspot.

Max seemed to welcome her renewed dependence on his facility for everything from breakfast to clean knee braces. He lifted his head at the squeak of her crutches on his waxed mess floors as if straining to catch a bittersweet melody, and later wheeled gladly at the click of her cane as it resonated his wide porches. When at last she could balance unaided down the flagstones of her dormitory, eyes wide and fingertips outstretched, his expression was worthy of Bob Cratchit before a mended Tiny Tim. Max personally led her through her exercises with a patience that seemed unlike him; he was patient *for* her. When at the end of her tether she asked why he bothered with a "tennis player" who couldn't touch her toes, quipping, "They shoot horses, don't they?" Max chided that he did not believe in planned obsolescence. If he would take a lifeless CD player in for service he would certainly repair an athlete.

As she made incremental progress, a camaraderie grew between coach and client that might ordinarily have cemented the bond between husband and wife. Now that Willy had been restored to his custody, Max enfolded her with consoling solicitude, as if her marriage were a grueling kidnapping attempt mercifully foiled, of which he was loath to speak and thereby recall her ordeal. When his private line jangled in the library, he handed her the receiver with a you-know-who shrug, no comment.

Though Max always slipped off to give her privacy, he needn't have bothered. The arithmetic regularity of Eric's calls bespoke duty more than impulse, and what besides duty would drive anyone to repeat such conversations?

Eric was full of complaints. The players' bus drivers didn't speak English and didn't know the way to the stadium. Practice courts were double-booked. His luggage was lost for two days, the plane was three hours late. Some disorganized tournament director did nothing but waddle from court to court trailing cigar ash. The courtesy car chauffeurs were forever sneaking off to the pool. The food was too rich and fussy, and he missed the plain broiled chicken at Flower of Mayonnaise. The toilets in Germany were perverted, offering up your feces on a throne for examination. Everywhere it was murder to find space to jump rope. A nagging ache in his right arm might be nascent tendonitis...

As Eric's querulousness mounted, so did Willy's incredulity. Here she was lurching about the Connecticut boondocks like Igor, game for little more than a stiff round of Snakes and Ladders, and he was on the international ATP tour competing with the crème de la crème of the sport, staying in chic hotels and ordering Black Forest gateau while she gnoshed one more overdone flank steak from the cafeteria. And he was *complaining*?

As Willy fumed after one more session of intercontinental bellyaching, Max pointed out how she might feel if instead Oberdwarf raved about what a marvelous lark he was on. What if he lavished praise on the exotic delicacies at his table, his posh digs, the breathtaking view of the Alps out his window? "He doesn't want you to think he's having too good a time without you. It's an ancient marital gambit. I peeved away to my wife all the time. Not that it worked. She was always sure I was covering up. To give the woman credit, she was right."

"So he's lying."

"Oh, I don't know. You've learned yourself that the hotel routine gets old fast."

"Motel Six's get old. He's in Europe."

"No, they all get old. There's only one thing on the tour, if you're the real McCoy, that doesn't wear thin. Which is also the one thing, if I don't miss my guess, that he's bashful about discussing."

Max's intuitions were on the money. Eric hanged himself regardless: if he griped he was ungrateful; if he rhapsodized he was rubbing-the-nose. But if he couldn't win with Willy, he compensated on the court, and it was precisely these victories that he short-shrifted over the phone. Often by the time Eric was finished moaning about greasy paella riddled with shrimp shell, the call had got too expensive to go into any detail about the second round in Madrid. And this from a man who used to burst into their apartment to deliver the blow-by-blow of an incidental practice match. Moreover, he was often disparaging about his performance, whereas previous to the Chevrolet he hadn't a discouraging word to spare about his game.

"But you did *win*, didn't you?" Willy once pressed in exasperation.

"Just."

"What was the score?" She picked distractedly at a flap of skin on her right palm.

"Mmm..." He pretended to not quite remember. "6–4, 7–5, something like that."

"Straight sets. That's not scraping by, Eric."

She could feel him recoil on the other end; the note of accusation in her voice was unmistakable. No doubt he was racking his brain for what he had done wrong this time. In the absence of an answer, or in avoidance of one, he changed the subject. "So how's tricks at Sweatspot?"

Several other patches were moulting off her fingers and thumb; the lifting skin was hard, thick, and yellow.

"Oh, I brought my forehead to my knee yesterday," she informed him dryly. "Cause for champagne."

"Honey, that's terrific!"

"Yeah," she slurred. "Just swell. Next week I'm allowed a light jog. One mile, then a whirlpool bath. In case you're wondering what it's like to be eighty-five, I can give you some previews."

Next to the phone, she had amassed a pyre of skin scraps on the library table, all that remained of her tennis calluses.

In truth, some of Eric's triumphs were truncated. He was contending in a higher stratum than domestic satellites, and his shimmy up the ladder had slowed to a more laborious clamber. Still the program was on track; by the end of September Eric was ranked 169, and Willy had slid to 357. They were no longer parallel trains chugging forward at varying rates. Willy's engine was stalled for overhaul at the station, while her husband's caboose rattled off to the horizon. All she could do was gimp to the edge of the platform and wave.

They were living in different worlds. Traveling, Eric accumulated a battery of exotic images that set him apart. How luscious it might have been instead to mock the tournament director's cigar ash together, to later reference German toilets and snicker. So many jokes came down to I-guess-you-had-to-be-there, and Willy wasn't.

At the unsatisfying conclusion of their phone calls Willy grew doleful, and not only on her own account. Eric had cherished a wife who could fully appreciate the nuances of a tennis match. Now to this very soulmate he felt bound to telescope, dismiss, and skate over the focal narratives of his life. Only when he was cut down in the first round in Stockholm did he indulge the whole set-by-set story. When instead he confessed to advancing to the quarters of the Brussels Classic, he spoke in the furtive, abashed tones of a man who has been arrested for public indecency.

In early October, Willy found herself about to hang up, having run up a ruinous bill jabbering how it was nice to have the regular students back at Sweetspot rather than the buy-your-way-to-glory kids of the summer school, into which any slob with cash was admitted. "I'm sorry this is all so boring," she hurried. "I can run gently now, and I'm hitting the free weights pretty heavy for upper-body strength. Talk to you in a couple of days?"

"Willy—don't you want to know how I played in the quarters today?"

"Oh, I forgot, how did it go?"

"How could you forget? I spoke to you just last night, I said the quarters were this afternoon, and I'd call this evening to let you know how the match went. I stayed up late, though I was dog tired, just so I could catch you your time after dinner."

"I'm sorry, OK? But Belgium seems pretty far away from here, my knee has been killing me, and your quarters are not exactly on the top of my mind."

"That's obvious." (Breathing.) "When you've made it through three rounds," he continued, "I would never *forget* about your quarter-finals. I doubt I'd think of anything else all day."

"That's because my setting foot on a tennis court would be headline material."

"No, before—And this is the Brussels Classic—"

"You mean it's not like the rinky-dink tournaments I used to enter," shot out before she could stop herself.

"Just forget it, Willy."

"*Well?* Did you win or didn't you?"

"You don't give a damn." The dial tone was unusually loud.

"I tried to call you back," said Willy morosely. "Turned out I didn't have the name of your hotel."

When still smarting from the reproof of his dial tone, she had located Fodor's *Belgium* in the library, and rang down the list of hotels for an Oberdorf among their guests. Hurling self-recrimination, whispering ardent apologies and promises to be kinder, Willy imagined that their subsequent reconciliation would be warm, weepy, and remorseful. But after ten fruitless inquiries, she'd been forced to give up. Now Eric had waited a week to call again, and in the interim Willy had journeyed from tortured and ashamed of herself to surly and pissed off. Eric had never been incommunicado for so long; his implicit castigation lifted the onus from Willy to castigate herself.

"So," she continued heavily. "*Did* you win the quarters?"

"Yes, but you'll be happy to know I was knocked out in the semis."

"I've never once said I was happy when—"

"You haven't had to."

"I'm really sorry, sweetheart, because you came so close—"

"Please don't bother, Willy, the crocodile tears don't wash. I guess you can't help being, well, a little begrudging. But I can't help being hurt, either. It's... the situation. Maybe in your place I'd... it's hard to say. But everything between us will straighten out when you get back on the road."

"*If* I do."

"I warned you about attitude."

"And I warned you about mine." The line crackled. Their talk was halting, but at least a relief from their usual diversionary prattle. It was time they faced what they were avoiding.

"You have no idea what it's like," Willy proceeded with difficulty, "having such a crucial part of your body ripped to ribbons. And to live with this tepid reassurance that you've a 'fifty percent' chance of returning to 'nearly' normal. I'm scared, I'm mad, I hate everybody. Of course you're going to be generously included. My whole life is on the line."

"I'm part of your life. I'm not on the line."

"Oh," Willy whispered sadly, her voice catching, "but you are."

"Don't—"

"Listen to us!" Willy pleaded. "Think of how we used to talk! Now we fight or we're fake... we have nothing in common—"

"Maybe it seems that way, but that's temporary!"

"You're doing it again," she admonished gently. "Always the answer to what this situation is doing to us is to change the situation."

"Of course. It was circumstances that put us at each other's throats to begin with."

"You don't have to be so diplomatic, Underwood. I'm the one at your throat. You've been an angel. Solicitous, encouraging, and incredibly tolerant."

"I don't know about that," he demurred. "If I were really angelic, I wouldn't be in Europe while you go through all this awful knee shit. But once you're on your feet again, we'll go right back to being a team."

"I wonder if we've ever quite been a team, Eric," she said mournfully. "Neither of us is the type. Besides, what if my knee doesn't sufficiently recover? Then you're just married to a shrew?"

"You're not a shrew," he lied. "You're in a lot of pain, in every way, and I'm sorry I'm not always sympathetic. But I get lonely over here, Wilhelm. Sure, the tennis is great, but nobody else within three thousand miles is rooting for me to win but me."

Willy allowed herself a droll quip. "That's a considerable cheering section, as I recall."

"Fuck off," he said fondly. "I mean I need your support. I have no one else to talk to."

"I can't even remember what you look like, Underwood," Willy admitted. "I have a photograph, and whenever I think of you I see the same frozen smile. I can't remember you moving around."

"I'll be back soon," he assured her. "But first I've got to, uh . . ." Eric was indistinct.

"What?"

"South America. I'm heading to Buenos Aires—"

Willy's soft, yearning confessionalism flew right out the window. "Oh, well be sure to write." The *T* on her palate was cold and precise, like a knife ticking china.

"But then I'm definitely flying home for a break."

"Yes, it would be nice to see you before the year is out," she clipped.

"I miss you," said Eric, with feeling.

Willy returned, "I miss you, too," in a rote monotone. He deserved better.

In all honesty, Willy missed one thing more than her husband, and that was tennis. Without tennis, her days were aimless. She watched too much television. Though diligent at what exercise she was permitted, weights, sluggish jogging, and ceaseless iso-tonic stretching left her body feeling lumpy and inert. Willy pined as if for a lover; Eric seemed to have eloped with the sport itself, wooing it on a honeymoon to Europe.

At long last Max extended her Pro-Kennex over the breakfast table. Willy's *crude gratitude* at shaking hands with her best and oldest friend was bound to give way in short order to irascibility at being rusty. But what Willy needed now far more than victory was to recapture her pure aesthetic joy, a ten-year-old's exuberance born in the obscure and unlucrative shade of a public park with her father. Tennis in its Eden had been conceived without enemies, with *partners* rather than oppon-ents, and anyone who outplayed her had been not foe but resource. Too bad, she reflected wryly, she hadn't got married at ten as well.

All the latter summer a mellow sun had taunted from outside the weight room window, her favorite season frittered in the stuffy fitness suite, late, lean evening light squandered on sitcoms. A life has a finite number of summers, horribly count-able. To have lopped off half of one was a loss that could never be restored, like the missing segment of a finger. Now that it was nearly November, a chill bit the air; court seven rasped with brown leaves. Max had insisted she wear sweats to keep her knee warm, in addition to dragging on the hated, constricting brace, the old-lady beige of support hose. But Willy wasn't complain-ing. She clasped the cold grip of the racket, pressed it against her cheek, and kissed it.

In all, it was more marvelous than she remembered. Because you couldn't remember. That was why, as Max had averred, the sport never wore thin. Like love or pain, tennis could be recalled only by repetition. You had to do it to have it.

"Easy does it!" Max scolded.

"Send me something hard! Stop hitting right to me!" She couldn't stop laughing.

"No leaping up and down, stupid!" he barked. "... Now look what you did!" Willy had frozen in a crouch, and eased upright, working her knee. Max tore to her backcourt, and had his arm under her oxter in seconds.

"Max, don't be hysterical. So it's a little stiff."

"Come back inside."

She pushed him away. "In a pig's eye! Get over there!"

When they had used up the practice balls, winners littered Max's side. She loped to help collect them, tossed three in his basket, and breathed deep for the sheer, sharp crack of the air in her lungs. "Max, I'm OK," she announced, stooping beside him. "I can play!"

Though she'd done no such thing her whole married life, Willy could no more help dropping the balls and throwing herself into his arms than Max could help wrapping them around her back and lifting her off the court in a circle. Even when the turn was done and he gently rested his protégée onto her toes, he didn't let go, and she didn't let go, until she kissed what deserved to be kissed instead of a thankless, inanimate racket.

"Honey, I played today! I'm so happy!" This was their first upbeat phone call since Eric's departure for Europe. Memory of that embrace on number seven niggled; in the course of the call, she told Eric she loved him three times.

And, a first in four months, meant it. She adored her husband, she adored Sweetspot, of course she adored her coach because she adored the whole world. If this meant Eric was right, that the answer to situational woes was situational redress, a darker correlate shadowed this revelation that Willy was in no mood to contemplate. It was Eric himself who claimed that no individual was omnipotent; that "there was such a thing as accident, as a bad break," and therefore even to be lifted by circumstance was to remain at its mercy. If events could summon Willy's love for her husband, events could as capriciously send it packing.

"My knee," she went on breathlessly, "is right as rain."

"Right as rain" was an exaggeration that Willy decided to perpetuate. Through the hitting session she had refused to heed the sharp, electric jolts shooting up through her thigh. If she did not acknowledge the pain, there was no pain. More, if she mentioned the slightest strain to Max, he would scoop her off the court and condemn her to the dungeon of the weight room for another month. He'd bring in that humorless physiotherapist, who would put her back to lifts of three ounces and those odious, interminable stretches. And with a peep of apprehension to her husband, Eric would ring Max's private line from Buenos Aires and lay into her coach for letting his wife off her leash before she was ready. Better to keep the twinges to herself.

Since the Tanqueray, a part of her body that had previously melted into her overall person had been selected out for special consideration and so had become distinct, separate, a set of complex ligaments, cartilage, and bone whose workings she now knew more intimately than she wished and whose competence she could no longer assume. Objectified, the hinge had taken on a character, vacillating between servant and master, friend and enemy, but in any case one of those pestilent relations who is a part of your life whether you like it or not. The knee had been unruly, but penalized, as Max said himself, far out of proportion to its crime. While its fate was touch-and-go, Willy had attended to the advice of its counselors down to the finest detail. Now that the obstreperous chunk of gristle was out of intensive care, it was time to get tough and stop being so indulgent. If at first the knee required tenderness, now it demanded discipline, and no amount of squealing *You're hurting me!* or *Yikes!* or *I can't!* would temper its new regime.

The night of her first practice session, Willy sat at the desk in her dorm room and wrote out a daily training schedule for the next several weeks:

12,000 rope-jumps (not 8!)
46 miles treadmill, 7 mph warming to 9 mph
2 hr. ground stroke practice (Max will stop at 1)
1 hr. volleying
1 hr. serving practice
Weight room circuit every other day; INCREASE LB's!

While the exclamation points were rousing, the pen was painful to hold. Since July her hands had evolved into the soft, white, padless extremities of a debutante. A single hour on the court had raised blisters.

That Willy expected her ten-year-old's glee to dissipate did not make its rapid evaporation any the less disheartening. Within the week Willy was disgusted. All her strokes were creaky, and she could not control the accuracy of her serve within two feet. She hadn't been away from the game for four months since she was five, and now she understood why.

More, it is actually easier to turn a deaf ear to the wailing of one's own child than to the petulance of the body. Stabs in her knee regularly delayed her that vital fraction of a second. Willy's resolve, her enthusiasm were at record highs. The mind was willing; the body was reluctant. The accident had left its legacy of mistrust. Once its ligaments were stretched and its supporting muscles warm, the joint appeared reliable, yet she could never be unreservedly confident as her weight transferred to her right leg. A whisper of nervousness, a girlish sense of delicacy were perhaps now with her for life.

Willy's consternation that her ranking was in free-fall ate her hollow. Wheedling failed to convince Max to let her enter an indoor tournament before the season was through. She couldn't do it without him—she hadn't the money—and frankly her game was not yet up to snuff. After six months of retirement Willy calculated that she would dive from 214 in June to the early 500's in January. The waste, the wanton waste, made Willy want to vomit. In her mind her points were soldiers; she was their general kept in chains while one by one her conscripts were captured by foreign troops. After reading the sports pages, Willy crumpled them into balls.

Eric had made it through the quarters in Buenos Aires, thereby raising his ranking to 159. Naturally he couldn't pass up the mid-November National Indoor in Nashville. The promised "break" after South America came down to: when the season was over he would come home. In the meantime she was to find vast consolation in the fact that at last they were sharing the same continent.

Well, then, in December he could find her at Sweetspot. If his earth-shattering career was such a cardinal priority that he couldn't skip a single tournament to see his wife, who'd been to hell and back in his absence, then he could very well come to her for once. As for Christmas, Willy was damned if she would interrupt her training to celebrate a holiday of no canonical importance to her, or to visit Eric's neurotic, quiz-show family. Much less did she wish to visit her own relatives, all of whom were fervently hoping that 1995 would be the year in which silly Wilhemena turned over a sensible new leaf and embarked on a life as a poorly but at least steadily paid and safely pusillanimous bank clerk. So Eric didn't like it at Sweetspot; tough. She wouldn't rush back to New York to fetch him his slippers. And if he didn't like it either that she and Max were getting along like a house on fire, too bad. He would have to be, as Gert would say, *mat-yure.*

It was to the rhythm of these mutterings that Willy jumped 12,000 times each day on a deserted indoor court or in the unattended rec room. She moved around, for though Max had not forbidden the exercise, she hadn't asked for clearance either. Willy figured that if she could not outdo Eric with his fancy-schmancy tricks she could at least best him with numbing, mindless endurance. The rope itself conjured Eric, and for the entire hour and a half she mumbled to her spouse. It must have taken a total of 150,000 skips, however, to work up the nerve to announce her Christmas plans when he could hear her.

"You're making some kind of *point*?" Eric asked coldly from Nashville.

"It's easy to forget, but there are still two careers between us, and I have to—"

"So that's the point," he interrupted. "Now that I get it, will you meet me in our own apartment, please?"

Mr. Room Service, Mr. Top Ten of Tomorrow was accustomed to having his way. "I need intensive practice before reentering the fray. I can't afford to pay—"

"I have plenty of money," he intruded wearily. "Enough for you to practice at Jordan two, three hours a day."

"It's not my money."

"We're married, for Christ's sake. It's *our* money, you idiot."

It had been Willy's idea to segregate their finances. To Eric, she had cited her need to calculate Max's cut of her winnings after expenses; to herself, she had cited a vague feminist conviction that a girl should have her own cash.

"I didn't earn it," Willy insisted. "I've had a setback, but I haven't lost my self-respect."

"You'll take money from Max, but not from your husband?"

"Max and I have a business relationship."

"Sure you do."

In stony silence, Willy wouldn't rise to the charge.

Eric carped, "I'm supposed to squeeze onto that single bed in your dorm room for six weeks?"

"You can sleep in another room, if you need your beauty rest," Willy said coolly.

"Are you threatening me?"

She regretted the remark, but wouldn't take it back, so proceeded to make matters worse. "This isn't negotiable. I need my coach. Max means Westbrook."

"If you need Upchuck more than me..."

This was getting out of hand. "I need both of you, damn it. You'll have been suiting yourself for coming up on five months. For once you could accommodate me."

"I want to go *home*," he finished forcefully. Sadly, she knew exactly how he felt.

FIFTEEN

E RIC SQUINTED. "You look thin."

"What did you expect?" Willy raised her chin. "That I've been flat on my back popping Cheez Doodles?"

They had kissed once on the station platform, lips tight; Eric didn't like public display. "Why do you interpret everything I say as criticism?" he asked in dismay. "I'm concerned, is all. And you're pale."

"You may not have noticed in South America, but up here it's winter."

"It was snowing in Nashville; I figured it out." He trailed behind her to the car. "Willy, you're *goose-stepping*."

"I've been given a clean bill of health."

"Recently?"

As Eric scrutinized her askance, Willy assessed her husband in return. Among the other washed-out Amtrak passengers his tan looked out of place. He was more nodular than she remembered, the Adam's apple, nose, and forehead lumpy and tuberous. In the snapshot she referred to he was smiling; this uneasy man's features were wrung like a wet towel.

Conversation en route to Westbrook was choppy; they were too used to speaking on the phone. Newly visible, Willy felt exposed. She let him into her dorm room and checked her watch, though the last hour had dragged so that she knew the time almost to the minute. "I've got to go work out," she said hurriedly by the door. "I guess later we can go out to dinner." The "I guess" leeched eagerness from the proposition.

"Do you have to exercise now?"

"I always do. In fact, I'm running late."

"There's exercise and exercise..." His scraggled eyebrows raised. Groucho Marx.

Willy wasn't being difficult; she really didn't get it. "Come again?"

"Not before the first time."

She wasn't laughing.

"I was hoping we could, ah...stay in your room awhile. Get reacquainted." He seemed embarrassed. Married almost two years, they should have been comfortably frank.

"I'd feel guilty if I skipped my routine, and we've plenty of time, right?" She urged a smile, and joked wryly, "That is, unless there's some tournament you have to save it up for."

"I'm sorry about that, Willy," he responded in earnest. "I've decided my abstinence thing was retarded."

"Aw, I was just kidding." Willy was still standing in the door.

"I'll get some winks, then. I'm pretty tired."

"Yes," she said. "You look tired."

"Willy?" he called as she collected her jump rope from its hiding place under her underwear. "You are glad to see me, aren't you?"

"Of course," she said formally, and fled down the hall.

Willy lucked out and found an indoor court free; students were cramming for exams. Though Har-Tru was kind to leather, the rope's central section had frayed from use. *Ta-dum, ta-dum...*

The phases of each monotonous rope-skipping session replicated the rhythms of a prison term. The beginning went surprisingly fast, as perhaps would the first months in San Quentin. The early middle was the worst—the routine already grown tyrannical, an appalling preponderance of servitude to go. The vast middle-middle was almost restful, with no tempting parole in view; the walls of any cell must evolve to the walls of the world. The killer was glimpsing release. Some days in her last one thousand Willy thought she might scream; it is said that a convict may experience his final weeks of captivity as longer than the rest of his sentence.

Bobbing in the middle-middle, Willy caught a flicker by the EXIT light. Eric, no doubt. Realigning a quarter turn, she kept her back to the door with the pretense of having seen no one. He didn't emerge, but lurked in shadow. To demonstrate that she was no slacker off the road, Willy spun into a sequence of scissors, heel clicks, and double jumps.

"Very impressive."

The voice was low and level. As she shuddered at its gravelly timbre, the rope smacked her ankles and lay still.

"And how many of those do you do a day?" The figure strode measuredly into the light.

"Oh," she said offhandedly, wiping a drip from her temple, "a few thousand. You know—"

"No, I don't know. So tell me. How many thousand?" The voice was even, coaxing, but it was also a voice that someone might use before he was going to hit you.

Willy folded the rope loosely, as if she were calling it quits. "It varies—"

"I don't believe you. You're a slave to numbers. Rankings. Miles per hour on the treadmill. So I think you do the same number *every day*."

She knew she should fudge, but Willy was proud of her stamina and couldn't bring herself. "Twelve," she squeaked.

"I take it you mean not twelve hundred but twelve thousand?"

Willy nodded; she was cringing.

"Now, for whom is this performance?"

Max was extending his hand for the rope. Had Eric done the same, Willy would have withheld it, indignant. But she relinquished the Everlast to Max. Maybe she could get another one in town somewhere.

Willy gestured to the empty court. "No one's here."

"Let's not be so literal. A performance doesn't need its audience to be physically present. Is this theater for me?"

"Maybe, in a way..."

He shook his head sadly. "I don't think so. I think it's for *Oberdick.*"

"He just got here!"

"Nope. He never left." Max lay the Everlast on his palm like a whip. "What is it you want? To beat him?"

Willy and her husband were 350 ranking places apart. The notion of exceeding Eric any time soon was preposterous. "I'd be content to be as good as he is. To keep up."

"You don't even want to fucking *beat* him?"

She stepped back. "I guess I'd like to impress him. To make him proud of me. So I might want to beat him...a little bit..." She added mournfully, "Since with Eric, beating him and impressing him are the same thing."

Max lashed her rope on the court. "*Why* do you think I took you on in the first place?" The crack of the rope echoed off the arched ceiling. His modulated tone had broken, and Max was shouting. "What drove your motor when we met? Did you pound line drives for two hours so I'd take you out for a soda?"

"No, I—" Willy shrank back. "I liked practicing line drives."

"And I'd buy you a soda anyway." Max advanced on her, snapping the rope tight between his fists like a garrote. "My approval was a perk, not what made you tick. I took you under my wing because you didn't give two hoots what anyone else thought of your game. No matter how much I required of you, you required more of yourself. You used to please yourself. And now you're just one more little girl out to please Daddy. They're a dime a dozen. He's fucking ruined you. It makes me want to fucking cry."

Willy turned her back, running her fingers across the net. "I may use Eric as a yardstick. But I also want to get in shape for the coming season. In tip-top shape. Is that so terrible?"

Max had come up behind her; he wound the rope around her waist, tugging the loop tight as he brought his hands together at her stomach. "Your knee is swollen," he whispered in her hair. "I can see it, even with the brace. Skipping, you favor your left leg. Is that why you kept it secret? You knew I'd see." He kissed her bowed neck. The Everlast's wooden handles bobbled on her shins. "It was so awful," he groaned, "when you fell. Your leg twisted at that sickening angle. And I couldn't even run up to you. I had to stay back and let..." He sighed, and the moist straggles at her temple fluttered. "Later, watching you hobble...Don't make us go back to that. Please be careful."

Max leaned down, nuzzled his cheek against her ear, and kissed under the lobe. The skin must have been salty. Since she didn't stop him, he was obliged to stop himself.

Showering, Willy turned the pressure up high to pelt Max's smell from her skin, willing the agitating memory of his advances down the drain. Instead she considered his allegation that the source of her inspiration had become displaced. But wasn't it human enough, when you loved someone, to want to make them happy even more than yourself? Was it so dreadful to have grown less selfish?

For a tennis player the shift was lethal. Tennis players were selfish and good ones stayed selfish. Lovers were a cheat, a way out; if she jumped rope to impress Eric, she might escape the more exacting demands of her own expectations. It was too easy to delight lovers; they were inclined to be delighted. Eric would make excuses for her, about her knee, about being out of practice, about being a girl. One's self was not so easily fobbed off.

Toweling down, Willy noted that her knee was indeed puffy. Bent, her whole body ached, as it did all day lately. Yet Willy still kicked herself: in meeting Eric's train she had skipped serving practice, and had to cut her run to four miles.

Max's formulation was skewed. True, her private slave driver had towered to six-three, sprouted broad forearms and sharp shoulders, and developed a 120 mph serve beside which her own would forever look feeble. But when she envisioned its face, her taskmaster had Willy's eyes.

For the next week she saw Eric only evenings, attending to line sprints, weights, and ground stroke drills during the day. Though Max had commandeered her jump rope, Willy borrowed and knotted one of Eric's, careful to confirm that Max was occupied before tiptoeing to the rec room, shoving a desk against the door, and playing the radio to cover the clicking sound on the floor. Though she tried to keep Eric and Max apart, when they ate in the cafeteria the two men's mutual presence was unavoidable. Granted, she was too familiar with Max; she made compulsive private jokes while her husband shoveled his meal in silence. Maybe she even flirted a little, which was naughty, or worse than naughty. But Willy could no more conceal her intimacy with her coach from Eric than she could hide her remoteness with her husband from Max. Max was so much easier to talk to.

Every night she and Eric made love. He was hungry, and vowed he'd been celibate on the tour. Willy patently believed him. An absolutist, Eric married = Eric faithful. Though even rote fidelity beat betrayal, she'd have preferred an admission that he'd wrestled the odd demon on her account.

Willy still found her husband attractive; after so much tennis, his body was tight, neat, and deliciously stringy. But she was so tired, she felt so heavy, that feeling below the waist took effort. She had to remind herself to become aroused. And no matter how deeply he pressed on the narrow single bed, his presence felt indefinite, delayed, sealed up; it was like fucking by mail. His whisper in her ear sibilated, its tones thinning as if filtered

through a telephone line, and the call of her name echoed plain-
tively as if shouted down a canyon from a mile away. Drifting to
sleep, she wondered what they might do to get closer, then
remembered that most couples converged by having sex and they
had done that.

A gingerliness to his touch was new, and when they bent to
sleep like a 22 he would ask whether her knee was comfortable;
his fingers were feathery. She almost asked him, *Be a little rough
with me,* but they'd been apart so long that she didn't want him
to think that in the interim she'd got into anything kinky.

After five days he proposed, why not hit a few with her own
husband?

"I supposed you wouldn't want to rally with me anymore,"
she shrugged. "You've cracked the top 200. I've slid to the fives.
You're out of my league."

Eric insisted, but in practice he rallied as he stroked her in bed.
He was too lenient and helpful. Far from trying to defeat her, he
let her good shots go, nodding from his baseline with a whistle.
The copious compliments actually hurt her feelings. That she
could no longer excite his rivalry was the ultimate insult.

"Can you even remember the days," she remarked dryly when
they were done, "that *I* used to give *you* advice?"

"You still do, and it's very valuable—"

"Bullshit, I can't tell you a thing. Even more astonishing
historical trivia?" Willy mentioned lightly. " *You* were once jealous
of *me.*"

"When was that?"

"Get out of here. When you lost the Jox in the first round or
something, and then came up to watch me win the New
Freedom? You were pretty pissed off at that party."

"I was not," Eric maintained. "I kept in the background to
give you the limelight, which you richly deserved."

"You thought I was a fat-headed jerk!"

"I did not!"

"You refuse to admit you were jealous?"

"Willy, that was two years ago; why are you getting worked up? What does it matter?"

"It matters," she growled. "Good God, why not apply for sainthood already."

"I'm sorry, but I was very happy for you and I wasn't jealous."

Willy stewed the rest of the day. Eric tended to rewrite the past so that his shit didn't stink. In fact, the memory of his stiffness at that party, not to mention his ducking to the john during match point, had grown strangely precious.

After two weeks, instead of switching off the light and collecting her in his arms, Eric lay back with his hands behind his head. "I'm feeling like a fifth wheel, Wilhelm. Tomorrow I'm taking the train to New York."

"What's at home that you don't have here?" she asked on an elbow. "Courts, weights, videos, games—"

"Yeah, all those games we play."

"—You don't even have to cook your own food."

"I want to buy some Hanukkah presents for my family. I want to see my father, and thank him for his help. Even tennis—after so much and more coming, I need a break."

It was decent of him not to mention that by-the-by his wife was also cold, aloof, and hostile. He turned out the light and rolled over. Tentatively, Willy slipped a hand over his hip.

"Why don't we just go to sleep tonight, huh?" he mumbled. "You're always so wiped out. Get some rest."

He patted her hand, and indeed on release from what she never used to regard as a marital duty Willy's mind had gone black and her body limp before she'd time to withdraw the hand from his pubic hair.

Eric was packed before breakfast, and after slurping a cup of coffee stood on the mess porch by his bags. Willy was aware of keeping an extra foot from him, as if avoiding a magnetic field.

"I don't suppose," he said flatly, "you'd even consider coming with me."

Willy loitered by the rail, wishing he'd phrased the statement as a question; maybe that would have made it easier to say yes. But she had taken a certain tack, and now appeared stuck with it. "No," she said gloomily. "I guess I've got to stay... I could drive you to the station."

"There's a bus taking students to Old Saybrook in ten minutes. I wouldn't want you to miss out on an hour's *practice*. You'd never forgive yourself. Much less me."

Hugging Eric good-bye, she clawed her fingers into his coat, like one more desolate Sweetspot boarder deserted on these steps and left to the mercy of strangers. Only after the bus had plowed down the drive too far to flag it down did she remember it was December 14, and she hadn't wished him happy anniversary.

Willy's eagerness to outdo herself dropped a notch the day Eric left. Though she'd prevailed upon him to leave a rope behind—he'd no idea that the exercise was verboten—the inherent absurdity of repeatedly hopping over a swinging leather thong brought her more than once to a stupefied standstill. Mortified that she could indeed be losing her drive, she levied an extra, punitive three thousand.

At dinner, with students cleared off for the holidays, the mess was bereft. Ordinarily fighting to be heard above the roar and clink, Willy missed their vibrant clamor. Sitting next to Eric, she'd been a fountain of banter; now she couldn't think of word-one to say to her coach.

"You and Undershorts," Max hazarded, "don't seem chummy."

"Relations are a little strained."

"Maybe it's for the best he left, then. Discord is distracting."

"The trouble was," she said sharply, "it wasn't distracting enough."

That night Willy dreamed that she was late for a tournament. She told Eric at her side, *I'm never going to make it if I don't run.* Eric advised, *You'll never make it, so relax.* Willy began to hoof it anyway; the stadium was miles away. But the more she poured on steam, the more nominal her advancement became. She was virtually running in place. Willy grazed her fingers across her monumental thighs, which were hard, striated, and stationary. The muscles were so heavily developed that they'd turned to stone. At last she gave up. Easing to a walk, she could proceed more rapidly than at a sprint. Eric reached for her hand, and the dreary overcast sky burst with sunlight. She would still not make it to the tournament, but suddenly a mere tennis match wasn't of the slightest importance. Willy laughed, kissed Eric's hand, and proposed that they order the broiled chicken.

At Christmas, Willy's regime was given a kick in the pants from a call to her family. Gert had passed her final round of tests to become a fully fledged CPA; according to Gert, Daddy was "thrilled." One by one they each got on the line and expressed lavish concern about Willy's knee. Their accord in urging her to reconsider her choice of profession now that her father's prediction of calamity had come to pass betrayed a powwow over pumpkin pie behind her back. Well, screw them. For a few refreshingly irate minutes after the call, Willy felt seventeen.

There was now a goal to shoot for. On the basis of her ranking previous to injury, Max had secured Willy a wild card for an indoor event in Providence at the end of January. Yet when Max conceded that Willy was nearly tournament-ready after New Year's, his eyes narrowed, and he didn't commend her improvement with any enthusiasm.

By mid-January, Willy had got lax about checking on Max's whereabouts when she jumped rope. He was a burly man, and when the thong beat tellingly out of synch with the radio, the desk blocking the rec room door proved a feckless impediment. This time he didn't ask for the rope, but tore its handles from her hands, jerked open a window, and tossed the Everlast onto the snow-covered porch roof. In the draft, Willy clasped her arms and shivered. She chilled easily of late, though she'd always been hardy in the cold.

"Come with me." Hooking her collar like the scruff of a cat, Max hauled her downstairs, across the icy flagstones, and into the unattended health clinic in the next outbuilding. "Stand on that scale."

Willy did as she was told, and jumped. Maybe the needle was stuck.

"*Ninety-eight!* What is this shit? You should be one-ten! Tell me," Max snatched her T-shirt again, "are you throwing up? I told you at the outset, no eating disorders, Will. They *bore* me."

Willy wrenched away and stepped off the treacherous scale. It was obviously calibrated wrong. "I haven't puked since I was twelve," she said stiffly, tugging at her stretched-out collar.

"So you're just hopping it all away, are you?" Max taunted. "Why should I pay for a dishrag to go to Providence?"

"My game is in great shape, you said so yourself."

"But you're not. Your skin is the color of oatmeal. I hate oatmeal. Your hair has no luster. Your eyes are dull as frozen dogshit. We're going to pass on that wild card, kid, I'm not letting you go. Providence would be a disaster."

"Max, no! I've got to go!" Willy wailed, knowing full well that Max never made empty threats, never changed his mind, and was never moved a millimeter by petulance, promises, or imprecation. "After I've worked so hard! After all those exercises!"

"*I've* worked hard, too. It's cost me plenty time and money just to get that knee of yours to bend more than six degrees and bear more than five ounces. I don't go to that much trouble as a roundabout way of returning one of my players to the hospital. What the fuck are you trying to do, kill yourself?"

Glowering, Willy picked up a towel and smeared her face. "Some days that's an appealing idea."

Max grabbed her wrist, forcing her to look him in the eye. "Don't you *ever* say that. Not even as a joke."

She twisted her wrist from his grip. "Don't fret. I'm not the type."

"You are."

Willy snorted.

"Oh, fine, maybe not with razor blades," he jeered. "You may not like to hear this, but when I ran across you in Nevada your skills were way behind your potential. I snapped you up anyway because what you did have was power—a tenacity, a fire, a singlemindedness that's a lot harder to find than pretty forehands. But, Will, kiddo? Boomerang that power back in your own direction, it's gonna *take your head off.*"

SIXTEEN

For the next six weeks, even with his students returned, Max didn't let Willy out of his sight. No more rope, no more treadmill, no more line sprints. Two hours of practice, end of story, after which he force-fed his diminished protégée until she felt sick. Meanwhile, Max remained adamant about Providence, which came and went. Ever after the name of that Rhode Island town, which means "divine guidance," would resonate with the suggestion that the gods were no longer leading Willy in the right direction.

Recuperation from overtraining brought new banes. For two months Willy hadn't menstruated at all. Max rescheduled her debut match to coincide with the return of Willy's period.

There are periods and periods. Her mother subscribed to the grin-and-bear-it school, and Willy had never been one to lay in bed to bleed. Sure, she'd played through them before, doping up with ibuprofen. But this one was a record-breaker for Willy's fourteen mutinous years of reproductive life. Standing straight to serve was an effort, and by the third game in the first set Willy had to request medical dispensation to dash to the locker room. It was embarrassing to explain her distress to the male umpire, but the tampon was soaked and oozing into her white overpants, and would soon bloom onto the dress. She took advantage of the break to vent her bowels, liquefied in the hormonal onslaught.

Five Advils hadn't made a dent in the cramps; her intestines were empty and gaseous. This was *only* her period, Willy recited, believing what she'd been taught: that because menstruation happens to all women (or perhaps because it happens to women) it was a trivial complaint. Still, the notion beckoned that if the same frivolous incapacity assaulted her unsuspecting husband, he would promptly check himself into a hospital.

The match was still close and went three sets, but an attack of vertigo in the tiebreak swirled Willy out of the first round like the flush of a toilet.

In her second attempt, Willy was playing fantastically well. All the spectators who approached her afterward agreed, sharing her outrage. Since Willy had entered a zone, she was playing the lines. But the difference between great tennis and punk tennis could come down to a single inch. Umpires distinguished between the two, since the days were long gone that an opponent could be relied upon to call shots fairly in the interests of good sportsmanship.

But maybe someone had slipped this umpire a C-note; maybe he didn't like her uppity attitude; maybe he was petty-power mad and abusing his clout out of sheer badness. All that was certain was that every time her shot was anywhere near the line the ump called, "*Fault!*" When her adversary's backhands bounced three inches deep, the squat, pudgy arbiter picked his nose.

Willy tried everything. Arguing, refusing to resume play— she'd learned all the gambits from ballgirling for McEnroe. Defiance dug the man in; badgered, he doubled his chin, which dimpled like a crumpet. Yet suffering injustice in stoic silence didn't soften his calls, either. The little toad, he couldn't hit a tennis ball himself if it were attached to his racket with a bungee cord.

When not even the small crowd's hisses shamed the ump, Willy had to aim so glaringly inside the court that she molly-coddled would-be winners into common returns. Although she *knew* the danger in this situation was not losing points but her temper, some information remains belligerently theoretical. Willy mumbled, "Don't let that worm get to you," to no avail. In the third set, when she was sick of babying the ball after having been in prime form at the outset, the umpire called even one of her safey-safey shots long and that was the limit. Willy blew a gasket and began to hit out.

Hit out in every sense. The umpire smiled, like an infant passing gas. When later that year Jeff Tarango walked out of Wimbledon over prejudicial line calls, Eric would be disgusted and Willy would acquire a new anti-hero.

Nevertheless, only as her third tournament approached did Willy begin to feel well and truly cursed. She and Max had allowed two nights before the match in Ocala for Willy to get acclimated to the baking Florida sun. Through the first evening's dinner, her lips tingled. "So you'll have a cold sore," she growled in the bathroom mirror that night. It always seems bigger to you than to the rest of the world, and it will go away.

Except this particular outbreak was bound to seem pretty goddamned big to the rest of the world. Tossing that night, Willy kept licking her lips and rubbing them together; they were hot, and itched ferociously. The area of irritation was so vast that she wondered if she'd eaten something to which she was allergic.

Rinsing her face the next morning, Willy lifted her head to glance in the mirror and gasped. Her whole mouth had exploded. Two patches of tiny raging blisters had invaded her chin.

"Good God."

"Oh, *Max*," Willy wailed. "Shut the door!"

Willy insisted they order breakfast from room service. Max took the tray from a bellboy while she hid in the john.

"Will, dear," Max intoned when the boy was gone. "You can't play tennis from the crapper."

"I won't show my face until you buy me some makeup."

Max obliged, but commercial makeup has its limitations, especially applied to a surface with a life of its own.

"It's turning into bubble-wrap!" Willy cried from the mirror, from which she could not be parted.

"Will, we've got to go practice."

"I'm not leaving this room."

"You are tomorrow, kid."

It was out of the question to attempt a last-minute withdrawal because of cold sores. The WTA would consider the ailment spurious, and slap her with a fine.

Forlornly the next morning Willy spent another five minutes examining the damage. By now the sores were suppurating. Makeup only made matters worse. Resigned, Willy dabbed off her dripping paint job, donned dark glasses, and moped down-stairs. At the taxi stand, a teenage boy pointed, "Hey, VD lips!" and sniggered.

Unfortunately, you cannot play a tennis match with your head in a paper bag. Though the sores were painful, nothing about a face like boiling marinara should have technically hampered her game. But above all tennis may measure confi-dence, of which Willy had zilch.

When Willy shook hands with the victor at the net, the girl whispered, "That happened to me once. I couldn't have hit a beach ball. I just wanted to go home. I heard you were terrific. Better luck when that clears up."

It was the sweetest thing that any opponent had ever said.

Meanwhile? Eric didn't get periods, Eric never got a cold sore, and if Eric had any problem with umpires it was that they fell in love with him.

No, Eric was frolicking about the globe collecting computer points in his basket like a kid picking up Easter eggs on a hunt he was too old for. But they had both concurred that another five-month estrangement was no-go. Tallying the expenses of his last departure, Eric adjudged that for his phone bill he might have flown home twice. He promised to space his tournaments more widely, and play fewer per year. More magnanimity from the well-endowed, which Willy yearned to return in kind.

But Willy didn't need to be magnanimous. She managed to be home all the time. Organizing a tournament schedule, you had to decide whether to allow for success. Satellites took up to three weeks, and required as many for advance registration. Defeated in the first round, after one day you were footloose. The alternative was to assume you'd lose early and double-book. But if you planned on losing there was no point in entering in the first place. Consequently, Willy allowed the usual three weeks between tournaments, then post-calamity had most of the month on her hands.

Though she could always head to Sweetspot to groove strokes, training was no substitute for the taut schedule of the journeyman on a roll—when you sweep off from the finals to grab your bags at the hotel, lunge into a taxi and tell the driver to step on it like in the movies, weave through other passengers at a jog to arrive panting at the departure lounge, where the plane is already boarding, and buckle up as the turbines rise in pitch. Sure it was tiring, sure you got fed up with hotel coffee the color of chicken broth, but Willy missed the grind; she even missed moaning about it. Because lately Willy packed (unheard of) the day before a tournament and arrived at the airport an hour ahead of takeoff like all the other saps who believed what the airline told them over the phone. And she was never in a motel long enough to make much of a fuss about the coffee.

Ticketing was expensive. Each time she lost early her reservation had to be changed, and that cost; what she now owed Max Upchurch Willy shuddered to contemplate. She might have taken the odd day to explore the country, but once she'd lost in a city it was spoiled. In that event Willy was free to play the happy homemaker if she liked, though the one afternoon she did go buy new curtains she was too depressed once back home to thread them on the rods.

Coinciding with Eric's return for a breather in late April, a phone call from *Tennis* magazine was not unwelcome. Willy wasn't a publicity maven; even *Slick Chick's* replacing her in its spread hadn't broken her heart, except inasmuch as it emblemized that unprecedented choke in the Chevrolet. But the season had been so catastrophic so far that Willy was relieved to be popping up on their screens at all, and readily agreed to an interview.

"Why you?" asked Eric distractedly, rewinding the Borg–McEnroe final, now flecked from constant replay.

"Has it become that surprising that anyone would be concerned with my career?"

"Don't be so touchy. I was only wondering what the peg was."

"They didn't say." Willy smiled wanly. "Maybe they're doing an article on herpes simplex, and I set some kind of record." Three full weeks later, the sores had not healed in the centers, and gray, shadowy scars etched her chin.

The journalist, Jeremy Roman, was fresh-faced, squeaky-clean, and sporty.

"You play yourself?" she asked idly, showing him a chair. It seemed chivalrous to solicit the interviewer when she was structurally the center of attention.

"Strictly amateur." He waved his hand. "I'm a hack."

She sensed he was proud of his game. "I forgot. Most pros couldn't spell *t-e-n-n-i-s*, much less write for it."

Roman chortled, and Willy settled on the couch, spreading one muscular calf across the other shin. She'd worn a simple sundress and bright leather pumps. She might have frumped to the door in sweats, but Willy, still recovering from "VD lips," was glad for an excuse to look alluring. Besides, he might want a picture.

"So, just to warm up," the reporter began, placing his microcassette on the coffee table and arranging a pad on his knee. "What's your husband's favorite food?"

Willy's hand draped her knee at an elegant angle, her back sinking in the pillows. "Broiled chicken and fried rice."

Jeremy scribbled on his pad.

"I'm partial to plain chicken myself."

The journalist wrote nothing.

"This is pertinent?" Willy inquired.

"Oh, we just need color. And when did you two meet?"

"Almost three years ago. The first day, Eric—that's my husband—swept me off my feet. Literally. Though I was warned off marrying a tennis player, I obviously didn't take the advice."

Jeremy turned up the level on his machine. "The people who told you not to marry a tennis player—so far, have they been right?"

Willy drummed her fingers on her other arm. She was uncertain how honest to be with a reporter. The question was doubly difficult because she wasn't sure what an honest answer was. "Of course there are tensions..."

"Such as?"

She chewed her lip, playing with the last little cold sore scab. There were tensions that a faithful wife was not to mention. Like the *tension* that the bastard was outdistancing her on the tour by a mile. That was supposed to be swell. Go team. All for one and one for all. The taste on her lip went salty; in dabbing a tissue to the spot Willy pressed herself to keep her mouth shut. "We rarely see each other."

"For the record, how old are you two?"

"Eric's a year younger than me. I'll be twenty-six next month," she said firmly. "That sounds old, I know. But I don't think the game is benefiting from the trend toward younger stars. They don't have the emotional resilience to handle the tour. You've got to be able to hunker down. Frankly, you need the courage to fail. To survive injuries, bad patches, and still land on your feet. That requires guts and resolve—not to mention patience—that most teenagers don't have. If you look at the history of the really young phenoms, as soon as they encounter adversity, they crumble."

Willy assumed the man's squiggling was to remind himself to transcribe this section of the tape. But readjusting on the sofa, she noticed that he was doodling daisies in his margins.

Oh, maybe the microcassette tempted her to pontificate. But could she be blamed for holding forth, after three tournaments in a row sent her home, tail between her legs, after the first round? To bask in this no-account's attentions was irresistible. Already the air filled her lungs more richly, her shoulders squared, and for the first time in months she felt beautiful. No one had shoved a microphone in Willy's face in nearly a year.

Having blackened the centers of his daisies, Roman noticed that she was finished. "When you learned of the award, how did you feel?"

"Award?" asked Willy blankly.

Award! Willy racked her brains to imagine for what she might be singled out this of all years. Most Star-Crossed Paid-Up WTA Member Who Has Not Jumped off a Bridge? Willy didn't care; she'd take it.

"Most Impressive Newcomer of the Year," said Roman impatiently.

"*Newcomer*, but I—"

"It was announced six weeks ago, and we just haven't had the space to..."

Having begun to scissor her other leg on top, Willy let the calf back down. "Oh," she said heavily. "Eric's award."

"Didn't your husband tell you?"

"Of course he did," Willy assured the journalist, hoping her face had not turned too bright a red. "It's just that Eric wins so much lately, it's hard to keep it all *straight*." Willy uncrossed her legs and crossed her arms instead. "What is the purpose of this interview, would you mind telling me?"

"Sorry, thought I explained on the phone. We do dozens of profiles, and they get kind of monotonous. So we thought we'd take a new angle, and interview the wife this time, get the woman's perspective, you know? Like, what are some of the stresses of holding down the fort when your husband's on the road? When he's back, do you hit the town, or after all that hotel fare does he really look forward to a home-cooked meal?"

"Maybe you'd better get this rolling, Mr. Roman. I have a practice game at four-thirty across town."

"Say, that's a good detail. You play tennis, too?"

The practice game had been a lie. Once she'd finally pushed Jeremy Roman out the door, Willy kicked off her pretty shoes and yanked the bobby pins from her hair. Roman hadn't wanted a picture after all. Slumping on the couch and crumpling her summer dress, Willy aimlessly flipped through the *Times*. The "A" section had run another feature on the First Lady. Hillary's health-care reform bill had been shit-canned. She was widely regarded as having botched it. White House advisors had prescribed a more muted role. The president's wife now made only a few modest appearances. Her new blouses tied in bows at the chin. When she accompanied her husband abroad Mrs. Clinton gathered hen parties for tea and sandwiches. She gave speeches on women's issues—day care and child-rearing. Hillary had started her own newspaper column, which eschewed politics for household hints. The *Times* had reprinted the First Lady's favorite recipe for oatmeal cookies. Eyes small and black as raisins, Willy clipped it out.

The door slammed. Hair still wet from showering at Jordan, Eric poked his head in the kitchen. "Why are you banging pots?"

"To make dinner."

"Fuck that. Let's go out."

"I can't afford to go out."

"My treat." Eric took the pan off the stove and poured the water down the sink. "What's this Hamburger Helper crap? I thought the interview this afternoon would put you in a good mood."

"Right, humiliation always cheers me up." Willy filled the pan with water again, and brisked to the cutting board to whack an onion in half. She wasn't adept in the kitchen in the best of times, which tonight wasn't. The knife sliced the tip of her finger. The exposed white onion tinged pink, darker between layers, where the blood coursed to each end. Damn it. The onion juice stung like fury, but the injury wasn't serious and the last thing Willy wanted was a lot of dither over a stupid cut. That kind of pity was cheap, and this evening she was disinclined to let Eric off quite so lightly.

"With that look in your eye, you've no business playing with knives." Eric hustled her out of the kitchen. He didn't notice the cut, and sat her down on the sofa. "Now, tell me what happened."

She hadn't bound it with a napkin, so the finger kept oozing, dripping silently on the white upholstery. It hurt. It hurt a lot, actually, but a sharp stabbing sensation at every beat of her heart seemed apt. "Why didn't you tell me about winning the ATP's Most Impressive Newcomer Award?"

"Oh, that." Eric waved his hand exactly as Jeremy Roman had, in dismissing the tennis aptitude that the reporter was secretly smug about. "Just a statistical thing. Which player new to the tour advanced the highest number of rankings over a year. The computer spit my name out. It doesn't mean anything."

"It means enough to *Tennis* magazine to do a profile on you. From the wife's perspective, of course. So she could coo and prate on your behalf."

Eric rubbed his eyes. "Nuts."

"*Why didn't you tell me?* Have I made you ashamed of your own accomplishments? Or are there so many awards coming in that some of them slip your mind?"

"Honey, I knew how you'd react."

Willy stood up, leaving a rich stain on the couch ribbing.

"How's that?"

"Willy, your hand—!"

"Never mind my hand. How would I react?"

"Let me see that—"

She whipped the finger away from him, spattering the Plexiglas table. "*How?*"

"You'd get mad! Look at you now!"

"Yes, I'm mad now, because I narrowly missed making myself look like a prize chump. I thought, absurdly it turns out, that that journalist wanted to talk about *me.*"

Eric busied himself wadding tissues, holding them out toward her finger.

"Typical," she taunted. "Tend some trivial cut instead of noticing where I'm really bleeding from!"

"Don't be melodramatic!"

"This is *drama,* not *melodrama.* Heard of it? No. You want to shove everything under the carpet. Your solution to becoming a big shot while I dribble off into oblivion is not to *mention* you've become a big shot. Just don't tell Willy about the award because she's so mean-spirited and envious that she'd throw a fit."

He threw the ball of tissues on the table. "I'm only trying to keep the peace."

"Whose peace? Which one of us is at peace?"

"Not me, that's for sure."

"I don't see why not. The crowds love you, you're making money, you're on your way! Why aren't you happy as a clam?"

"Because you're not."

"In other words, I'm ruining your life?"

"No, Willy, and I'm sorry about the confusion over that interview, but it's not my fault! And it's not my *fault* that I won an award, is it? That I'm a good tennis player? I'm supposed to feel creepy about that, like I'm doing something awful to you? Because that's the way you make me feel; every time I win a match it's as if I'm winning it to spite you."

"Sometimes I think you are," she said quietly.

"You're talking out of your ass, Willy, and *please* do something about that cut, it's driving me crazy."

Willy put the finger in her mouth and sucked.

"What is it that you want from me?" he shouted. "When I walk up to the baseline, what's going to make you happy? I have to do something, I can't just stand there. So even if I were to run my professional life wholly according to your whim, in consideration of your *feelings*, do I serve an ace or drill the ball into the net?"

A forthright answer ("drill the ball into the net") was unacceptable. "Don't be ridiculous."

"If my ranking goes down, too, that's not going to raise yours one single point, is it?"

"I just want a little sympathy—"

"I *have* sympathy. It doesn't seem to do you much good."

It didn't. "That journalist didn't even know I *played* tennis!"

"Whose fault is that? Why didn't you tell him?"

"It's my fault. My fault for having become a nothing. My fault for being ranked 696. That you feel badly now is my fault. Everything's my fault. You're perfect, you're good to me, you've become a dazzling athlete, everything's going your way except your hideous marriage. I'm probably the only mistake you've ever made in your whole life."

"Sweetheart, no." At last she let him wrap the tissues around her finger. "I've never regretted marrying you."

"What's happening to me?" she sobbed. "I love you, so why can't I act like it? Why am I so mean to you? That you can't even tell me when you win prizes? And I don't blame you! I want to be happy for you, but I can't! You're right, I just get mad, and it's horrible, I hate it. You come home and you've won another big match and this anger rises instantaneously in my throat like heartburn. And then I feel gross, gross to myself, bitter and ugly and twisted. How can you *stand* it?"

Eric pulled her into his arms and murmured, "I know it's hard to feel happy for me when you're not happy for yourself.

And I know you love me, because you do act like it, most of the time. But I can see how, when I come home, and things have gone great for me and rotten for you, well, I must make you worried on your own account. I know you feel excluded. I mean, no matter how I try to tell you it's your win, too, you don't believe that."

Willy's chest shuddered. "You wouldn't buy that 'it's your win, too' stuff if it were the other way around."

"No," Eric conceded with a smile, smoothing her hair, "probably not. So I guess you feel lonely. But you're not alone. And I doubt I could have ever come this far without your help. One of the things that gets me through the grind of the road is knowing I have you to come home to. If this tennis thing weren't something we were doing together, I might deep-six the whole tiresome business. But just try to remember that when I do win a tournament, or some nickel-and-dime ATP award, it's not something I'm doing *to* you, OK? I want your ranking to turn around as much as you do."

"Why can't I win anymore?" Willy whimpered into his shirt. "I used to be great! I used to feel great! Now I feel like a slug!"

"Sh-sh," he stroked her head. "You've had crummy luck. You're in a slump. You'll pull out. It's a bad time. You'll see, in the end all these travails will make you stronger. You'll look back on this year and be proud that you didn't give up. It's just a bad time," he whispered again. "A slump."

As if to embody the metaphor, Willy went slack in his arms.

SEVENTEEN

A CAREER IN DECLINE, as opposed to ascent, rarely obliges with cathartic event. Failure is apt to be marked by what doesn't happen. True, a few lives do yield up turning points: the day a banker is arrested for embezzlement, the Tuesday in November a politician loses what the party has agreed will be his last Senate race. But more typical is the career that sinks in a leisurely fashion, with no single cataclysm at which instance its custodian can take stock. Disappointments accrue—another promotion denied, a flutter of résumés "on file," a dusty accumulation of "we had many applications this year" postcards referencing prizes gone to strangers or (worse) to someone you know, and whom if you did not dislike before now do. But no single catharsis provides for the venting of great grief; instead, many little griefs preempt a moment of reckoning. Always, promise beckons—a want ad, an untried contest, a friend's advice, a fresh attitude on waking Saturday. *Mere setback,* a voice whispers. *A fallow period, adversity to overcome.* As Eric would say? *A slump.* Bingo, you're seventy.

As professions go, tennis allowed more reckonings than most. Besides confronting the outcome of matches themselves, players shuttled a published hierarchy of who's who. Still, more tournaments continually beckoned. A pristine year on the computer enticed another go. Quick-fix solutions tantalized: a new racket, redoubled jogging, a switch from power to finesse. Until at least the knell of thirty you could deceive yourself.

It was consequently difficult for Willy Novinsky to get her hands on her own despair. Careers are prone to total in slow motion, like a car crash that takes decades; the phone never rings in the middle of the night. A blighted aspiration has all the earmarks of a missing persons case: nothing certain, no date to circle on the calendar when catastrophe occurred, just an absence, going on and on, and the front door stays shut. Failure is one long no-show, a surprise party when the guest of honor stands you up; a *Great Expectations* with unraveled lace and a cake full of rats. When should Willy stop waiting for opportunity to knock? And when she'd waited this long, why not one more day, and another after that?

Naturally, like the night Willy cut her finger, there were scenes. In fact, they grew monotonous: the tears, entreaties, accusations, the streaking to the sofa with the bedspread in tow. Eric's ritual pleading to come back to bed developed a weary trace of sarcasm. For her husband could only recite trite, impotent platitudes that might have been lifted wholesale from *The Little Engine That Could*. Willy would deride his counsel to "believe in herself" as bland and simplistic. Eric would bunch on his side with all the blankets, but neither of them would sleep.

Willy didn't blame him for getting bored. She was constantly sounding the same alarm—*I'm foundering, this is killing me, anything that kills me kills us.* But the alternative was to be lulled complicitously into Eric's contented domestic fiction: that they were an industrious two-career couple, each with their own tournaments to play, careful to arrange a week out of six to trudge famished hand-in-hand to Flower of Mayonnaise for the broiled chicken. In truth they were easing over a dark maw, as if the floor of the 112th Street apartment were wafer-thin and with too heavy a tread they would plunge a story. By the spring of 1996 their stereo plug had developed an erratic connection. Eric was too busy to fix it, Willy too lethargic. Every time one of them stepped on or near the cord the music stopped. They had literally begun to tiptoe around their own home, lest the tinkle of normalcy cut abruptly off.

"Wilhelm, pour us another round of your dee-licious ice tea, will ya?" Gary Sidewinder routinely helped himself to her nickname, deploying the Germanic *V* and its aura of mock obedience, as he likewise helped himself to Willy's husband.

The two men were brainstorming around the dinner table, surrounded by the dog-eared *ATP Rulebook* and registration blanks, the phone at hand to explore another permutation of the spring's airline schedule. Sidewinder had set his glass on bare wood, and condensation was bleaching a white ring on the table. To Willy, who replaced the highball on its coaster, this carelessness was typical. Gary was accustomed to other people taking care of details. He was a middleman, a delegator; in other words, a parasite. He did nothing that Eric couldn't do for himself besides pander to her husband's vanity.

Which Eric was fully capable of fostering as well, except that a pushy advocate allowed her husband his fabled modesty. Humility, like magnanimity, was a luxury of the prosperous. When Willy affected the same unassuming air, it came off as low self-esteem.

"Nah, you don't want to stay in that fleabag," Sidewinder advised. "The Hilton in Tokyo is top-drawer."

Gary Sidewinder was Eric's agent. He dressed like Tom Wolfe: white suits, sea-green tie, jade cuff-links, and sea-green socks, set off by a canary button-down and topped, when donned at the door, with a Panama. But Sidewinder relied on hirelings—dry-cleaners, bellboys who'd have his suit pressed within the hour. Accordingly, his tie was spattered with salad dressing, and the white jacket was badly creased. He appeared less dapper than once well-heeled and down on his luck. Since

Gary always looked as if he needed a wash, maybe he couldn't get anyone else to shower for him.

"Speaking of accommodations, Slick, ever think of moving out of these digs?" Sidewinder was recommending. "Mean, this apartment's got a cramped, graduate-student feel. Like you expect jug wine and fish sticks in the kitchen. With your income, you could shift into a doorman building in the eighties..."

Willy had never had an agent. Oh, she understood what Gary was for: to negotiate with the ATP over which tournaments her husband would deign to play, to haggle down fines (as if the well-bred Eric Oberdorf would ever do anything censure-worthy on court), and, of course, to lure sponsors. Gary was an instrument of the *family* interests.

"Gotta say, I wondered if you shouldn'ta gone for the Slams last summer," Gary declared. "But the way your points stack up now, I figure you made the right move. Even if you scraped through the qualies, players have an *attitude* about qualifiers. That puts you at a disadvantage. Lotta tennis is psychological in my book..."

Duh, thought Willy, rubbing butter into the white ring.

"This year," the agent went on, "is your peach for the picking, my man. Just get to the quarters of the Italian again and you'll stick at a solid 75. That's in the running. Makes for a superior mind-set. Gotta watch yourself in the Slams. Go down in an early round, and from then on that event has a bad smell—"

"Willy's the one who advised me not to go for the Slams last year," Eric interrupted.

"Wilhelm's got smarts."

"Willy knows a lot about tennis, Gary."

"Sure she does," Sidewinder purred.

"I've thought of writing a book," Willy quipped on the way back to the kitchen. "A sequel to Brad Gilbert: *Losing Ugly*. Three hundred individual tips on how to throw a match to your grandmother with cerebral palsy."

"Kids with cerebral palsy don't usually live to be grandmas, sweetheart!" Sidewinder called after her. "The question is *which* Slam." They'd talked this out a dozen times, but Sidewinder loved saying *Slam*. "You're most at home on hardcourt. Down Under's Har-Tru now, but that's behind us—and I can respect, I mean *respect*, that you wanted to take January instead to work on your marriage. Besides, lots to be said for initiating a bright-lights career in your own country. I don't see there's two ways about it. It's the U.S. Open or bust. Leaves you all summer to gear up. You given any more thought to getting a coach?"

"Nah," said Eric. "I've got my wife."

"He has this proprietary swagger because he 'discovered' you," Willy growled when Gary was gone. "As if you'd never gotten anywhere until you signed with Pro-Serve. He tells you where to stay, what to eat, and meanwhile he treats me like room service. He's a leech, and I wish you'd get rid of him."

"I know Gary's a little oily—"

"A *little?*"

"But I'd never have been able to pull in sponsorships by myself at my ranking."

"At *your ranking*," Willy mimicked, whisking lunch dishes from the table. "As if 75 were shameful. I hate when you little-ole-me. It's so fake."

"75 is a long way from giving autographs." Eric bustled to help with the plates. "It was Gary who conned those companies into investing in an up-and-coming instead of another up-and-been. They're small sponsorships, too, but they do line our coffers."

"They line *your* coffers."

"Fine, have it your way. The money's all mine, you can't have a dime." Eric's latest tactic was to acquiesce.

Willy sloshed Sidewinder's undrunk tea down the sink.

"I wish you wouldn't run yourself down around him," Eric mumbled.

"Aren't you attractively self-deprecating? You 'can't give auto-graphs'?"

"No, that stuff about *Losing Ugly*. It's different."

"You bet it's different. I genuinely give myself a hard time, and your meekness is a fraud."

Eric lingered in the doorway, absorbing her spittle like a sponge. The last year had taught him passive forbearance. "What do you think about aiming for the Chevrolet again?"

"Why would *you* play the Chevy?"

"I meant you, stupid."

"No, even a training-wheels tournament like the Chevy—which you wouldn't touch now with a ten-foot pole—'stupid' can't get into anymore."

"You could play the qualies," Eric suggested.

"You won't even play the qualies for a Grand Slam!"

"My opting out of the Big Four last year was your idea."

"Which was probably dumb," said Willy, loading their new dishwasher. "If it hadn't been for me you could have taken the ATP by storm a year ago. You could have snubbed Gary and his travel agents because you'd be tooling around in your own private jet."

"Bullshit, you were dead right. Better to take my time, get a handle on the level below—the German, the Italian. And it worked. I'm in a much better position this year... So what do you say? About the Chevy?"

"Oh, please stop condescending to me!" She broke the iced tea glass, but they could now afford to replace it with a hundred more. "I'm ranked 864! I know that, I recite the number to myself at night like counting sheep. But I didn't *used* to be a nonentity, so I know the ropes; I can run my Tinkertoy schedule by myself. I wish you wouldn't be so fucking *solicitous*."

"What, I should run on about my plans all the time, ignore your career?"

"What career?"

"There's no talking to you when you get like this. Forget it."

Eric retreated to the living room and slid in a CD. (Though

Willy had made do with a cassette player for years, they now owned three hundred silver Frisbees.) When Willy tromped out for the last lunch dishes, she disturbed the wire again, and the Sibelius ceased abruptly midchord.

"Really," Eric appealed a last time. "Your advice last spring was right on target. I'd have gotten nothing in the Slams but abuse. This year we'll do great."

We'll do great, will *we*? Women must have some genetic predisposition to hiding out in kitchens. Willy rested her forehead on the wet counter. Sure she'd talked Eric out of breaking down the gates of the All England last year. But not because Eric wasn't ready. Willy wasn't ready. And the long, strenuous discussion had produced nothing but delay. Willy still wasn't ready. She never would be.

The next morning Willy was jangled awake by the phone. She didn't set her alarm for 6 A.M. anymore. There didn't seem much point.

As she groped for the receiver, Eric's long arm pinned her to the mattress. "Hello? Right, Gary…Chump change, but doesn't hurt. Free shades, anyway. Thanks."

When he hung up, Willy growled through the cord dragged in her face, "You assume it's for you."

"Wasn't it?" asked Eric, getting up. He was fond of facts, and used them to protect himself from what they meant.

"Move the phone to your side of the bed, then," Willy grumbled, grabbing the set. "You're right, it's always for you. Another company offering you an electrolyte contract. A tournament director dangling a guarantee—" She gave the phone a yank, and the jack popped from the wall.

Eric picked up the jack and stuck it stoically in the socket. "You broke it," he announced calmly. "The plastic tab snapped off."

"Buy another one. You're rich." Willy grabbed her clothes. Lately she felt uncomfortable when Eric saw her naked.

"I'm not rich. For the first time I'm making a living wage. That doesn't mean you can start smashing things up. For once what you've broken doesn't cost much," he lectured with Daddyish self-control, "but the repair will be a hassle."

"Don't worry, I'll end up taking care of it. Just like I buy all the groceries, and vacuum, and take out the garbage, and clean the toilet—"

"I've said we could get a maid."

"You've got a maid!"

The polarity widened; it always widened. The more mature reserve her husband marshaled, the more childish Willy became. If anything, awareness that she was being puerile made her more so, from the same punitive strategy she employed at her blackest on the court: hitting an even ghastlier shot as fitting reprisal for the gaffe that preceded it. For no matter how disgusted Eric became with Willy's petty invective and hypersensitivity, Willy was far more disgusted with herself. Since additional disgraceful behavior seemed appropriate penance for disgraceful behavior, her tantrums tended to snowball.

Banging about the apartment, Willy concluded that Gary was right, the place had got cramped. The foyer now spilled two dozen rackets—all, barring Willy's three Pro-Kennex frames, gratuities from Eric's sponsor. How distant the era of one treasured, beloved trusty—like the Davis Imperial, whose wooden laminate she'd lavished with lemon oil as a child, neurotically ramming the frame in its press the moment a game was over. In the old days there was no such thing as *one of my rackets.* When she'd recently come upon the battered Imperial in the Walnut Street attic it had looked doleful—once so faithful, now abandoned, like a sidekick in grade school who gets dumped when you become popular in junior high. The small face and arcanely tight throat had dated all out of proportion to its time. These days Willy would no more play a match with the Imperial than drive to the court in a horse and buggy.

But Eric's state-of-the-art freebies were impersonal and interchangeable. He was like a man with too many friends, who wouldn't notice when one or two didn't call for a year. Willy might have filched one, but they were all the wrong grip size, intensifying her awareness that her husband's bounty had not fallen to her own hand. Eric's rackets collected at his feet, begging for the privilege of being played with, and she had come to disdain them as she might human sycophants.

The Plexiglas coffee table had long ago topped up with used balls, and the floor rolled with plastic cans. Eric brought his discards home for Willy, but the ambiance of his rejects was distasteful, like one-night stands thrown over for fresher game.

And the clothing! How Willy missed his threadbare shorts and limp socks draped over the radiators, the stench of cut-rate sneakers reeking from under chairs. How she had loved to nuzzle her cheek against his flanneled three-for-ten-dollars T's. Nowadays? Eric sent out his laundry: collared knits with loud logos and clever underarm netting for air. Even Eric admitted the designs were hideous, but he was paid for wearing them.

Willy glugged boiled water into the *cafetière*, and plunked it, sloshing, on the dinner table. As the coffee steeped, Willy left to wrench the bedclothes in order, leaving Eric barricaded behind the *Times*. She shot a cool glance at the dusty line of tournament trophies over her bureau. They were arranged in chronological order, from the cheap chrome figurine of the Montclair Country Club Championship to gaudier chalices, cups, and crystal bowls. Two years before Willy had anticipated adding a third shelf, but the few recent additions were the dwarf sort for semis or quarters. Midget achievements had fit easily on the remaining board.

As she stooped to tuck the sheet under the mattress, a glaring neatness nagged the corner of her eye.

Eric had never built his own display shelf. He'd piled his trophies on his dresser higgledy-piggledy, though he was a tidy man. The overflow had lined the baseboard; Willy was prone to trip on the clutter of her husband's success.

"*Eric!*"

He took his time. "What now?" he asked warily from the doorway.

"What have you done with them?"

"Done with what?"

"Your trophies. They used to be all over the place, and now your dresser is crowded with exactly one comb."

He shrugged. "Too junky."

"You didn't throw them out?"

"Probably should have. But as you're ever eager to point out, I'm too conceited for that, so I stuffed them in the closet." As if to emphasize this renewed concern with order, he whisked up a wad of socks and stuffed them in the hamper. She didn't know why he bothered with laundry anymore. With several unopened cartons from sponsors beneath the bed, he had enough new clothes to use them once and throw them away, like tennis balls.

"Besides," Eric noted, carting two more pairs of shoes—gels and air-pumps, with fuchsia and aqua stripes—to the closet, "those trophies are garish."

"If you think they're kitschy or boastful, I should take mine down, too."

"No, don't!" Eric cried as she stretched for the Montclair Country Club Championship and tossed it on the bed. "Those are history!" Hastily he revised, "I mean, they're precious."

"Because they're an endangered species?"

"Because they're yours." Eric returned the chrome figurine to its place. Flakes of waning silver came off on his hands. Willy pushed him out of the way and rose on her toes, toppling the New Freedom trophy with her fingertips. The bowl nicked the dresser and clunked onto the carpet.

"You're being infantile!"

"I'm being adult for once," she countered. "Why keep my trophies in view and yours with the shoes? All those shoes?

You're the one treating me like a kid, wanting to magnet my drawings to the refrigerator."

Defeated, Eric allowed, "Put yours away, too, then. But I thought you were proud of them."

"I was. But now they mock me. You're right, they're history. I'm too young to live in the past."

Resolutely, Willy edged two cups forward and pitched them on the mattress. Likely pained by watching Willy crane her neck, her six-three husband laid a hand on her shoulder and removed them himself. Eric lined the tributes lovingly in order on the bed, then insisted on shrouding each in tissue paper and wedging the mementos into stiff cartons left over from a shipment of shirts. While he packed, Willy glanced in the closet and her heart melted. Eric had tumbled his own trophies, unwrapped, into a battered, open-topped box.

"Underwood?" she asked timidly, vowing to make fresh coffee; by the time he was finished, the pot would be cold. "If you were married to somebody else—like, a real homemaker, or some insurance executive, or another super-successful player—would you stuff your trophies away like this, as if they were dirty secrets?"

"Of course," he said gruffly. "They're vulgar."

"Then mine are, too—"

Eric crushed a sheet of tissue and threw the wad on the bed. "They don't *mean* as much to me as yours do to you! Tennis doesn't mean as much to me. It's something I'm good at but I don't *love* it. And in no time I'll be too creaky to play professionally, I'll have to do something else, and that will be *fine*."

Willy looked at her hands. "Ironic, isn't it?"

"No, it's not. There's a connection. You want to be a champion too much. That's why you seize up. If you didn't care so damned much, you might get farther."

"Apathy is the answer?"

"No, but a dose of easy-come wouldn't hurt. A few extra-curricular pleasures."

"Like what?"

Eric gripped her shoulders and wheeled her to face him. "Like *me*."

Willy's faltering fortunes may have transformed her husband into one more affliction, but they had just as utterly revised her vision of herself. Characteristics that she'd once have considered fixed, impervious, revealed themselves as subject to the elements, like a hat in the rain. It transpired that confidence, for example, was not some inviolate trait, but the offspring of encouraging events, and therefore vulnerable to disaster. Willy had never thought of herself as quiet, but her voice had measurably ebbed—unless she was screaming—so that Eric had often to prod, "Pardon?" on long-distance calls. The tonality of her speech had musically transcribed to a minor key, and there was a tentativeness about her assertions that in another woman Willy would have found objectionably deferential. Certainly she had always adjudged herself energetic, yet now she slept unprecedentedly long hours, and rarely rallied the vigor to make it to the cinema. If on one of his dutifully scheduled weeks home Eric proposed a movie, she'd accede early in the day, but by nightfall, up against trooping out the door, would instead sag into a chair and claim, truthfully anyway, that she was tired. Though Willy had prided herself in the past on a cynical bite, she had always been, in regard to herself and the fineness of life in general, an optimist. Yet now that acerbic edge had flipped inward, carving graffiti on the walls of her head. While she'd have previously expected—maybe gullibly, stupidly expected— for matters to turn out well enough in the end, lately she gave intelligent credence to every new day's potential for catastrophe. It was an unwelcome education. She'd have given her eyeteeth to go back to being an idiot.

Effectively living with a stranger, she sometimes reminisced about Untrammeled Willy as she might have about a bosom buddy with whom she'd lost touch—her Davis Imperial. On the other hand, she was disillusioned with the joie de vivre her doppelgänger had exuded. Elation hadn't been intrinsic to Willy after all, but was the mere by-product of occasion. Wistfully Willy imagined the go-getter she'd be on a winning streak instead—consuming sports pages and tennis magazines; sharing gossip about boyfriend bust-ups in locker rooms; game for new ethnic cuisines, controversial plays, and late-night sneaks into locked motel pools. Now even were that mischief maker to return Willy would never quite trust the vivacity again. She'd cast an uneasy eye at her own springy step, so easily shuffled by a woeful tennis match. By the spring of 1996, Willy was forced to accept that a self was not an unassailable constant, but a ragbag accumulation of batterings and bolsterings, not only an agent but a consequence. Even happy people were victims of a kind.

For if taken as a lot the accomplished were buoyant and looked on the bright side, was their airy disposition to their credit? Why, there were days Eric had to *pretend* to be in a bad mood. Similarly, was it sheer coincidence that the disappointed were collectively misanthropic, distinguished by an aloof, smoldering abstention and a sadistic pleasure in bursting other people's bubbles? Torture subjects testified that the stalwart who could undergo any mutilation and keep his integrity was a 007 myth. At a point, every martyr cracked. Every damn one.

Meanwhile, the whole outside world disclosed itself as treacherously subjective. Neither good nor sinister, dull nor fascinating, luminous nor black, the exterior universe possessed no innate qualities, but was nightmarishly reliant on the grind of her interior lens. That the Boat Basin in Riverside Park would not, at least, remain a sublime and halcyon copse atrot with friendly dogs unnerved her, for the same Hudson walkway could transmogrify into a bleak and trashy strip, its dogs ratty and hostile, the vista of New Jersey grim and aggressively overfamiliar. Sweetspot as well could flip-flop overnight from tasteful clapboard haven to slick, elitist preserve for the spoiled

rotten. Willy resented having responsibility for the fickle
landscape outside her mind as well as in; there was no resort. As
the seafarer craves dry land, she yearned for anything ineluctable
and true, immutably one way or another. Instead Willy was
smitten with the awful discovery that even the color of a
lamppost was subject to her own filthy moods.

On single evenings in Riverside Park Willy remembered
herself. It would actually slip her mind that her ranking was on
the edge of oblivion, and personality, malleable or not, is among
other things a habit. If only because she had so often in the past,
Willy would swing Eric's hand and playfully corral him into the
river rail, bantering with garrulous lunatics while the sun
returned to its originally sumptuous vermilion and sank good-
naturedly into Hackensack. She could tell from the expression
on Eric's face that in such twilights she was pretty again, her
forehead smoothed out, the muscles around her mouth
loosened so that its corners lifted naturally like seabirds from
houseboats, her hair whipping free of its stern nylon tie. But
there was, in his eyes, a new element—of gratitude, of
mournfulness, as if he were seeing her from a long way off or
were gazing at youthful photographs of a lover since grown
haggard.

Willy might have been grateful herself for these respites,
which attested to the chemical impossibility of a misery that is
perfectly unremitting. Surely glimpses of the woman he'd fallen
in love with must have discouraged her husband from cutting
his losses and bolting for the door. But in a way resuscitation
was cruel—like the gift of an orange to a prisoner who would
return to bread and water, or the wickedness of a too-brief
remission in a terminal case.

The rudimentary fact of Willy's downfall overshadowed its
causes. But in the vast free time available to early-round rejects,
it was impossible not to ponder: what had gone wrong? Willy
could only surmise that she was defeating herself. This last year
her opponents had hardly to lift a finger; Willy was playing both

sides of the net. Whatever quantity that she once aimed outward now pointed in the opposite direction, as in Bugs Bunny cartoons where Elmer Fudd's blunderbuss is U-turned to explode in his face. Why she would wittingly warp the barrel of her own gun was another mystery, but a tennis career was too short to allow for the unraveling of the soul—as was, no doubt, any life. By the time you understood it, it was over. So Willy could only draw conclusions from the crude statistics: she was about to turn twenty-seven; she was ranked 864. Ergo, her career was finished.

Yet if personality is partly a habit, so is ambition. Mechanically, Willy continued to file applications to the lowly tournaments that would admit her. She took the train to Sweetspot, numbly tromped to practice, and ran six miles a day in an anesthetized haze. Faith in one's self has all the earmarks of religion, and is equally susceptible to crisis; Willy sleepwalked through the motions of aspiration as the lifelong churchgoer will continue to rouse and dress on Sunday mornings long after he's ceased to believe in God. If nothing else, she did not know what else to do with the day. She had set her sights from childhood on Flushing Meadow. Having charted no alternative destination, Willy continued to shamble in the same direction, like a downed pilot in the desert who hasn't a prayer of reaching civilization before he runs out of water, but who keeps slogging over dunes because the unthinkable alternative is to lie down in the sun and wait to die.

EIGHTEEN

THOUGH AWARE SHE WAS changing, on no single day did Willy look in the mirror to face an ogress, any more than an aging woman confronts on a particular morning, *I am old.* True, gratuitous smiles at shopkeepers and compliments to practice partners sprang less spontaneously to Willy's lips. But the nefariously gradual pace of her transformation allowed time to adapt. New Willy considered a couple of minor incidents that year with Eric merely strange. Old Willy would have found them sinister.

Back in January, when Eric had grandly forfeited the Australian Open to *work on his marriage*—a phrase that likened their relationship to the chore of filling out joint tax returns—he had asked her to post an application for Portugal's Estoril Open on her way to pick up bagels that morning. Willy had tucked the envelope in her parka and slogged a block up Broadway to Mama Joy's. In the aftermath of the blizzard of '96, great bluffs lined the walk.

Maybe the extraordinary arctic vista had been distracting. It wasn't until the snow had melted, refrozen, and turned black in February that Willy encountered the creased envelope still snug in her parka. She peeled open the flap, to discover that Estoril's due date had passed. Nervously, Willy buried the application in 112th Street's basement trash cans. The Portuguese cup was worth $100,000.

"Damnedest thing," Eric informed her long-distance in March. "I called the Estoril today, and they never received my application."

"That's strange," she said, pulse thumping. Was she that far gone? Had she forgotten her errand accidentally-on purpose? "Maybe something went wrong with the mail."

"Ironically, I was calling to get out of it. I'd originally wanted practice on clay, but Gary and I are having second thoughts about the French. Meanwhile I've been offered a wild card from Key Biscayne—more money, more points, hardcourt. It's lucky the application got lost, because the fine for late withdrawal in Portugal was outrageous."

Willy felt a pang. Key Biscayne was one of the two coed international events that Max had mentioned long ago, and now there was no way she and Eric were entering together. "That's wonderful, sweetheart," she said faintly. "You just can't lose."

He didn't. It was largely thanks to Key Biscayne that Eric advanced to 75.

The second incident was less ambiguous. The day Eric came home in April, he schlepped in the door with a terse, "I'm back." Dumping his bags, he went straight to the refrigerator and rattled its empty drawers. "Willy!" he barked into the fridge. "All my clothes reek. Take my laundry in, will ya?"

He stalked out of the kitchen and selected three rackets, propping them on the doorjamb. "I've got a practice game at Forest Hills later this afternoon," he announced. "I'll come by later and pick up my stuff. For now my legs are killing me from those shitty economy-class seats, and I'm going to Jordan to jump rope."

"Right away?" Willy asked in incredulity. "You haven't been home for five minutes."

"Some *home*," he groused, standing in the doorway. "You know, I've been on the road for six weeks. I come back, there's not so much as a crust of bread for lunch, and this place is a pigsty."

The door slammed. So much for how-are-you-honey, much less let's-get-reacquainted-in-the-bedroom. Cramped transatlantic flights may have made Eric crabby, but being treated like dilatory hotel staff made Willy far crabbier. She glowered at the battered leather duffels, tattered with torn routing tickets to London, Frankfurt, and Tokyo. So she was supposed to paw through his stinky sports clothes? Think again, buster.

In the foyer, his rackets peered back at her with prim expressions, awaiting the return of Master. Though their covers were sumptuously padded, the pampered Princes now lay at the mercy of their governess. Willy had always treated her own rackets with respect, never thrashing them to pieces against a fence as Andre Agassi had done with no fewer than forty rackets a year in his youth. But Eric had bought a wire cutter to replace the plug on the stereo and hadn't got around to the repair; it seemed profligate to invest in an implement never put to profitable employ.

She unzipped the top Prince; it cowered. Working the blades of the wire cutter into the sweet spot inspired all the murderous glee of slipping a knife into human gut. They were expensive strings. With a snip the whole frame shuddered. At first the grid remained intact, as a stabbing victim might remain standing a moment before pitching forward to the pavement. After a minute, however, the center of the face subtly loosened, quivered, and unraveled like the composure of the mortally wounded. She zipped it back in its body bag.

Quickly, she did the other two accomplices and arranged the rackets back in order.

"Can you believe," said Eric on his return from his match, "that all three of my rackets had busted strings?"

"All *three?*" Willy marveled.

"Plane pressure, temperature change—"

"I guess you couldn't play."

"I borrowed a spare off Leonard. In fact, I fell in love with his Wilson. When my racket contract is up for renewal in August, I'll have Gary approach Wilson instead."

She had indulged mindless, fruitless vandalism, but vandalism was by its nature fruitless, and for the first time Willy wholly understood young boys with dim prospects who took Louisville Sluggers to bus shelters.

Maybe Willy indulged the odd deviant behavior in an effort to make herself feel something, if only guilty. For repeated battering on the circuit had bludgeoned all her senses. Colors waned—vistas outside her Amtrak window appeared two-dimensional and faded, like poor landscape reproductions in cheap hotels. Samuel Barber's "Adagio for Strings," which once moved her to tears, now sounded tinny and thin—peevish, self-pitying, and lachrymose. When she had heaped curry onto chicken thighs, Eric leapt for water; Willy covered hers with cayenne and couldn't taste a thing. When she left the unlit oven turned on, she didn't notice; the gray choke of natural gas too well resembled what Willy smelled all the time. As for sex, it took ages to come. The protraction had grown embarrassing. Eric was a patient lover, but patience is not what any woman, in bed, aims to tax.

Yet it was on the tennis court that this flattening was most pronounced. Hardcourt green no longer lured with the permeable lushness of a meadow or sea, but looked painted and easily flaked to expose a raw, ashen composition. The dimensions of the court seemed smaller, like the house of your childhood visited when you were all grown-up. The once elegant lines of the game, winking with intrigue, now looked insipidly simple, like the hopscotch chalking of a dull girl.

The single stimulus that could always provoke a reaction of some kind was Eric Oberdorf. But despite the rare flood of self-annihilating adoration, itself not always welcome, Willy had to allow, as the summer of Eric's first Grand Slam approached, that if she added up all her feelings for her husband on a given day and divided them by the total, the average was dislike. It was frightening. Recognizing the distinctive, self-assured sweep of his stride from two blocks away, not so long ago Willy would have broken into a run, arms open. Now she was inclined to wait, irked at his swagger. Even little things that used to charm her, like the huge quantities of food he ate, now got on Willy's nerves; *she* could never devour all those carbohydrates without getting fat. Flashes of hastily regretted hatred were one thing, but this unblinking glare at the man who was supposedly the love of her life was wildly unfair, to both of them, and could not continue much longer.

If grown-up birthdays serve any purpose, they are for taking stock. On that milestone in May Willy demurred from attending Eric's second round at Forest Hills's Tournament of the Champions, and stayed home to brood on the alternatives for her future:

1. *The Mrs. Eric Oberdorf Option.*

Graciously Willy throws in the towel on her own career, devoting herself to the more prodigious talents of her husband. Eric advances rapidly to the Top Ten. He is pursued for presidential endorsements, harassed to play charity exhibitions, and paid to lend his name to the "Obie," a new Wilson racket. When her husband breaks Bjorn Borg's record for straight Wimbledon wins, Eric booms to the crowd how he could never have made it without the constant encouragement of his devoted wife. Willy beams.

On tour, she tries to be of use in little ways, unpacking in each hotel, ordering sandwiches, vetting calls. Other seasons she stays back at their mansion in California, for the children need one parent to stay put once in a while. For her own part, she sometimes plays a friendly doubles match with neighbors on the backyard court in Palo Alto, after which she pooh-poohs her disreputable performance and serves lemonade. But she never misses the Slams, and when the set gets tense the camera always seeks her out in the stands. At home on the couch, she has practiced leaping with delight at his final put-away volley in the fifth set, genuflecting and glancing heavenward like Brooke Shields.

2. *The Shrew Solution.*

Snipping Eric's racket strings dwarfs to small beer. Eric no longer stores his trophies in the closet but carts them to his parents' apartment, where they will be displayed with doting *oohs* and *ahs*, since the last time he arrived home with French Open crystal his wife shattered it with a sledgehammer. The "accident" was embarrassing, since the presentation trophy is on temporary loan to the winner for the year, and Eric had to pay for another to be specially cut. He has likewise learned not to take his wife on tour, because she stages abusive, drunken scenes in hotel lobbies. More than once she has been ejected by court security, booing and throwing bottles at her own husband at the seemly All England Club.

The closest Willy comes to hitting a tennis ball herself is kicking the damned thing out of the way when it's dribbled between the liquor cabinet and the TV. Fat, unkempt, foul-mouthed, and slanderous, Willy has become a serious liability for Eric's bid for the Senate when he retires. It doesn't look good, either, that they've had no children, though there's been little likelihood of kids. Eric has avoided his wife's bed ever since Willy was arrested for calling in a bogus bomb scare during his first U.S. Open final.

3. *The Absentee Wife Ploy.*

Too self-respecting to serenade as second fiddle and too weak-stomached for hard booze, Willy withdraws. She sleeps ten to twelve hours a day; her dreams are exotic. She reads novels set in Tahiti, or science fiction; she has left the planet. Her interior life is rich and ruminative, but from the outside she appears catatonic. She is pleasant but docile; Eric has to repeat himself several times before his wife responds, "Sorry?" Eric's career seems to be going well enough, but Willy couldn't say how well exactly. His results neither delight nor distress her; they no longer *apply*. She has exhumed her Davis Imperial from her parents' attic, and hits for hours against a backboard as she did as a child. She has given up flesh-and-blood opponents. If she cannot compete, she will not compete, and for years now Willy hasn't thought of herself in terms of other people at all.

If Eric does break Bjorn Borg's Wimbledon record or endorse presidential candidates, he can have the tinsel of celebrity with her blessing. Willy has ceded the spotlight. All that she asks in return is to be left alone.

She eats little or nothing, and her body has grown so ethereal that any day now she will be able to fly while she is still awake. It isn't that she has no feelings, but her emotions are pastel: bemusement, whimsy. She has no relations to people that she could not also have to objects. In bed, Willy is acquiescent; he is welcome to whatever he can lay hands on. If Eric wins or loses she murmurs, "That's nice, dear," or "That's too bad, dear," and sometimes she gets the appropriate responses mixed up. She functions, and doesn't appear a danger to anyone or to herself, but she's heard Eric quizzing psychiatrists in the study about whether his wife has lost her mind. In fact Willy has not lost it but crawled into it, and she likes it there.

"You left an option off the list. Try adding *Willy gets her act together*." So Eric had won at Forest Hills—he had that blithe, refreshed look.

Willy whipped the envelope from Eric's hands. On its back, an embellished scrawl listed, *1) Willy becomes a good little wifey, 2) Willy becomes a big bad wifey, 3) Willy becomes one of the disappeared*, and was heavily framed by dense, jagged scribbles.

There'd been no need for three alternatives; they all came down to the same answer: suicide. "That's none of your business."

"We're married. What happens to you is my business. *To* you," he mumbled, dropping his sports bag on the floor. "That's your problem, you let things happen *to* you."

"Every day I've got a different problem." Willy crumpled the envelope and free-threw it to the trash can. She missed.

"You're a great tennis player," he retrieved the balled paper and arced it into the can—a swish, "you're underachieving like fury, and the trouble is all in your head."

"Isn't that the ultimate terminal injury?" she asked calmly. "To my head?"

"Willy, you've said yourself that the difference between good and great players is character."

"So my flaws are central to my very nature," she elucidated matter-of-factly. "*Character* is the very definition of what you can't do anything about."

He threw up his hands. "Do you not *want* there to be a solution anymore? I swear, sometimes I think you enjoy wallowing in this! Like a pig in shit!"

Eric was breathing hard; he rarely permitted himself to insult her. Her husband's rare flash of anger freed Willy to remain sedate. The reserve had a delicacy; she could see how he'd acquired a taste for it. And she was more than happy for Eric to sample the grapes of wrath.

"That's right," she said quietly, folding her arms. "I enjoy being poky and disreputable; I lose for fun. The disparity in our performance is destroying our marriage, and I enjoy that, too."

"Nothing's 'destroying our marriage'! We said 'for better or for worse.' *I* meant it."

Oh, the phrase had echoed before. But long ago Max had been right: Willy had initially anticipated doing better to Eric's worse. This had been a day for fantasy futures, so a fitting one to admit what she'd foreseen at her wedding: Willy would rise to eminence. *She* would hit the international tour, *she* would endorse presidential candidates, *she* would have her agent to lunch. *Eric* would pour the tea.

Maybe the vision had been invidious, Willy reflected, a *Mrs. Eric Oberdorf* in reverse: Mr. Willy Novinsky. But one aspiration wasn't horrid. In her original pipe dream, Willy was consoling—and how she yearned for once to stroke his bowed head, to pour a stiff whiskey for her disconsolate partner. Surely it wasn't his dejection she wanted so much as a chance to play the foul-weather friend, the good woman on whose devotion he could rely when the world had turned its back. But the world never turned its back. He was a winner. They doted on him. She wasn't his Rock of Gibraltar, but a millstone around his neck. Willy couldn't remember the last time she bucked him up, cheered Eric with *You're a great tennis player*, and concocted strategies to turn his luck. She might well become a classic helpmate, if only sometimes she could be the voice of confidence when his own had fled, the bolsterer enfolding him in bed, reminding him (lying) that there's more to life than tennis.

It was sapping, always thinking one thing and saying another. "Better or worse?" she repeated, sinking to the sofa. "I guess I'd hoped to be the one to do better."

"And I would do worse?" Eric remained standing. To sit down was to resign himself to this conversation.

"I should say no, that I'd like us to do equally well. But parity is inequality waiting to happen." Willy confessed, "Honestly, I'd have preferred to keep the edge."

"You said I was good when we met. You should have trusted your own judgment. Why would you of all people marry a second-rate player? More to the point, why would you want to?"

"I'd have thought even a couple of years ago that I craved proper competition," she said dolorously, propping her feet on the Plexiglas table. "Now I think I'm not so grand as that. Maybe I'd do better with a husband who couldn't hit a ball in the court if his life depended on it."

"But my life *does* depend on it," he chided. "So I can't believe that you want me to fail. Not in your heart."

It was precisely this innocence of Eric's that Willy traded on daily. If he could visit her head for ten seconds, he would die.

"Willy, I don't like this situation any more than you do." Eric vigorously collected newspapers. "I will do *anything* to help you turn things around."

Willy faced the window. His persistent kindness was a torture. "You always get to be so sweet, and all I get to be is beastly."

The syntax was peculiar, except that Willy's experience of her marriage lately resembled having been dubbed the ugly stepsister in the school play. And the only alternative to being hideous was to lie. She could at best conceal her envy, but she was powerless to forbid it. When Eric toted one more trophy home, where she awaited empty-handed, she might cry, *Well done!* or *I hate you!* but the only difference was what she said. Tinkering with the gut indignation itself—feeling gracious rather than acting that way—was beyond her. She could as easily fall in a lake and refuse to get wet.

For Willy had never understood whether you could be held responsible for your own emotions. As far as she could discern, circumstance had dealt them discrepant menus as the waiter had at Lutèce. Rather than lack prices, Willy's listed different entrées: rancid resentment, gristly consternation, and prickly spite, all with an aftertaste of self-reproach—a sort of collective squab. After swallowing her pride, Willy's only just dessert was humble pie. Meanwhile, Eric's menu cataloged an emotional haute cuisine: tender solicitation, sweet concern, and creamy largess. In fact, she wondered if Eric himself wearied of his princely diet, got full to his eyeballs with his own decency, and coveted her shrieking fits. He was an aggressive, complicated man. Nobility and forbearance morning to night must have bound him like a woman's corset.

"This state of affairs isn't easy for me either," Eric objected, hands on hips. "I have problems, too."

"Oh?" Willy asked archly. "Name one."

"When I win, you suffer. So what's in victory for me? How do you think I felt at Forest Hills today, with my opponent's girlfriend cheering in the front row? Where were you? And I come home, you don't even ask if I won!"

"It's obvious you won, Eric. Waves of self-congratulation come off you like a smell."

"See?" His hands flailed; his voice grew louder. "I bust my butt today, and I'm supposed to apologize. Besides, how can I ever take pleasure in my game going well when you go to bed sobbing?"

"I'd pay money for your problems."

"They'd cost you a bundle, because I've got plenty. The more highly I'm ranked, the more other people are counting on me. The pressure's enormous. I have to keep reproducing successes month after month—"

Willy laughed. "You sound like Monica Seles bitching to reporters about the tyranny of obsequious fans in restaurants. Be honest: would you trade places with me?"

"You claim you want to be 'sweet,' but when I give you a chance to sympathize with me for once, you won't take it."

"*Answer* me. Would you trade places?"

He sighed and flopped beside her on the couch. "No."

Willy stroked the long dark hairs sprouting from his hand. "Have you ever considered what it might be like if the tables were turned? If I were the one whizzing around the world and making stacks of money while you moped back here after being sandbagged in some squalid satellite?"

"I can see how I might feel...a little left out."

She studied Eric's face, incredulous. *A little left out?* In the understatement was a refusal to do what she requested, a small favor in the scheme of things: to try and really think how he might feel in her shoes. Then, any efforts in this direction had always seemed mere feints. Winners first and foremost did not wish to imagine themselves as anything but winners. The refusal was superstitious: *Don't look down.* Besides, since triumph filled the rankest bastard with goodwill, the victor, halfheartedly forming his fictional failure, always pictured a similar magnanimity in defeat. In fact, one source of friction between Willy and her husband was Eric's tacit presumption that he would surpass her even at losing.

But he was right. A hologram of Eric the Megaflop materialized perfectly before her on the coffee table, and it bore little resemblance to her own bilious tearing of hair. Had his career come up snake eyes and hers a natural, Eric would be a gentleman. When she won, he'd buy flowers. His brittle congratulations would never strike him as cold or less than sincere. In public, his rigid bows to her glory would impress others as gallant. Eric's performance as her unreserved advocate would be so well acted that he'd be persuaded by the theater himself. Only a pervasive vacancy would pester him at times, as if the doors in his mind were all shut and locked and he found himself out in the hall.

Abruptly, he'd fall in love with someone else—a younger, pretty woman with a hesitant manner who had, more's the pity, never picked up a racket in her life. (He was teaching her to play. They had a lovely, goofy time, though she displayed, sadly, little aptitude.) Eric would come to his wife remorseful, perplexed, declaring that he'd had no more warning than she, but the thing was done: behind his own back his love for Willy had died. Mystified and affronted, his tone would imply that he, not she, had been betrayed. He would describe their shattered marriage like a vase he had knocked over by accident, whose several pieces defied glue. Of this she was sure: in confessing his tragic disaffection, nowhere would the information feature that she was ranked number three in the world and was worth several million dollars while he, a stickler for pulling his weight, was part-timing in a sporting goods store. Since Eric could not apprehend her vision, Willy had to stop herself from exclaiming, *Why, you self-deceiving sack of shit!*

"Can you at least grant that your being ranked 864 while I was 75 might put our relationship under strain?" she asked dryly.

"Not that long ago I *was* ranked in the 800's, and you were ranked—"

"You were on your way up and you knew it. Me? I've hit the skids. I'm through."

Eric sighed and shook his head. "When we met, I'd never have figured you for a quitter."

"A quitter is the last thing I'd have figured myself for," Willy concurred agreeably. "But isn't there a point at which giving it another go is delusional? Pushing on for its own sake, rather than striving for a goal you've a hope of attaining? Isn't there a stick-to-itiveness that starts to look pathetic? For heaven's sake, I'm twenty-seven."

"You're twenty-six."

"Twenty-seven," she corrected. "As of today."

Eric covered his eyes. "Oh, God, Willy. I'm sorry." But when he lowered his hands, he was clearly relieved. Forgetting her birthday was a catastrophe on a scale he could handle.

"Don't worry, I'm not in the mood for cake." She reclined to the far side of the sofa.

"You're twenty-seven, not eighty-five. And you're still on the computer—"

"Would merely remaining on the computer be good enough for you?"

Eric stood again, pressing his palms to his temples. "What *would* be good enough for you, Willy? At what ranking would we no longer have this fucking conversation?"

"What do you want to hear, that I'd only settle for number one?" she asked drolly. "That I'm going to play my darnedest until I've won all four Grand Slams? Is that the way a real *winner* thinks, and if I'd be happy with number two you'll say that's my 'problem'?"

"Shut up and answer me. Would number ten be acceptable, you wouldn't snuffle when we went to sleep? 25? 50? 110? What's the number, Willy? At what ranking will this apartment be livable again?"

Tolerantly, she entertained the question. Even from this distant a vantage point Willy could see how top billing could pall: clothing contracts would become a curse, having to wear those dipshit dresses; sleazoid agents would grow irksome; importunings to play tournaments would quickly lose their flattery value, and she would groan on the eve of one more twelve-hour flight to Australia. She might even start chucking trophies in the closet herself. In short, the goal was dreck; once attained she would dismiss it. But that, in a sense, was the real aim; to disdain celebrity, you had to be famous.

"Sure I'd like to be a star," Willy admitted. "But anything in the top 200 would be comfortable. Just so long as I made a living doing what I love."

"So you won't be at peace until you've scrambled to the top 200?"

"250, then!" A familiar gorge began to rise.

"What if it's 251? Screaming fits, crying jags?"

"What's the *point*?" Willy's smooth demeanor was slipping.

"275, 350, what's the difference? No one is stopping you from *loving* the game. Nobody stops hackers in Riverside from *loving* the game, or playing it."

"That's horseshit!" Willy cried. "When you've been demoted it's not the same. No way a concert violinist gets the same thrill from fiddling in his room as performing in Carnegie Hall. Especially after being fired for playing out of tune."

"If he really cares about music? Sure he does. But for all your talk of 'loving' tennis, Willy, I don't witness much affection these days. I've seen you packing for a match. You look as if you're marching to the gas chamber."

"So that's another of my *problems*, is it?" Willy's foot was on the Plexiglas table, and with one heft she kicked it over. The top flopped forward onto the carpet, and hundreds of dead balls spilled over the room. Stonily, Eric righted the box and, one by one, pitched them back in.

NINETEEN

Eric's REDOUBLED SEARCH FOR remedies signaled a better appreciation for the urgency of their situation than Willy gave him credit for. The only solution he did not pursue was to close the disparity in their rankings by deteriorating himself. Eric rose to 58 by July.

But he came home the moment the crowds collected their picnics. Between times, he coached her. Though he refused to play formal games, in long hitting sessions at Riverside Eric tried every tack, from cajoling, hectoring, and abuse to adulation and applause—each of which Max, too, had tried in turn. Though when Willy relaxed she did return to the deep, plunging consistency of earlier incarnations, competent practice was no guarantee that in match conditions she wouldn't clench into her own worst enemy. And even these recitals were imperceptibly impaired; by what Willy could, but wouldn't say.

Lowering himself, Eric entered with Willy in a mixed-doubles satellite. He reasoned that they would benefit from playing as allies. But as soon as his foot touched the baseline, Eric the Attentive became Eric the Asshole. He either took over their whole court, poaching balls that landed three feet into his wife's territory, or covered the net so effectively that the ball never reached the backcourt. He didn't trust her, and he was a singles player by nature. Any oncoming ball belonged to him by right. They got into such arguments by the second set that the couple gathered a crowd, the onlookers riveted less by the stupendous rivalry between duos than by the shots that Eric and Willy fired at each other. With Eric on her side, of course they won, but having touched the ball only a handful of times Willy didn't regard the win as hers. Feigning injury, Eric withdrew their "team."

The next togetherness scheme was to play in the same tournament, to relive and optimally rewrite the Chevrolet. Once more this dictated that Eric play beneath himself, but as long as the small-draw coed tournament didn't interfere with his own schedule he was willing.

The men's and women's first-round matches were played simultaneously on adjoining banks of courts. Halfway through Willy's second set, which was going well, one of her aces roused a cheer. That her match was attracting attention stirred Willy to hit with a vengeance. Yet her next doozy inspired no reaction. Midway through an unexceptional point, whistles rose once more. The sound track and picture were out of synch, as if the game were poorly dubbed.

Disconcerted, Willy glanced up to find the audience in her bleachers standing and craning their necks to see over the green-netted fence at her back. On a changeover, Willy mumbled to a spectator in front, "What's the hoopla about?"

"I don't know what he's doing here, but there's a top 100 player behind you. His name's Over-something. He's amazing!" The woman whispered, "I do hope there's a seat left. Good luck!" Waving, she slipped out the gate.

In no time all of the spectators at Willy's courtside had either left or clambered to the top rows to get a better view of the Oberdorf match. Deflated, Willy frittered her lead. With his wife eliminated, Eric was stuck playing out the rest of the sordid tournament, which he resented. At his wits' end, as a belated birthday present Eric sent his wife to a sports psychologist.

**

"Why do you want to play tennis professionally?"

"It's all I've ever wanted to do since I was five."

"That's not an answer...And you don't have to lie down, unless you're tired."

The psychologist had a wandering eye. When his left pupil traveled toward the window of its own accord it seemed to pine for the summer's day, hankering for the baseball games across the way in Central Park. Yet only the eye had a noticeable taste for sport, and she wondered what had drawn him to this specialty. His middle thickened and arms spindly, Dr. Milton Edsel didn't appear to have indulged in anything more vigorous than croquet. She couldn't pin his accent; if anything, his articulated English seemed foreign from lacking one. Well-educated immigrants borrowed a tongue conscientiously, like a library book they were loath to deface.

"There may be one activity in everyone's life that expresses them—that *is* them," Willy speculated. "Maybe for some people that's dancing, or painting a picture; maybe it's just thinking. For me, it's tennis. The first time I connected with a ball was like coming home."

"But nothing in what you describe explains why you have to play tennis for a living." The doctor's therapeutic approach, it evolved, was to be obstreperously stupid.

"That's what Eric says," Willy groaned. "What, I'm employing you to talk me out of my profession?"

"I'm concerned that you tell me you 'are' tennis. Perhaps in that case the sport is too important."

"That's what Eric says," Willy grumbled again. "He thinks I take my ranking too personally. That I regard it as my ranking as a person."

"Is it?"

Flustered, Willy, too, looked out the window. "Yes. And don't." She held up her hand. "No lectures. The WTA ranks me on everything about myself that I care for."

"Do you care for yourself?"

"Not when I play badly."

"Why do you think you play badly?"

"Because I don't care for myself?" she posited caustically. "Neat circularity, but there's more to it."

"You were once ranked—?"

"214. My coach claims I should have kept going; that I had the aptitude to be a real little earner. But lately Max tends to describe me in the past tense."

"What do you think happened?"

"Eric happened."

"You bring up your husband often."

"That's what Max says."

"Other people are always telling you things. I want to know what you think. Why are you here?"

"Because my ranking is a scandal. I practice, I play great; I start a match, I stink the place up. For two years I've played like garbage."

"You like to say bad things about yourself. Your voice—it has joy in it."

"Self-laceration is one of my only remaining pleasures," Willy grumbled. "I know this doesn't make sense, but I gave my affection for myself away to someone else."

"Do you mean you fell in love?"

"That's the more conventional way of putting it," she grunted. "I injured my knee badly two years ago. Other people think that's where my trouble started. *I* think it started the tournament before, at the Chevrolet. That was the day my husband surpassed me numerically. We were both in the finals. He won. After which, I choked. I choked like you wouldn't believe."

Finally Edsel smiled. "Remember my job. I would believe."

"I was so grateful when I got married. I'd never had boyfriends to speak of, and I was lonely. My coach—" She decided to skip it. "Let's just say I wanted my coach to be my coach. To love my *game*."

"You also wanted your husband to love your game? Since, according to you, Ms. Novinsky, you *are* your game?"

"I guess. And now I've disappointed him."

"Eric has told you that he's disappointed?"

"No, I—okay, I've disappointed myself. Eric claims he doesn't care whether I win, that he loves *me for me*—"

"You say that sarcastically."

"I mean it sarcastically. What's me without what I do? I'm not the same person I was when I was winning, Dr. Edsel. I've become a complete shit. And it sounds crazy, but I feel betrayed."

"By yourself again?"

"By *Eric*. I was glad for a man who understood my way of life, but I hadn't bargained for a companion who would make me look like dog doo in comparison."

"Maybe I'm missing something. Do you believe that if your husband were to lose his matches your standing would improve? You're not ranked on the same computers." Edsel was deploying it again: belligerent witlessness.

"How can I avoid comparing myself with the tennis player lying next to me in bed? And listen, Eric is incredible. When we met his strokes were ragged, he couldn't keep the ball in the court. A year or so later, I was living with a McEnroe. Or excuse me, a Stefan Edberg." She added dryly, "Eric thinks McEnroe was rude."

"You told me Eric is number 58. That is no McEnroe. Do you exaggerate your husband's ability?"

"Maybe. A little."

"Leaving aside that he's a man and can hit a harder ball, do you think his talent is much greater than yours?"

Willy sat up straighter and cocked her head. "No. No, I don't. If I could get over being a head case, I'm at least as talented as he is."

"You realize that it doesn't matter. That his ability has nothing to do with yours."

"Yes, *rationally*, that makes perfect sense." Willy was starting to get mad.

"And what is wrong with being rational, pray?"

"Dr. Edsel, you don't understand! I've started to despise my own husband! And it's not fair! He does everything he can for me! He's a mensch!"

"I see. So not only is he John McEnroe, but he is a paragon in other respects. Maybe I should meet this husband. I don't think I've ever met such an ideal person."

"Stop making fun of me. He may not be perfect, but he doesn't deserve what I've become. I hate Eric, I hate myself, I even hate—"

"Go on."

"Tennis." Willy bowed her head. "Maybe that's what I'm being punished for."

"You have used the passive voice."

"You sound like my father."

"Do you like your father?"

"He's a disappointed man. He wants his kids to be disappointed, too. His sick version of intimacy, I guess."

"Just as you want your husband to be disappointed with you. Why can't you imagine being close by both being successful?"

"Great fantasy, doesn't help. Do you have any idea what it's like to watch the person you live with get *everything* you want? Money, trophies, acclaim, a future—while I run up debts. How would you feel if you were defrocked, or whatever it is you people get, and meanwhile your wife waltzes off to her office every day and makes a couple hundred thou a year on sports therapy?"

"Fortunate. Our mortgage payments would keep pace."

"But would you feel like a man?"

"Do you wish to feel like a man?"

"Hell, yes. Any woman worth her salt does."

"I think," he smiled a second time, "you are a very good player."

"That's what Eric says," she grumbled. "Except Eric's compliments feel condescending. They're like insults."

"And his insults must feel like insults. So everything out of his mouth offends you."

"Boy, don't you just wish you were married to me?"

"Did your father push you very hard?"

Willy snorted. "My father didn't push me at all. When I was young that made me angry, and I was out to prove he'd underestimated me. Now I'm worried he planted some seed of doubt that's grown into an oak tree in my head. Poison oak."

"Poison oak is a shrub."

"You sound just like Eric. He's a pedant."

"That is the first negative thing you've said about your husband. Yet if you 'hate' Eric, you must think ugly thoughts about him often."

Willy rubbed her forehead. "It's not Eric's fault he's a tennis prodigy. When I think mean things about him, I feel ashamed. At least my tumbling in the ranks is my fault. All Eric did was marry me."

"Are you frightened that at some point you will no longer be able to play tennis professionally at all?"

"Of course. In a couple of months I could fall off the computer altogether, which as far as I'm concerned is dropping off the edge of the world."

"You said you had a serious injury two years ago. What if the accident had been worse? Since you 'are' tennis? What if you'd never been able to play again? How would you have coped?"

"But it wasn't worse," she said hotly. "I'm fine."

"I'm sure you are," Edsel soothed. Though he glanced decorously at his lap, his left eye swivelled to look straight at her, as if it could see things the good eye couldn't. "But even if we jump-start your career again, you will face much the same brick wall in a few years."

"I recognize that an early retirement in tennis is inevitable, and quitting the tour would be difficult for me in the best of circumstances. I just want to leave this part of my life behind me *with* something, you know? Tennis is all I care about. If I've made a fool of myself in it, I'd rather...die." She looked away, embarrassed.

The therapist remained placid. "Literally?"

"*Some* days. You think I'm a baby." When Edsel didn't rise to the charge, Willy scowled. "I am a baby. Knowing that doesn't mature me by ten minutes."

"Tennis is 'all' you care about. Don't you also care about your husband?"

"I do," she said impatiently, "but I won't submit to marriage under any conditions, so maybe I don't care for him enough. I thought when we met that Eric would be a reprieve from the pressures of the circuit. Now not only my career's on the line when I play, but my marriage, too. Eric's no safe harbor; he's an added pressure to prove myself. That's why I choked in the Chevrolet. I may not seem that way now because I'm such a goddamned mess, but I'm a proud woman, Dr. Edsel. I'm not the housewife type. I detest cooking and cleaning, and the prospect of being some toadying schmoe while my husband gets famous makes me gag."

Edsel's wandering eye roved in her direction and for once the pupils synchronized. In the single coherent glance glimmered a nascent affection. "Let me get this straight. Your estimation of yourself depends on tennis, since you 'are' tennis—"

"I wish you'd stop repeating that. It sounds retarded."

"Does it?" he asked innocently, and bent back his next finger. "Your marriage is on the line—the baseline. Your association with your coach is, I assume, contingent on performance?"

Willy raised her chin. "It is a professional relationship."

The wandering eye curved her way again. "And you're not close to your family? Or rather, you can only bear their waiting for you to fail when you've demonstrated that you're not a flop?"

She'd come in here vowing to maintain a dignified reticence, but Walnut Street had been on her mind. "My sister, Gert, has been rubbing her hands the last two years like a greedy kid about to come into an inheritance. The high-and-mighty's falling-on-butt presumably redeems her killingly sensible existence. My mother is waiting for me to crawl back in the womb, where I belong, or better yet check in early to The Golden Autumn and drool in the halls so she can wipe my chin and spoon me strained peas. My father... created me in his own image, and was aghast when he recognized his own credulous face. He's been stepping on it ever since as a substitute for stepping on his own. How would *you* feel walking into that rat's nest with a ranking of 902?"

Edsel had kept his *yourself, your marriage, your coach*, and *your family* fingers bent back with his other forefinger. "You have few friends?"

"Tennis is demanding, I—"

"No friends." Edsel appraised his bent fingers with his good eye. "What else have you left?"

"What's the drift?"

"Everything in your life, according to you, is dependent on your success in tennis. In sum, not only does your choking in the occasional tournament not surprise me, but I am staggered that you're able to wobble a ball over the net at all."

Willy looked back at the psychologist steadily; she couldn't make him out. "Are you ridiculing me?"

"You mock yourself so incessantly that you perceive ridicule from every corner." Edsel slipped his pencil through the spiral of his notepad. "Your situation is not uncommon. Women are by and large more emotional than men in sports. That's both a strength and a weakness. In fact, strengths often convert to weaknesses, and we need to see if yours can be switched back again. Self-criticism has helped you to set high standards for yourself, but now the lash is out of control and is flaying you to shreds. Comparing yourself with others has spurred you in the past, but now makes you feel worthless. And maybe something in you wants to perceive Eric as your superior. At any rate, men don't like to be overshadowed, even in the nineties. When we love someone we feel a nagging impulse to do what they want. Maybe you are losing on purpose, as a favor to your husband, do you think?"

"I'm no altruist, Dr. Edsel. I find that theory frankly incredible."

"An idle thought. Or perhaps you are short-circuiting. All other tennis players are the enemy; your husband is your friend; your husband is a tennis player. It doesn't compute. In your mind I can see quite an electrical fire."

"Might Eric," Willy drummed her fingers on the couch piping, "have a part in this?"

"I'm sure he does, but how do you mean?"

"I've wondered if he'd have gotten so far without me around to show up. If I've inspired him to clobber me."

"The person you are describing is not a paragon at all, but a very cut-throat, competitive, even destructive man."

"Yes," she said brightly. "Like his wife."

"I'm going to give you an assignment," Edsel announced, putting down his notebook. "I want you to play for fun. You must have done that as a girl. Those were good days?"

"The best."

"Try to remember how you felt then. The vibration of the strings in your grip. If you hit the ball out, enjoy hitting it out. Because do you feel 'at home' on the court nowadays?"

"On the contrary, I feel banished."

"Go *home*," Dr. Edsel ordered, and Willy stood to leave.

He touched Willy's arm on her way out the door. "I think you should decide why you are coming here. Do you wish to save your career or your marriage?"

"At this point? Save one, save the other."

"Perhaps we should try and decouple them."

"*Decouple* is an ominous choice of words, Dr. Edsel."

"What if I were to tell you that you will not rescue your tennis game without breaking up your marriage?"

Willy paled. "I might find a new therapist."

"Don't be alarmed; it was a hypothetical question. For now, go play for fun. If you stop having a good time, quit and try again another day."

Willy headed down the hall. "Ms. Novinsky," he said quietly behind her. "You're limping."

"Willy, what's wrong? Honey, you're crying!"

Willy parted her hands around her mouth. "I did—" She stopped to inhale; the air wheezed.

"Take your time." Eric fetched a Kleenex.

Willy kept her eyes closed, and when blindness didn't allow sufficient privacy she angled her face toward the wall. It took concentration to get the words out, and her enunciation was precise, like Milton Edsel's. "I did my 'assignment.' I went to Riverside to have *fun*."

"You don't look as if you did your homework very well."

"I played Randy, remember him?"

"Gold chains? All mouth no strokes."

Willy groaned. "I lost."

"You're joking." Eric made her another appointment.

"We live in a culture of celebrity. Yet only a handful achieve renown. How do you think that so many nobodies manage?"

"I haven't an inkling." Willy had brooded on the question before. "All that *managing* boggles my mind. Edsel, are you urging me to give up again?"

"You may have to allow yourself to give up in order to keep going. If you continue to equate failure with death—the death of everything that matters to you about yourself, the death of your marriage—the prospect will terrify you into choking. Somehow scads of your peers adjust to a life that falls short, often desperately short, of their desires. They are not all Stepford wives or suicides or even divorcées."

"You sound like my mother: 'Don't get your hopes up.'"

"Hope, but don't put quite so much at stake."

"Staking everything used to distinguish my game. I've always been wholehearted. My parents protect themselves by expecting to fail—they, like, prefail, as if anticipation softens the blow. Which it doesn't. Did I ever tell you about this dinner in high school? After I was in the finals of the New Jersey Junior Classic, and my parents couldn't come?"

"Couldn't, or wouldn't?"

"They always had excuses. Department meetings, a flat-liner in the nursing home. Let's just say they never changed their plans. But they promised we'd 'celebrate' that night. Anyway, I won. I came home pumped, right? And my mother's putting dinner on the table. Some mushy tuna casserole with soggy noodles, creamed spinach. Bananas and custard for dessert. My stomach *sank*."

"What did you expect?"

"Steak! Champagne! Cake! It was a *victory* dinner!"

"How could your parents have known that you'd won?"

"That's the point, Edsel. My mother made the same food she serves in her nursing home: bland, pale, and soothing. She fixed a *consolation* meal. Then when I blew my stack, she cried. No matter how many trophies I hauled back, they always prepared the hankies for when I came shuffling home in tears . . . Why are you smirking?"

"Because you can see defeat even in casseroles."

"Just come right out and say it: I'm nuts."

The stray eye rolled to the ceiling, but the fixed one humored her. "Maybe your mother could only show she loved you through comfort. It's hard to feel close to victors. They don't seem to need sympathy."

"It's lonely at the top?" said Willy flippantly. "Ask Eric."

"Let's go back to your assignment. You thought it would be easy, didn't you?"

"Oh, I just leapt at one more opportunity to fail at something. I can't even have a good time."

"I told you to stop if you began to get upset."

"It was the middle of a match, Edsel. What was I supposed to do? Tell Randy, 'I'm sorry, but I'm beginning to have feelings of self-revulsion and my psychologist tells me I have to quit'? Give me a break."

The wandering eye sank toward his cheek, dolorous. "You often describe yourself in terms that make your situation seem comical. Yet I don't hear you laughing."

"It *is* comical! Edsel, I read the papers. All over the "A" section, Muslim genocide, Africans hacking each other to bits. These people have *real* problems. And meanwhile I'm blubbering because I can't win a tennis tournament. My career is zip in the big picture, of no moment even to the game. Other women with good backhand slices will take my place. I bow out? Big deal."

"Putting your plight into perspective doesn't seem to cheer you up."

"I hate self-pity," Willy muttered. "Which only makes me feel more sorry for myself."

"When a young woman tries as hard as she can to achieve what she wants most, and her aspirations are frustrated, do you not think that story is a little bit sad, too?"

"I don't know," Willy admitted, hands behind her head. "In every novel I read, the hero prevails. He has to suffer adversity, of course, or there wouldn't be a book. But by the end it's always *Rocky*. No one writes about people who bite the dust. So I keep expecting that one day I'm going to turn my own page and in the last chapter everything turns out swell."

Edsel got up and rummaged his shelves, returning with a beaten copy of *Jude the Obscure*. "Read some old books," he recommended. "This era doesn't suit your state of mind."

"Hardy? My father loves him."

"Yes." Edsel smiled. "I thought he might."

Sessions with Edsel didn't salve Willy's anxiety but brought it to a pitch. Mid-July she was entered in the New Jersey Classic, staged on old turf in Newark, where she'd competed in the juniors. Maybe that was what set her off. After all, it was humiliating to hack through the qualifiers when she'd won this same tournament six years before.

Nobody paid attention to qualifying matches, one reason they were difficult to concentrate through. While the stands ambled with chatting players, Willy went down in the third set's tiebreak 15–13. She hurled her racket at the microphone, barely missing the umpire, and the sound of the frame striking the mesh amplified over the loudspeakers to a small nuclear explosion. Cited for "gross misconduct," Willy would have been defaulted if she hadn't already lost. Eric had come along for moral support, which was unfortunate. He turned chalk-white, and wouldn't speak to her the whole train ride home.

Just as well. Yes, she had lost her temper. Yes, or in a way, she was sorry. Yes, it looked bad to chuck her racket at the umpire, to scream obscenities in public, and yes, she knew that Eric was touchy about appearances.

But she was not simply *sorry*. Previous to hard times, Willy had given little thought to the brutally harsh gestalt of the *good loser*. Victors, of course, were expected to be mannerly, but grace fell to the winner's circle like manna from heaven. Willy's own gallantry in triumph—extolling the fine fight, her opponent's mastery—had only redounded to her glory; the grander the adversary, the nobler the champion. And look: already proven the superior athlete, she was munificent as well! The chivalry was always sincere; Willy could only be grateful to an antagonist who so cooperatively bungled the last point. It was such a breeze to love your enemy when he was beaten that *good winner* wasn't even a pat phrase.

But what was extorted from the vanquished? He could not weep, curse, or flee. While champions could give over to instinct—to their free-flowing generosity and élan—the defeated was compelled to suppress his every impulse. It wasn't bad enough, was it, to lose, to drown in a rush of dismay and self-disgust? No, a second subjugation awaited après-game. Willy had obliged at the Chevrolet: expounding on that fat cow's brilliance while elucidating her own deficits, paying homage to the last person on earth she was in the mood to praise. Forcing losers to display genuine generosity—that is, generosity with a price—was like hitting up the destitute for charitable donations. A *good sport* was a considerate liar, who successfully disguised his every true emotion and so spared one and all the medical unpleasantness of his intestinal cramps, the obscenities in his head, the spasms of his heart. How much would it have cost Eric and that handful of onlookers to forgive a brief display of pique and a few well-earned profanities?

The graciousness exacted from the also-ran was a travesty for losers everywhere, who deserved emancipation as much as the wheelchair-bound or overweight. As Edsel had emphasized, the world was dense with losers. How many comers climbed to the pinnacles of their professions? The vast majority foundered, so why was there no spokesman for the second-rate, the runner-up, the penultimate, the huge disheartened horde? Would no one defend their right to hurl their rackets? All the way home on the PATH train, Willy knew she was supposed to apologize. Her refusal was a political statement.

"You only care about how I behave," said Willy, throwing T-shirts into her suitcase. "Never mind how I feel, just so long as I don't embarrass you. I failed to convert *five match points*, two of which I double-faulted down the drain. What normal human being wouldn't *scream*?"

"Any mature adult with a little self-control." It was an old, unresolvable difference: Willy placed a premium on honesty, Eric on decorum. "You worry me, Willy. Flying out of orbit like that. You never used to throw tantrums in public."

"What do you know about losing? You haven't a clue how I feel!" All through an avalanche of socks. The number of times a year Willy and Eric watched each other pack gave the relationship a tumultuous texture, as if they were always trooping off to Mother in a huff.

"Edsel doesn't seem to be doing you much good. I wonder if we should find someone else."

"Typical American solution. Go get *help*. And if the latest painkiller doesn't do the job, switch brands. Well, in case you care, Edsel's too *reasonable*. 'So your husband is about to play the U.S. Open while you can't make it through the qualies of a satellite; *why* should that matter? Why not be *happy* for him? And oodles of people flunk at what they do, what makes you so special? Join the club!'"

"Uh-huh. And what does Upchuck tell you instead? Since I *presume* that's where you're going."

"At least he understands—"

"That scumbag isn't sharing your agony. He sees we're having trouble and he's dancing. Since you obviously go up to Wetspot and pour your heart out. But he doesn't give a fuck about your career!"

"Then who does?"

"*I* do!"

"Who's literally invested in it? Max!"

"But *what* is he buying?" Eric sputtered. "He's making down payments on your ass, Willy. Lying in wait—"

"You find it incredible that anyone would stick by me because they thought I was talented?"

"Willy, you're ranked 924, you've been costing him thousands for over two years, and he still pays your health insurance, finances your plane tickets, and eats your hotel bills, not to mention giving you the run of his camp—"

"School."

"*School*, with permanent access to a dorm room he could be letting out to a younger, more profitable client."

"Why are you doing this? I'm not a big enough train wreck, you have to tear off some extra parts yourself?"

"Because I'm tired of going along with a charade that's entirely at *my* expense. He's making a fool of me, Willy. Just because you're having a rough time doesn't mean I have to take humiliation lying down. *Why* would he lavish all that money on you? When he's the most prominent coach on the eastern seaboard, and could take his pick from top 200 players, who would reward his attentions in cash? At this point, *how* are you planning to pay him back?"

"Thanks," said Willy, slamming her suitcase shut. "Not only am I a zero, a black hole to pour money down, but I'm a whore."

"What you are is *vulnerable*. He sees you're weakened, that you and I fight a lot, and that some other man slipping a hand down your shirt might make you feel wanted. But *I* want you. That ought to be enough. I'm warning you: I don't give a fuck if you're ranked 5,007. But call me old-fashioned, I won't be made a cuckold. I've had plenty of opportunities on the road and I've spared you the details because I never, ever consider screwing around. Then I come back here and you can't see through that dirty old man in Connecticut. I have to wonder what bullshit lines you might fall for."

"You're wrong, dead wrong—What are you doing?"

"Just checking." He was rifling through the cabinet under the sink, where Willy kept her diaphragm.

When Willy peeked in the library, it was late, the lights were off. She assumed that Max had already called it a night until a flicker from a video alcove threw light on the opposite shelves. Willy picked her way around the reading tables to find Max seated before a screen, scotch at elbow and the remote control cradled in his hand. She stood behind him to watch the video: tennis.

"She's fantastic," Willy remarked. He hadn't moved since she walked in, but didn't start when she spoke.

"Isn't she?" Max agreed, still riveted to the tape. "Graceful, quick, ingenious. And beautiful. Small but perfectly proportioned. What a fire under that woman."

"New acquisition?"

"Ancient. But one of my best." Max turned and cocked an eyebrow at the twist of her features in the glow of the tube. His lips parted in wonder. "You really don't recognize yourself, do you?"

"That's *me*?"

Max laughed. "You are far gone. Jealous of yourself." He hit the pause; Willy's face froze in a grimace. Max rewound and reran the point. "New Freedom; I took the camcorder. You were miles ahead of the field. They weren't good enough to tie your shoes."

"I'm not good enough to tie my own anymore."

"Hey, there's always Velcro. Drink?"

"Sure."

"What brings you up here at this hour?" Max switched on the lamp in his usual corner and unlocked his liquor cabinet.

"Is it OK? You're glad to see me?"

"I'm glad to see you." He took the opportunity to touch her neck, just. His hand was warm.

"I was bad."

"New Jersey qualies?" He handed her a whiskey the size of an apple juice.

"Long tiebreak; one rabbity return of a shot I should have clouted." She shrugged, accustomed to telescoping protracted disaster. "I mean I was badly *behaved.* Tried to decapitate the umpire with my racket. My language was unladylike. Eric went apoplectic. Does it matter?"

"I've always found your temper rather magnificent. I'm sorry I missed it." He clinked his glass against hers, and they plopped into perpendicular armchairs.

"Max..." Willy wet the edge of the tumbler and traced its perimeter. "Why don't I feel competitive with you?"

"I'm a has-been."

"You can still run me around the court standing in place. Why don't you make me mad?"

"Simple answer? You're not in love with me." His delivery was deadpan. "Complicated answer?" Max proceeded when she didn't rush to correct him. "We have a hierarchy. I'm your teacher. Hierarchies preserve the peace. Why do you think the divorce rate's gone up? The old system worked. Marriages were spared head-to-heads because the battle was over before it began. Be your mother's yes-massa sort of wife, Oberachiever would never piss you off. You'd just be grateful for his kindly pointers." Before Willy could protest, Max raised a hand. "Too bad you can't do that."

"I don't get it. According to you, if Eric didn't beat me, I wouldn't respect him. If he does beat me, I don't respect myself. How do two people ever—?"

"They don't, commonly," said Max lightly. "Only two choices, Will: fight or knuckle under. Don't capitulate, and he still trounces you?" Max smiled. "You might kill him."

Willy squirmed. "I read an article a while back about the marriage of two engineers. The husband got laid off, and couldn't find a job. The wife was in a more generalized field of engineering, and made a bundle. He did, he murdered her. I told the story to Marcella and that bunch, in the locker room? Other women. They were all sympathetic with the man. But in the same conversation they expected me to be over the moon about Eric's meteoric success, not homicidal. How do you figure?"

"Nothing's changed," said Max, topping off her drink. "A wife's subservience to her husband is still considered par for the course. Vice-versa is *unnatural.*"

"How did you hack it, married ten years? You were famous."

"The apples-and-oranges ruse. Pretend your occupations don't compare. Which they do, of course; other people rank your status whether you like it or not. Still, Angela handled my tournaments with a muscular condescension. Had some design business of her own... I never knew much about it. And Angela made my life hell when the crowds went home, which leveled the score remarkably."

"I've tried that solution. It widens the score. The victim racks up bonus points for long suffering."

"Think Oberjock could bear your ESPN interviews, while he made sure that in the apartment you never visited there was always ass-wipe in the can?"

"In a word? No."

"If you could do a deal with the devil, would you switch places with him?"

"Funny, I asked him the same thing. Sure, I'd trade 924 for 58 in a millisecond."

"At the price of turning your husband into a pumpkin?"

Willy's hesitation was slight. "Yes."

"Some love."

"I'm young and selfish."

"I'm not."

She looked at him harder, and stopped playing with her glass.

"Watching you the last two years has been so ..." Max spread his free hand helplessly in the air, then dropped it. "If Lucifer handed me the contract, I'd sign tonight. I'd deliver you my clipping file if I could, as a present."

"And you'd take mine? No way."

Max put his drink down and knelt at her feet. "You could have my Top Ten ranking. I'd inscribe your name on my All England cup. I don't care."

"You won't convince me that you don't care about tennis."

He took her hand. "I don't care about *my* tennis. I'm beyond ambition, kiddo. What I want the ATP can't offer."

"You only want what you don't have." Willy fought a rising agitation. "The grass is greener."

"Your grass is very green indeed." He wrapped his hand around her neck, and kissed her. He'd done that before, but had always pulled back with a pretense that it hadn't happened. This time he didn't pull back. It happened.

"I said we had a hierarchy, Will," Max whispered hoarsely a few inches from her face. "You thought I meant I was on top.

Not so. You've been in the driver's seat since you were seventeen. So go ahead. Dominate me."

He pulled her forward and kissed her more deeply. As he swept her body to the floor and pinned her on the carpet, he did not feel to Willy like a man who was being dominated.

TWENTY

WILLY ALMOST SKIPPED BREAKFAST, but avoidance was delay. Which dictated Max's table; to sit anywhere else would be more awkward yet. Ordinarily a hearty eater, Max was propped before a lone cup, his face drained and inexpressive. Summer camp was in full swing; the rowdy shriek and tussle of kids jangled Willy's nerves. A good proportion of this year's intake were overweight. Their parents couldn't have hoped that the little porkers would play Wimbledon so much as that on their return home there would simply be less of them. Sweetspot-turned-fat-farm no doubt depressed its proprietor, or would have depressed him on mornings he was aware that he had students.

Willy nodded and assumed a seat opposite, stirring her cup and blowing on the coffee. Max sat immobile, at rest. He seemed relaxed. If the night before he was "beyond ambition," this morning he was beyond something else.

"You expect," he introduced in a craggy monotone, "to do some line sprints, a few weights, and then of course I'll spend a couple of hours with you on court."

"Unless you have other—"

"But that's what you expect."

The coffee tasted awful. "It is what we usually..."

Willy could meet his eyes only in sorties, but Max stared at her squarely. "After sliding so far, your gall remains intact. Maybe that hollow of yours isn't all that cavernous. Your ego is remarkably robust. I wish I could say the same for mine."

Willy bowed her head, her stomach acid. The gray sludge in her cup looked like liquid dread.

"Since we do have a *business relationship*," he continued, "might you join me in my office? Before you avail yourself of my facilities? Consider yourself as having an appointment."

In his office, Max was bulwarked behind his desk, surrounded by copies of dunning letters rich with five-figure sums. This was the Max Upchurch whose implacable edifice met the parents of fat children, parents who would pay through the nose for every ounce he sweated off their kids. This was the Max Upchurch who had no intention of engraving his All England trophy with any other name than Maximilian E. Upchurch.

"Our contract," he began, clasping his hands, "bound me to cover your expenses in exchange for a cut of your *earnings* the first five years of your pro career. You turned pro at twenty-one. You're twenty-seven. Our contract," he paused, "has expired."

"What do you want to do about it?" She didn't take a chair.

"I originally had in mind a somewhat different arrangement, but last night you apprised me that my alternative proposal was not suitable." He said *syewtable*, like a Brit.

"I told you years ago that it wasn't *syewtable*."

"I can take a long time to get the message."

"But you've got the message now."

"Entirely," he said, tracing a light red scratch on his left arm. "So maybe we should proceed on a more à la carte basis. You are welcome to rent a dorm room on the premises for $700 per month, or $1000 with board. Court time is $15 per hour—"

"Spare me—"

"*My own time*," he overrode, "is $100 per hour, and that is a discount."

"I'm bowled over by the break." A light, cold sweat had broken out over Willy's forehead.

"A C-note would not be nearly enough compensation, I assure you."

"Is all this because I wouldn't fuck you last night? Revenge?"

"I'd call it justice," said Max, mock-aggrieved. "Your ranking doesn't merit a renewal of our arrangement. My investors would be rightly irate. I couldn't even argue that you were a hard-luck case; your husband is well paid. For this year I can write you off as a tax deduction . . . You're smiling?"

"That I'm a *write-off*. Literally."

"My business is one of calculated risks."

"And you've been calculating."

"You haven't been."

"So I should have kept my shirt off? To keep you on board."

"Might have worked for a while, too," Max conceded. "But integrity is expensive. Why most people give it a miss."

"What about yours?"

"What have I done to be ashamed of? I carried you for over a year I didn't have to. And there's an injury clause in your contract. After your ligaments tore, I could've cut my losses. In fact, if I'd documented that you were done for, your insurance would've paid me a lump sum of fifty thou."

"Why didn't you?"

"I'm a nice guy?" Max supposed.

"You don't sound as if you believe that."

"I've felt nicer. Ask Angela: when it comes to subdividing property, I'm merciless."

"Is that what we're doing?"

"You're the property. And uncharacteristically, I cede all claims. Please don't imagine that I'm kicking you out. I'm treating you the way I would any other player at your ranking, at your age, with your prospects. Isn't that what you wanted? And Eric can afford to buy you a bit of coaching, rent your room. Husbands have been financing their wives' costly, eccentric hobbies for hundreds of years."

Blinded for an instant by the same blazing fury that her

husband could ignite, Willy had to consider if maybe she loved Max, a little, after all.

"We've worked together for a decade," said Willy, the *good loser*. "Are you taking everything back?"

"You do have one of my rackets."

Willy nodded at the files on his desk. "You get to keep your racket. No, I meant all those *Good shot*'s. *The Well done, Will*'s and *You've got what it takes, Will*'s. Did you really mean *Nice tits*?"

Max winced, as if pricked by his own brass tacks. "When I came across you in Nevada you had more raw talent than any client I'd taken on in five years." The compliment seemed to tax him; he dropped back in his chair.

"So what went wrong?"

"Talent's only the half of it, Will. You know that."

"You used to say I had the other half."

"Your heart was once in the right place." His eyes scrunched. "It shifted."

"My decline is all Eric's fault?"

"It could be partly my fault," Max allowed, and taking some responsibility for her downfall appeared to cheer him. "I may have undermined you—"

"Yes. You did."

"Ironic, isn't it? Pretty girls throw themselves at me all day long. You might have been flattered."

"If I were Marcella. But I've never made a very good *girl*."

"And of course there's one more thing. Which may reduce psychologizing to empty gab." His gaze indicted her. "The Tanqueray."

"It healed," she jumped in.

"Not quite, Will. You might put one over on Eric. But how could you hide it from me? Look at the way you're standing."

Willy glanced down at her bent right knee. The majority of her weight rested on her left foot.

"You favor the left all the time," Max noted. "And there's a diffidence... You don't trust it, and maybe you shouldn't. Because it hurts, doesn't it? Sometimes all day, or when it rains. During practice you grimace twenty times in an hour. Your admirable stoicism amounts to a hill of beans."

"I did my exercises," Willy insisted. Standing symmetrically, she blinked, hard.

"And how. You might have recuperated properly if it weren't for all that mindless rope-skipping." He added bitterly, "*Eric's* routine."

"So I'm damaged goods?"

"Tennis players arc a commodity. Even good ones are a dime a dozen. It's not enough to manage a brisk walk without collapsing." Max spread his hands. "You have to be perfect."

"This is my parting gift? An excuse?"

"You need one."

Only while clearing out her dorm room did Willy realize that for the first time in years Max had used her husband's real name.

When she opened the door Eric jumped, guiltily, as if she'd caught him over a girlie magazine with his pants down, though he was only wrapping a new racket with a rubber grip.

"You're back early," he observed, his face flushed.

"Since we both know I only go to Westbrook to fuck my coach, I thought I'd skip the pretense of practicing my strokes."

"That's not funny," said Eric mutedly. He rushed to help her unload, but didn't remark on the fact that she'd returned with twice as much luggage, most of it in plastic bags. His motions were jerky, and he didn't look her in the eye. "Hungry? I got some—"

"No." There was a starkness to this day that Willy intended to preserve. She didn't want props.

"Say," Eric raised, wiping his hands on his shorts as if something wouldn't rub off. "I got some good news."

"How unusual," said Willy.

"For both of us. I got an offer that I couldn't refuse."

"You're not in the habit of refusing offers anyway."

"I, uh, I got a coach."

Willy stood in the middle of their living room, like a guest whom no one had invited to sit down. The apartment looked bedraggled. She didn't care; with the drape of sponsorship sports clothes and conspiracy of alien rackets, this didn't feel like her own place any longer. It was harrowing, to yearn to go home when you were already there. "Oh?"

Eric collected the crimped strip of his racket's original grip. Skirting around his wife to the trash can, he gave her wide berth, like a squash player midpoint avoiding the arc of his opponent's swing. "It's only six weeks to the Open. I've one warm-up scheduled, the Pilot Pen in August. Gary's been pressuring me for months, and maybe it's time I stop being so pig-headed, like, this is the big time, a Slam... Maybe I don't know everything, and if I'm going to get some, ah, help, now's the time."

"I fail to perceive why this turn of events is good news for me."

"Well." Eric blushed. His laundry had been sent back damp; he began folding garish sports shirts drying on chairs. "It's, you know... Max."

Willy remained standing in the same spot. She was practicing distributing her weight evenly between both legs. Straight and bearing a full fifty-two pounds, the knee began to ache. A ligament with which she'd grown intimate was tightening, slowly, like a violin string tuned gradually from D to E.

"This way," Eric went on hurriedly, "you and I can head up to Connecticut together. Spend more time—"

"You couldn't find," she said evenly, "any other coach?"

"Willy, you've said yourself that Max Upchurch is the best there is in this part of the country. Why should I opt for less? And what better recommendation than yours?" Though Eric could not have acquired his new confederate long before, the speech sounded rehearsed. "Max said he could have me up to

Sweetspot, then leave the summer kids to his pros and accompany me to the Pilot Pen. I thought, if you had nothing else on, you could come along."

"*Nothing else on.* You mean, get chucked from the qualifiers of another satellite."

"You could give me pointers, right? Tell me what I'm doing wrong?"

"I think you know what you're doing wrong." Her tone was ministerial.

Eric avoided looking at his wife. "Max wants to do some intensive, really hands-on work with my game."

"As opposed to getting his 'hands on' me. And you'll escort me to Sweetspot. As a chaperone."

Eric's folding was usually precise, but the roll collar on top of his stack was off center. "Willy, this decision is totally impersonal."

"According to you everything is impersonal. Your rise in the ranks, my fall. You helplessly succumb to your own monstrous talent; I'm blighted by an abstract bad luck. I'm beginning to wonder if we have a relationship at all."

"Look, I need a coach, and Max is the obvious choice. His name popped up constantly when I asked other players for suggestions. And *he* came to *me.*"

"So he phoned you this morning. And nothing he said suggested that I might take this *personally*?"

Eric concentrated on bunching his socks. "Why can't we share a coach? We share everything else."

"We share nothing, Eric. For the last two years, I doubt there's been a single minute of the day when you and I have felt the same way."

"That's not true. I also feel frustrated, angry, powerless—"

"On my behalf." Willy picked Eric's freshly gripped racket off the Plexiglas table, inspecting the label. A Wilson. So he got the new sponsorship after all. Not that he'd mentioned it. That would be indecorous. "Tell me," she requested calmly. "Are you to pay him one hundred an hour? Discount rates, of course."

"No, like with you—a percentage. He asked me my current gross, and said he'd settle for ten percent. If he makes any difference at all, it'll be worth it."

"He makes a difference," said Willy, creaking the strings of the sweet spot in line. "To me, at least. You know, you really are amazing, *Underwood*. You've assumed half a dozen of my signature strokes, and refined them. Moved into my apartment, and installed all your fluffy free clothes. Ingratiated yourself with my family—as a *real* tennis player they can believe in, not one of their own sorry-ass kids. Sometimes it even seems as if you've been downloading my computer points into your file. And now you've helped yourself to my coach. From the sound of your amicable arrangements, I don't see why you and Max don't get married. Because I've been swapped for a newer model. Like your racket." She looked up wonderingly from the strings. "You sort of *are* me, aren't you?"

"You're talking crazy."

"The new, improved version." She hefted the Wilson, patting the frame on her palm. "Willy Novinsky without all those icky, human flaws. No holes in your molars. With a proper rah-rah Daddy, not some dour, unpublished Montclair nothing. Best of all, a *boy*."

Eric shoved his clothes aside on the dining table; he'd nothing left to fold. "You're going off the deep end again—"

"That was the problem with the old version. Obsolete Willy had *feelings*. Little moments of hesitation, specks of doubt as to whether she was just the greatest fucking thing that ever happened to the game of tennis. And the moods—the *disreputable behavior*—we've had complaints! So our updated model is a *gentleman*."

Eric advanced with his hand out. "Calm down."

"He *never* loses, which doesn't stop him from being an expert on how to go down in style. Max—funny how suddenly you two are on a first-name basis; what ever happened to 'Upchuck'? Max himself said this morning that a tennis player has to be 'perfect.' He's found his archetype in one phone call."

Eric grabbed for the Wilson, and she whirled to the dining table.

"No temper," she said, sweeping his pile of neatly folded shirts to the floor. "Always concerned for the welfare of the less fortunate; I'm sure you'll make many a charitable donation as a millionaire. And good at everything! Scrabble, German, mathematics—as if you had the microchips installed."

The brandished racket smashed the glass over the New Jersey Classic poster, and shards tinkled to the floor.

"Willy, get a grip," Eric growled.

"Don't worry," Willy eluded her husband, chucking couch pillows in his wake, "*Mrs. Eric Oberdorf* can clean all this up. She can tidy," she kicked his dozen sycophants across the floor, "all your *sports equipment*—"

"Get a hold of yourself!"

"—and bake *cookies*!" This time she aimed for the MOMA print on purpose, and its glass shattered.

"Give me that!" Picking his way through the shard-strewn rackets, Eric tripped over his jump ropes.

"You're not my husband," Willy lifted the racket overhead, "you're my *replacement*!"

Willy did not remember heaving the Wilson downward. Like flow in good tennis, the stroke expressed an absolute confluence of intention and execution. Because if she'd thought about it, she wouldn't have done it.

Eric cupped his right eye. He was kneeling amid the scattered rackets with his head bowed. For a long moment he did nothing but breathe; Willy did nothing but stare; until between his fingers red began to seep, drizzling down his hand. *Pat...pat...* Blood dropped onto a vinyl racket cover like the first few drops of rain on the court when the sky has turned black and though you keep hitting, you know the game is over.

"Eric!" Willy stooped and fretted over his damp, thinning hair. "What did I do? Oh, God, I'm sorry, I didn't mean to—

Let me see!" She pried weakly at his fingers, which remained tightly clamped. His body was trembling and hunched into a fetal ball. For a minute, perhaps two, he wouldn't speak or remove his hand from the wound, and she knew that for those minutes he was entering the life in which his own wife had blinded his left eye.

When at last Eric edged his fingers away, blood was everywhere and it was impossible to see the scale of the damage. Willy ran to moisten a towel, and returned to dab gingerly at the perimeters of his socket and help him to the sofa, through murmurous remorse. "Honey, can you see? Tell me please, *can you see?*"

He took a deep breath, and underneath the coagulating ooze an eyelid fluttered. The breath held, and held, then rushed out. "It's blurred—but yes—I think so."

"Shut your right eye. How many fingers?"

He took the towel and wiped the left eye. "Six?"

"No, two, Eric—!"

"I was joking."

The four-hour wait in St. Luke's emergency room allowed Willy so much opportunity to embellish her apology that Eric asked her quietly to give it a rest. Willy forced herself to examine the wound, a deep laceration over an inch long, slicing through Eric's wild eyebrow. Later when the doctor inquired what had happened, Willy was about to bare all. Eric interceded that he had stumbled into the corner of an open kitchen cabinet.

Remembering how her husband had held her hand when she fell in the Tanqueray, Willy slipped her palm into Eric's as the doctor squirted Novocain across his brow, the excess anesthetic drizzling down his face like the tears he hadn't shed. She wished he'd squeeze hard, as she had crushed his fingers on the New Haven court, but Eric's hand was curled, lax, and dry. He kept his eyes closed while the doctor assessed eight stitches, warning his patient, "Hope you're not too vain. This is going to scar."

She was about to quip that Eric was the vainest man alive, just not about his face, then swallowed the remark. Ribbing didn't seem appropriate.

Willy insisted on taking a taxi home, though it was only three blocks. By the time they shuffled in the door the wound had swollen, reducing his eye to a slit. The socket was purpling. Willy had got her wish: she'd wanted to console her husband, and his life was so charmed that to do so she'd had to bash his head in.

The apartment was a shambles. Glass, rackets, and tennis shirts littered the floor. Hastily, Willy gathered the couch pillows and plumped them on the sofa. The sopping red towel was still wadded on the cushion where they'd abandoned it for a fresh one. Its crimson had soaked the upholstery. Next to this sticky puddle and its livid adjacent handprints, the rusty drips on the piping from Willy's kitchen cut the year before looked trifling. She smoothed a fresh sheet on the sofa and led Eric to lay down. Though he said he could use one, when she fixed him a brandy he slumped stuporously before the snifter and left the cognac untouched.

Willy rushed to stack his rackets lovingly in the corner, collected and refolded his clothes, and had begun clinking shards into the trash can when Eric spoke at last. "I don't think you're in the right mood to do that now."

Eric was right. Her careless handling of the jagged edges tempted a competing injury. Obvious, and classless. Willy used a broom.

"I might have put your eye out," she mumbled, sweeping.

"Yes."

"That would have ruined your depth perception. Before your first Grand Slam."

"Yes," Eric repeated flatly.

"You'd never have forgiven me."

"You'd be surprised what I could forgive. But that's not a limit you want to test."

"Since I could have blinded your eye, I might as well have."

"Even the law recognizes the difference between an act and an attempt."

She held the broom handle forward like a microphone. "Do you think I tried to put your eye out on purpose?"

"Please don't get worked up again," Eric appealed, dropping his head back. In the lamplight, the gauze glared. "That's not a question worth asking."

"I've become...dangerous. You're not safe with me in the same room."

"Typically, you would blow this out of proportion. Excoriate yourself enough and you'll manage to turn things around so that *I* feel sorry for *you*. Supposedly you don't want my sympathy, but I'm beginning to wonder."

"I don't deserve sympathy. I'm a witch."

"Try deriving a smaller lesson and you have a better chance of learning it." He spoke with no inflection. "Like that you're so keen for expressing your emotions, but that there is a place for self-control. Or that you may be a woman, but a powerful one who can do a lot of damage if you're not careful. I'm not an icon, Willy, I'm an ordinary man, and you can hurt me very badly."

"If you were a wife, you'd be in a battered women's shelter by now. You'd be surrounded by counselors convincing you to press charges, to demand a restraining order. In the courts, if you murdered me in my sleep you could get off with pro-bation."

"If you don't stop turning a minor incident into a Greek tragedy, I *will* hit you and then we'll be even. Is that what you want?"

Willy dumped another load of glass from the dustpan and looked up. "Wouldn't you like to?" She located the offending Wilson and held it grip-first toward the couch. "Be my guest."

To her surprise he grabbed it, and wrenched her to his side. Curling Willy under his arm, Eric chucked the racket to the floor. "Do me a real favor," he murmured. "My head is pounding. I'm shaky. I'm exhausted. Get me three aspirin, and come to bed."

As they shambled to the bedroom, for fifteen feet they enjoyed a picturebook marriage: it was hard to say who was leaning on whom. Willy fetched Eric his aspirin, brushed her teeth, and paused at the sink. Whenever they were both home she inserted her diaphragm before going to bed, to avoid having to get up and interrupt matters should the mood strike them. The optimistic habit persisted, if the mood had waned. But tonight, shrinking from the implicit self-protection, from the effrontery of expecting that this of all nights he would want to make love, she left the contraceptive in its case.

Yet when Willy slunk under the sheet Eric slipped his hand into her hair and pressed her temple to his heart. For whole minutes he held her head against his breast, close and motionless, his chest barely rising from the slow, shallow breath of fear—much the way he'd cupped his palm against the eye that afternoon, as if he were frightened of another kind of blindness, which might also entail a darkness on a whole side of his life. At last, satisfied somehow, able to see into at least the next few minutes, Eric released the pressure on her crown, trailed his fingers to her back, and exhaled deeply. He reached for her hand, but this time didn't try to bend it backward, commend her resistance, match his strength to hers. If there was any contest, it was over which of them felt weaker or less interested in a contest of any description.

Softly lacing her fingers, Eric traced tiny circles on her knuckles. Willy propped on an elbow and felt the urge to blurt again that she was sorry, but he'd had enough of that. "I . . . " she mumbled, and the next words caught, "*love you.*" A chill crawled the nape of Willy's neck, her eyes shot hot. Still trembling slightly from his trauma, Eric raised from the pillow to kiss her and so seal her sense that this most rudimentary of marital avowals was what he far preferred to more regret. There had been so many apologies, and they had healed nothing.

Willy's eyes brimmed and sluiced over both cheeks, washing her clean as the flood of tears shed in this bed on her own account had never done. She shuddered, and sank. The few inches to Eric's shoulder felt like a long, vertiginous drop.

Landing, her body relaxed—relaxed and gave way as it hadn't in years, so that only now did Willy realize that she'd been holding herself stiff, that she'd been fighting, even in her sleep tugging against something but never free. But all of Willy's struggling had only pulled their knot of problems tighter. As the tension left her limbs, her legs entwined loosely with Eric's like snarled shoelaces that were finally coming undone.

Eric placed two fingers in a Cub Scout salute on Willy's waist, right where her hips, though narrow, still flared a little. He loved that tender, supple curve, duplicated nowhere on his own body, itself drafted in hard right angles. The two-fingered salute to her distinction was an old signal, and with it his prick rose, traced an arc over his thigh, and semicircled of its own accord to nestle against her ribs.

"Honey," Willy chastised him, "you're so tired. And you're hurt—"

"Sh-sh," he hushed, stroking the curve. "I want to." He meant that he was tired, yes—other nights Eric had hefted her full weight overhead with those steely cabled arms, but this evening all his muscles had retreated, and barring the single rousing at his groin his body was limp. And that he was hurt, certainly—but that the doctor's ministrations in St. Luke's had managed only the feeblest repair. The laceration over Eric's eye had also opened a gash between them, and Eric would suture this wound with a blunter but more powerful needle.

Willy stilled her husband, and plumped his pillow beside each ear so that his head lay steady. Resting a hand on his clavicle to emphasize that he mustn't do any of the work, Willy straddled his hips and eased down onto the instrument of their mending. She couldn't help but remember watching the doctor's needle puncture Eric's brow, in and out, in and out, and for a moment Willy felt a little sick but that passed. She and her husband had done this so many times, but tonight Eric seemed to be piercing a place that had resisted his penetration for at least the last two years. She wondered briefly where he'd been jabbing all those other times and what it had felt like for him, maybe like sewing on a perforated button, stabbing blindly through the material from underneath, and hitting hard, unyielding plastic when you miss the hole.

He'd found it, that tiny point of entry, where there was no obstruction and no terminus, so that tonight he seemed to slide up and through her torso until she could feel him as a lump in her throat. Willy gazed down at Eric's face to find it puffy, bruised, and improbably gracious.

"It's all right," he said quietly. Though he was already saying as much without words, he didn't want to be misunderstood. "You worked yourself into a state, that's all. I know you wouldn't do it again. I love you, Wilhelm. You'd have to whack me a hell of a lot harder to change that."

"Thank you," Willy whispered, which she'd been taught as a child was the best, simplest response when someone does something nice for you, better than abashedly stuttering, *You're too kind, you needn't have.* Real forgiveness was always an option, not a requirement, and she wondered if there was ever such a thing as being too kind.

Studying the bandage over his eye in the moonlight, its gauze crosshatching red from seepage, Willy was mystified how she could ever have confused the only bona fide ally she possessed in all the world with one more enemy. It wasn't as if there weren't enough genuine enemies out there already: her sister, who wanted her ordinary; her coach, who wanted her punished for the very same loyalty that he revered when she applied it to tennis; all those official opponents on the circuit, who wanted her beaten and brought to her knees. For once she faced not another catty singles aspirant out for Willy's prize money but her partner and champion: a tall but not especially large man, with his own troubles, as isolated as Willy herself, as easily assailed, as readily floored by a single blow as she had been felled by one tumble in New Haven. Eric, too, was desperate for an island of respite in a rising tide of hostile adversaries, as Willy was for "safe harbor" in Edsel's office. So Eric Oberdorf was normal-sized after all, and alone in league with her against the vast, monolithic Them whom Eric had identified at their first dinner in Flor De Mayo: a morass of humanity who if they did not wish her ill at least, maybe worse, were indifferent to Willy Novinsky's fate altogether. Alas, this accurate glimpse of her spouse was rare and bound to be temporary, but she tried to capture the moment all the same. As she came, Willy felt a mesh drop from between them, and a fresh, clear, unimpeded expanse of bright, floodlit air rush forward once the curtain fell. If four years ago Eric had introduced her to tennis without the ball, tonight they finally invented tennis without the net.

TWENTY-ONE

B Y THE NEXT MORNING Eric's face had ballooned, his eye
mooned underneath with a mulberry crescent. Its lid was
fat. When they eased off the bandage to change the gauze, it
stuck. The gash had oozed during the night; peripheral blood
and fluid had solidified with the main scab. Leery of picking at
the wound, Eric left the extra gunk, which made the cut look
even worse than it was.

Willy might as well have hit herself on the head. In fact, better
that she had. However Eric's injury throbbed, no dull ache could
have approached the sharp accusatory stab of looking up at that
violet mess and remembering it was all her fault. Willy alternated
between avoiding his face, and eating it with her eyes like crow.

Eric exacted one compensation: Max Upchurch. Eric called
to accept her former coach's terms within her earshot, and Willy
said nothing.

In voluntary penance, she insisted on coming along to that
evening's dinner with her in-laws, which Eric was reluctant to
reschedule. Though he was tight-lipped, maybe the sorrowing
attentions of his mother appealed to him. Willy's tenderness was
tainted with guilt, and he shied from her hand as if it weren't
quite clean.

"Come with me on one condition," he allowed. "That I hit
my head on a *kitchen cabinet.*"

Willy was reminded of how many women in her mother's generation had run into doors.

Willy had avoided the Oberdorfs for nearly a year. She hadn't the energy for another bicker over whether women players should earn the same prize money as men or "didn't give the same bang for the buck," or to riposte Axel's digs at her ranking. And Axe was already marketing Eric's prowess when his son was ranked 972; the ballyhoo with Eric on the cusp of the U.S. Open boggled the mind.

Alma's shock on opening the door prompted Eric to explain before he'd said hello. "Gracious," the regal, willowy woman exclaimed, touching her daughter-in-law's elbow. "I've never got him to walk into *my* kitchen."

Alma hustled Eric into the ebony-trimmed bathroom, sitting him on the alabaster toilet lid while she re-dressed the cut, dabbing it with orange Mercurochrome. The neon antiseptic was lambent with childhood. Though he pretended impatience, Eric visibly basked in his mother's caresses. So all the while Willy had been yearning to take care of her husband, he had likewise yearned to be taken care of.

"I hear you've been beating up on my son again!" Axel grappled Willy playfully and ushered her to the living room. Cheeks tingling, she fumbled unsuccessfully for a quick retort.

When Eric joined them Axel played doctor. Building herself a chair with the Velcro-edged blocks while Eric furnished his "kitchen cabinet" run-in with lush detail, Willy detected the estrangement that any lie, however small, instantly inserts between people.

"Ready for the Open, then, kid?" Axe asked rhetorically. "Said you might get a coach. Any movement there?"

"I got a coach," Eric said hurriedly. In the last two years he'd run out of neutral subjects. "And how's tricks at Mt. Sinai?"

Surprisingly, that was it. Now that Eric really was a star, Axel's praise, no longer needed, was subdued; he segued agreeably to the rise in prostate cancer. Though Eric had treated it to many a rolled eye, he must have missed his father's outsized veneration. It wasn't true, then, that everyone loved a winner. Very few people did. Since they didn't care for losers either, Willy surmised that on the whole they were awfully hard to please. Maybe her sister's determined mediocrity reflected Gert's drive to be liked.

At dinner, they were a foursome. In contrast to the rambunctious, contentious tussle Willy had encountered in 1992, the polite quiet around the huge teak table was depressing, a portent of retirement.

"So how's Steven?" asked Eric.

"Got him working on Bob Dole's campaign," said Axel, puffing his chest. "Learning the nitty-gritty of elections. Come in useful when he runs for office himself."

"How likely is that now?" asked Alma quietly.

"Boy's just gotta find his feet again."

His mother turned to Eric and explained, "Steven is stuffing envelopes. He finds it soothing."

"Is he still in that studio on Avenue C?"

"We have been informed by his psychiatrist," Axel intruded sourly, "that Steven's capacity to open his own can of Chef Boyardee is something to be *proud* of."

At a distance, Willy had followed the fortunes of Eric's brothers with as much fascination as their father had dismay. To Axel's indignation Steven had failed to get into Yale or Harvard; the boy was left with no illusion that Dartmouth was just as good. Steven took the most demanding courses in the catalog, and on holidays was forever holed up in his room to study. Yet spectacular effort had not translated into spectacular marks. Though the boy was stupendous at memorizing facts, his negligible powers of original analysis earned him steady *C*'s.

At the end of Steven's sophomore year something had happened. Shying from the word *breakdown*, Axel described his second-born as "taking some time out in the real world." But from the sound of the family's evasions, Steven's world had become all too real. More than once Alma had bolted from dinner in tears.

Eric inquired, "He still working for the Development Office at Columbia?"

"The med school let him go," said Axe glumly. "Despite my threats to pull my alum-fund check. Kid kept calling in sick. Christ, all he had to do was answer the fucking phone."

"Sometimes answering a telephone can be quite terrifying," said Alma, studying her smoked trout but eating none of it.

"Since when? Alma, you rock-a-bye that boy like a basket case, he's going to stay a basket case!"

"What's Mark up to?" Eric intervened. The Oberdorfs, like Eric and Willy, were short on neutral subjects.

"Summer school," Axe growled, disgust gathering like a cloud. "*He* wanted to gallivant around Europe, to collect *material* for his future oeuvre of films." Axel sneered. "On my meal ticket, of course. But I wasn't about to be hoodwinked a second time. His freshman year I said, You have your grades mailed here, buddy, and don't expect to intercept the envelopes the way you snagged the ones from Horace Mann. What do I get sent? Both semesters, three incompletes each! I told him, You know Eric never took a single incomplete at Princeton, and you're at NYU!"

Eric interrupted, "NYU's no tiptoe through the tulips, Dad."

"Wants to be a hotshot film director," Axel went on unimpeded. "Which supposedly gives him an excuse to watch *Wagon Train* and *Gidget Grows Up* 'til 5 A.M. Then has the nerve to point to Eric here and say, Look at my older brother, he's flying high on *talent*. I try to tell Mark, Eric practices three hours a day, jumps rope, weights, why I don't even know what-all. But he *earns* his money, he *earns* those trophies—"

"Bet that went down like a lead balloon," Willy murmured.

"Speaking of which, son," Axel brightened, "thought I might give Steven a ticket to your first round to cheer him up. Get him a seat in the player's box?"

"Maybe," Eric mumbled. "I'm just not sure watching me play the U.S. Open is the best therapy for Steven now, Dad."

Eric looked haggard, beyond the bruising around his bandage. He had to ask his father what the boys were up to because none of his brothers ever gave him a call. He must have been wondering if trophies came with prize money as compensation for what they did to the rest of your life.

"Where did you ship Robert this year?" Eric completed the trio of updates with depleted enthusiasm.

"Outward Bound."

"Going to make a *man* of him?" asked Eric ruefully.

"I hadn't in mind nearly so large an evolutionary leap," said Axe, shoveling salad.

The phone rang. Alma suggested they let the machine pick up, since they saw Eric so rarely. As Alma fetched the main course, the message recorded in the next room: "Dr. Oberdorf, this is John Flinders from Outward Bound. Robert was caught using drugs, and you know that calls for immediate expulsion from the program. Could you call me to discuss this? Robert was sent back from the Rockies yesterday, and is on his way home."

No one at the table looked astonished.

"Jesus Christ," Axel griped, "what the hell are we going to do with that kid underfoot the whole summer, Alma?"

"He won't be underfoot, dear," she assured him. "When he ends up in the precinct lockup, you can refuse to bail him out, just like last time."

"Bad enough Robert got booted from Hotchkiss," Axel fumed. "But I'm damned if he's going to drop out of Williston at sixteen. Way it looks from here, Eric, you'll be the only boy out of four to get a degree."

"Steven has only two more years —"

"Yeah, but to get a diploma somebody would have to glue the kid together long enough to sign his name."

"And whose fault is *that*?" said Alma, lips pressed.

"His fault, Alma."

"You can't take credit for Eric without also taking the blame for an emotional cripple, a compulsive liar, and a juvenile delinquent," she returned with controlled anger.

"Eric takes credit for Eric! Though you have to admit, I must have done something right..."

Having eaten little of Alma's lovely meal, the party retired to the living room, where the modular furniture was breaking down. The bright primary-school colors of the cubes and cylinders had grown dingy, their Velcro tired, so one had always to be pressing the geometric shapes together again. Once rearranged by the children daily into new and amusing confab- ulations, these constructions hadn't changed since Willy was last here. Back then there'd been talk of replacing the avant-garde toys with proper furniture. That the Oberdorfs had not done so suggested the same dispirited *We really should* of her own parents and their terminally brown house.

Axe gestured to his usual throne, insisting Willy take the chair. Willy assumed the focal hot seat uneasily. Here it came. Dessert.

"Eric tells me you're climbing the wrong direction on that ladder. What'sa problem?" Axe squared his shoulders on the couch construction, his chin raised like that of a sparring partner, tempting the old one-two.

"With a ranking of 961, I'm running out of rungs." Rather than keep her arms close to her chest, Willy rested them on either side and left her body open. Any decent pugilist would have been appalled. "I have one more satellite, while Eric plays the Pilot Pen. If that goes as smashingly as usual, by the end of August it will have been a whole year since I made so much as the third round of any tournament at all."

"Sounds pretty discouraging."

"As lame as you can get," Willy rejoined. Her father-in-law looked consternated. Not only would she not put her dukes up, but she was getting in the odd biff on herself. "In that case I will no longer be a ranked player." Willy's smile was inviting. "*Poof,* I disappear."

"Got your work cut out for you, then," said Axe gruffly.

Willy picked at a callous on her palm, digging it off though it was vital to her forehand. "Maybe not."

"What's this, you're gonna lay down and give up? I don't believe what I'm hearing here." He seemed personally aggrieved, as if Willy were depriving him of sport.

"There is a point at which tennis gives up on me."

"But look at Seles." Axe stabbed his finger. "Out of the game for two years, comes back sharing the number-one spot with Steffi, takes no prisoners!"

"No one is saving my ranking for me while I collect my thoughts. And I'm twenty-seven. In tennis terms, a crone. As you pointed out yourself, I was kaput by the time we met. Had I listened, you'd have saved me a great deal of trouble."

"Hell," Axe grumbled. "You look in pretty good shape to me."

"On the contrary, I'm shattered," she volunteered pleasantly. "Tennis isn't so different from boxing—it's the brain that takes the biggest beating."

"Come now, it can't be as bad as all that!" Axel appealed to Eric with a look, but his first-born's eyes were shut. Eric had been tossing it-can't-be-that-bad for two years, and obviously welcomed a relief pitcher.

"I've long belonged to the never-say-die school," said Willy, "except there's nothing splendid about the denial when you're bending over a corpse. So I've considered appealing to Eric's sponsors to sell sporting goods. I might try for an administrative job with the WTA. Or coach the handicapped for the Arthur Ashe Foundation. Any other suggestions?" To her own ears, her voice lifted with a disconnected, absent quality. Perhaps there was an ultra-reasonableness, a runaway sanity synonymous with losing your mind.

"Get back to it, of course," Axe recommended brusquely.

"Thought you wanted to be a tennis star."

"I did. More than anything. Too bad for me." Willy shot him an airy smile, and her father-in-law drew back in horror.

"The problem is," she proceeded mellifluously, "I'm not qualified for squat. All I can do is play tennis. I'd join Eric's entourage, except it turns out I make as lousy a fan as I do a competitor."

Willy clasped her hands. For the moment, she was visited by a freestanding pragmatism, a clarity that came from appraising herself with the same casual brutality that she employed in perceiving other people every day. While the sensation was restful, her body felt heavier than usual and more dense, sinking into the furry cubes. Mustering the energy to go to the bathroom was inconceivable.

"Have you thought about having a family?" asked Alma.

"Nope," said Willy curtly.

"But I was given to understand when you two got married that my son had found a partner in more than one sense," Axe carped. To Willy's surprise, he seemed anxious to efface the image of his daughter-in-law as a harried matron with a brood. "Eric said when he first brought you over here that you beat the daylights out of him."

"Oh, *that* didn't last. He crushed me on our first anniversary. As he might have done from day one, but your son has a kind streak. Now I think back on it, his throwing all those games was incredibly sweet."

"I used to think I was gifted, until he came along." Willy nodded at her husband fondly. "Eric taught me what real talent was about. Effortlessness, for one thing. But most of all, he has the mental equipment: resilience, tenacity, and if you don't mind my saying so, arrogance. He disdains other players, so they don't intimidate him. Eric's a natural champion. Me, I come from defeated stock."

"Hold on, I saw you play three years ago," Axel weighed in. "Maybe I was reluctant to admit it at first, but I had to agree with Eric that he'd married a real winner."

"Yes, your son has proved terribly loyal," said Willy wistfully. "I wish I could say the same for myself. It was his idea to lie to you, but that awful gash? I did it."

As Alma's pupils dilated with alarm, Eric opened his eyes at last. They were angry. Exaggerated by rings of violet discoloration, his glare looked dangerous. "You'll have to forgive Willy," he intervened sternly. "My injury upset her, and she's not herself. She thinks it's her fault for not having closed the door of the *kitchen cabinet.*"

"Certainly no call to blame yourself for household accidents," Axel muttered, indicating no appetite for intervening in a dispute that produced eight stitches, as if, were Willy truly that violent, he might get hit. "Why not," he cast about, "I don't know, go back to basics? Thought you had some big shot coach."

"We've divorced," Willy announced.

"*What?*" Eric exclaimed. He knew nothing of her "appointment" in Max's office.

"And little wonder." Willy's laughter pealed. "I played some swaggering Italian in Riverside Park last month? An amateur, right, a *bad* amateur, never played a pro match in his life? Beat me 0–6, 7–6, 6–2."

Eric leaned forward. "Willy, it's getting late—"

"It's only ten o'clock."

"All right, then, *I don't feel well,* OK?"

Willy obediently collected her bag. "Say, why don't we have a game some day?" she proposed gaily to her host. "The way I'm playing lately, you might surprise yourself."

Just perceptibly, Eric shook his head at his father.

"No, Will," said Axe, clapping her shoulder more gingerly than usual, as if whatever it was she'd come down with might be contagious. "You'd drill me, and an old man can live without public humiliation. Stick with the pros."

Moving a ruthless man like Axel Oberdorf to charity was the crowning insult of Willy's career.

"When you lost in the qualifiers this week, how were most of the points lost?" Dr. Edsel prodded.

"Unforced errors."

"Does that not suggest to you a deliberateness, even resolve? You've referred to 'playing both sides of the net.' You were once a fine athlete. Are you not playing the other side awfully well?"

"Yes, yes, I hate myself," Willy droned, bored with self-examination.

"I don't think so." The contention jarred. "You have a flair for the dramatic," Edsel explained, his errant eye ranging the room in one direction as he roved in the other; he had her covered. "Is it not much more operatic for your ranking to become wretched, nonexistent, rather than modestly inferior to your husband's? In the grandiosity of your decline, I see signs of self-affection."

"What's this, the old I-enjoy-wallowing number?"

"Failure can become an ambition of its own. In its attainability lies its allure. And you have a histrionic side, Ms. Novinsky. You carry historical baggage as we all do, but nothing you've told me about your background suggests that you have to be losing every match you play. Your consistency betrays design."

"Like, better to be a bum than a mediocrity?"

"Notoriety is a kind of distinction. This dramatizing of yours keeps you in the limelight. You claim to preserve a sense of proportion, but in truth you play the tragic figure to the hilt. And slyly, you make your husband feel responsible. Were you to have maintained a ranking at least in the 200's, he'd have surpassed you, but the situation would not have appeared grossly intolerable. In truth, it would still have been intolerable to you. So to emphasize the indignity of being outflanked, you exaggerate the disparity."

This was the longest speech Edsel had delivered for weeks. That while losing her last match Willy had felt physically peculiar—heavy, tender, cramped; her period was late—she decided to keep to herself. Edsel was so pleased with his insight that to compromise its glory would be rude.

"Sport is theater," he expostulated. "You have cast yourself as the underachiever, the gifted athlete with a fatal flaw. Theater is a trap. I suspect you are as good an actress as you are a tennis player. The character you're portraying is unappreciated, tortured, slighted. I'm sure your husband's income is a frustration—it denies you the gutter, which may be why you've been so loath to avail yourself of his funds. You court poignancy as a proxy for acclaim."

Willy groaned. "This sounds familiar."

"Yes," said Edsel, patting his hands together as if rendering himself faint applause. "Doesn't it."

"Admit it," Willy charged. "You're happy."

Her father's cocked head completed a crookedness; he always sat in that ragged armchair as if he were snapped in two. "I am happy," he said, "that one of you has made a living off this tennis business, however improbably."

Willy couldn't sit down. The den was tiny for pacing, with its *brown* carpet, *brown* paneling, *brown* upholstery—oh, God, it was so fecally dour she could be sick. "But if it had to be one or the other of us, you're pleased as punch it's Eric. That way your own flesh and blood doesn't challenge your beloved worldview."

The psoriasis on her father's face was in a shedding phase. Ashen flakes drifted to his collar, as if the friction of daily disappointment were wearing him away. "I am only 'pleased as punch,' Willow, that you have a husband you can be proud of."

For years Willy had assumed that her father's unflappability was designed to disarm; now she suspected his placidity was intended to do what it actually did: enrage. Likewise both her parents' aggressive hear-no-evil naïveté about her marriage, about how *proud* she must be of Eric, amounted to sadism, a preachy moralism, a willful gullibility. Willy had come home plenty of times and sullenly reported her husband's latest achievements, but never had they registered her tone, the seething through her teeth as if their daughter had lockjaw.

"But luckily you don't have to be proud of me," Willy grumbled. "You have too much invested in the conviction that it's pathetic and delusional to hope for anything. If I made it, you'd have to question whether, if you'd been really determined and told those publishers to shove it, you might have become a writer after all. Christ, you didn't even tell us you wrote that stack of books. I had to come across them by accident in the attic!"

"I didn't see any reason to burden you girls with my stillborn aspirations," he returned calmly. "But yes, a *stack* of books. Doesn't that indicate some dedication? Which failed to bear fruit. It's true I have an 'investment,' as you said, in believing that the meritocracy in New York publishing is imperfect, that some talent goes unrecognized. But I've also allowed for the possibility that I might not have what it takes."

"So that's supposed to keep me warm at night? 'Oh, well, I guess I'm not good enough, just like Dad?' Which is what I was told incessantly as a kid. Tennis is half confidence—or lack of it—and you sure did your job on that front. Now I'm collecting on your hard work in spades."

"Recently I'd been getting the impression you were blaming your husband. Now your ranking is all my fault?" Willy thought she could detect a smile. Theories about her parents always sounded more credible out of their earshot.

"You haven't helped," Willy muttered uncertainly.

Her father folded his newspaper neatly into the tube he'd learned to construct as a paperboy in his childhood. It was an old, compulsive habit, for which Willy felt a pang of reluctant affection.

"Try to imagine a little girl, eight years old." Her father held his hand out above the arm of his chair. "This high. She loves to play tennis, you take her to the park, she is uncannily good at it. But she's just lost her baby teeth, and not that long ago you were changing her diapers. She sees some pros on TV and says that's what she wants to be when she grows up. It's sweet. But how seriously do you take her? Do you start throwing thousands of dollars at her pipe dream, or might that be too obvious a channeling of a parent's own egotism?"

"You take her seriously when she starts winning junior tournaments right and left. You take her seriously when she becomes number three in New Jersey even though you won't let her compete as nearby as Pennsylvania!"

"We had two children, Willow. I don't think either of you grew up wanting for much, but my salary at Bloomfield was small. How would you feel if you were Gert, and your parents were sacrificing your summer camp, your trips to the shore so that your sister could play tennis all over the country? Might you be justifiably angry, and wouldn't you grow to hate that sister?"

"Your diplomacy didn't work. She hates me anyway." Willy collapsed to the adjacent chair.

"Gert does think you're a prima donna," her father conceded. "But I can't see how that's my fault."

Willy glowered.

"If I *had* pushed you," her father continued gently, "tennis could have become a duty, a trial. As it was, you pushed yourself, which builds real confidence. In fact, I wonder if you haven't pushed yourself so hard that you now resent the pressure as much as if it had come from me."

Willy had sunk from fury to funk. She'd been in a lather on the number 66 bus, mumbling accusations so that people in adjacent seats looked askance, but now everything her father said sounded so *sensible*.

"Hey." Her father patted her knee. "It's a beautiful summer evening. It's stuffy in here. Let's go for a walk."

"I don't feel like it."

He stood and appraised her. "I've never seen you so pale in this season. You usually have such a lovely tan."

"I can't train at Sweetspot anymore." Willy tried to control the quaver in her voice without success. "My membership at Forest Hills was up this month, and Max didn't renew it. I can only practice on city courts, and I lost so badly to some hacker in Riverside that I'm too embarrassed to show my face."

"Come on," her father coaxed softly. "You've never refused a walk with me on a night like this."

Head bowed, Willy creaked out of the chair like a resident in her mother's nursing home.

Down Walnut, a warm breeze bathed Willy's face, shushing in oaks and maples. The barn-shaped Dutch Colonials and sturdy Queen Anne's bulwarked the street, enduring and safe. Fireflies glinted, and with brief girlish inspiration she caught one. It so docilely submitted to capture that Willy softened and let it go.

"If it would have meant something to you, I'm sorry that I didn't share my frustration over not becoming much of a writer." Her father's voice was low and lulling, like the wind in the trees. "I simply sealed that off as another life. You're too young to understand, but most lives are made of several. I put those books behind me. It's not as if I never think about them, and you know yourself that I regard most of what's published as pretty piss-poor. But I'd hate to think you've concluded that my life is only bitter and mean as a consequence. There's much more out there than career success."

"Like *what*?" she asked sulkily.

He waved at the neighborhood as they wended onto Park Street. "A walk on a lovely summer night. Music—that Samuel Barber you used to play over and over. Spinach gnocchi at Rispoli's, and an old Sherlock Holmes movie on the late show. Or the look on your mother's face when I announced that we were finally going to go to Japan." He shrugged. "And sorry to raise a prickly subject—but tennis."

They had ambled instinctively to the public park where Willy had learned to play. The streetlight shed patchy orange on the decrepit court, like a vista only partially remembered. Its surface was cracked and crumbling. The gate, once locked after dark, was partially off its hinges and swung wide. Willy shuffled onto the macadam, toeing the rubble of backcourt. It looked like her life, in shambles.

"I still play once in a while," said her father.

"You and I haven't in years."

"Well, I couldn't hope to give you much of a game. You've pasted me since you were ten."

Willy was about to add something gratuitously self-deprecating about how he might have a chance now, but decided, *Enough of that.* "I would love to play you. Just for fun."

"That's what I like to hear. For fun."

"I shouldn't be here, Daddy," she admitted. Willy couldn't recall kicking across this court in the dark before. It looked wrong, dim. She always recollected these lines incandescent with sunshine. "Today Eric was playing the quarters of the Pilot Pen. I should have gone. I couldn't bear it."

"You're right, you should've been there. Eric deserves your support. He needs it."

"He deserves it all right, but sure doesn't *need* it."

The Novinskys were not a gropey family, and her father's hand on Willy's shoulder was awkward. "You worry me, Willow. I never see you enjoy an ever-loving thing. I'm sorry if my trying, foolishly, I suppose, to protect you from getting your hopes dashed backfired, and you assumed that I didn't have faith in your talent. I just never wanted you to think that our love for you was in any way conditional on whether you won kudos for our family. The affections of the rest of the world are conditional enough.

"But you've got to take some eggs out of that tennis basket. Not that you shouldn't keep trying. But any career is full of pitfalls, good and bad luck, the sometimes malign or negligent influence of other people. If you let that side of your life be everything, you deliver to others, and to forces that have no feelings or loyalties at all, the power to defeat you utterly. Profession, it's just a game. In your case, a literal game. But the best things in life aren't only free, you can't even earn them: fireflies on a summer night; watching your own daughter pick up the backhand with the ease that most kids pick up nits. And now you've got the rarest gift of all: a boy who loves you. I could see it in his eyes the first time he walked into our house, and that's why we were attentive, not because we liked his tennis stories. I'm warning you, if you waste that, the most precious thing on earth that you not only can't go out and buy, but you can't go out and *look for*—"

"Daddy," Willy choked. "He's about to play the U.S. Open!"

"Honey, I know that must be a little hard to swallow. But somehow you've got to find a way. If you don't, you'll never forgive yourself."

Abstractly, she knew he was right—as she always knew, abstractly, that in preparing for a winter jog the temptation was to bundle up too much, and presently she'd be puffing down the road in all that gear, melting and claustrophobically hot. But time and time again, the abstract information was no use. Time and time again, she swaddled in sweats because she was chilly right then, only to smother over six miles because she hadn't quite believed what was only an idea and not an immediate agony. Clinical information you often got in time; visceral confirmation arrived reliably too late.

Abstractly, she recognized that love was paramount, that a good man's devotion could not be measured in anything so trifling as tennis trophies. Abstractly, she grasped that the best recompense for a stymied ambition was Eric's kiss on her temple after gnocchi and Sherlock Holmes. Abstractly, she could see how if she allowed passing travails to derail the only other thing of value in her life, *she would never forgive herself.* But all these insights floated unattached, hovering weightlessly over the crumbled court of her childhood—as worthless and impertinent to the moment as the principles of quantum physics.

Incapable of acting on his well-intended but ultimately wasted good advice, Willy threw herself into her father's arms and wept, grieving over her own calamitous lack of foresight.

TWENTY-TWO

"YOU'LL BE PLEASED TO hear I lost the semis." Eric slammed the door.

Willy didn't protest though for once she couldn't have cared less whether he made it to the Pilot Pen finals. "I'm sorry," she said mechanically.

She was sitting at the dining table, bent at the broken angle her father had described in Montclair, fingering the list from the WTA that arrived in that morning's mail. Though the sheaf contained one thousand names, "Novinsky" was nowhere to be found. Scanning the last page, she could as well have returned from beyond the grave to find a stranger's surname on her buzzer. The WTA had posted Willy Novinsky her own obituary.

When she leaned forward to rest her face in her hands, her breasts bulged up from the walnut, firm and tender. Willy had always regarded them as a nuisance to bandage out of the way, and now no running bra could pin them, boyishly immobile, to her chest.

"Of course, if you'd *come* you could have watched me walloped firsthand. Missed a thrill." Eric was banging around the apartment, pitching his rackets in the foyer, disturbing the others, and they fell.

"I had something else to attend to."

"You had to wash your hair. Visit a sick friend. Should have reserved those lines for our first few dates. Would have saved me a peck of heartache."

"Yes. I'm sure you wish I had."

Eric stopped flinging sports clothes from his bag and grimaced. "I take that back. I shouldn't have said that."

"Oh, Eric." Willy massaged her forehead. "If I only said what I *should*, we wouldn't carry a conversation."

"Can you even remember the last time you watched me play?" Eric resumed. "And are you ever planning to attend one of my matches again, or from now on am I on my own? Me, I've opted out of tournaments to urge you on. Organized my whole summer schedule around helping you find your game. I've rallied with you, played the same gig, entered that mixed doubles, dug up Milton Edsel…what do I get in return?"

"Grief," Willy volunteered.

"So what about the Open? I'm playing in the goddamned U.S. Open next week; can I expect my own wife to show up, or will you have 'something else to attend to'?"

She let him rant. He'd earned a tirade and more, though his timing was poor. "I'm doing my best to generate you an additional spectator."

He appeared to read nothing into the coy remark but evasion. Eric marched off to stuff his sweaty clothes in the hamper. Losses usually put him in a shrugging, fuck-it humor, but this evening the Pilot Pen had triggered something else. He seemed to blame her. Fair enough, Willy should sometimes experience the irrational imputation on the receiving end.

"Has Max been any help?" she asked, doodling desultory spirals on the ranking list.

"Good God, *interest in my life!* That must have cost you. As a matter of fact, he takes great pleasure in bossing me around. And he wants to change so much at this late date—grip, stance, you name it—that he may have taken me on to sabotage my first Slam."

"No, shaping you into a champion would make much more effective revenge."

"For what?"

She sighed.

"He's a cold customer. I don't think there's much chance we're getting married . . . My." Eric checked his watch. "It's only nine. Time for another cozy, romantic evening. Maybe we could head to Flor De Mayo and relive our glorious getting-to-know-you, the prelude to all this wedded bliss." The *S* hissed. He'd reverted to the proper name of the restaurant. Presumably he reserved pet monikers for people he felt close to.

"I don't have much appetite."

"You never do. I might add, for *anything*."

"I did seven weeks ago," she said precisely.

"Oh, right. The guilt fuck." Eric picked up tennis magazines and straightened the bedspread covering their bloodstained couch. His fussing impugned her—dragging around the apartment all day she might at least have found time to clean up —but he hadn't the nerve to say so out loud. "You eat so little lately, it amazes me how you've put on some weight. What, are you bingeing in secret now? Christ, when we met you were so well adjusted."

"You're the victim of wife-swapping, my dear. I'm not the person you married."

"A clever dodge," said Eric, working a shard from around the Gay Nineties volleyball player. Willy had left both frames hanging with their glass still shattered, their remaining splinters pointed reminders of the night she lost control. "You're not yourself, so you can't be held responsible for what some impostor does."

Willy slid forward on her elbows, pushing the WTA rankings aside. "Eric, please." She rubbed her cheeks; the skin was tight and dry. A persistent metallic taste leaked from her gums, as if she'd been sucking on a nickel.

"I'm sorry I'm not in the finest of moods, because I just lost a very big tournament in front of hundreds of people—incredibly, *total strangers* will turn out to watch me play—and I'm about to enter my first Grand Slam and that makes me edgy. Except, whoops!" Eric pitched a shard to the trash can; a three-pointer. "I forgot. I don't have problems."

"Eric, I'm pregnant." She blurted it out. The subject was hardly going to arise of its own accord.

As he flushed, the pink scar slicing through his eyebrow went scarlet. "God, I—" He was holding another fragment from the poster, and waved it around, unsure where to put it. "I feel like such a heel, I—"

"Don't put that in your pocket."

He fished it out. Placing it on the table, he looked embarrassed. Having seen his share of sappy sitcoms, Eric must have felt duty bound to lunge for her groceries and insist she sit down, but she was already seated. And the burdens Willy shouldered were not so easily lifted as paper bags.

Eric knelt by her chair. "Honey, that's great."

Willy cocked an eyebrow. "Is it?"

"You know I didn't want to wait until we were decrepit. Kids deserve young parents. The timing's good."

"For whom?"

"For us."

She looked at him askance; of late they rarely shared the same pronoun. "One minor sticking point. How many pro tennis players have you seen waddling around the court with a beach ball in their shorts?"

"Of course you'd have to take some time out—"

"Honestly, at my age isn't 'taking time out' a euphemism for retirement?"

"But we're not talking hypothetically here." Eric got up off his knees. "You're pregnant—physically pregnant right now—so the question's not *Well, is this the absolute, exact moment you'd choose to have a child?* I'm not right-wing about abortion, Willy, but I don't like it—"

"Oh, who *likes* it?"

"*I don't like it*," he repeated. "And we don't have an excuse. We've got money, we're married, neither of us is in junior high school. If you think childbearing would be a strain on us right now, I guarantee you that flushing our own kid down the john would do us more damage by far."

Willy screeched her chair back. "Are you threatening me?"

"Are you seriously suggesting that we not take this child to term because of *tennis*?"

"Don't sound so derisive when it's what you do for a living."

"It's not important!"

"Tennis seemed awfully important to you when you walked in the door tonight." Willy circled the room. "But I'm supposed to blow it off. Oh, sure, I'll carve one, two years out of my prime, no problem!"

"Some prime," Eric muttered.

Willy wheeled. "Whether or not I have been down on my luck the last two years, I've devoted my whole life to this sport."

"You're only twenty-seven. You've no business talking about a *whole life*."

"It's all the life I've got. And now you expect me to throw it over for your scruples. Have you taken one minute to think about what would happen? Even though tennis is 'unimportant,' Daddy would keep slugging away—zipping all over the world, sending postcards, and asking Mommy to put Junior on the phone. Who'd do all the work? And what kind of a mother am I likely to be when every time I look at my own kid I can only see sixteen tournaments a year that I'm not playing?"

"Nothing would keep you from going back to it."

"What, go on tour with a stroller? And leaving aside that pregnancy itself can total your body, I'd have to start at ground-zero again—"

"You're *already* at ground-zero!"

They faced each other, breathing hard. Willy's face flashed cold; her raised hands blanched white.

"For two years," said Eric, lowering his voice, "I've said it's salvageable, Willy, you've got the goods, Willy, you just have to get your head in gear, Willy, you're so talented, give it another try... And meanwhile you scoff at me for being a Pollyanna, for massaging you with platitudes, though I've never known what you expect me to say instead. You're all washed up? All right, then. *You're all washed up.*"

She couldn't remember Eric saying something cruel that he did not immediately take back. She waited. He didn't take it back.

"It's bitter medicine." Eric grasped her by the shoulders firmly so that she couldn't wriggle free. "But there's more on the line now than your pride. Most women these days hit their peak in tennis by twenty. For a long time I did believe you could turn it around, so I haven't been full of shit. But this 'slump' of yours has gone on long enough that what began as some bad breaks and a passing surfeit of anxiety has blossomed into a full-fledged loser complex. Which could take years for you to beat, if then. You know I know tennis history backwards and forwards. I've come across *no one* who has gone down so far for so long and has bounced back to become a top player. It's too late, Willy. You were once a remarkable athlete, but something happened. What that was I'm frankly beyond caring. But you won't sacrifice our child for another year of agony. Wilhelm, I said I'd help you any way I could, but this time not to put your shoulder to the wheel, but to *let tennis go.*"

Fleetingly, Willy wished her husband were a violent man. How much better if he'd hauled off and smacked her. True, Eric's homilies had often been torturous: *Don't let them see you sweat*; *Show your grit*; *Half of any success is determination.* His barrage of mindless clichés had demonstrated little appreciation for the bruising she'd taken, for how incessant humiliation sapped the very quantity she called upon to persevere. And coming from a man who had little experience of disgrace, his sermons had inevitably come off as glib. But no insensitive, brainless aphorism had ever cut her to the quick like this unadorned advice that she should quit. Willy had regularly spewed her husband's spoon-fed pabulum encouragement back in his face. Yet served up instead this indigestible hard cheese, Willy could only swallow. There was nothing to say.

Her posture erect, Willy swiveled calmly to the New Jersey Classic poster. Systematically, she worked the paper out from under the thin silver frame, avoiding the slivers on its edges. Having peeled the masking tape off the cardboard backing, Willy rolled the freed poster into a tube, secured it with a piece of tape, and rested it by the front door. Equally methodical, she disassembled the MOMA print. The figure's brightly striped swimming costume was inappropriately gay and goofy, like pajamas. His handlebar mustache tilted at an inserious angle, and the ebullience with which the man leapt from the frame with that orb at his fingertips had grown alien. For anyone to get so much pleasure out of a silly ball was childish.

Willy's knee had seized again; it was difficult to bend it without wincing. Whisking to the kitchen, Willy kept her legs straight as a toy soldier's. She returned to the living room with a box of black garbage bags. After lifting off the top of the coffee table, Willy leaned it on its edge against the sofa. The chronology the ball discards once documented had already been disturbed when Willy tipped the table on her birthday. The disorder was no loss; the history the dead balls recorded was complete. Besides, the layers of muddied Penns and Dunlops was merely the sediment of a moderately promising tennis player whose gifts had come to nothing and whose name not even the sport's fanatics would ever know. Willy removed the balls three at a time, laying them in the bag, cautious to assure that none of them rolled off.

When the box was empty, Willy twist-tied the bag and dragged the several hundred balls to sit by the tubes at the door. Standing at the nearest window, Eric studied a patch of the Hudson reflecting the lights of New Jersey through the black

trees of Riverside Park. The moon was full. She could see only
the back of his head. His crown was beginning to bald; a second
moon shone in the lamplight between branches of black hair.
Maybe, as with her father's face, something was wearing him
away.

When she took a second garbage bag to the bedroom, Eric
remained at his lookout. Kneeling in the closet, she moved Eric's
copious tennis shoes out of the way, keeping the pairs together.
The boxes were stacked in the back. Within them the trophies
still nestled in tissue. Before hefting them to the door, Willy
checked that the cartons contained her own trifles, confirming
that she wasn't chucking Eric's tributes by mistake. This house-
cleaning was the least painful—trophies were chaff—or would
have been the least painful if she felt anything at all. Instead the
only twinge was from her knee, stabbing from her stoop in the
closet.

Yet at the next renunciation, Eric would have noticed a flicker
of hesitation if he'd been watching, which he was not. The
recently disturbed rackets in the foyer were mixed up, and she
had to sort through them to retrieve her own from among the
Wilsons. Pro-Kennex was a lesser-known make, though you
could hardly call it an off-brand. While Willy no longer played
the same racket for years as she had the Davis Imperial in her
childhood, nonetheless she had employed successive generations
of this uncommon line since college. Sticking to the same brand
had given the series a sense of heritage and relation.

Willy felt sorry for the rackets. This early retirement was not
their fault. Had Eric not been standing by the window, she'd
have apologized out loud. But there was no point in leaving
them for her husband; the grip sizes were too small, and he was
contractually obliged to play Wilsons in public. Willy supposed
that she could have donated the equipment to the Salvation
Army. But Willy's rackets had standards, and she was loath to
subject these stalwart allies to the loose wrists, late preparation,
and poor follow-through of some bargain-hunting slacker.

Surely they'd prefer a dignified burial. She might have carted them to the cans downstairs slung on her shoulder in their cases, but she didn't want them to see. Willy placed them in a black bag with the kindness of binding firing-squad targets with a blindfold.

With a third bag, Willy went for the mop-up, though her motions had slowed. For brief beats she would forget what she was doing. Must be the pregnancy; they said it made you spacey. On the desk facing the main room's second window, she located the *WTA Rulebook* and dumped it in the bag, leaving the ATP's. Blank tournament applications littered the desk; she sifted each pile to weed hers from Eric's. One completed form lay sealed in the out box. Before adding it to the rubbish, Willy tore off the uncanceled postage and slipped it in a drawer. Though he was wealthy now, Eric wouldn't approve of waste. Done. The remaining papers were dominated by USTA mailings: regulations, lists of hotels, and time schedules all pertaining to the upcoming U.S. Open.

Collecting the ranking list from the dining table, Willy returned to the bedroom to prize photographs and clippings from the wall. She was willing to leave any pictures that did not have tennis rackets in them, that were not of tournaments, that hadn't been snapped on courts.

There weren't any. Even the shots of her family were marred by the crosshatch of Willy's strings; where she balanced on her father's shoulders at eight, a telltale green shimmered behind her flying hair. In every picture of her married life, she and Eric wore sports garb, or were caught after practice mopping sweat. All the more recent snaps of Willy captured that unsightly brace masking her knee, like tape over pornographic posters in Times Square. Last of all were their wedding pictures—Willy in high-heeled sneakers, Eric in white flannels kissing over a net: tennis. They all went in the bag.

Once every scrap of grip, flash of hardcourt, and pleat of tennis dress were excised from the montage, little else remained besides residual yellow gum and the tiny perforations of pushpins. Willy herself was expunged. The sticky remnants and minute holes suggested that the enterprise was flawed—that every history, however edited, leaves marks. Yet notably, as she eradicated tennis, Eric as well vanished from the wall.

Lugging the detritus to the elevator and hauling it to the cans in the basement took longer than it would have with assistance; Eric didn't help, though he also didn't stop her. Yet on her return upstairs, Willy wondered at how little time it had taken, really. "You must be hungry," she said evenly.

"Not anymore."

But it was only ten-thirty, and they both felt the same lifeless desperation to evacuate the premises that one might at the scene of an atrocity. Though even the voracious Eric was bound to stare dumbly at his chicken as if it were papier-mâché, they shambled out to Flor De Mayo after all. That's what they both called it: Flor De Mayo. Right before she shut the door, Willy caught the eerie gray loom of the New Jersey Classic frame, its cardboard blank, like the decor of a woman who has no interests.

Willy had left a single souvenir behind on the bedroom wall: Eric's mutant eyebrow hair, pulled from the same spot now marked by a knit pink scar, as if the one hair had drawn blood. Still taped shyly on the edge of the ravaged collage, the scraggle was once plucked to prove what her father had cautioned: that some trophies can't be earned or sought but have to be offered.

"*Where the fuck have you been?*" Once more, the door slammed.

Willy sat on the couch, eyes to her lap. What she'd just put Eric through was so overtly abusive that it didn't bear contemplating. Instead she considered Edsel, with whom she'd canceled yesterday's appointment, and hunched with the old high school cringe of having cut class.

"I came back from Flushing Meadow early so we could spend the evening together," Eric railed, "and no sign of you. I waited, and waited, it got late...I called your parents, I called Max, I even called *my* parents. I'm playing the U.S. Open *tonight*, Willy, and I got *no sleep*. And I've just come back from the police."

"I'm sorry."

"Yeah, I've heard that a lot lately. Where *were* you?"

Her lips parted, and nothing came out. To allow the words to escape would amount to being publicly sick. She looked to Eric in mute appeal; it wasn't that she would not speak, but could not. Overnight Willy had tutored her husband in helplessness, and he had learned his lesson.

Eric raked his fingers through his hair, making a *pfffff* sound as if trying to slow his breathing. "You're OK, though?"

"More or less."

"Come here." He held out his hand. Willy rose, and Eric clutched her to his chest. "You look pale. I'm so relieved you're all right." Eric squeezed her until Willy was too weary to hold on anymore. Then he led her to the couch. She wished he wouldn't be so nice.

"Listen," he said, "you scared the daylights out of me, but maybe that shocked me into something. I want to make you an offer." She nodded. "You know I'm always mouthing off about what jerks tennis jocks are. Last night I was thinking, maybe I'm a hypocrite. I want to beat them but I also want to join them. So maybe you think I'm an asshole. And maybe you're right."

"I don't—"

"Hear me out. This whole gig, even for me, is at most for another ten years. And obviously the danger is that you get out, you're not qualified for anything but one of those moronic commentating jobs."

"But you could also—"

"Hear me out. I know how hard it's been for you to watch me get somewhere and even make it to the Open, when that's all you've ever wanted for yourself. When you love the game so much, and I only like it. It's not fair, is it?"

"But you do so well partly because—"

"Let me finish." He clasped her hands. "People our age think there's all the time in the world to have a family. But this country is coast-to-coast with couples blowing thousands a whack on treatments to conceive. You never know when it's your only chance. So I want this baby, sweetheart. And I know the way you described it, that would be no good, with me on the road most of the year, you up to your eyeballs in Gerber and baby shit. So I wanted to propose a deal: if you have this kid, I'll quit."

Willy looked at her husband in bafflement. "Quit—tennis?"

"Lock, stock, and barrel. Except for kicks. Teach the kid to play, which would be a riot. Or you and me. Long summer afternoons in Riverside, just rallying, until the sun sets, until we can't stand up we're so whipped, and we limp off for chicken and rice. Like it used to be."

"Oh, honey." Willy's shoulders caved inward. "It can never be like it used to be."

Eric had cherished his hologram; he looked cross. "I don't see why not."

"So you mean, like the Open. Tonight. You're not planning to go?"

"No, I'll play." He squirmed. "You know, I'm obligated."

She laid her hands gently on his. "Admit it. You've worked hard for this. You *want* to play."

"Of course I want to! But after the Open, that's it."

"What if I asked you to withdraw from the Open as well?" Willy tested.

Eric was still. In his silence, she could see that he was bereaved. "I guess I'd say," he proceeded slowly, "that maybe you were being—unreasonable. But. If you really insisted. Yes. I would withdraw." By the time he got the words out, he looked spent.

She touched his cheek, guiding his head to face her. "Look at you. How much giving up this one tournament would cut you

up. Think of all the others. 'Unreasonable,' you said. Of course
bartering your career for a family would be *unreasonable*. Do
you think you could ever live with such a bargain? That *I* could?
You're on a roll now, riding an emotional crest, but later you'd
hate me."

"I could never hate you," he said staunchly.

"Is that right?" she asked, looking him in the eye. "Your deal
isn't on, Eric, because I have nothing to trade."

His expression went blank. "What?"

"Last night I checked into a clinic."

"Something went wrong?"

"Nothing went wrong."

He stood up, stricken. If he was driven to go, he did not
know where. "Without asking me. Or telling me. Or talking
about it."

"There was nothing to discuss."

When he turned he was smiling, though the grin had an ugly
twist. "You're really trying, aren't you? Like, beyond the call of
duty, the whole nine yards."

Willy frowned. "Trying—?"

"To force me to leave you."

"I wouldn't say—"

"*I* would. Why else? Why did you do it?"

The cramps in Willy's uterus had started in earnest—thin,
stiletto stabs. She pictured a pair of fencers, unskilled at their
art, who kept missing each other and foisting their foils in her
walls. The pain gave her focus, and she was grateful for it.

Willy bowed her head. "I can't have a child as a substitute for
a life."

"Nobody was asking you to. Lots of women—"

"But that's how it's felt the last few days. You practicing in
Flushing Meadow while I stay home and take my vitamins. I
know some women can flourish through their children. I can't.
I'm too selfish. You said the timing was good. I thought the
timing couldn't be worse: give up my profession and have a

baby. It made me feel like someone else. Some lumbering vehicle for posterity. I started resenting the child for its opportunities, the same ones I've squandered. I could see it learning—"

"A baby's not an *it*."

"It is now," she said sharply, then averted her eyes. "I'm sorry. She, if you like. I could see our daughter learning to play tennis. You taking her to the park, just like my father... With our genes combined, think what a natural she'd be, how talented... until she enters her first tournament. And all the while I'm on the sidelines keening, *Don't get your hopes up.*"

Eric faced her with an expression that Willy recognized from the baseline. She had long attributed his success in sport to nonchalance; on court he was fearless because losing didn't scare him much. Maybe she'd been unfair. If Eric's commitment was to himself and not to the game, that didn't make the commitment any less fierce. He won because he never gave up. He was suited to tennis because up until the very, very last point you could win, however dire the score. Right now he embodied the defiant optimism of receiving down 5–0 in the fifth set and refusing to roll over.

"It won't work," he said stolidly. "I'm not leaving. If you want to end this marriage, you'll have to do it yourself."

Willy's sanitary napkin had soaked through. The pad squished between her legs; a bubble formed and popped. The inside of her thighs felt damp, and a sweet, cloying smell rose from her lap. They'd said she'd bleed, but she hadn't been prepared for this Red Sea. The blood must have seeped beyond her thin summer skirt to the sofa. One more dark stain.

Willy wadded the skirt in her hands. "You didn't fall in love with a loser."

"You're more than a tennis player, Willy—"

"Not to *myself.*" She looked up. "I know you love me, but I no longer know why."

"That's for me—"

"It's two-way. For your love to do me any good, I have to be able to see how you could feel that way about your wife. Can't you grasp why I might be in love with you?"

"I have my points," Eric allowed warily.

"Well, my points have always been a wicked slice backhand and a deadly drop shot."

"Not to—"

"To *me*! You're not listening!"

"We can work through this—"

"*Please*," Willy pleaded. "You've only been sweet to me. I wish I could say the same in reverse. I've treated you abominably, think I don't know that? And my every bitchy remark sticks in my own craw. Awful as you might find living with a cow, it's much more horrible to be one."

Willy would have liked to roam the room, but she didn't want to expose the puddle on her skirt. Sitting while Eric paced, she felt like a suspect whose confessions were bound to contradict a detective's painstakingly constructed case. "When you finally told me a few days ago that I was 'washed up' in tennis, I couldn't believe you said that out of spite. I have faith in your judgment, and I think your advice was ironically kind. When I threw all that stuff away, I wasn't being melo-dramatic—"

"Sure you weren't."

"All right, I wasn't *only* being melodramatic. I was driving something home to myself. But chucking a few trophies was barely a start. It's going to take me a long, long time to adjust to not practicing three hours a day, not flying off to a new city every month, not spending most of my waking hours rehearsing points I might have handled by coming to the net or staying back. My every routine has been centered around tennis, tennis, tennis, and now I've got to learn to think about something else, to care about something else. For the life of me I don't know what that will be."

"Try a family. Try your own husband."

"Would you want my whole world to revolve around you?"

"You'd never do that. I have every confidence that you'll come up with a new course of—"

"We're not talking about a hobby, a passing fancy! Giving up tennis, it's like cutting out my liver! I don't know *who I am* without that sport."

"Tennis," he snarled. "I'm beginning to wish that when I picked up a racket at eighteen I threw it in the fire."

"But you didn't," Willy admonished. "My father told me last week that a life is made of several lives, and that I wasn't old enough to understand that. Maybe I am, just; maybe I can see it. But I have something to go through, and it's going to be excruciating. I have to re-create myself from scratch. At twenty-seven, I have to go back to the age of five and come up with something else I want to be when I grow up."

"Then let me help you!"

"You can't, Eric," she stopped him softly. "You're deep in the top 100 now, about to play your first U.S. Open. You're the last person on earth who can help. Because I have tried and tried to construct a scenario I could live with: becoming your right-hand supporter, bowing out and yielding to the greater talent, raising our children, who'd be so proud of their father. But I kept coming back to, *What do you do, Mommy?* I know there's such a thing as gallantry, stepping aside, and I admire the pants off of people—men and women both—who can manage it. But I've searched myself, and I can honestly say that I don't have that much grace in me. You know yourself that tennis is egocentric, and in some ways it's made me what I am. Maybe I can change, but it's going to be agonizing. I still can't picture you hitting a last victorious volley and my being overjoyed. Think of yourself for once, Eric. Don't you deserve a wife who at least wants you to win? It's no more attractive to me than to you, but I wonder if I won't always be a little bit bitter. No matter what else I find to do, for the rest of my life I'll grieve for my game. When I say that out loud it sounds petty. But it isn't petty to me."

As a fatalism had begun to dog her in matches, loss begetting loss, a momentum to their discord had carried her to this blood-soaked couch. There was an inexorable logic to this end point, like the logic that losers lose. Her arguments were solid. Countless afternoons she had labored at this riddle, always arriving at the same solution, like the answer to one of Eric's undergraduate equations. Every time, she factored herself out, and for the past few minutes her very voice had taken on the factual calm of a mathematics lecture.

Yet if this was an impasse with which she had sometimes threatened him, more often threatened herself, in the brandishing of their ruin it had become by definition a hobgoblin of the future and thereby a myth. The breakup of her marriage was not an event but an *eventuality*. Willy felt less anguished than perplexed. She had never meant the threat as anything but empty. She had thought the unthinkable only in order to frighten herself out of it.

Eric should have recognized that she was begging him to make her shut up. Later she was destined to wonder if, had he clapped his mouth on hers rather than allowing her to keep talking, the confrontation would have turned out otherwise. Then, perhaps not. That was a mistake that couples often made: *if only* she hadn't thrown ... *if only* he hadn't said. But without hurling dinner, or screaming this or that, the crisis would have arisen over something else instead. Variables need filling.

"If I'm about to move on to another life, Eric," she continued heavily, "you're a part of the old one. The prospect of capitulation embarrasses me, though I don't seem to have a choice. It's going to be dreadful enough, but the one thing I can't bear is for you to watch."

"You seem to have it all worked out," he said glumly. The tension had left his body. His shoulders only dropped that final notch when a match was over.

Willy looked at her husband in horror. She couldn't believe he was letting her get away with this.

Eric glanced at his watch, which was still keeping time in the old life. "I have to go to Flushing. This is your apartment. You still get the *credit* for leaving me, but I'm the one who should move out. After the match tonight, I'll go back to my parents'."

Eric left for the bedroom, and returned tucking his passport into his back pocket. Though he was headed only for Queens, he was readying himself for a different country.

"One thing," raised Willy, pinkening in chagrin. "Did I ever beat you? For true?"

"Willy Novinsky," he said, his weary facial muscles falling like rubble down a slag heap. "No one has ever beaten me so completely."

"And I...I did give it my all, didn't I? At least assure me, I did really, really try?"

"You tried," he said, "at *tennis*."

Eric shouldered his sports bag and paused. "I know there's little chance—" He dug out his wallet. "But just in case, this is yours."

He laid the U.S. Open ticket on the empty Plexiglas table, and walked out the door.

It was early afternoon. Sun blazed obliviously through the windows, beckoning little girls to tennis courts. Disoriented on the sofa, for an instant Willy forgot herself, wondering if she might pick up a game in Riverside on such a radiant day, then pulled up short: she had just broken up with her husband; she was recovering from an abortion; she had thrown her tennis rackets away.

She could take up squash. It was a nice little game.

One year of study would complete her B.A. Columbia had an adult education program, and was just across the street. She could take out a loan.

Willy's eye fell on the fragment of glass that Eric had left glinting on the dining table. It was sharp. She could finish her degree and translate Spanish for the United Nations, or she could slit her wrists.

In truth this second option seemed at least as viable as the first. But Willy's imagination was too vivid: in Technicolor she envisioned raising the shard over her arm, plunging the edge vertically along the veins, keeping her resolve intact to repeat the exercise on the other wrist. Nothing but a line for a moment, and then—

She might have dwelt on the idea longer, but that would have meant indulging more of Edsel's self-dramatizing. After year-in, year-out of running and weights and line sprints, her homage to the body was too binding. Willy stood up shakily and dropped the glass in the trash.

She felt peculiar for being present. With all the components of her life disposed of, something had risen from the sofa. Apparently it was possible to survive yourself.

Willy changed out of her bloody skirt and replaced the sanitary napkin. When she forlornly wound up one of Eric's jump ropes, she had an inkling that it was hers now; that he would never come back for any of his belongings in this apartment. Tempted by the rope, frantic to throw her hours at an activity that was bludgeoningly stupid, Willy knew that a punitive session of skipping would risk hemorrhage. Still, the blaring silence of the apartment became a kind of violence, and Willy fled to Riverside Park.

Occluded by trees, the 122nd Street courts were just audible from the Hudson overlook where Willy slumped over the wall. *Pock ... pock ...* Such a harmless, casual sound, it recalled what public parks had always tendered: balance. For every shot, a return; for every triumph, a comeuppance. With the perfect partner, tennis offered up that implausible American ideal of equality. In this archetypal vision, the weekly ebb and flow was entertainment, full of ribbings, vows of revenge next Wednesday at four. But sometimes with the most seemingly suitable of partners, one of you came out conclusively ahead. Surely that's when you were no longer *playing*, and parted ways.

Drawn irresistibly by the pocking sound, Willy shuffled down the muddy path and past the flaking green benches to hook her fingers on the chain-link fence. The couple on court number one weren't very good. In fact, they were terrible. But neither seemed perturbed by their abysmal chop and thwack. The girl fumbled more than one return because she was laughing. Their balls were bald, and when one sailed into the woods they let it go. After hitting one competent pass, the girl lifted her racket overhead and clicked her heels midair. She looked so happy. Willy couldn't remember any of her own shots, the most ordinary of which were ten times more spectacular than that little down-the-line, giving her remotely the same degree of satisfaction since she turned pro.

"Hey!" The parks attendant sidled beside Willy at the fence. "Will-*eee*!"

"Those two look like they're having a ball," said Willy wistfully.

"Yup, it's a real nice day," he returned. For the lackadaisical attendant, tennis was no great test of character, but synonymous with weather.

Willy followed the amateurs on court number one with the close scrutiny of watching a Grand Slam final, as if the couple had mastered some devilish trick of which the Top Ten were ignorant. "Did you know," Willy introduced conversationally, "that most professional tennis players are miserable?"

"That so," said the paunchy official, who didn't care. "By the way, where you been? Haven't seen you down here for ages, girl."

"No," Willy reflected. "I haven't really been here for years."

That evening Willy vacuumed. She wanted the noise, white and erasing. She was pretending not to know what time it was, but there was no use pretending by herself. If nothing else, the ticket lay on the Plexiglas to remind her. It was eight o'clock, and as she'd known she would since Eric left, she turned on ESPN.

Over the *wahah* of the vacuum, Eric's game had already
started. His renown from the Sörle upset had assured that this
would be one of the few televised first rounds. He looked skinny
on screen, though the camera was supposed to add pounds. His
hair was lank and weedy.

But more disconcerting was his game—the game that,
however unrefined, had first caught her eye in Riverside like a
rough diamond; the game she'd watched cut and shined facet by
facet and had filled her with the covetous longing of a cat
burglar; the game she would have recognized from a mile away
except not tonight because tonight she didn't recognize it at all.

There was a drag to his step, and Eric's anticipation had
always been stupendous. None of his returns had sting. He
often double-faulted. When she turned off the vacuum cleaner,
she could hear the commentator remark how Eric Oberdorf had
been mooted as a promising new talent, and this was a very
unimpressive performance indeed.

One of Eric's secrets had long been that he did not admit the
possibility of defeat. Since it wasn't part of his universe, he
would no more try to fend off failure than wear garlic to protect
himself from werewolves. Willy had taught him surrender.
Pandora, she had opened the box of nightmare disappointments
into his life.

The match was short. Eric went down in straight sets. Willy
switched off the TV, and for hours wrestled with whether to
call his parents at about the time he might arrive at Seventy-
fourth Street. If she didn't blurt that their breakup was all a
horrible mistake and please come home, at least she could
offer condolences about the match. But by eleven o'clock,
Willy had stayed her own hand. Eric knew her terribly well.
No matter what she said, no matter how she modulated the
timbre of her sympathy, he'd see through her in a flash. Eric
had lost in the first round of his first Grand Slam, and
something in Willy was glad. That was why she shouldn't call,
and couldn't ask him back.

Reading group questions

By convention, spouses are meant to regard themselves as a team, on the same side. How could Willy love her husband, and yet begin to hope he loses on court?

Do you find Willy—or at least her plight—sympathetic? Or is her moral obligation to be supportive of her own husband so profound in your mind that you cannot forgive her bad attitude?

Do you know any couples that have had problems with rivalry in real life? Have you ever had similar problems with your own partners? Competition doesn't only emerge in issues concerning career, but sometimes in smaller situations: who can competently work the DVD player, which of you can recite the full name of the president of Iran?

Have you ever fiercely wanted something for yourself, and then watched someone else get it, or achieve it, when you didn't? Was it difficult especially if this other person was close to you? Perhaps *more* difficult the closer you were? If so, why is that?

In the instance that Eric weren't another tennis player, but did something completely different for a living, would the tensions between them be less pronounced? Might she be able to wish him well as, say, a businessman or visual artist, even if she herself had fallen on hard times on the tennis circuit?

Along these same lines: tennis stars Andre Agassi and Steffi Graf married. So far, they seem happy. Do you think they've had an easier time of it because Steffi had retired by the time they wed?

How much is *Double Fault* really about tennis? Can you conceive of this novel written about another field of achievement altogether? If so, why do you think the author chose to write about tennis players?

Try to imagine this same plot with the sexes reversed—more like the relationship between Judy Garland and James Mason in *A Star is Born*. Near the end of such a book, would Eric, down on his luck and humiliatingly outdone by his own wife, seem more readily sympathetic —having been "unmanned"? That is, might we still feel, despite all the advances that women have made, that it's more natural for the man to be the more successful spouse in a marriage?

On the other hand, might young women these days be especially disappointed to find themselves inexorably playing the weaker role in a marriage, perhaps repeating the same pattern as their mothers did—now that women are supposedly "liberated" and free to compete on a level playing field?

Men consistently beat women at tennis, if only because they're bigger and stronger. Does the fact that Willy can beat Eric at the beginning of the novel strain credulity? In any event, why should Willy take it to heart when he beats her at last? Isn't her losing to a man who's on the way up in the rankings inevitable?

Compare Willy's and Eric's families. How might these differences have influenced their characters?

To what degree do you believe that Willy engineers her own professional downfall? Might she want to succeed too much? But you can't really blame her for her injury, can you?

The book's title is obviously a play on words, implying that both parties in the marriage have some responsibility for what happens. Willy's "fault" is pretty obvious. But in what way is Eric to blame? Or is he?

Eric is much more generous than his wife. But have you ever had the experience of everything going swimmingly for you, and discovering how much more kindly disposed you become toward everyone that surrounds you? Isn't it easier for Eric to be supportive of his wife when she no longer presents a threat? Isn't the kind of generosity required of Willy much more demanding?

Why did Willy not seem to even consider keeping her baby? Isn't her career pretty much over anyway?

The experience of falling in love can feel eclipsing; it becomes hard to keep a hold on who you are. Is it possible to resent people you love for the very fact that you love them, and to come to hate the very things about them that you most admire? Besides, in the case of Eric, aren't people who are good at everything—and you have surely met such people—a little infuriating?

One of Willy's most tragic losses at the end of the novel isn't just her marriage, but her first and greatest love: *tennis*. She has destroyed her own pleasure in the sport. How do you picture her life after the last page? What will she do for a living? Will she marry again? If so, will she have learned her lesson? And what lesson would that be?